I0542396

Wildfire:
A Paranormal Mystery with Cowboys & Dragons

Mina Khan

The characters and events portrayed in this book are fictitious. Any similarity to real persons, living or dead, is purely coincidental and not intended by the author.

Wildfire:
A Paranormal Mystery with Cowboys & Dragons

Copyright © 2013 by Rashda Khan

Cover design by Ana Grigoriu from Kingwood Creations

Interior art by Fahmi Khan

Editor: Jennifer A. Boggs

ISBN: 978-0-9853032-8-0

All rights reserved. No part of this book may be reproduced in any form by any electronic or mechanical means —except in the case of brief quotations embodied in critical articles or reviews— without written permission.

For more information: minakhan@wcc.net

Dedicated to everyone who keeps me writing.

MINA KHAN

CHAPTER 1

Fear incinerated sleep, left her mouth tasting of ash.

Lynn Alexander's parched throat ached. Her mind plucked at reason. She'd been dreaming of fire again. Wild, angry flames. Billowing smoke. A faint voice pleading for help. Through it all, someone —something— watched her. Waited.

"Come here." Another voice, dark and intimate, had commanded from the depths of the fire. "Come here, little girl."

Then a man's face emerged from the smoke and flames. Strong and grim, with rugged angles, sensuous lips and intense green eyes that glittered with blistering heat.

Panic pressed on her windpipe. Lynn wrenched her head sideways, blinked back tears and stared at the pebbled texture of the wall next to her bed. Ragged breath caught in her lungs and she focused on the present to escape the grasping remnants of the dream. She tuned in to the soft swish of the fan, the quiet roar of the air conditioner, the wild thrashing of her heart.

A nightmare. The same damn nightmare she'd been having all week. An insidious whisper echoed in her head: *Not a dream. A vision.*

Like before, like when her grandmother died.

Dread rolled through her, cold and certain.

Who was the mysterious man? The person in trouble or the murderer she hunted? A prickly knowing grew inside her, jamming at the base of her throat. The tightness turned needle sharp, and then popped. A single thought formed: *Save Jen.*

Tangled in bed sheets, she twisted around to snatch her cell from the nightstand. The clock blinked three a.m. in poison green numerals. Jen would be mega-pissed if the phone woke her at this ungodly hour in the middle of the work week for no reason. Worry itched between Lynn's shoulder blades. But what if this was a true warning? She'd rather risk her best friend's wrath than her life.

Clutching the phone, she speed dialed Jen. No answer. *Pick up the phone. Pick up the damn phone.*

After six rings, she snapped the phone shut and threw off the covers. Lynn leapt out of bed, and stripped out of her sweaty clothes. She grabbed the backpack she always kept ready by her bedside, shoved the phone into a front pocket, and slipped her arms into the extra-long straps. She knew she shouldn't risk exposure, but she had to get to Jen. Protect her from whatever danger threatened.

Naked, she rushed to the French doors and threw them open. The cool October breeze embraced her and dried the sweat clinging to her skin. She stared into the night, glad of the darkness. Being one of the rare shape-shifters in the family garnered her a room with rooftop access. Closing her eyes, she inhaled the dank smell of the bayou and summoned the change.

Heat crackled across her skin, filled her mind, as blue-green scales rippled over her body giving her tan a bronze sheen. Lynn's core dissolved to molten lava, reformed and hardened. Muscles stretched and grew stronger, bones pushed and molded flesh. Nubs emerged from her back, elongated and flared into wings. A deep burn spread from her gut, igniting cell after cell, until she shook like a live wire juiced on raw power.

Her leathery wings flailed behind her as she stumbled around a bit before settling into the new weight. One would think a five foot one and half-inch Asian American woman would transform into a delicate, miniature-poodle type of dragon. Not so. In dragon form, Lynn was seven feet of sharp scales, sinuous muscle and steely strength.

She raised her face to the moon and launched from the roof. Below her, Buffalo Bayou wound through downtown Houston glittering like a net of diamonds under the silver moonlight. The tremendous beat of her wings drowned out her worries for a moment.

Lynn considered her ability to shift, the visions, and the sometimes overpowering instincts of her inner dragon as undesired complications. Except for the flying. She loved that. Of course, *Obaa-chan* had called her abilities gifts from her Japanese ancestors.

Her gut clenched at the memory. With her grandmother, she'd arrived too late, and then—

She'd failed *Obaa-chan*. She wouldn't fail Jen.

The earth fell away as she shot into the dark velvet sky and toward the distant stars. Images of fire spiked through her thoughts, knotted her insides. Adrenaline thrummed through her veins. She rocketed over the tangled mess of highways and overpasses, pumping her wings hard and fast, glad not to have to use a vehicle. About a year ago Jen had moved to an artist's colony in Paradise Valley, six hours west of Houston by car or an hour by wing. She wanted to be there *now*.

A few headlights rushed underneath her like fireflies on a mission. Even those disappeared as she left behind the glass and concrete jungle of the city. One good thing about flying at this odd hour meant fewer people were about and the darkness hid her. Just to be safe, she flew high enough that she'd easily be mistaken for a plane or UFO. Anything but a dragon. A dull ache throbbed through her straining wings. She hissed out an annoyed burst of flame, and forced herself to slow. Work smart, not hard. Wind currents shifted and supported her as she rode one thermal, then skimmed another. She leaned into the moving air as she threaded through wet clouds, muscles taut with purpose.

A grin parted her lips as she spotted the collection of pale spires on what Jen called Salvation Row because so many churches competed for attention on the same block. San Angelo, the nearest small city to Jen. Almost there. A jolt of fresh energy buzzed through her, making her flagging wings beat harder.

Soft darkness wrapped around her as she headed further into the countryside. Innumerable stars spilled across the sky, shining with a fierce light. She drank in the brilliance. Her gaze traveled into the distance, then locked onto a part that looked murky and dull. As if something had bitten off a chunk of the sky and swallowed the stars.

Her vision haunted her mind. Unease skittered under her scales.

As Lynn crested the double peaks of the Twin Buttes, the bite of smoke tickled her nose and the air steamed and boiled. Below her, fire blazed across the rolling plains toward a darkened cottage like a dragon desperate to devour.

Goaded by the wind, gold and orange flames leapt in wild abandon. Thrilled her. How hot would it blaze? Which direction would it lunge? How far would its sooty claws reach?

Mesmerized, she slid into a glide and pulled in a deep breath. The aroma of the fresh fire made her eyes drift closed in pleasure. The raw scent of sulfur and ash, and underneath that a hint of—

The unmistakable musk of a male dragon. A warm tingle spread through her veins. The face from her dreams ghosted into her mind for a moment. Foe or friend? Her eyes flew open. Her head swiveled this way and that. Nothing to see. Lynn shivered with the premonition that she'd be meeting him soon.

A name, a memory, seeped back into her consciousness. *Jen.* She blinked and peered through the smoke. The cottage stood dark, quiet, and peaceful. Utterly unaware. Recognition filtered through. Jen's home. About to be consumed by fire.

She wanted to hurtle to the ground and rescue Jen. But now the unknown presence, cold and powerful, surrounded her like an invisible wall, stopping her. Lynn stilled and searched some more.

Nothing moved aside from the usual night creatures fleeing from the writhing, surging flames.

Had the other dragon shadowed into invisibility? Her scales stiffened. She wished she could melt out of sight. Never easy, the molecular change had become more volatile since *Obaa-chan's* death. She flickered in and out like a defective light bulb. "Damn, damn, damn." Her tail snaked back and forth in frustration.

Come closer, little girl. A whisper emerged from the dark.

The words filled her mind, turning her to ice. The acrid smell of smoke and charred flesh singed her nostrils. Once again she saw her grandmother's blackened and shriveled body in that burning warehouse.

Her mind screamed. *Save Jen. Save Jen. Save Jen.* She jerked back to reality, and found herself falling from the sky. Frantic flapping, a sharp bank to the left and a clumsy somersault later, she regained her flight. She couldn't handle another death on her conscience. Lynn tore toward the flames.

Only to pull up short and hover over the fiery path. Every bit of dry grass, brittle branch, and dead leaf smoldered and burned. How the hell did a dragon put *out* a fire?

Laughter rumbled behind her. The flames jumped higher, licking and tasting the air.

Lynn swung around to face the blaze. She wished she could smash through the roof, grab Jen and fly to safety. However, no flying creature could carry something equal to its own weight and still fly. She huffed out a breath.

Maybe she could just block the flames with her body. Fire couldn't harm her dragon form. Then another idea bloomed. She pulled back and rose higher. Stretching her wings to their full twelve-foot span, she beat the air.

The fire flared and stood its ground. The flames hissed and snapped at her.

Trembles sped across her aching wings. Lynn winced, but continued the movement. The air churned and roiled, then obeyed. Pushed the flames, turned them in a slow U. Away from the house. Away from Jen. They burned back toward charred ground. No fuel, no fire.

A deep growl rolled across the sky like distant thunder, followed by the plaintive wails of sirens.

She ignored the growing din and continued to flap until the fire raced further away. A few more, slower flails, then Lynn wrenched away from the burning earth.

Her eyes narrowed to slits. A tawdry display of red and white lights raced toward her, overshadowing the muted silver of the dawn sky. Humans. Or rather, clueless human authorities. Panic followed by camera phones and guns. Great.

The change rushed over Lynn as she tumbled toward the ground.

CHAPTER 2

Lynn crash landed smack dab into a Texas Sage. Her breath whooshed out. Woody stems cracked and splintered beneath her weight, and retaliated by poking and scratching her bare skin. Finally, she lay caught in a web of branches. Silver green leaves clumped back together to hide her sprawled figure.

Dazed, she blinked at the pin-pricks of light beaming through the leafy canopy and listened to the sirens. Her skin burned with fresh scrapes. She blew out a shuddering breath. Weariness wrapped her like a blanket, urged her to close her eyes. Just for a moment. Or until all the uproar ceased. *No. No. She needed to see Jen, make sure she was okay.*

Her eyes popped open. Tension twisted her muscles as

she scanned her surroundings with her mind. Emptiness echoed back. The male dragon was gone. Had he ever been there? Or was her mind playing tricks again? The sirens grew louder, nearer. No time to change into clothes. She scrambled out of the foliage and came face to face with an outcrop of prickly cacti covered in red fruit, bright yellow flowers and pale thorns. Life could have been worse. Much worse.

She edged past the cacti and ran naked to Jen's porch, backpack bumping behind her. Her breath came fast. Almost hyperventilating, she pounded on the door.

When the door flew open, Lynn stared at her friend. Short lime green hair stuck out in all directions, faded purple Winnie-The-Pooh pajamas, and heavy black rain boots. God, she'd missed that round, sweet face for the last year.

"Oh my God, Lynn! It's so good to see you!" Jen blinked. "Wait, what are you doing here? Naked."

"Getting ready to moon your fire department."

She followed Jen's frantic glance over her shoulder. The headlights of various vehicles spilled across the end of the drive. Fingers dug into her right arm, dragging her inside. The door slammed shut.

"Bathroom's the second door on the left," Jen pointed toward a shadowy corridor. "I'll go outside and talk to the cavalry." Then she ducked out.

Lynn dashed to the bathroom. Once inside, she leaned her sweaty body against the door and slithered to the cool tiles. Damn, that'd been close. Her mind kept returning to the vision, the fire and the invisible presence. What the hell was going on?

Breathing in deep, calming breaths, she gazed at the aquamarine walls as her heart calmed to its normal rhythm. She shrugged off her backpack and pulled out underwear, a t-shirt and sweatpants. After dressing, she twisted her loose curls into a topknot and stepped out, ready to investigate.

Following the light and noise leaking through the windows, Lynn made her way through the darkened living room to the front door. The door squeaked as she opened it and stepped out onto the porch.

Jen and an older man, wearing a Stetson and shoulder holster with a gun, stopped talking and turned around. Ice-blue eyes raked over Lynn . He chewed on an unlit cigar, making his salt-and-pepper mustache jog.

"Ah, there you are! This is my best friend Lynn Alexander, visiting me from Houston." Jen's bright voice jarred against the backdrop of billowing smoke, spewing water, and firefighters. "This is Rick Anderson, Tom Green County arson investigator."

He tipped his hat with one hand, while removing the cigar with the other. "Welcome to Paradise Valley. How long have you been here?"

Lynn ignored the panic widening Jen's eyes. "I got in late last night."

Her eyes followed his gaze to her bare feet.

Dirt and bits of green grass flecked her toes. Her dragon curled into a tight ball in her stomach. Shit. Shit. Shit.

"You've been outside already?"

No point denying the evidence. How could she have been so stupid? "Ah, yes."

"Yeah, when the radio started blaring, it woke us up." Jen's hands fluttered in the air like frightened sparrows. "And I couldn't believe the fire was at my house."

"So I stepped out to see if it was true."

His eyes narrowed. "It's smarter to run away from a fire than towards it."

"I think we kind of panicked," Jen ended with a short nervous laugh.

Lynn folded her arms across her chest and squared her hips. "When I realized what was happening I ran back to the house."

Silence simmered for a few long seconds. Then he nodded. "Well, that explains one set of footprints we found." He tapped his nose with the cigar. "Strange thing is we didn't find your footprints going away from the house. Why is that?"

Damn perceptive man. Lynn shrugged. "Maybe I scuffed them running back."

When he continued staring at her, she returned a cool look of her own. "You're the investigator, once you figure it out let me know."

"Well, that was just from my initial survey," he shrugged. "We are still studying the scene and we'll figure it out."

"I'm going to put on a pot of coffee and fix something to eat." Jen's voice sounded over-bright like canned Christmas music. "After such an early start, I think everybody could use caffeine."

"I know I'd appreciate it." Anderson turned away from them and ambled down the steps.

Was Jen out of her mind? A fire needed investigating and she wanted to make coffee and cookies? A not-so-gentle shove sent Lynn stumbling toward the door.

"Come on, you can help me make sandwiches."

Sandwiches. She was a dragon not a soccer mom. Lynn opened her mouth to address the issue.

"Ah, Miss Alexander?"

Now what? She pictured fluffy white clouds in her mind and turned to face Anderson. "Yes?"

He stood staring at Jen's battered old station wagon

under the lacy shade of a mesquite tree. Hers was the only car in sight, other than the fire vehicles. "How did you get here?"

Fortunately Jen came up with an answer while her brain still scrambled. "Bus. I picked her up at the bus station."

"Well, you weren't kidding about late then." He chuckled. "That last bus comes in close to midnight."

"Try closer to one," Jen said.

This time she didn't need any prodding. Lynn beat Jen to the door and held it open.

Once the door shut behind them, Lynn grinned. "We still tag team pretty well," she whispered.

"Of course." Jen waggled her dark brows. "The grand adventures of Mizz Loca Latina and the Wasabi Shrimp continue."

"I always hated that Shrimp bit."

"Hey, life made you short." Jen grabbed Lynn's arm and pulled her down a dimly-lit hallway.

They emerged into a cheerful little kitchen, with sunny yellow walls, apple green cabinets and scuffed, but clean, cream-colored linoleum floor. A riot of painted butterflies, sunflowers and leaves ran rampant across the top of the walls. The pattern repeated itself on the wooden kitchen table and chairs.

A familiar jealousy tip-toed across Lynn's heart. Oh well, some people were born artists and others turned into fire-breathing beasts. She dropped into the nearest chair and pillowed her head on her arms. "Is Anderson anal enough to check out bus schedules?"

Jen shrugged while rummaging through her cupboards. "If he does, he'll find out I'm right."

"So now you're an artist and a know-it-all?"

"That'd be O Great Know-It-All to you." Jen switched

on the coffee-maker. "Nah, mom wants to visit and dad can't get time off work. So I just checked on the buses."

"What if he checks the passenger list?"

"I don't think he seriously considers you a suspect, he just gives people the third-degree automatically."

Lynn shivered. "Anderson is like a Rottweiler or something."

"Don't take it personally. It's a small town and they tend to be suspicious of strangers." Jen plunked down a tray with bread, peanut butter, jelly and plates on the table. "Your smartass reply didn't help matters. Ever try being tactful?"

An eye-roll seemed appropriate. "I'm not here to make new friends."

Jen glanced down at the tray. "Darn, I forgot the knives." She sauntered back toward the cabinets, but the rigidity of her shoulders betrayed tension. "So what *are* you doing here?"

"Just wanted to see you."

"Uh-huh, in the middle of the night when there's a fire at my front door." She jerked open a drawer and searched through it. The clatter of metal cutlery filled the silence between them. After she snagged two dinner knives, Jen hip-bumped the drawer close. "How long are you here for?"

"As long as you want me around." Lynn scraped her chair back and stood. Telling Jen about her messed up life could wait.

"So you remembered me tonight, after almost a year of hardly any emails or phone calls, you just chose to fly rather than drive, then there just happened to be a fire. All coincidences, right?" Jen sighed as she placed the knives on the table and pulled out a chair for herself. "Let's try this again without the BS."

"If you'd answered your phone, I wouldn't have had to fly down."

"Darn, I must have left my phone in the car again," Jen said, shaking her head. "And you're avoiding my question."

Friends since kindergarten, the woman knew her too well. Lynn glanced away from Jen's dark, questioning eyes and looked at the sunrise framed in the window. "I-I had a dream. A vision. Whatever." She shrugged. "I just had this bad feeling and wanted to make sure you were okay."

Jen's shoulders relaxed, dropped lower. "Thanks. I appreciate that."

Lynn glanced away toward the back door, paced back and forth. The dragon inside twisted and turned, unsettled. "I should be out there investigating the fire. Helping."

A rude snort greeted her words. "You seriously think Anderson and the others will let you, an untrained civilian, get close to the scene?"

Lynn folded her arms and glared at her sandwich-making friend. "I could teach them a thing or two about fire."

"Yeah well, they don't know that and I think you'd like to keep it that way." Jen nudged the clean knife forward. "You want to help? Grab a knife and get to work."

Swallowing her irritation, Lynn dropped into the nearest chair and picked up the knife. If Jen wanted sandwiches, she'd get sandwiches. She slapped and spread the peanut butter and jelly onto two different pieces of bread, pressed them together and then cut the sandwiches into four triangles. The first one was a mess.

"It's good to see you and yes I do want you to stick around," Jen reached over and tapped her left bicep. "You look leaner and meaner. Nice muscles."

"Thanks, I've been working out." Too many sleepless nights spent exercising.

"Are you still working at the PR firm?"

"Nope, I'm writing the Great American Novel." Writing had always been her thing. But it had changed after *Obaa-chan's* death. Instead of flowing out smooth and playful like a word stream, it came in jagged bursts that left her hurting. She couldn't form the words into neat, pretty sentences or clever, catchy jingles any more. Now the words pushed and shoved out of her. And truth always showed through, raw and naked.

Lynn looked down at her sandwich and shook her head. "I-I couldn't continue working there after Rob and I broke up. But thanks to *Obaa-chan* I don't have to worry about money."

"So what happened with Rob and the engagement? All I got was a mass email four months ago saying the wedding was off."

The knife clenched in one hand, Lynn looked her friend square in the face. She didn't want to talk about her ex. "Why are you interrogating me?"

"Well, maybe if you'd kept in better touch I wouldn't have to." Anger and hurt flashed in Jen's eyes.

Lynn ducked her head. She seemed to have a special talent for pissing people off, especially the ones who cared about her. "I'm sorry. I haven't been a very good friend."

Jen leaned forward and placed a hand on her left arm. "You're here, aren't you? I just want to know you're okay."

Tears burned Lynn's eyes as she managed a nod.

A staccato burst of knocks interrupted. Lynn whipped around ready to leap from the chair as Jen yelled "Come on in!"

Anderson and a red-faced man crowded into the kitchen. Both looked sweaty and grim. They nodded a greeting and headed for the coffee maker. Again the tell-tale trace of dragon musk tickled Lynn's nose, made her grip the edge of her chair. She eyed the newcomers. In silence the men selected mugs from the choices Jen had set out. Anderson grabbed the pot and poured. They carried their cups over to the kitchen table and claimed the two empty chairs. Behind them, pink, orange and gold clouds streaked the sky, reminding her of the fire.

Jen smiled at the younger man. "This is Dan Roberts, Tom Green County Sheriff and volunteer fire chief for Paradise Valley. My friend Lynn."

Anderson took off his hat and placed it on the table. Roberts stuck out his hand. His slow grin transformed his homely face into comfortable. "The man with too many hats at your service."

Lynn met his gaze. Weariness. His hand engulfed hers for a brief, warm shake. No sparks or anything out of the ordinary.

"So any ideas what caused the fire?" Jen shoved the plate of sandwiches toward them.

The two men exchanged looks, Anderson leaned forward.

"A cigarette butt."

What? Lynn sat up straight. Not a dragon, but something so ordinary? "How do you know that?"

"The fire spread in a wide arc and left a charred trail. We just followed it to the point of origin." He bit into his sandwich.

"Given how dry it's been, it could have been worse, a lot worse," Roberts said. He took a drink. "But the wind must've changed and forced the fire around. Moved it away from the house and killed the momentum."

Anderson nodded. "I thought I heard thunder earlier." He gazed out the window and searched the bright morning sky. "Maybe, we'll get some rain."

Lynn grabbed another slice of bread. Her hand shook. She needed to get the conversation back on track. "Where did the cigarette come from?"

Roberts shrugged. "A vagrant might have camped out by the fields and got careless with his smokes. We found some footprints in the dirt." He nodded toward Lynn. "Besides yours."

She plunged her knife into the peanut butter and focused on the work at hand.

"I have been seeing more homeless people around." Jen's brows scrunched up. "But they usually hang around in San Angelo, in areas with more traffic."

"Well, that's the more benign version." Anderson set down his half-eaten sandwich.

Lynn swallowed past the knot of cold fear in her throat as she turned to stare at the fire investigator.

Anderson continued, "Someone might have set the fire on purpose."

The knot unraveled and plummeted to her stomach. Had her friend made an enemy? She couldn't imagine anyone *not* liking Jen, but things happened. "So which do you think it is?"

Blue eyes locked onto her, studied her. "We are still investigating." Anderson brought the mug almost to his lips. "Did you see anything when you ran outside?"

Lynn shook her head. "No, just the fire." That might not be the complete truth, but it wasn't a lie. She hadn't *seen* anything.

He took a sip of his drink.

Roberts cleared his throat. "Jen, I have to ask, have you ticked anybody off? Or noticed somebody hanging around?"

"No and no." Her voice trembled at the edge of tears. "If I did, I didn't do it intentionally and I don't have a clue about who, why, where and when."

Lynn patted Jen's shoulder and glared at Roberts, who turned pink and focused on his cup.

The door swung open and weary firefighters trudged in one after another. Soon the kitchen hummed with talk of weather and fire, shuffle of feet, and the soft clatter of spoons and cups. Through it all, the smell of dragon musk grew and thickened. Lynn's nose itched with every breath as if she'd left behind the cozy kitchen and strolled into a smoky bar. What the hell? Was her nose going crazy too?

Anderson sprawled back in his chair, nodding at people. His gaze traveled around the room. "So where's Jack Callaghan then?"

Roberts' eyes widened. He twisted around to scan the room. "I-I didn't realize he was missing." He lurched to his feet. "Anyone seen Callaghan this morning?"

Jen's gaze flickered from face to face as heads shook in the negative and murmured "No's" poured out. Anderson and Roberts exchanged a tense look.

A loud burst of beeps and the crackling of radio static interrupted them. Lynn almost dropped her coffee mug. She set it down on the table and opened her mouth to ask questions. But snapped it shut as Jen held up a finger for silence.

An electric quiet gripped the kitchen. A spike in the muskiness almost had her reeling. Lynn gritted her teeth and held onto her sanity. Someone in here had to be the dragon. Her gaze ricocheted from face to face. All eyes stayed glued to a little black radio on the far counter. People leaned forward, listening.

"Paradise Valley and Water Valley Volunteer Fire Departments responding," a voice blared from the radio. "Structure fire at 3016 Wren Road. Crosses Aspen Lane and Pine Road, county map coordinates L and 4, section 18. All volunteers please respond."

"I'm so damn sick of all these fires," a man said, setting his mug down next to the sink.

The hair on the nape of Lynn's neck stood at attention. All these fires? How many had there been? She watched as firefighters abandoned their mugs and sprinted out the back door. Within minutes the kitchen had emptied.

Jen rushed about gathering bottled water, cookies, towels, some blankets, and a first-aid kit. She threw them all into a wheeled cooler.

"Where are you going?"

"There's a fire at the Jarvis house and our volunteer fire department is going to it," she said. "So, I have to go. You can come along or stay and take a nap."

"You're a firefighter?" Lynn hurried out the kitchen door after her friend. Excitement skittered through her. Maybe she'd find something concrete at the scene of this new fire.

"No, I'm the fire department's treasurer."

"Treasurers help fight fires?" Lynn arched an eyebrow. "In their pajamas?"

Jen looked down at herself and laughed. "Ah...no and no. Could you load up? And you might want to put on shoes." She disappeared down the hallway.

Lynn finished loading the car and buckled herself in. She drummed her fingers and counted backwards from a hundred. Both she and the dragon chaffed at being forced to wait and to use a vehicle.

On sixty-six, the door opened and Jen slid into the

driver's seat. "I essentially stay out of the firefighters' way. Everyone turns up to help however they can." She took a deep breath and started the old station wagon. "I'm usually on the sidelines if the firefighters need water to drink, the victims need comforting or, God forbid, if somebody needs first aid."

"Do you know the people whose house is on fire?"

"Like I said, this is small place."

"Okay, I get it— small community. Everyone knows everybody, everyone helps everyone." Lynn leaned her head back against the seat. "Just don't start singing Kumbaya."

Jen cut her a glare.

"So, who's Jack Callaghan?"

Her friend's knuckles blanched on the steering wheel. "He's my landlord and my nearest neighbor."

"How come he didn't show up at your fire?" She angled her head toward Jen. "That wasn't very neighborly of him."

"Being a neighbor here doesn't mean right next door, he's about two miles away." Jen's face darkened, grew pinched. "But he's part of the volunteer fire department and he *should* have been here. I hope he's okay."

God, Jen was such a softie. Where most people would run away from an injured bull, she'd try to help it. And yes, where most people would have panicked and fled from a dragon shifter, or attacked, she became BFF. "You know him well?"

"Pretty well," Jen said. "Jack's one of the nicest guys I've ever met. He is gentlemanly, straight forward, and big brotherly."

"Hmm, full of praises aren't we? Do I sense a spark of interest here?"

The car almost swerved off the road.

"Let me repeat myself: *big brotherly*,'" Jen scowled. "He's a good friend though."

Lynn righted herself in the seat and looked around. "Holy Wasabi."

The dry, brown West Texas countryside turned uglier with swaths of charred pasture on both sides of the road. Blackened trees stood silent witness. Soon the stink of smoke seeped into the car despite the closed windows. Her blood tingled and a thought resurfaced. "How many fires have there been?"

"The Jarvis fire will be the fourth one this month." Jen's lips tightened into a thin line.

Too many. And these last two were too close. Lynn stiffened as a twinge of intuition hardened inside her. She hadn't seen anything, but she'd definitely sensed something. Smelled him. While her other faculties might be backfiring, she trusted her nose. Or had until now.

"Do you think…." She paused and rubbed her chin. "Do you think it's something like me?"

"A dragon? But that's not possible."

"You know better." Jen knew all her secrets.

"But…but I haven't seen any Japanese or half-Japanese around here," Jen said. "To be a descendant of the Dragon king's daughter, don't you have to be somewhat Japanese at least?"

As young girls, they loved hearing *Obaa-chan* tell the story of Kiyohime, a daughter of Riyojin, the dragon lord of the sea. She fell in love with a human and approached him as a beautiful teahouse waitress. After a brief affair, he spurned her. In her grief she turned into a dragon and killed him.

Lynn sighed as a dull ache pulsed at her temples. The story of a grief-stricken dragon losing control seemed too close to her reality. "Jen, dragon myths exist in all cultures. I don't think all shape-shifters have to be twenty-five-year-old Japanese-American females with a black belt in karate and a taste for sushi. There could be a gun-slinging Texas cowboy version."

"But I thought you are all supposed to be guardians of the world?"

Nerves slipped and slid around inside her. "Yes, at least those of Japanese origin are supposed to be. As punishment, Riyojin forbade Kiyohime to ever set foot on land and said that her descendants would all be guardians." Lynn kneaded her forehead. "However, there have always been rogue dragons, those who misuse their power. That's where most of those dragon-slaying stories come from."

"*Madre de Dios*," Jen whispered.

"Of course, the fire-starter could be nothing more than an ordinary human who got careless like the sheriff said," Lynn put in. "Given my history, dragons pop into my head way too easily." But not this time. Not when her senses were overloading with dragon musk.

"I left Houston so I could paint in peace and quiet. Now this…" Jen ended on a sob. "Whatever or whoever this person is, I want him stopped."

The dragon slithered in Lynn's belly. She reached over and clasped Jen's hand. Whether human or dragon, the arsonist was going down. She wouldn't lose another person she loved.

When they reached the fire, Jen maneuvered the car between two fire trucks, parked and jumped out. Lynn shadowed her. Firefighters, dressed in yellow, milled about pulling hoses and shouting orders. Flames leapt out of windows, even as three steady streams of water doused the tiny wood-frame house.

Black smoke choked the air. Her dragon swirled inside her. She lifted her face to the sky and sniffed. The acrid tang of fire laced with a musky scent. The first whiff sucker punched her. Robbed her of breath. Of thought. Desire shot through her veins making her knees buckle. Male dragon pheromones. Must be a powerful one given her reaction.

Lynn took a deep breath and allowed her gaze to roam as she grasped Jen's shoulder to steady herself. Jen turned, a frown creased her brows. "Are you okay?"

Yeah, I'm almost orgasming here. Yay me. Her cheeks flamed. She nodded and pulled herself together. "So, who's who?"

Jen pointed out Tom and Brenda Jarvis before heading toward them.

Lynn squinted at the burning house and then back. With her hair pulled into a pony-tail and her face devoid of any makeup, Brenda looked young and fragile. Much too young to lose a home like this. A tow-headed boy stood by their legs.

The despair reflected in their faces seemed to shout accusingly at her. Your kind did this. A dragon did this.

Lynn swiped at the corner of her eyes. She had to get this bastard. The beast inside her rumbled its discontent and paced in agitation.

Tom glanced at them and then watched the fire again with clenched jaws. "We had all of Timmy's birthday presents hidden in the house. Now there'll be nothing." A tear rolled down his soot-smudged face.

"You're alive, Brenda's alive and little Timmy's alive," said Anderson, who stood next to the man. "That's a lot to be thankful for. Other things be damned." He chewed his unlit cigar with added ferocity.

Timmy grasped his father's hand. "It's okay, Daddy."

At this, Brenda sobbed harder. Lynn stared at the family, her throat dry. Would she ever have a child? A family? She rubbed the bridge of her nose. Misery must really love company because no other reason for her to contemplate passing on her freaky genes and messing up a few other lives.

Jen pulled Brenda into a hug and walked her to the station wagon. She sat the girl in the passenger's seat and cleaned her sooty face. All the while, Jen talked to her in a low soothing voice, telling her everything would be okay. Lynn smiled, proud of her friend.

The smile disappeared as her dragon stirred and sniffed. Its muscles clenched and unclenched. The skin at her fingertips stung as claws ached to unsheathe.

Shakespeare's words popped into her head. *By the pricking of my thumbs, something wicked this way comes…*

Lynn drew in a deep breath. The dragon shifted into a ready crouch. She turned.

Timmy had followed his mother and now stood behind her. Firefighters worked around and behind him.

She stared at the wide-eyed, sad-faced boy. Was he the rogue?

For a moment, she couldn't breathe because of the fist in her gut. The tightness hovered at the threshold of pain. She blinked and marshaled her thoughts. A child couldn't be setting all these fires. And the dragon she'd sensed earlier had felt older, more male.

Little by little, the tightness eased its clutch. Lynn smiled and opened the driver's side door for him. The boy climbed in and sat stiff and silent as she inspected him for cuts and bruises. Taking Jen's cue, she wiped Timmy's face and arms clean with a wet towel and offered him water and cookies. He grabbed both. Poor kid.

"You must be Timmy."

He nodded. "Timothy Jarvis. But everyone calls me Timmy."

Lynn introduced herself. "How old are you?"

"Seven, but I'll be eight next week."

"Wow, that's just five days away, you're a big boy.

Timmy nodded sagely as he twisted and turned the steering wheel.

"Do you have any pets?"

Timmy went still. "Lucky," he whispered. He tried to push past Lynn. "I have to go."

She cursed her big mouth. "Tell you what, I'll go with you." Lynn grabbed one of his hands. He dragged her toward his father.

"Daddy! Daddy!"

At the ear-splitting call, Tom Jarvis turned and squatted with open arms. Timmy tugged free of Lynn. But instead of running to his father, he took off for the burning house yelling, "Lucky! Lucky!"

CHAPTER 3

The dragon bellowed and fumed inside Lynn's head. Its fire swept through her, burning, consuming. She broke into a run, hands fisted at her side to control the urge to change.

As a protector, she wanted to sweep in and pluck Timmy away from the flames. The creature thrashed, trying to break out of her skin. She kept her gaze anchored on the boy's figure. His spindly limbs pumped and flew. She'd catch him just before he reached the burning house. It had to be this way.

Yet, her mind argued caution. Changing into dragon would only add to the panic. Turning invisible, even if she could pull it off, would be pretty noticeable too at this point. She blew out a breath as tension tap-danced in her stomach. And what would happen afterwards? A shudder ran through her. Mass hysteria and probably a posse. Not to mention the rogue would be alerted.

Tom and the fire marshal darted in front of her as they joined the race. A firefighter grabbed at Timmy as he rushed by, but was rewarded by a swift kick in the shin. Another tried to tackle the boy, and instead stumbled into the other. In the confusion, Timmy got away and darted into the house. Anderson grabbed Tom in a bear hug and restrained him when he tried to follow.

The two firefighters pursued Timmy into the smoky, black opening where the front door had stood. Lynn stopped a few feet from the house, panting. The dragon seethed. Why was she waiting when she could save all three? She closed her eyes and focused, reining in the beast with her will. Wait. Wait. Let firefighters do their job. This was not the time to expose herself.

"Oh God, oh God, oh God," Lynn muttered. She edged closer to the house, her body trembling with the need to change. If they weren't out in three minutes, she'd go in, turn dragon and drag all of them from the house. Lives saved would be the only consequence that mattered.

She checked her watch. After two minutes that seemed to stretch into years, the yellow-suited firefighters emerged. One carried Timmy and the other a fat, terrified ginger cat, presumably Lucky. Thank God. Drained, Lynn trudged back to the station wagon. She shouldn't have said anything about pets. The boy could have died. A breath shuddered out of her. She should've been in control. But then lately, her control over things had been fragile at best. Not her actions, not her life, not her dragon.

Desperate times called for cookies. She grabbed an

oatmeal-raisin and bit into it. Ate without really tasting anything. Leaves crunched nearby. Lynn whipped around. The approaching firefighter looked like a space alien in his bunker gear, helmet and breathing apparatus. He stopped in front of her.

Lynn steeled herself. OK, she'd earned a lecture. She took a deep breath and tamped down the beast. The guy helped save Timmy, he could berate her to his heart's content. Her pulse pounded in stereo.

It was a scene out of the movies: the hero standing there, a knight in shining armor— or in this case, a smoking suit. He reached up and took off his helmet.

Her dragon lunged, then fell back. *Yikes.*

The man from her vision stood in front of her. He was real. And he sported a big-ass shiner. Cool green eyes — the right one surrounded by purplish-black bruising— studied her. Flecks of gold danced in their depths like sunlight.

Her stomach clenched. Both dragon and woman trembled.

The firefighter was a big guy, like those hulking football players. Tall, well over six feet, with wide shoulders and a thick, muscular neck. Danger spiked the air around him.

"Are you going to share that?" The firefighter nodded at the half-eaten cookie clutched in her hand.

What? Shouldn't he say something more dramatic? Or, at least, lecture her on responsibility? "I think you deserve more." She handed him two chocolate chip cookies and a bottle of water. He sat on the ground and leaned against the car. The cookies disappeared in two bites and then he guzzled water from the bottle.

Lynn stared at him, taking in his flushed face and the sweat-dampened dark curls sticking to his head and neck.

A strange feeling fluttered in her stomach.

He looked away from the fire toward her. "Thanks for the cookies. Can I have another?"

Lynn handed him a third cookie. Their fingers brushed and a light buzz ran up her arm. She dropped it to her side, rubbed her fingers against her jeans.

He devoured the last cookie and swallowed some more water. "I didn't get your name."

She closed her mouth. "Lynn."

"I'm Jack." He held out his hand .

Jack. Jen's Jack? He didn't seem big brother material to her. She stared at the knuckles, cuts and scrapes on skin tanned golden by the sun. She forced herself to present her hand.

Warm, strong callused fingers wrapped around her skin. Heat traveled from the touch, bloomed inside, spread lower. She tried to pull her hand free.

His grip tightened and he squinted at her in consternation. Did he feel the strange charge too?

Tension thickened the air as his gaze burned into her. Panic clogged her throat. Her lips parted on a silent gasp. Finally, he blew out a breath, relaxed his hold. She snatched her hand back.

Why had he appeared in her vision? He didn't look like he needed rescuing. "Thank you," she said. "For saving Timmy."

He glanced away. "Just doing my job."

"If I'd just held on tighter or realized what he was going to do." She turned away, grabbed a water bottle and took a drink. Paced back toward him.

His gaze bore into her as if looking past the skin to the dragon and beyond. "I'm the guy Timmy kicked and got away from, and his father was pretty fooled too," Jack said. "So unless you have some sort of secret ability the rest of us don't know about, there's nothing more you could have done."

Her hand jerked and she ended up with more water on herself than inside her. Sputtering, she screwed the top on the water bottle and wiped her face and neck with the back of her hand. Could he sense her animal? *Takes one to know one.* God, she was turning into a cliché queen like her grandmother.

She glanced at Tom, Brenda, Timmy and Lucky locked in a tight family hug. Tears pricked her eyes. She turned and looked hard at Jack. Would the rogue stop to help the family? Who knows? People could be unpredictable. After all, didn't she flame-broil a Miata in the not-so-distant past?

"What?"

"Nothing." She stepped closer, inhaled. A hint of rich musky maleness teased her nostrils, made her heart skip. Her chest tightened and tingled. Dragon or just a prime human male? With all the smoke and ash in the air, and being a rather inexperienced dragon, she could miss an older, more controlled shifter.

Something had riled her beast up. Of course, just minutes before the creature had mistook a seven-year-old as a threat. Her abilities were seriously fried, couldn't be trusted.

"You're staring at me."

Lynn wanted to slap the smirk off his face. Instead she folded her arms across her chest. "I'm just amazed how dirty a firefighter can get."

He laughed and glanced ruefully at himself. "You did catch me in the banana suit." He gulped some water. His sweaty, soot-smudged face broke into a grin. "Tell you what, next time I'll make an effort to clean up." He winked. "Just for you."

Lynn pulled in a quick breath as fireworks exploded in her stomach. Oh. My. God. The man had potential.

"Hey Jack, got a minute?"

She bestowed Roberts with a grateful glance. He stood a few feet away with Anderson.

"We need you to answer a few questions," the fire investigator added in a frosty tone. He pushed his hat back and stuck out his chin.

Jack's expression turned stony and his gaze burned. Just like in the vision.

Lynn's pulse sped up as she watched the too still tableau.

Roberts shook his head at the two men and stepped forward. "All I want is a friendly chat."

Jack lumbered to his feet. "I'll see you around."

The dragon pushed against her skin, wanting her to step closer, to touch, to breathe in his scent. Her face warmed as he stalked away. *What the hell?* She needed a man like she needed a dragon in her life.

Lynn slumped in her seat as Jen drove them back home. She remembered *Obaa-chan* sitting cross-legged in the sunroom, teaching her about life. *All material things are impermanent.* Seeing the house destroyed —literally devoured by flames— brought that truth home to her. *Our attachment to material things causes suffering.* The sad, soot-streaked faces of Tom, Brenda and Timmy came to mind and tears threatened again. The family had become homeless within minutes. But how could they not be attached to their home, affected by the loss?

"You okay?" Jen glanced at her.

Lynn nodded, leaning back into her seat. "I hate fires."

Jen pulled over and stopped the car. "I know."

"I hate being part dragon. I hate that the dragon loves

fires."

"You didn't start the fire. We don't know who did, but it wasn't you."

Protector and destroyer were two sides of the same coin. Who knew which one would come out in a toss-up? "I wish there was something I could do."

"The Paradise Valley community will make sure they get clothes— probably used ones, but at least it's something," Jen said and restarted the car. "Plenty of food and whatever cash can be scraped together. But there's only so much." She paused. "You could make a donation."

Lynn nodded. "I will, but I want to do more." She cocked her head. "How come there wasn't any media there? I mean this was a pretty major fire and if more people knew about the situation, perhaps more help would come."

Jen sighed. "The *San Angelo Herald* is the nearest paper. They send out people whenever they can, but if something's going on in the city and the small staff is tied up..." She shrugged.

"Maybe I can write up a few paragraphs about the fire and the Jarvis family and mention the assistance effort," Lynn said. "We can send it in to the *Herald*."

Jen tossed her a wry grin. "That'd be a good use for your journalism degree, better than writing ad copy and jingles for a soulless PR firm."

Lynn bit her lower lip. "They might not even print it."

"Never know until you try."

Jen pointed out Jack's house as they passed it. The ranch house stood surrounded by ancient live oaks. The spreading canopy of branches and leaves hid much of it in cool shadows. Lynn took in glimpses of red brick and dark wood. The house looked mysterious and aloof.

A movement among the trees closest to the house made her draw in a sharp breath. Did somebody step back into the shadows?

"Something wrong?" Jen asked.

"I thought I saw somebody."

Jen slowed to a stop and they peered at the house. No one. The leaves shivered from time to time and shadow and sunlight played tag.

"I don't see anybody now."

"You probably saw a branch move in the wind or something," Jen said, driving on.

"Maybe." Lynn glanced back. Uneasiness still prickled her neck. She just couldn't shake the feeling someone stood in the shadows watching them.

Fire *would* avenge.

The dragon master hoped the discipline and routine of his daily run would help calm him. If nothing else, he hoped he'd be too tired to think anymore. He ran through downtown San Angelo, trying to lose the frustration burning his blood, smoking his thoughts. Too many things had gone wrong. He'd almost got caught. A breath raced out of him.

He shook his head. *Focus. I am the dragon master.* His gaze flickered over the closed stores and empty streets. Podunk town. Seven o'clock Wednesday evening and the place stood desolate and bleached by the sun. Dry heat itched across his bare neck, face, arms. Eighty plus degrees in October. Only in West Texas. Absofuckinglutely *loco*.

Lynn had distracted him. Thrown him off his game. An image of the shimmering blue-green dragon hanging in the early morning sky like a fantastic illusion filled his mind. A real live dragon. The same one he'd seen before.

She'd distracted him even though he'd been expecting her. Ever since he'd visited Jen and seen their picture on a side table in the living room, he'd been thinking and planning. He'd used Jen as bait to draw her out and she'd come. Satisfaction, warm and sweet, shot through him. He'd stood hidden among the trees and gaped like an idiot. Until she'd fanned the blaze away from the target. Then anger had brought him back to his senses, but too late. The damn fire brigade had arrived by then, with sirens blaring and lights flashing. Hero-wanna-bes.

He cut into a service alley behind the library. He knew all the back ways in the area and this would get him to the river quicker. The parking lot stood deserted, but further down three scruffy men, scarecrows in tattered clothes, scavenged through the dumpster. Right in his path. He wanted to be alone. No small talk, no hassle. He stuffed his hands in his pockets, ducked his head and picked up speed.

His thoughts returned to fire. Fire was his thing, his to control. Yet, he'd messed up. The Jarvis house hadn't been scheduled until next week. But after the artist fiasco, he'd lost control. The beast inside had demanded another fire. He'd rushed the job, only to land himself a second damn disaster.

The fire should've devoured the house, ground it into ashes. Instead, it stood like a charred and smoking rebuke to him. His business associates would be pissed.

Damn town. He should have never returned to San Angelo and Paradise Valley. The whole area gave him the heebie-jeebies for some reason. He gritted his teeth. Fuck everyone and everything. His roots were here and he belonged here as much as anyone else. He had every right —and intention—to stake a claim.

The wind carried the smell of rotting food and piss.

His gut churned with every breath. He focused on the ground and crunched across the gravel. No eye contact, no whining for change or cigarettes. The others moved like shadows in his peripheral vision. Almost past them.

"You lost or something?"

The gravelly voice stopped him in his tracks. He turned and looked at the three guys. Two of them were bent and broken by age and hard living. The one in the middle was younger, even had some muscle tone as revealed by his open shirt. He had blond dreadlocks, no shoes, and wore his sneer like a medal. Spokesman for the Homeless Losers Association.

The dragon master firmed his stance and let his arms hang loose at his sides, flexing his fingers in a slow rhythm. A good brawl would settle his rage. "I'm exactly where I want to be. You got a problem with that."

While the other two exchanged nervous glances and inched back, the bimbo in the middle squared his shoulders and puffed his chest out. "What if I do?"

"Fix it then." He smiled and winked. "I'll count to three so you can come up with a plan."

"One." The older guys scattered like buckshot.

"Two." Adrenaline coursed through him as his brain followed ingrained patterns. His foot shot out and landed dead center of the kid's chest.

"Oof!" The younger man doubled over.

The hunger for prey overtook him. The dragon master shoved the heel of his right hand up and into the blond's nose. A sickening crunch sounded, followed by a howl.

The boy clutched his nose and fell to his knees. Blood seeped between his fingers and ran down his front. Wide, tear-bright eyes stared at him.

The dragon master froze with his right hand fisted and pulled back. A little bit more force, and he'd have killed the kid. What the fuck was he doing? This man was neither business nor personal. Just unlucky and stupid. Shafted by life. Could have been him a few years earlier. Except he'd fought back. Punched life in the gut.

He lowered his arm, stepped back. To calm himself he rubbed the ring on his finger —the only inheritance his mother had left him— and stared at the defeated man. He should save his anger for those who deserved it.

The other two guys watched him from a safe distance. Fear plastered their faces. He turned and walked away, until a soft keening stopped him, made him retrace his steps.

The kid hugged himself and rocked in place on the cracked concrete, watched him with wide blue eyes. When he stopped, the kid ducked his head behind his arms.

The dragon master pulled out his wallet and grabbed a twenty dollar bill. "Get something for your pain."

A frightened gaze darted between the money and his face. "What? Why?"

"I've been in your shoes."

The kid snatched the bill and tucked it away.

Feeling somewhat better, the dragon master turned away again. His steps quick, almost jaunty, carried him toward the corner.

"You said you'd count to three."

He shrugged without stopping. "Smart men don't fight fair."

He exited the alley onto a wider street lined with old-fashioned buildings —dressed in Victorian curlicues and flourishes. Letters carved into stone identified former aliases, while newly painted signs proclaimed the latest reincarnation. Schmidt's General Store now housed Elaine's Antiques. Tomorrow it could be bulldozed and replaced by one of those chain pharmacies. Change, the one constant of life.

His thoughts turned to his problem. Lynn. An image of her standing at the edge of the Jarvis fire seared his mind with white-hot clarity. Her midnight hair whipping around her shoulders as she stood in trembling readiness watching the house burn.

Recognition had slammed him at his first glance at the picture, at the first whiff at Jen's fire. Lust had seized him at the second fire. He'd seen her, smelled that sweet, light scent, a year and a half ago at the loft fire in Houston's warehouse district. Good times. Of course, back then she'd been slighter and softer, hysterical with fear and grief.

She'd been, what, a teen in dragon years?

Now, she carried the aroma of sandalwood and sex; a potent mix that had sought him out. Once he'd caught her scent, nothing else mattered. Even the fire didn't matter. His blood had raged, until he'd found her in the crowd at the Jarvises.

The dragonlet had grown, changed, into a beautiful female dragon and human. A groan escaped him as he remembered her round, high breasts pushing against her tank top. How would those long, lean legs feel wrapped around him? His body jerked as need tore through him. Damn, he was acting like a hormonal teen. Breathing raggedly, he picked up his pace.

Control yourself, his mind whispered. Remember. *Retribution. Fire.*

Lynn had moved with such grace and speed, like something dangerous and special, like him. He'd lingered at the fire too long just to watch her, listen to her. He'd risked getting caught. Thank God for those ugly, yellow fire suits.

His feet pounded across the Oakes Street bridge and toward the saddle-shaped museum building. The smell of smoke drifted in the evening air. He drew in a deep breath. People must be lighting their BBQ grills. His mind burned with images of Lynn.

It'd be nice, very nice, to sit with her, in their own backyard, grilling, enjoying a cold beer. Kissing her. To take her in his arms and dance. He closed his eyes and braced against a tree, drew in panting breaths, as waves of yearning crashed through him. An ordinary evening in the life of two ordinary people. Ah, but he wasn't ordinary. He had a destiny, a purpose. He couldn't afford such simple pleasures, such distraction.

"Getting involved would be like playing with fire." He chuckled at his own wit as he headed for the Concho River. Finally, he flopped down on the concrete steps leading into the water and stared at the dark silhouette of the Concho Mermaid. "Lynn." He liked saying her name. So short and sweet, so perfect. "I know it's a bad idea," he addressed the statue. "But it's tempting."

Several formations of birds, black squiggles in the sky, flew overhead. Desire for Lynn once again beat its wings within him. His breath stuttered in his chest. "And now I'm talking to a damn statue." He laughed. "I'm losing my mind."

The dragon master stared at the disappearing light reflected on the river. Darkness edged in from all sides. Lynn. Lynn. Lynn. He stood and headed back, his hands clenched into fists. He needed to save his strength to call the dragon.

"I can't allow her to do this to me," he whispered. "No one controls the dragon master

CHAPTER 4

Thursday had started off terrific.

Re-energized by ten hours of deep sleep, Lynn felt great. Almost cheerful. She'd borrowed Jen's station wagon and driven over to meet with the Jarvis family. The interviews had gone well. She had the bones of a good story. Then she'd gone clothes shopping, grabbed lunch, and picked up a bottle of wine to share at dinner. All in all, a productive and positive day.

She should've been suspicious.

Instead, she drove toward Jen's listening to Sheryl Crow singing the old George Harrison song *Here Comes the Sun* on the radio. The phone erupted into a series of shrill rings. By the time she'd parked on the side of the road, her backpack sat silent. She pulled out her cell and flipped it open. Her mom.

She hated to spoil the day by returning the call, but *Obaa-chan* taught her never to shirk duty. Besides, she'd left town without telling her parents and they were probably worried sick. Lynn eyed the low-battery icon and hit speed-dial. Maybe the conversation would be short and sweet.

Her mom picked up on the first ring. "Hana-chan? Are you okay?"

The shape-shifting gene had skipped a generation and her mother had never forgiven either *Obaa-chan* or Lynn for it; in fact, she went out of her way to avoid anything to do with dragon business. Until *Obaa-chan's* death had forced her to get involved. Now her mother wanted to replace her grandmother, to the extent of using the same term of endearment. *Not happening.* "I'm fine."

"Where are you?" The question dripped with suspicion.

Talk of tingling dragon senses and visions would only make her mother uncomfortable. Keep it simple. Lynn shoved a handful of wayward curls out of her face. "I decided to visit Jen."

"You could have told us before you left. That'd be the considerate thing to do." A sigh filtered down the line. "Did you at least pack your pills?"

Lynn bit her tongue. Pill. What an innocuous, deceptive word. In reality it was a prescription tranquilizer designed to combat anxiety disorder and insomnia in one fell swoop. Only problem was even after waking up from eight hours of dead, dreamless sleep, the pill didn't let her go. She'd weaned herself off the pills as quickly as she could and flushed them down the toilet. "I forgot."

"Lynn Hana Alexander, I can't help you if you won't let me." Her mother's voice rapped across her like a cold, hard ruler biting into skin and bone. "I'm a trained medical professional, people actually pay money for—"

Blessed silence. Lynn shut the dead phone and tossed it into the passenger seat. Well, that didn't go too bad. She restarted the car and pulled back onto the road. Long stretches passed without a house or another vehicle.

A loud bang cracked the air. The car fishtailed as Lynn clutched the steering wheel. "Holy damn wasabi!"

Did someone just shoot at her? She twisted hard and straightened the station wagon. It clunked forward like a dying rhino. She jammed on the brakes, ducked low and mentally scanned the area for danger. Nothing pinged her internal radar. She took a deep breath and sat up again, peered at the world through the bug-spattered windshield. Nothing but cotton fields, broken by scrubby trees and brush, lined the sides of the road. Definitely, no gun-toting maniac. She took another breath. Exhaled.

"And my luck strikes again," Lynn muttered as she threw open her door and trudged to the front left wheel. Uh-oh. The gash in the tread stared at her. Shit. She squinted at the sharp rocks littering the dusty rural road.

Her dead cell wouldn't be any help. And she didn't fancy changing in broad daylight and flying the rest of the way.

Memories of several Saturdays spent changing perfectly fine tires under her dad's watchful gaze came to mind. Not her best teenage memories, but now…"Huh, I guess Dad did know best."

She grabbed the jack and the tire iron from the trunk and got to work as the hot afternoon sun branded her exposed skin. Finally, she groaned and straightened. Her arms and shoulders ached. Sweat ran down her face, trickled between her breasts as she stumbled back to the trunk.

After some rummaging, Lynn found the spare. She grasped it with both hands and froze. Tires shouldn't be spongy. *Oh Jen. That girl lived in her own world.* She dropped the flat spare to its former resting place and wiped her hands with an old red bandana she found in the trunk. What now?

Lynn slammed the trunk shut and trotted to the driver's side. She sunk into the sun-warmed seat and turned the air on full blast.

"Crap! And double crap!" Could things get any worse? She thumped her head against the steering wheel.

Lately lots of things seemed to be going wrong. Heaviness weighed her down. What had she done to earn all this bad karma?

Obaa-chan would have said the universe was trying to send her a message. Well, the universe needed to cut all the mystical hints and go straight to English or Japanese. She closed her eyes and leaned back.

A rumbling growl filled her head. Lynn's eyes flew open and she saw a cloud of dust approach. Hallelujah! She thumbed her hazard lights on and climbed out.

A beat-up green pickup, almost double the size of her car, slowed and stopped. As the dust settled, the driver— a tall, lean man with broad shoulders and long legs— stepped out. She couldn't see his face because of a battered straw hat pulled down low. The scent of dragon musk and sweat drifted in the air. The gravel crunched under heavy footsteps. Lynn fought the urge to step back as he got nearer.

He wore snug jeans and a gray cotton work shirt; both were dusty, greasy and torn in places. His hands could do with a good wash too. Worse, they were scratched and bleeding. What had he been up to? The dragon inside stretched and shook. Lynn folded her arms in front of her and firmed her stance.

He tipped his hat at her, pushing it up somewhat at the end of the greeting to reveal more of his face. Jack.

Her skin tingled with awareness of him. She tightened the grip on her arms.

"Well, hello there, darlin'. Need a hand?" His voice resonated, deep and smooth. A late-night radio voice. His gaze traced over her body. Made her insides somersault.

On hearing about her tire dilemma, he nodded. His lips twitched with a hint of amusement. "I'd be happy to give you a ride."

A startling image of her on top and him underneath flashed through Lynn's mind, leaving her throat parched. "Um, I wouldn't want to trouble you."

She glanced at his pickup, checking for the stereotypical gun rack or tell-tale stickers supporting some crazy cause. No gun rack and only one sticker urging people to drink more wine to conserve water, but Lynn wasn't entirely reassured. The man made her dragon fidgety. Could he be the fire starter or just plain trouble?

"It's no trouble and you don't seem to have too many choices," he said. "I'm going into town, you can ride along. We can pump up your spare and pick up the parts I need."

She gave him a slow once-over. "What happened to you? You look worse than the last time I saw you."

He flashed her that smile again, boyish, charming and rueful.

Lynn sucked in a quick breath. Her present situation called for a clear head and sharp reflexes, not emotional turmoil and confusion. She didn't need or want pins and needles.

"Excuse my appearance, but I was having some trouble with the stripper."

Her mouth fell open. Oh. My. God. What had she got herself into now? "What did you do to the poor woman?" She shifted her feet, allowed her hands to fall free at her side, loose and ready.

"What woman?"

"The stripper."

He looked confused. Then a blush edged across his sharp cheekbones. "The cotton stripper." He shook his head. "That's a machine. It strips cotton from the plants. It's been breaking down on me. That's what I'm going to get parts for."

"Oh," Lynn said, not quite sure if she believed him.

Jack stuffed his hands in the pockets of his jeans. He cleared his throat. "So are you riding with me? Or you can stay with your car, and I'll take your spare and be back."

Neither option appealed to Lynn. But the uneasy dragon trawling inside her, probing and scratching against her skin, told her Jack Callaghan merited a closer look. "Let me grab some things, and I'll go with you."

Lynn ducked into her car and grabbed her purse. She eyed the gift-wrapped wine intended for Jen. While she could probably take him, self-defense 101 advised to use anything and everything at hand. Of course, she could always incinerate him. "Not so fast, Miss Trigger-Happy Dragon," she whispered. "Better stick to human tactics."

Lynn grabbed the bottle and felt reassured by the weight. If push came to shove, she'd break it on Mr. Callaghan's so-very-charming head. Then she'd kick his ass to the nearest jail.

Jack glanced sideways at his passenger. Lynn sat at the edge of the seat, pushed up against the door and stared straight ahead, clutching her things close. He understood grabbing the purse, but why would anyone grab a wine bottle to go pump up a tire? Women.

Her nostrils flared, and then scrunched up like she smelled something bad. He was all sweaty and dusty. Maybe that's why she sat as far as possible?

The back of his neck burned when she caught him gawking. He cleared his throat. "So, how long were you stranded?"

"Not too long. Thanks for the rescue though."

"My pleasure, darlin'." He offered her a smile and a wink.

She studied him back with a cool gaze. "What do you do again?"

Hmm, a challenge. He could deal with that. "I'm a cotton farmer, that's why I was stripping cotton."

"Right." She returned her gaze to the horizon.

He sighed. Life was unfair. The day he got to rescue a woman he wanted to impress, get to know better, he also looked like he'd been wrung through the stripper. Jack stifled a laugh at their confusion over strippers.

Turning his eyes back to the road, Jack smiled. He'd been expecting Jen because he'd recognized the car. When the dust cleared and he spotted Lynn instead, the gorgeous cookie lady from the Jarvis fire, he'd done a double take. He was sure the heat was playing games with his over-worked mind, or he was seeing things as a late side effect of the recent brawl. He really needed to control his temper better. His smile slipped into a scowl.

All he'd wanted was a nice cold beer, some casual conversation and a relaxing evening after a hard day's work. Maybe a woman who knew how to flirt and make him forget his troubles. Instead, he'd run into a bunch of drunk cowboys. As soon as he'd walked into the bar, all conversation had stopped. He should've walked right out again.

Being a stubborn idiot, he'd ordered his beer and tried to ignore the snide remarks about the character of Callaghan men. It was when the guys started speculating about Callaghan women —specifically his sister— that he'd lost it. No one disrespected Annie.

Jack clenched his jaw. Hell, he wasn't going to let people's ugliness drive him from what was his, nor was he going to be a prisoner in his own home. The headache pounding behind his right eye made him wince. Yeah Callaghan, but you let them push your buttons, waste your time and then you screwed up at Jen's. Some friend.

A rustle drew his attention back to Lynn. Nice. Her chest rose and fell with every breath, round, firm breasts stretched the material in the front of her tank top, the swell of golden skin peeked out deliciously from the neckline. Desire coursed through him. Maybe his luck was changing. It's not every day he got to pick up a good-looking woman on a dusty farm road.

Jack's gaze returned to the blue-green dragon inked around Lynn's tanned and lean bicep. Add to that a sexy angular face with dark, exotic eyes, faded jeans ending in dust-covered combat boots and a curtain of hair so black that it glinted blue in the sun. Would it feel as soft and silky as it looked?

She hinted of danger and wildness, promised secrets that invited slow discovery. Want thrummed in his veins, demanded to be fed. He gazed out the windshield. Definitely not one of the practical farm women of hearty Czech and German stock who lived in the area. Lynn seemed different from any woman he'd encountered before, and he'd encountered quite a few. Something about this woman just buzzed him in the gonads every time he laid eyes on her.

"Something about her I can't deny," he hummed under his breath.

"What?"

"Ah, nothing." He coughed into his hand. "I was just humming an old country song."

"Oh." She flashed him a grin.

Had she picked up on the words? He looked away.

"So, how long have you lived in the area?"

"My family's been here for generations." Jack took in the countryside. Mesquite trees, scrubby cedars and spiky cactus rushed by. "You aren't from here are you?"

"That obvious, huh?"

He shrugged. "Yeah, but this is a small place. A new face sticks out."

"I came up from Houston to visit Jen." She uncrossed and crossed her legs.

Heat licked his body, making Jack squirm. "Jennifer Delgado? The artist?"

She leaned forward and narrowed her eyes at him. "How did you get to know her?"

Whoa. Did she give everybody the third degree or was he just special? He ran his tongue across his lips.

He could've said they'd met at a Fire Department meeting, which they did. Or he could have told her Jen was his renter, which she was. Maybe it was the tone of her questions, or maybe he just wanted to have some fun. "I rescued her."

"Rescued her? From what?" Lynn sat straighter.

"She was out jogging and found herself surrounded by a pack of cougars."

Lynn squinted at him. "There are cougars out here? They move in packs?"

His tongue seemed to have a life of its own around her. "This *is* the Wild West you know," he said. "Yup.

This is cougar country darlin'."

"So what happened?"

"Well, I was out on my usual morning ride on my horse, Sundance," he said, "when I heard an awful yowling. Cougars make this unearthly noise that makes your blood run cold."

Glancing at her, he noticed Lynn's eyes had widened with interest and her lips parted, revealing a flash of teeth. Sexy. Encouraged, Jack continued. "So I started shooting in the air and spurred Sundance. That helped scatter the cats a bit. Anyways, I just scooped Jen up, pulled her across the saddle, and got the hell out of there."

Oh well, he was already so deep in bullshit he might as well go for a swan dive. "Then came the Indians."

"Indians?"

"Sorry, Native Americans," he amended. "Swinging tomahawks and letting out war whoops."

"Just the kind to make your blood curdle, right?"

That made him smile. He caught her pointed stare from under arched eyebrows. Her lips twitched and laughter danced in her eyes. Jack gave Lynn his best shit-eating grin. "Sorry, I just couldn't resist."

She cracked up laughing.

Jack sucked in a breath as the sound filled the cab. A warm, heady feeling rushed to his heart. Lynn's arms hung loose by her side, her head fell back, as laughter shook her, transformed her from attractive to heart-stopping. And he'd done it. He'd made her laugh and come alive.

"Good story," she said when she'd stopped chortling.

Jack nodded his thanks and gave her the true version of meeting Jen. By the time he finished, they'd arrived at Herb's Parts House, the John Deere dealership. He parked the pickup and opened his door. "I'll leave the air on for you."

"No, no, I'm coming along," she said. "I've never been inside a parts house before."

They walked in on the proprietor —she assumed Herb— visiting with some of the older farmers and ranchers in the area. Lynn inhaled the smell of sawdust and machine oil and turned toward the excited voices.

"So, this city slicker from San Antone stopped by and made me an offer for my land," said one of the grizzly old men.

The others nodded.

"I says to him thanks but no thanks. You won't believe what the young whippersnapper did then."

"What did he do?" Herb asked from behind the counter.

"Why he looks me in the eye and says 'you'll regret this someday, Mr. Tavistock'."

"An' what did you do?" another man asked.

"Why I pulled out my shotgun and said 'if you don't get off my property, you'll be having regrets a whole lot sooner, son'."

A round of guffaws filled the room. Then Herb and the others noticed them and fell silent. Oooh boy. Jen had said people here tended to be suspicious of strangers…except none of them were looking at her. All the cold stares aimed for Jack.

His spine rigid, Jack stepped up to the counter. "Howdy y'all."

"What can I help you with, Mr. Callaghan?" Polite laced with definite chill. Herb stood with his beefy arms folded above his beer belly. *What was going on here?*

As he entered into a discussion about plates, augers and nuts, Lynn browsed in the aisles looking at the 5-

gallon oil cans, chainsaws and other equipment on the shelves. She kept her ears tuned. Herb promised to call around for the stripper parts, but expected it to take a couple of days. The old men whispered and she managed to catch only a few words. Callaghan. Trouble. Fires.

A tingle spread through Lynn. The dragon odor in the truck had been heady, but then she'd been smelling them everywhere in Paradise Valley. Here it was sharp and strong. Either her imagination had run amuck or there was something wrong with her nose. She tucked hair behind her ear and cocked her head toward the conversation. Stilled.

"Thanks. I'll be expecting your call." Jack's strangled voice intruded. She turned in time to catch him tipping his hat to the men standing around. Some nodded back grim-faced. Others simply looked through him.

Lynn almost trotted to keep up with Jack's long strides out of the store. Once they walked out into the sunlight, he slowed. A sigh escaped from him.

"Sounds like a stripper really is a machine. A troublesome one at that."

"You got that right." He grinned at her. "Come on, let's get that tire fixed."

They headed to an air pump located by the shop area. A comfortable silence settled between them while Jack worked on the tire. Lynn squatted next to him and watched.

"So, how'd you get that black eye?"

The air hose slipped out of his fingers. He grabbed it before it clattered to the ground. "Those Indians and strippers ganged up on me."

Did the man never answer straight

CHAPTER 5

The fool woman had ridden a horse to the damn rendezvous.

Sitting tall and straight on the pale Arabian, in her straw cowgirl hat, a crisp white shirt and blue jeans, against the backdrop of a lurid sunset, Kate Harrington portrayed the perfect picture of old money in the West.

The dragon master watched the ghost white gelding shift and snort among the weed-choked headstones and broken angels of the cemetery. She leaned forward, pressed her body close to the animal, and whispered. One hand caressed its neck. The horse settled. In one graceful move, she extended a long, lean leg out and over, and swung herself to the ground.

He stepped out from behind the cluster of live oaks.

Kate's storm-blue eyes widened, then narrowed. Her face showed no other emotion.

"Wouldn't it have been more practical to drive?"

She looped the reins loosely around a branch. "Wouldn't it have been more practical to be an accountant than an arsonist?"

He smiled. "Touché."

"And wouldn't it have been more practical to meet in a restaurant than a forgotten cemetery?"

No. Too many damn eyes and ears. "You wanted a meeting, you got one. What's the emergency?"

Her lips pressed into a prissy line. She took her own sweet time sashaying forward, stopped a foot away from him. "Your stupidity."

The chaos of birds calling out to each other as they raced to their nests, settled into the trees for the night echoed in the air. He focused on the raucous calls and released a deep breath.

"Excuse me?"

"The first fire was a flop, and the Jarvis fire wasn't supposed to happen yet."

"What's it to you? The Jarvis house was damaged enough for your purposes." The dragon master flexed his fingers, wanting to wrap them around her slim, white throat. "Just do your part and sweet talk them into selling the damn property."

"Don't worry about my part." She huffed out a breath and folded her arms. "Do you seriously think people won't wonder about two fires so close together?"

"You're not my boss. I don't owe you any explanation."

"I didn't choose to work with you either."

"Give them back the money and get out of the deal."

Her gaze flickered away as she paled. Adrenaline

pumped through his veins.

"You've spent it, haven't you?" He pushed closer into her space and ran a finger down the side of her face. Smelled her gardenia scent laced with sweaty fear. "You're up to your neck in this shit, aren't you?"

She jerked back. "You're not my boss and I don't owe you any explanation."

The dragon master smirked. "Yeah, but I'm the guy they'll sic on you if you don't deliver."

She shivered in the cool evening breeze.

He circled her. "I'm going to enjoy working with you."

"Just don't get in my way or get the cops too interested." She pushed past him and strode to the horse at a fast clip. She presented a ram-rod straight back to him. Was she brave or stupid? Probably both. Bitch.

He watched her gallop away. And smiled.

CHAPTER 6

Lynn followed the mouth-watering smell of grilled meat and Jen's off-key singing to the kitchen.

"Ah, the woman still lives," Jen looked up with a grin as she chopped the cilantro for the *pico de gallo*.

"And she's starving." Lynn watched her mix the tomatoes, onions, jalapeno, and then the cilantro.

"It's almost 8:30 at night, did you get the story written and sent?" She handed the *pico* to Lynn, then poured two glasses of water and placed them on the kitchen table, along with a plate of cheese quesadillas.

"Almost written." Lynn dropped into the nearest chair and took a bite of the warm, spicy quesadilla and savored the ooey-gooey cheese and charred chicken. "Mmm, I've missed your cooking."

"Just my cooking, huh?" Jen quirked a pierced eyebrow at her.

Lynn licked her lips and tore a paper towel off the roll on the table. "What else is there to miss?" She cut a glance at her friend. "Mizz Loca Latina."

Jen snorted. "You're one to talk, wasabi shrimp."

Lynn choked on a laugh and had to wipe at her eyes. Oh how she missed this easy banter. She'd gone too long without talking to Jen.

"God, we were so immature." Lynn took another bite of quesadilla.

"No, we knew how to be crazy and have fun."

"Speaking of crazy…" Lynn told Jen about arming herself with the wine bottle.

"I'm glad you didn't waste that wine on him." Jen giggled. "All this is funnier because Jack is really a great guy. Speaking of wine, want some?"

Maybe a couple of glasses would help her unwind and forget the strange flutter that started beneath her breast bone and dove deep between her legs at the mention of Jack. "Great idea. I'll take a glass or two or more."

Jen arched an eyebrow. "And then you'll hit the floor."

The phone interrupted with loud rings. As Jen rushed to answer, Lynn searched for the bottle opener. She found it in the third drawer and turned waving it around in triumph. She stopped cold at Jen's pursed lips and monosyllabic answers.

Lynn mouthed "Who is it?" She pointed at the phone for emphasis.

"Please hold," Jen stabbed a button. Then holding the phone in one hand, she glared. "Rob, your very unhappy ex-fiancé."

"Oh, shit." Lynn dropped into a chair at the kitchen table. Tossing the opener next to the wine she grabbed the phone.

"What's going on?" Jen asked.

"Let me deal with him first." She sighed and hit the hold button. "I told you not to contact me. How did you get this number?"

"Your mother."

Aaagggh. Her mother really needed to stop interfering in her life.

"Lynn what the hell is going on? Why'd you disappear without a word?"

"I left a note."

"Oh yes, the note. Do you seriously think that cryptic message was adequate?"

Lynn held the phone away from her ear and waited until his voice died down.

"Yes. It had all the relevant details— the wedding is off and we no longer have a relationship."

Jen's eyes widened as she whispered, "You left a note?"

Lynn turned her back to her friend. "That's the bottom line right there."

"I think I deserve an explanation."

What you deserve is a kick in the balls. Lynn closed her eyes. She wanted to throw Cyn in his face, but then he'd ask how she knew. Next, he'd ask about the fire. She swallowed.

"Lynn, I invested time and money in this relationship. Not to mention emotions."

"Oh, please, go cry a river on our friendly neighborhood wedding planning slut." The last bit ended in a growl.

"What's that supposed to mean?"

"It means, I know about you and Cyn." The words leapt out of her.

Silence on his end. "How?"

"That's not important."

"Wait, were you at my place the night of the fire? Did you have something to do with that?"

Keep breathing. She'd gone to Rob's house that night intending to reveal her biggest secret. Her dragon had definitely come out, just not according to plan. "Oh, I know about the fire too," Lynn said. "As for the cause, what did the fire department say?"

"Spontaneous combustion."

Thank you, guardian angel. "Well, there you have it. Goodbye."

"Wait babe, she came onto me."

"And you couldn't say no because..."

"We can't cancel the wedding." A string of muttered oaths followed. "I haven't told Mother or anyone else in the family."

"What? I broke up with you four months ago!"

"I know," he said. "I thought you'd have calmed down by now."

Lynn pinched the bridge of her nose and counted to ten. "I'm calm and I'm still not marrying you."

"Come on, Lynn! How will I ever live this down?"

"I don't care. I can't marry you because you obviously don't love me."

"I do love you." His voice dropped to a throaty, sexy whisper reminding her of too many shared intimate moments.

Hot tears pushed at the edges of her eyes.

"I-I got scared and I made a mistake." He paused. "Please baby, let me make it up to you."

"I'm sorry Rob, this isn't something you can kiss and make better." Lynn cut the phone off and shoved it back into its charger.

"OK, chica, spill the beans."

Lynn groaned and turned. "I think I need wine and something unhealthy for that."

Jen's dark eyes focused on her. Without a word, she turned and dove under her kitchen sink. She pulled out a package of Extra-HOT Cheetos and put them on the table, uncorked the wine and filled the two glasses. "Emergency supplies are here. Now, talk."

Lynn talked and sipped. The entire story —about how she'd caught Rob and their wedding planner boinking, turned dragon and then fried Cyndi's Miata— spilled out.

Jen listened, tight-lipped and nodding. At the end, she cleared her throat. "I always thought your relationship happened a bit too fast. You should have broiled Cyn's bare ass!"

Sighing, Lynn took a large gulp of wine and stared at the purpling sky. Flame orange clouds streaked the darkness, just like the dragon that churned inside her. "No, I should have just walked away. Instead I lost control. Just like I did with Dave."

Jen set down her glass, walked around the kitchen table and pulled her into a hug. "Sweetie, they both deserved it. Especially Dave. He tried to rape me!" She shuddered. "I'm damn glad you were there."

"Me too." Lynn pushed her face into her friend's shoulder, breathing in her warm, calming scent. Jen had found out about her dragon that night. "But there were two of us, we could have handled him without me turning into... into that beast."

"You were scared." Jen patted her back. "Damn, I was so scared that I froze. Your turning dragon pushed me to act."

An image of Jen swinging the shovel flashed through Lynn's mind, followed by Dave dropping like the sack of shit he'd been. A small giggle escaped her. "And when you act, boy do you act."

Jen gently pushed Lynn away and looked into her eyes. "Yes, we all do what we need to do."

Lynn fought back tears. "There's more." She closed her eyes and talked fast. "After the Rob and Cyn thing, after losing control, I had another breakdown."

"Oh, that explains the MIA for the last few months." Jen's head drooped. "I'd already moved. I wasn't there for you."

Lynn grimaced. "You can't always be taking care of me. Anyway, Doctor Mom came to the rescue again, even though I never told her the whole story."

"I think the dragon side of your mom came out when your grandmother died," Jen said. "She hardly let anyone near you." She cleared her throat. "She didn't even want to let me see you before I moved from Houston."

"Yeah, she got a bit overprotective." Lynn gnawed on her lip for a moment. "After *Obaa-chan* died, I had on and off visits from members of the North American Dragon Council."

"Dragon Council?"

"It's an oversight body, the members quietly keep track of dragon births, deaths and everything in between."

"They sound like Big Brother."

Lynn managed a half-hearted smile, one she didn't really feel inside. "They questioned me over and over about her death."

"What was there to question?"

Her gaze flickered away to a painted butterfly caught in a carefree dance. "I told them that someone else was there, that she was killed. Murdered." A sob tore from her throat. "But they didn't believe me."

Jen pulled her into a hug again and held on.

Lynn skipped over the period when they thought she'd killed *Obaa-chan*. Those memories —the accusing words and looks— still gave her nightmares, bled her dry. Her mind had crumbled under the pressure like a weak wall. Stop. Don't go there. She shied away as if from an attacking knife. "In the end, they decided she'd set herself on fire. Old dragons tired of life sometimes resort to self-combustion." A shivering breath escaped her. "And that I was a grief-stricken mess."

"What do you believe?"

"I don't know. With my dragon powers wacked out and me losing control…I'm scared." She grasped Jen's hand. "I'm scared that I'm going to lose to the dragon and turn rogue."

She let go of Jen and stared into her empty wine glass. "I'm scared that I will never have what Brenda Jarvis has— a family. If I can't control the dragon, people are not going to be safe around me." She blew an unruly curl out of her face. "Not that I really need a family to further complicate my life."

Jen slipped an arm around her shoulders. "I want you to get this clear. You're my best friend; you're very important to me and you deserve every kind of happiness. I'm going to be right next to you as we get through this."

Lynn nodded. "I know. I just wish I knew how."

Jen bit her lip. "Well, *Obaa-chan* always said," she began.

"A calm mind can conquer anything," both of them ended together.

Jen smiled. "Maybe, she did know what she was talking about. Meditating and focusing on the good of the dragons might be the answer. Like people, dragons can be good and bad. You have a choice."

Lynn nodded and snatched a couple of Cheetos.

"That's what I hope. I figure if I can do something about the fire-starter here that should bring me some good karma and balance the scales."

"Did you sense anything at the fire?"

"Not enough." Lynn licked her fingers clean of the neon orange powder. "I could sense a dragon, but nothing useful as to who it might be." Of course, her libido had recognized the dragon as male, but Jen didn't need to know that. She'd never hear the end of it.

The phone rang again. Startled, Lynn stared at it. Another ring shattered the silence. "Must be Rob ready for round two."

She pushed the talk button and returned the phone to her ear. "Hello?"

Rough breathing echoed down the line.

Lynn rolled her eyes. "Hello?"

"I can't stop thinking about you." The gravelly whisper scraped her nerves raw.

"What?"

"I dream of dragons."

A cold click ended the call. Lynn listened to the droning dial tone for a long moment, then jabbed *69.

The mechanical voice announced the last call came from an unlisted number.

Sheriff Dan Roberts shut the arson file and kneaded his forehead. The words had started dancing together and clues didn't lead anywhere straight. He looked up at the clock on the wall. 11:45 p.m. With a sigh, he pushed out of his chair and grabbed his car keys from the hook near the door.

As he stepped out of his office, he looked around and nodded at Jenkins. As an ex-military guy, the deputy did intimidation well. All he had to do was stand around, freeze his face and flex his muscles. "Let's go."

Jenkin's dropped his cards and unfolded to his six-foot two-inch height. He lumbered to the door and held it open. Another benefit of the military, the fellow didn't ask too many questions.

"We are going to the Chadbourne Street bridge downtown, contact me only if it's something you guys can't handle." He nodded to the remaining deputies.

One of the older guys snorted. "Going fishing at this time of night?"

"Yeah, fishing for information."

He swung through the outside door and jogged down the stairs to his personal vehicle. An unmarked Ford Taurus. He didn't want to announce his arrival and spook his prey. He clicked the car open and both men climbed in.

"I'm just looking to talk to the guys that camp down there, shouldn't be any trouble." He started the car and drove out into the street.

"So you're playing good cop to my bad cop?"

Roberts grinned. Jenkins was alright. "Yeah. You just stand around and scare the crap out of them, and I'll be Mr. Friendly."

He tapped the steering wheel. "But be prepared for anything. We might stumble across the arsonist. I don't expect to, but we might."

"Yes, Sir."

They drove past hulking, ornate churches lit up by spotlights. Stone angels and crosses stood silent and glowing like eerie sentinels on either side of the street.

"The old Sheriff, my dad, used to say it's best to catch people by surprise."

"Yes, Sir."

Half a block from the bridge, he killed the lights.

Moonlight illuminated the empty street. Decent folk were all tucked up in bed, unaware of all the life going on without them. Being Sheriff didn't afford him that luxury. He parked the car at the closed shop nearest to the beginning of the bridge. 11:55 p.m.

He twisted the key out and both men slid out of the car. The doors shut behind them with soft clicks. They fast-walked to the railing. Despite the full moon, darkness shadowed the steps. Roberts clung to the wall as he eased his way down. The smell of smoke wafted in the air, reminding him of long-ago camping trips.

They rounded the corner and came across men huddled around a bonfire built inside a metal trashcan. Some held their hands out toward the warm flames, while other stared mesmerized at the glow. A few lay scattered on the incline, already asleep or drinking from bottles hidden in paper sacks.

The tableau froze as he and Jenkins emerged into the light. Only the drinkers and sleepers ignored them.

Roberts pulled out packs of cigarettes from his jacket and held them up. "Just want to talk, that's all."

Jenkins took a step forward and folded his arms across his big slab of a chest. Roberts winced. He could see the whites of eyes and the twitch of muscles. He waggled the packs in his hands. "Got some smokes for your trouble."

A young blond with a bruised nose stepped forward, eyed the pack.

Roberts took a cigarette out and offered it to him.

The man grabbed it. "What you want to know?"

He held out a few more cigarettes and looked around. "Any other smokers in the group?"

Several men shuffled forward. The stench of old sweat and body odor wafted forward. Roberts kept on smiling as he handed the bribe out. "How come you guys don't go to the Salvation Army?"

"Don't like sleeping indoors."

"Can't stand the preaching."

"Don't got no room last time I checked."

Roberts nodded, feeling like a bobble head toy. "You guys out here two nights ago?"

Shrugs and murmurs of ascent rippled all around.

"Anybody go out to the country? Out by Carlsbad or Paradise Valley?"

Silence.

"Come on guys, we were getting along so well."

Jenkins twisted his head this way and that, until the bones in his neck popped in the silence.

"You can talk to me or to my deputy." He thumbed at Jenkins.

Wide-eyed gazes darted from one officer to another. Quick, jerky shakes of heads answered.

"Alright, anybody see anything interesting lately?"

Uneasy glances flickered around. Roberts shook the remaining pack in his hand. "I'm looking for information. Anybody see anything strange? I'll give you the entire pack if you give me something useful."

"What's this about?" The blond kid piped up again.

Roberts shrugged. "I'm the sheriff and I need to know about all kinds of things happening in my town."

"I saw something, maybe." The quavering whisper came from one of the drinkers.

Roberts ambled forward and held out a cigarette. "Yeah?"

The man licked already wet lips, revealing missing and rotting teeth. "Yeah."

"Where were you?"

The guy snatched the cigarette and brought it to his nose. Took a deep sniff. "Behind the library, near the dumpster."

Roberts held out another. "There's more here. So what time was it?"

The second cigarette got tucked behind an ear and hid by greasy hair. "Still dark. Sometime before dawn."

The timing fit Jen's fire. His chest tightened as he remembered her pretty face all puffy and red from tears and worry. He wanted to close the case, reassure Jen, hold her hand. The sheriff leaned forward. "So what did you see?"

"I was behind the dumpster."

"Doing what?"

"I got hungry in the night. So I was snacking on an old burger I found."

Roberts stared at the brown paper bag the man cradled in his lap. "So what you see beside the burger?"

A crafty light glinted in the old man's eyes and he flashed a toothless smile. "Another smoke might help jog my memory."

The old coot had nerves. Roberts snorted and handed over another stick.

"I was hidden behind the dumpster, when this large, black shadow swooped over me, swallowed all the light." The man took a swig from his bottle. "I looked up."

"And?"

His gaze shot away and boomeranged back. He leaned forward. "It was a dragon."

Roberts shook his head. The geezer ought to get points for originality. Most others just saw space ships.

The old guy's chin shot up and his eyes narrowed. "I know what I saw. A dang big dragon flew right over me and headed west, toward Paradise Valley where they'se been having the fires."

A boot sailed through the air and thwacked the

speaker in the head.

"Oww!"

"Shut the fuck up you old fool."

The sheriff whipped around toward the angry voice and saw one of the sleepers glaring over his shoulder. This guy looked like what he'd imagine Rasputin looked like. Crazy, gleaming gray eyes stared out of a dirty gaunt face covered in ropy, knotted hair. It ran from the top of the head into the moustache and beard. A dusty black overcoat covered most of his long, thin body.

"Some people are trying to sleep here." The man glared and then turned away.

Roberts' gaze landed on the boot lying near the whimpering old dragon-sighting guy. An old, scuffed and creased brown work boot. He studied the sole of the shoe. His mouth felt dry. The tread pattern seemed familiar. He nodded to Jenkins to bag it and made his way to the sleeper.

"Hey, you can't go about throwing things at people." He stood with hands on his hips, close to his weapon and handcuffs. "I might have to haul you to jail for that."

The man cracked his eyelids open and sent out a bleary stare. "Just trying to sleep."

Roberts eyed the other boot peeking out from under the coat. He stepped forward and tapped the foot with his own. "You got some nice boots there," he said. "Aren't you lucky? Where'd you get them?"

The man pushed himself up and hunched over his knees. "Found 'em."

"Where?"

A sullen glare. "By the library dumpster."

"Everything seems to happen around this dumpster."

Bony shoulders rose and fell. "I was there same time as the dumb ass claims he saw the dragon."

"Did you see the dragon?"

A laugh wheezed out of him. "I ain't crazy or drunk."

"So you were at the dumpster in the middle of the night."

The man moved his head in a slow shake. "It was morning, I was hunting breakfast."

"And you found the boots?"

"How about one of those smokes?"

Roberts tossed him the entire pack. "Tell me about the boots."

The man turned the pack around in his hands. "Thanks Sheriff."

"The boots?"

"A beat-up green truck drove up and a man chucked them out the window. I grabbed them."

"You see the man's face?"

The cigarette pack disappeared in the coat. "Nah, he wore a hat pulled low over his face."

Roberts massaged his neck and nodded. "I'll need the other boot."

"Fuck."

CHAPTER 7

Lynn basked in the early morning sun streaming through the bedroom window while she balanced on one leg, eyes closed, and pretended to be a tree.

She focused on her breathing, trying to follow *Obaa-chan's* advice and calm her mind. A calm mind can conquer anything. Now if she could just convince herself.

The weird phone call and writing about the fire had riled up the dragon again, so much that she'd felt the heat and smelled the smoke sitting in Jen's guest room. In the quiet hours of the night, fear of the unknown adversary had clutched her heart until she'd concentrated on Timmy's face as he watched the fire.

She'd started the article with that image and gone into how Timmy would be having a birthday soon without any presents. However, he would have his family and Lucky. She wrote about the hard work and heroics of the Paradise Valley volunteer firefighters, and mentioned Jack and the part he played. She ended with the community pulling together to help the Jarvis family. Lynn read the story almost half a dozen times before emailing it to the *Herald*. That'd been almost a half-hour ago.

She hoped the paper would print the story. Should she follow up with a call to the paper?

Calm your mind. Be in the now. Her arms reached toward the sun like strong branches, allowing her sorrows and worries to drop, spin and flutter away like dead leaves scattered by the wind of her will.

Exuberant knocking startled Lynn into planting both feet on the meditation mat. Her aching arms sagged to her sides. "Yes?"

"Phone call for you," Jen called out.

Damn, she was popular lately. "Can you take a message?"

"It's the editor of the newspaper, I think you better take it."

Lynn threw the door open and snatched the phone from Jen. "Hello?"

"Top of the morning, Ms. Alexander! This is Scott Hernandez, editor and publisher of the *San Angelo Herald*."

Worry niggled at her. "Did you receive my story? Were you able to open the document?"

"Yes, yes. I read your story about the fire."

He probably hated it. She hadn't written a news story since college. "I'd be happy to rewrite it if you need me to."

A chuckle sounded in her ear. "Hey, can you come down to the office and talk to my reporters about accommodating their editor?" He chuckled some more. "The story read fine. It'll be in the paper tomorrow."

Heat swarmed her face. "Oh. Thanks for letting me know."

"What I'd like to know is if you're free for lunch today?" Hernandez cleared his throat. "I have a deal you want to seal."

A woman on a mission, Lynn arrived at the *San Angelo Herald* building fifteen minutes before her lunch date.

While the editor had amused and intrigued her, what she really wanted was information. If anyone had the dirt on the local people, it'd be the newspaper guy. The challenge would be focusing him on her agenda rather than his.

The receptionist laid aside her crochet work and smiled as Lynn stated her business, and then buzzed the editor. "Your lunch appointment is here!"

Lynn had just sat down on the plush couch, when the newsroom door swung open and a big man bounded out, his right hand extended. "Good to see you Ms. Alexander."

She jumped up. He still towered over her as he pumped her hand.

Hernandez was younger than Lynn expected, maybe in his forties, with wings of silver at his temples that added a distinguished look. His dark gaze studied her with intense speculation. "Ready to go?"

She nodded. He stepped briskly ahead, leading the way, but stopped at the receptionist's desk. "Keep this boat afloat while I'm out to lunch, okay?" he said. "I'm counting on you, Abby." He gave her a jaunty salute and continued forward.

Lynn offered Abby a wave and rushed after

Hernandez. He barged through a second set of doors, before he stopped and sniffed the crisp, autumn air. "Perfect day for a walk. You don't mind if we walk to lunch, right?" He marched down the sidewalk not waiting for an answer.

Lynn hurried, doing her best to keep up and not trip in her heels. She should have worn sneakers.

"So, who are you? What's your background?"

She filled him in about her journalism degree and her previous public relations experience. "I'm between jobs at the moment."

He clucked sympathetically, without slowing his pace.

Lynn thanked the powers that be for the Don't Walk sign at the corner. She caught her breath as they waited for the light to change at Chadbourne and Beauregard. Her feet ached in the high heels and she could feel blisters forming. So much for the power outfit. "Where are we headed?"

Hernandez pointed across the street at Fuentes Downtown Café. "All the movers and shakers eat there."

She eyed several men and women coming in and out the doors, standing around shaking hands or talking on cell phones. In between the power suits, she glimpsed a scruffy man sitting hunched over on a bench right in front of the restaurant.

The man raised his head from the folds of an oversized, dusty black coat. Her gaze collided with glittering gray eyes set in a dirty face obscured by straggly salt-and-pepper hair and a beard.

Traffic ceased flowing, people turned to statues, the dragon within her tensed. Lynn drew in slow, labored breaths. Her racing heart petered to a sluggish rhythm, the blood in her veins congealed. She stood rooted to the spot and held the man's stare.

He sent her a mock salute.

Cold fear wormed inside her. She fisted her hands at her sides. The tips of her fingers burned to grow dragon claws.

The man's slim shoulders shook as if he were laughing at her. He leaned back and folded his arms.

Lynn blinked as a portly man emerged from the restaurant and blocked her view. Breathing easier, she angled her head this way and that to see around him.

The light changed and Hernandez rushed forward. Lynn pulled her attention away long enough to cross with him. As soon as they stepped onto the curb, Lynn tried to relocate the vagrant, but he'd disappeared.

She found herself surrounded by people. Several of them shook hands with the editor and said hello. Lynn pushed through the crowd and looked up and down Chadbourne. Adrenaline zipped through her as she caught the tail-end of a fluttering black coat turning the corner. She glanced back at Hernandez, then at the corner again.

Should she chase the homeless guy? She still had to get information from the newspaper man. Besides, what would she do even if she did catch the stranger? Ignoring the nervous knot in her gut, Lynn turned. Now Hernandez had disappeared.

Hoping he'd entered Fuentes, she plunged through the door.

He stood in the lobby, laughing and talking to a group of people. Lynn breathed a sigh of relief that he hadn't noticed her odd behavior. The restaurant owner led them to a booth at the back and left them with some chips and salsa.

After they settled in, Hernandez locked gazes with her. "You're a good writer, Alexander."

"Thanks." She slipped her shoes off under the table and almost groaned in relief. "You mentioned something about a deal?"

He drummed his fingers on the glass tabletop and jogged a leg in place. She wanted to put him in a straitjacket.

"You want a job?"

Lynn stared at him. "Excuse me?"

"A job. You're a good writer, who's out of work, and we're short staffed. So, how about it?"

She leaned back into the vinyl cushion, massaging one foot with the other. "I'm just visiting a friend here and happened to be at that fire. I don't know how long I'm staying."

Hernandez picked up the fork beside his plate and tap-tapped it on the table. "Why don't you freelance for us while you're here?" he said. "We could use good copy and we'd pay you per story. Nothing exorbitant, but decent."

Lynn almost kissed the guy. What a perfect cover for her to investigate the fires and ask questions. While she wasn't hurting for money thanks to *Obaa-chan*, extra cash would still be nice. But she didn't want to appear over-eager. "I don't know what to say."

"A thank you would do," he said. "Look at it this way, you'll get to try this out and you'll be free to leave whenever." He reached over and snatched a package of crackers from the small container on the table.

"True."

"It'll be a nice entry on your resume." He tap-tap-tapped the table with the packet.

Lynn leaned forward. "What kind of stories do you want?"

A waiter came by and took their order. Hernandez greeted him as Paul and asked about his studies and his family. After Paul left, he leaned back against the booth, the crackers still in hand.

"We've wanted to cover Paradise Valley better for a long while," he said. "So anything important that's happening in that community would be good."

"I can do that." She paused for a heartbeat. "Can I also do fire stories? Maybe an investigative piece? See if there's anything to link all the incidents together."

He stilled and narrowed his eyes at her. "What do you know that I don't?"

"Just a gut feeling I've got."

He set the package of crumbled crackers down and raked a hand through his hair. "I have great respect for women's intuition, but news stories can't be based on that."

Lynn folded her arms across her chest. Too bad she couldn't tell him about her dragon instincts. Hollowness bloomed in her stomach. Could she trust her dragon? It'd been acting off-balance and erratic lately. "Fine, I shouldn't have said anything."

"You didn't let me finish," he said. "Intuition, like rumor and gossip, is a great springboard for stories."

"There's no smoke without fire."

"Exactly. You first come up with an idea, and then you search for facts to either support or refute it."

"So, if I think these fires are a series of arsons, I need to get hold of facts next," she said. "Maybe I should interview the arson investigator."

Hernandez beamed at her. "You do have to interview him, but not just yet." Instead he told her to do some online research about arson and serial arsonists. He also told her to talk to area fire chiefs, the Sheriff's department, and law enforcement professors at the local university.

"If you go in with some knowledge, you'll be able to ask pertinent questions," he said. "Then Anderson will talk to you rather than talk *down* to you. That makes a difference."

Her respect for the man shot up by leaps and bounds. "Thanks, I'll do that."

The editor cleared his throat. "Does this mean you've accepted my offer?"

She grinned. "You have a deal."

They shook on it. "And thanks for this opportunity."

The waiter placed a sizzling plate brimming with fajitas, pepper and onion in front of her. The savory steam made Lynn's stomach beg for a taste. She took a warm tortilla and placed some meat and vegetables on it.

"By the way," he said, cutting into his cheese enchiladas, "did you know one of the most infamous serial arsonists in America was an arson investigator? John Orr."

Lynn stopped folding the tortilla. "You really are a fount of knowledge."

"Don't you forget that, Alexander," he said. "So you met the enigmatic Jack Callaghan. He was quite the hero in your story."

She swallowed her bite and shrugged. "I don't know if I'd call him enigmatic."

Hernandez shot her sharp look. "Well, you certainly seem to have a seen a different side to him, but he can be rather closemouthed. Callaghan's got this love-hate relationship with the area."

Lynn managed a smile. "Jack is some sort of Dr. Jekyll and Mr. Hyde?"

"Goes back ages," the editor said. After downing a bite, he continued, "The story is his great-great-grandfather owned a hardware-dry goods store here.

Then his great-grandfather added a grocery to it. Partnered with some Mexicans and Chinese in the area to supply vegetables and set up a meat counter. He sold everything from milk and beer to nails and barbed wire."

Lynn tasted a forkful of smoky re-fried beans. "Interesting, but where's the juicy bits?"

He leaned forward and lowered his voice. "When the region suffered a drought, farming and ranching went into a decline. People kept buying staples from the Callaghans, but mostly on an IOU basis."

Hernandez shoveled in another bite of enchilada. Lynn drummed her fingers on the table.

"After a while Mr. Callaghan called in the loans and took over people's lands. In other cases, he bought land but at dirt cheap prices. Anyway, he set up the Callaghan Ranch and became the largest landowner in the area."

"That's quite a story." Lynn gulped some water. According to her grandmother, sometimes dragon characteristics leached into human personality. Characteristics like greed and hoarding.

Hernandez shrugged his bullish shoulders. "It rubbed people the wrong way. To make matters worse, oil was discovered on different parts of the ranch in the early 1900s. Made the Callaghans richer."

Lynn balled her hands into fists as he took a hefty swallow of ice tea.

"The next two generations of Callaghans didn't help. Jack's grandfather built up a reputation for drinking, gambling and romancing other men's wives. His father ran unsuccessfully for political office, spent freely and spouted history and philosophy."

Characteristics like taking risks, over-indulging, and, even, bookishness. Of course, all these flaws also appeared in ordinary humans to a lesser degree.

A picture of Jack with his black eye flashed through her mind. Characteristics like temper and aggressiveness. She recalled the townspeople's cold reception at the parts store. "Don't tell me they hold a grudge against Jack because of the rest of the Callaghans."

The editor grabbed a chip and dunked it into the salsa. "People have long memories here, and a lot of them don't look beyond the fact that he's a Callaghan."

Before she could prod more, the waiter brought the ticket to the table.

Lynn winced as she forced her feet back into her shoes. He paid with an expense card and added a hefty tip for Paul.

Stepping into the sun again, Lynn glanced around but didn't see the vagrant. Hernandez set off at a trot, and she hurried to keep up with him.

"Welcome to the *Herald*," he said. "You can start with the county commissioner's meeting tomorrow."

"Tomorrow? On a Saturday?" Lynn stumbled.

"Yup, that was the only day all the commissioners could meet. Our commissioners are real dedicated, especially around election time," he ended with a wink.

Lynn managed to nod and wobble along. Nothing like being thrown into the river to learn to swim. Holy Freaking Wasabi.

Jack's name had popped up too many times for comfort. Lynn paced in her room, worrying a furrow into the carpet as she contemplated her next move.

Check out Jack's house. Without Jen. Sneaking around was risky business and she didn't want to get her friend in trouble.

She chewed her lower lip. Also, the way Jen had been gushing about Jack told her she might not be open to the idea of him being a suspect. Was she really not interested in the man?

Lynn's unease multiplied as the hunky firefighter came to mind. She rubbed her temples. Truth be told, Jack had been nothing but nice —tempting— since they'd met and she felt like shit for suspecting him. However, she couldn't ignore the jack-booted march of goose bumps along her skin. Maybe she'd find some kind of proof or clue that would settle the matter once and for all.

She changed into her running clothes and shoes, then slipped on her backpack, before hurrying to the kitchen.

Jen stood at the table picking up their dinner dishes. "Where are you off to?"

"A run." She took her plate to the sink. "Do you have a water bottle I can borrow?"

"You just ate. Don't you want to rest?"

Lynn rolled her shoulders. "No, a run should help work off some of the calories."

Jen shook her head and turned back to the dishes. "There's bottled water in the fridge."

She grabbed one and slipped it into the backpack. "Want to join me?"

"Eew, no." Jen scrunched up her face. "I'm allergic to exercise. Just get home before dark."

Lynn waved and ran out the back door, smiling about Jen's reaction. Some things never changed. Thank goodness. She did a few jumping jacks and stretches, then jogged toward Jack's place. The rural road didn't come with sidewalks, but fortunately there was little traffic. She ran along the bar ditch, checking out the new environment. The sweet smell of hay laced her every breath and the chirping of birds accompanied her pounding feet. Lynn relaxed as she slid into the familiar rhythm of the run.

Waves of anger reached out to her as she neared the Callaghan ranch. While the exercise hadn't winded her, the raw emotion did. She stood, panting, and scanned the overgrown pasture between the rough road and Jack's house. Her glance danced over thorny bushes and cacti peeking out from the overgrown grass, then the clumps of trees dotting the landscape. If she cut through the pasture she'd have to watch her step, but she'd definitely be less exposed.

Crouching, she pushed her way through, zeroing in on the house. She ignored the poke and prickle of the underbrush and focused on the feelings suffusing the atmosphere. Underneath the anger she caught the lingering odor of dragon musk. Shoving away the dread thickening inside her, she zig-zagged from one cluster of trees to the next.

Not seeing anybody, Lynn inched closer to the tree-shaded alcove by Jack's front door where she'd previously sensed the hidden presence. She ducked behind the thicket of leaves and branches, ready to battle whoever or whatever.

Emptiness greeted her. Her breathing eased, as she bent and searched the ground. Scuff marks in the dirt obliterated whatever footprints there'd been. A bit of white in the leafy ground cover under the window caught her eye. Using her left foot, she toed leaves out of the way. Someone had kicked several cigarette butts into the bushes.

Shit. A cigarette had caused the fire at Jen's.

Lynn rummaged through her backpack until she found the pack of tissues inside. The plastic crinkled loudly as she pulled a fresh one out. Damn, she was as loud as a dragon in a china shop. She squatted and gingerly picked a few of the cigarettes up with the tissue, brought it close to her nose. Stale odor of smoke, fading anger and dragon musk.

Slipping the tissue-wrapped clue into her backpack, she zipped it and listened. Nothing but a piping bird song drifted to her. Taking a deep breath, she unfolded herself and exited her hiding spot. Her mind urged her to get back to Jen's, but curiosity pushed her to explore. To come all this way and not at least peek into the house would be a shame.

After a quick glance around, Lynn hurried up the steps onto the porch and peered inside through the beveled glass and wrought iron decorating the top half of the door. All she could see was a hat rack/bench and a polished wood floor disappearing into the dark heart of the house. The interior seemed empty. Just to be sure, Lynn reached up and rang the doorbell. The muted sound of deep, church-bells floated to her. She shifted foot to foot and waited.

Licking her lips, Lynn tried the door handle. Locked tight. She stood, hands on her hips, and stared at the solid wood. Maybe there'd be a backdoor. Maybe it'd be unlocked. And maybe she was the queen of Thebes. Oh well, no harm in checking it out. She bounded down the steps and headed toward the back of the house.

Loud crashing through the bushes startled her. The snap of branches grew more frenzied. Dragon? No, a dragon wouldn't be running around so openly. Would it? What else could it be? In the wilds of West Texas? Anything. Feral hog. Cougar pack. Mutant skunk. *Oh God, please don't let it be a skunk.*

Growls thrummed in the air as the thrashing and snorting came nearer. She backed up a few steps before stopping herself. Flashes of gold glistened in between the leaves. The branches immediately in front of her shivered and shook. Her muscles tightened and coiled, ready for action.

A large dog burst through the thicket and pounced on her.

A dog. Just a dog. Lynn screamed as she landed on her back in the dirt, with her arms full of the hairy, slobbering creature.

The clatter of horse hooves pounded the earth and stopped inches from her. Defending herself from hot, wet kisses, Lynn looked up at two cowboys on horseback silhouetted by the sun.

"Cannon!"

The sharp command cut through the air and froze the tussling pair for a moment. The dog whined and looked over its shoulder as Lynn squinted at the shadowy figures, trying to place the voice. With a wag of his tail, the dog returned to licking her face with renewed enthusiasm.

Muttered curses buzzed in the air as one of the cowboys swung off his horse and hauled the dog off her. Jack.

"Come on, Cannon." Jack said, pushing the dog into a sitting position. "Sit, boy!"

Once Cannon had settled down, Jack squatted next to the dog and looked at her. "You okay?"

Caught in his piercing green gaze, Lynn found herself at a loss for words. He bent over her, close enough for her to see the gold flecks floating in his eyes. Before she could nod, the other man peered over Jack's shoulder and glared at her like she was a bug lying in the dust. "This is private property, yer trespassin'."

Jack's shoulders stiffened. "She's a friend." He flashed a wry smile. "You've already met Cannon, so named for his tendency to cannon through everything and everyone." Then he gestured at the other man. "This is

Sam White, my sister's ranch foreman. And Sam, this is Lynn Alexander, Jen Delgado's friend."

White grunted and held onto his scowl. "She's still a stranger and got no business skulking around."

Heat warmed her face and her gaze dropped as fast as a sinking stone.

"Head on back to the barn Sam, and take Sundance with you." Jack didn't bother to turn to look at the man. "There should be some wire stored in the back. I'll be out there in a little while."

White spat into the dust and grabbed the reins of Jack's horse. "Damn fool!"

Lynn wasn't sure whether the label applied to her or Jack. She watched the manager stomp off, cursing loudly about strangers traipsing around and causing trouble. Soon he disappeared into the distance in a drum of hoof beats. Cannon wheeled and galloped off behind them.

"Sorry about that," Jack said. "Somebody's been cutting the fencing between the ranch and my fields so Sam's kinda prickly."

She nodded. He studied her back quietly, his face empty of expression. "So, what brings you out here?"

Her tongue refused to work.

"What? You missed me already and had to visit?"

She looked up and caught the smile shadowing his lips. "No. I was out for a run and decided to take the scenic route."

"I'm glad you appreciate the view." The smile spread to a lazy grin.

She flushed. "I meant the countryside."

"Of course." He took off his hat and wiped his brow with a handkerchief. "Then you saw my place and couldn't resist another meeting."

She matched his smirk. "Don't flatter yourself."

"So, back to my original question." He settled his hat back on his head. "What are you doing here?"

Lynn found herself flushing again, along with a strange sensation bubbling inside her. When did she turn into a lava lamp? "Actually, I got turned around and was hoping to get some directions."

"Well, darlin' helping damsels in distress is my specialty."

The accompanying wink set off hot sparks inside her. Maybe her mom was right— maybe she and her dragon were off-kilter. She'd been around plenty of men before, and never felt so wired.

He wiped his palms on his jeans and held out a hand to her. "Here, let's get you up first."

She grasped his hand. Electricity jolted from her fingertips up her arm. Lynn let out a sharp, surprised squeak and stumbled.

Jack's solid arms embraced her in an instant. "You might have a twisted ankle."

An injury would be easier to explain than crazy hormones. The ploy might also get her into the house. "Ow. Ow."

He gathered her into his arms and lifted her off the ground. His warm, musky scent ignited a sizzle at the pit of her stomach, torching her insides and flaming onward. Lynn focused on a distant tree over his shoulder. *Focus. Focus yourself.*

A cool breeze soothed her skin as a beautiful sunset blazed behind him. The scene could be the ending of one of the old Western movies her dad watched—the cowboy ready to take his bride into his home. Ready to kiss and claim her. The last thought punched straight to her stomach and a fever burned her cheeks. Happily-ever-after only happened in romance novels and Hollywood.

He looked at her through the sooty fringe of dark lashes. "Now let's see what we can do for your pain," he drawled, his voice soft and sultry.

"Kiss and make it better?" Oh. My. God. Did she just blurt out those words? Was that breathy voice hers? Her mind and tongue both seemed to be going at the same speed— out of control. Lynn's heart cantered.

His eyes —green, green eyes— widened, glittered with interest and something more as he stood rooted to the spot, holding her against his thudding chest. Full, sexy lips and square jaw shadowed in stubble. She wanted to run her hands all over and discover every soft and hard inch of him. Her breath came in short, shallow bursts as his head drew closer. His warm breath whispered across her skin.

She managed a strangled laugh. "But an icepack would probably be more effective."

He chuckled. "Probably, but the other sounded a whole lot more fun."

"Oh." She dropped her gaze and found herself staring at the V of his tanned chest revealed by his unbuttoned blue cotton shirt. The desire to undo the rest of the buttons made her throat dry.

He pulled back, shifted her in his arms. "Well, um, let's get you inside and see what we can do."

Her gaze flicked up and clashed with his. Her mind whispered promises.

Jack marched around to the back of the house, up onto the back porch and kicked open the screen door and the unlocked backdoor.

Dammit, guess she was the queen of Thebes. A frustrated breath escaped her. *Okay, you're here to play detective. So detect.*

Inventory of the room might help her get her mind off

the fact that the damn man made her so weak-kneed that she had to be carried around. Lynn's gaze traveled over the cheerful yellow mudroom. A white washer and dryer set stood against one wall. A wooden table, a bench, and a shelf stacked with boots and shoes and umbrellas. Nothing out of the ordinary.

They passed through the kitchen/dining area and her gaze fell on a dark wood sideboard against one wall. Ferocious-looking flying dragons were carved onto each door. Two more dragons faced each other and formed the decorative top of the piece.

"That's a sixteenth century piece from Mexico that my great grandfather found during his travels," he said.

Admiration shone in his eyes as he looked at the sideboard. Lynn glanced back at the piece. "It's beautiful. You like dragons, then?"

He shrugged. "Don't really have much of an opinion on dragons, but my forefathers apparently had a taste for them," he said, walking through the shadowed house. "I just like the sideboard because of the craftsmanship."

Lynn leaned back in his arms and kept her eyes trained on the sideboard. Where she'd seen dragons and gone on alert, Jack had seen the creatures and thought of the craftsman, someone who'd spent hours making pieces of wood into functional art. His noticing and appreciation made her wonder if she needed to slow down and take in the details of life. Or maybe she was just coming down with something.

They passed a series of family portraits. All of the men sported dark hair, green eyes, high cheekbones and hawkish noses. The last face seemed softer, with rounded, ruddy cheeks and multiple chins. The one before it had twinkling eyes and a mysterious smile. He seemed to be a good-looking rogue. But the other two were almost identical down to the cold eyes and sneering lips. The first one had a flare of white hair giving the man a skunk-like appearance.

"Who's who?" she asked.

"Great-great-grandpa, followed by Great-grand pa, Grandpa, and my father."

He carried her through another set of doors and stopped just inside. Musky dragon smell hung in the air, soft and dry, like undisturbed time in a forgotten cave. "Can you turn on the lights? The switch is just by your head."

She flicked on the switch and light flooded the room. A number of animal heads —from deer to bear— stared down at her with glass eyes. She stifled a scream as her gaze shifted from curved horns to bared fangs. In the end, none of it had been enough. A shudder ran down her spine. Damn spooky. She pulled her gaze away from those eyes. "I see you are a decorating-with-dead-animals fan."

Jack laughed as he settled her into a gigantic leather armchair and pulled up a stool for her foot. "Not really," he said. "This was my grandfather's sanctuary and he was the great hunter."

He waved a hand around. "Then my father inherited it and added some of the furniture. I haven't bothered changing the décor."

She looked around. A lot of the things —like the heavily carved desk, the wet bar, the ornate crystal chandelier, the thick maroon drapes with gold fringes— didn't seem to fit Jack.

"So how come you haven't laid your claim?" she asked. "I thought all men marked their territory."

"I don't know," he said. "Just hadn't thought about it. I'll get the ice pack."

She watched him leave. An interesting man with hidden layers. Well, she'd unwrap him— the mental image that popped into her head warmed her all over again. *Figuratively speaking only*. She'd get to the bottom of the who and what of Jack Callaghan. She looked around the room until the display cabinet occupying a corner caught her attention. Curious, she padded over to it. Guns, of course. A few arrowheads and battered ancient coins. Her gaze fell on a dessert-plate-sized shimmering scale and she drew in a sharp breath. Silvery, with concentric rings of white on white, it was beautiful. "A dragon scale," she whispered. "A big one, too."

Trembling with equal measures of excitement and nerves, Lynn fumbled with the latch. Finally, it snicked open and she reached in. For a moment her hand hovered over the scale. Touching it, holding it, would make it so much more undeniably real. But she'd never seen such a large scale. How big was the dragon it came from? Even *Obaa-chan*, the oldest dragon she'd known personally, had been like thirteen feet, the size of a playground see-saw. She took a few calming breaths. This particular dragon must have been more like a Tyrannosaurus Rex.

Her fingers closed on the cool, smooth scale. She pulled it out and cradled it, spending minutes just staring at the thing. Finally, her mind kicked into gear. She counted the calcified rings, each representing a year. Damn, the thing had been about a hundred and twenty years old when it lost this particular scale. So, not Jack. He definitely didn't act like an ancient dragon.

She held the scale up to the light. The tension in her shoulders relaxed. The edges were almost transparent, so the dragon had lost the scale a long time ago. Good, then her chances of running into a ginormous geriatric dragon were pretty remote.

She gently returned the scale to its place in the display cabinet and latched the door again.

"What are you doing up?"

Guilt flushed through her as she turned. How long had he been standing there? "Curiosity got the best of me."

"Haven't you heard of the saying curiosity killed the cat?" He walked over to her and looked into the cabinet. "More worthless ancestor junk."

"They can't be totally worthless," she said. "Otherwise, why keep them?"

"There are some neat stories attached to most of those items," he said. "That musket for instance was used by my great, great grandfather when he was a foot soldier in the confederate army."

"What about the scale?"

He laughed. "My grandfather always told these tall fishing tales. The more he drank, the larger and wilder the fish got." He gazed at the scale. "Looks like at least one of his stories might have been true. That must have been a monster."

Lynn stared at Jack. Was he truly clueless about the scale? Or was he lying again? "Why didn't he get it stuffed and mounted like his other trophies?"

He glanced around the walls. "Maybe he ran out of space." He swept her off her feet and carried her back to the chair. "Let's take care of the foot, then I'll drive you back to Jen's."

Once he'd settled her into a chair, Jack knelt at her feet and quirked a brow at her. "Which one hurts?"

"The left."

His fingers slipped under her calf, raised her foot and placed it on a well-muscled thigh.

Lynn gnawed her lower lip as he pulled the lace out of its knot and carefully eased the shoe off. What took moments seemed to take agonizingly long. He peeled the sock off and revealed her foot.

She felt strangely naked as his cool fingers caressed and massaged her skin. How could such innocent touch be so intimate? Warmth pulsed through her, made her gasp.

His fingers stilled. "Sorry, did that hurt?"

"No." She licked her lip. "It felt good."

He smiled and his fingers worked their way up, slipped under her pants leg.

Lynn closed her eyes as all thought ceased to exist, aware only of the desire that thrummed and shivered through her body.

Fingers and heat traveled back down. Then a sharp jab of cold. Breath hissed out of her. Lynn's eyes popped open as she almost leapt from the chair.

He'd applied the damn ice-pack.

CHAPTER 8

Next morning Lynn beamed at the newspaper as she read her story and sipped coffee. The editors had made only a few minor changes. She ran a finger along the "special correspondent" designation following her name. "It sure felt good to use my laptop for something more worthwhile than checking email."

Jen nodded. Being an early riser, she'd read the paper first. "You have a writing talent. You shouldn't waste it."

"Maybe," Lynn said taking a sip of her coffee. "Writing an article like this is definitely more rewarding than some of the ad jingles I had to come up with."

"I know I prefer you out of work and writing cool articles rather than dying a slow corporate death." Jen arched an eyebrow. "Or writing a book you don't share with anybody."

Lynn sighed. Yeah well, some people had natural talent and calling, while others had nightmares and screwed-up lives. Sometimes, she envied Jen's creative and happy spirit.

Her friend glanced at her watch and hopped out of her chair. "*Vamonos!* We have to go!" They planned to ride together to the county meeting since Jen would be requesting a grant for Paradise Valley Volunteer Fire Department. Lynn chased after her.

When they arrived at the county courthouse, Jen screeched into a parking spot. "Let's go, let's go!"

Lynn followed Jen into the library, then up the stairs to the second-floor meeting room. They stood huffing in front of the closed door. A young girl, sitting at a table covered in piles of paper, handed them agendas along with a welcoming smile. "They're still in executive session."

"All that hurrying, just to wait," Lynn jabbed her elbow into her friend's arm.

Jen rolled her eyes and then introduced the girl as Lexie, the new intern at the county clerk's office.

"What are they in closed session about?" The lowliest person on the totem pole often gave details without knowing any better.

Lexie shrugged. "Some personnel issues and a land deal of some sort."

Just as Lynn opened her mouth to ask more questions, the girl's cell phone chirped. Lexie glanced at it and lit up. "It's the boyfriend. Hey, can you guys watch the table for a bit?" She waved at the table. "Hand out agendas and stuff if someone new comes by?"

Receiving their nods, she thanked them and took off

down the corridor giggling into the phone. Jen sank into the chair, as Lynn glanced at the agenda. Curiosity pricked her. What land development? Where in the county? She looked through the stacks of paper on the table. "Great, there's supporting materials for all the agenda items in the public session."

Jen shook her head. "Think of all the poor trees. I'm lobbying for them to put everything on CDs and made available to anyone interested."

"Not a bad idea, but not everybody has a computer or uses one." Lynn picked up one of everything. Her eyes fell on a stack of red folders that had spilled across the floor behind the chair. She bent down and restacked the folders, taking one for her pile.

The door flew open, and several men stepped out laughing and shaking hands. A tall, young man, dressed in a snappy navy blue blazer and chinos, stuck out among the more casual county bunch. Her gut tightened, and the dragon shivered under her skin. Surprised and suspicious at the sudden wakefulness of her beast, Lynn considered the young man.

Did he have something to do with the proposed development? He definitely looked city-slick— his clothes, the shoes, and the Bluetooth almost hidden by trendy longish brown hair with blond highlights. Yet, somehow, he reminded her of Jack. Maybe it was his bearing. Or maybe she just had Jack on her mind.

Both men were about the same height and coloring, but the similarities ended there. This guy seemed thinner, his face softer, rounder— overall, more boyish.

Then the stranger's pale gray eyes met hers.

Cold ghostly fingers brushed her thoughts. Lynn stiffened, then forced out a smile.

His gaze traveled down her body and then back again.

Red, hot lust slammed her. Lynn sucked in a breath. For an intense moment she could smell the guy's cologne, a spicy blend of lemons, oranges, and rosemary with a hint of musk.

"Henry, how about talking some more over breakfast at Fuentes?" One of the other men spoke from the group.

The man broke eye contact as he turned to answer.

The vortex of feelings, emotions, and sensations ceased as if a faucet had been turned off. Lynn dragged in a breath, her shoulders sagged in relief. Something was definitely wrong with the dragon.

Lynn hurried after Jen into the meeting room. What was up with the creature? Biological clock ticking? Or was this the dragon equivalent of menopausal hot flashes? Okay, so she was only five years away from thirty. Not horribly old. After all, in dragon years that'd translate to what, fifteen? Oh, great. Teenage hormones.

Unease tugged at her, all prickly and insistent. She glanced back.

The man stood watching her. He winked just before Lexie shut the door.

"Pigeon poop." Lynn's fingers hovered above her keyboard. Would the *Herald* print the phrase even as a direct quote?

Armed with a Diet Coke, her notes and a stack of documents, she sat at Jen's kitchen table typing her story on the county commissioner's meeting. She focused on the Paradise Valley Volunteer Fire Department's grant request as that had been the most interesting thing on the agenda.

Jen had marched to the podium and said: "The new fire engine we have, thanks to you and the federal government, sticks several feet out of the barn we've to park it in. So next time you see the engine and the back part is covered in pigeon poop, don't be surprised."

The audience laughed in response. Jen was a hoot. But obviously an effective hoot. The commissioners' awarded the VFD $50,000 of the $100,000 they needed.

Finally, after consulting her notes, she used the more dignified Jen quote in the story: "We need to build a new fire station that can adequately hold all our equipment and have an area for community gatherings." Lynn grinned. The girl owed her, and she'd remind her of it. Of course, then Jen could pull out a whole laundry list of what Lynn owed in return. Okay, no gloating.

She typed in the last period, leaned her chair back on two legs and reviewed the story. Short and sweet. The smiling faces of all five commissioners danced through her head. They had seemed almost happy to allocate the money.

Michael Ward, one of the commissioners had said: "We read in the newspaper what a wonderful job y'all did at the Jarvises. We want to make sure the volunteer firefighters have everything they need to continue doing a good job and keep the community safe."

Even now, hours after the meeting, Lynn basked in the warm fuzzies of the statement. Talk about a domino effect. Maybe many people wouldn't consider a freelance writer an Essential Employee, but she felt essential. She returned the chair to its upright position and glanced at Jen's studio door. Still shut. Oh well, she'd just have to read the story in the paper tomorrow. Lynn hit the send button.

She stood and stretched. Her stomach rumbled. Dropping the empty Coke can in the recycling bin, Lynn headed for the refrigerator. No chocolate, no dips.

Looked like Jen had already halfway shifted into the raw food idea she'd talked about. Lynn grabbed an apple and munched her way back to the kitchen table.

Her gaze settled on the stack of papers— material she'd picked up at the meeting and her notes. One more look to see if she could get a few more story ideas from any of them and then into the recycling bin the whole pile would go. Lynn plunked into her chair, ready to work. A bit of red, sticking out from underneath the stack, caught her eye.

Her heart leaped. She'd forgotten all about the folder. If it turned up something important, she'd have to send in another story right away. Fun, fun. She flexed her fingers, and pulled it out. Nothing on the cover indicated what lay inside. She flipped it open and began to read.

The studio door opened and Cyndi Lauper's *Girls Just Wanna Have Fun* poured into the kitchen. Lynn slammed the folder shut and looked up.

"Sorry, didn't mean to startle you, *chica.*" Jen stood, cleaning paint from her fingernails with a rag. Her hair stuck out every which way, making her look like a lime green porcupine. "My stomach told me to come out and fix lunch."

Lynn glanced up at the cat-shaped kitchen clock. Fifteen minutes past one. Where had the time gone? "Sorry, I should have fixed us something, but I got lost in paperwork."

Jen washed her hands at the sink and headed for the refrigerator. "Don't worry about it. So what's so interesting?" She pulled out salad ingredients and carried them to the counter next to the sink.

Lynn bit her lip and watched Jen slice and dice. Within minutes of reading, she'd figured out she held the conceptual design of the proposed land development.

Contraband material. Should she compound her sins by sharing the information with Jen? Oh hell, she was already in trouble. "Okay, this has to stay between you and me."

"Oooh, do tell." Jen's eyebrows danced up and down as she carried the tossed salad to the table and settled into a chair.

Lynn grabbed plates and utensils. She helped herself to heaps of spinach, artichoke hearts, mandarin oranges, and grilled chicken. "It's a proposal for developing thirty five hundred acres as a high-end subdivision— three hundred houses at about $400,000 each." She took a bite. Cheese. It needed cheese.

Jen's eyes widened as she let out a low whistle. "Where are they planning it?"

She hurried to the refrigerator and grabbed the hunk of Cheddar, then a knife. "Paradise Valley."

"Holy Purple Cow!" Jen glanced at the folder then at Lynn. She squinted. "Wait a minute, is this what they discussed in closed session? Where did you get the folder?"

Her face burned. "It was an accident. I must've grabbed it when I picked up all the additional information." She focused on cutting the cheese into slivers over her salad.

"Lynn, you shouldn't have this."

"I know."

Jen pushed away her half-eaten salad and jumped out of her chair. She crossed her arms and paced. "You are going to get in trouble for this."

"Thanks for the news flash." Lynn nibbled her thumb. "Only if they find out. I mean, they might know it's missing, but they don't know I have it."

Jen glared at her. "Lynn!"

She held up her hands in surrender. "I can't just hand this back to some commissioner, giggle and apologize for the silly mistake. No one's going to buy that." She twirled her fork, making the spinach dance.

"Well, you definitely shouldn't have read it."

Lynn sighed. "You're right. I shouldn't have read it, and I shouldn't have said anything to you."

Jen stomped to the table and reached for the folder, but Lynn snatched it away. "No, no, I should start doing the right thing at some point."

"Oh cut the crap!" Jen rolled her eyes and threw herself back into her chair. She grabbed the folder. "Heck, you're going to hang for it anyway."

She read with pursed lips. "Huh, they've designated two hundred acres in the middle for a shopping center."

"Well, right next to it they have a children's park." Lynn pointed at the much smaller green area on the drawing.

Jen snorted. "Yeah, look at the comparative sizes. Freaking developers!" She flipped back to the map locating the proposed subdivision in the county. "That's a lot of land, and the Jarvis property is right at the center of it."

Lynn pored over the spot Jen indicated. "I wonder if they've had an offer on the land." She needed to ask around.

Jen shrugged. "I can't imagine them selling. In fact, I can see quite a few people in the area turning down their offer. There's a lot of family history tied up in those properties."

"Even if the price is right?" Lynn glanced at the business card attached to the proposal. Something sparked in her mind, but she couldn't stoke it into fire just yet. "The representative, Henry Chase, looked rich and confident." She flipped through her papers and notes.

Jen frowned. "Maybe, money can make a difference to some people, but I doubt it. He came sniffing around here, but lost interest when I told him I was merely the renter."

Lynn bound out of her chair and rummaged through Jen's collection of pens and pencils by the phone. She grabbed a red pen and drew lines across the Jarvis land.

"Great, now you're defacing a document you shouldn't have."

"Hush, finders keepers." Lynn continued to draw, then pulled back and cocked her head to look at what she'd drawn. She rolled the pen to Jen. "Can you locate the other recent fires on this?"

After they plotted out the fires, Jen let out a low whistle. "Well, that's some interesting overlap."

CHAPTER 9

A grown man did what needed to be done without whining. Fortified with that thought and strong, black coffee, Jack strode into the shadowed library.

Was the room shrinking? He forced himself to breathe deeply, inhale the stale, warm air— dust-coated and dry, musty with the smell of old books, dog and a hint of mold.

Damn, he missed being outdoors in the crisp October air, feeling the sun on his skin, watching the blaze of autumn colors on the Flame Sumacs lining the fields. But he couldn't work at the farm since the machine parts he needed weren't in yet. Instead, he found himself stuck with fun things like paying bills and balancing accounts. *Holy shit. He'd die of excitement.* Jack groaned and promised himself a beer at the end of the torture session.

Setting his coffee down, Jack flicked on the lamp. Another thing he didn't like about the room— no windows. He fell into the large, red leather chair and looked out over the ornate and imposing desk. Twenty years dropped away leaving him a gangly ten-year-old, awed and lost, in Dad's library, in Dad's chair, behind Dad's desk. The thrill of the forbidden zigzagged through him.

Jack shifted around, trying to get comfortable in a chair with worn cushions molded to someone else's body. Lynn was right. Time for a change.

Lynn. Her voice echoed in his head: *Kiss it and make it better?* Damn, instant hard on. He shifted in his chair and shook his head. Bills. He needed to take care of bills. Distraction and finance didn't go well together.

Jerking open a side drawer, he pulled out the folder of current bills, then thumbed through all the ones with approaching due dates. He'd just scribbled his signature on the tenth check when the phone jangled. He snatched up the receiver with relief.

"Hi there neighbor," a woman purred. Katherine Harrington came from a ranching family with roots going as far back as the Callaghans and she lived not far down the road from him.

His spirits plummeted. For a moment, he'd been hoping to hear Lynn's voice. Ridiculous. Why on earth would she call? Probably didn't even have his number.

"Oh, hey Kate. How're you doing?" Jack asked as he leafed through a few other bills.

"Um, okay," she said. "Still adjusting to being single again."

Memory clicked into place. She'd divorced her lawyer husband in Dallas a year ago. Shouldn't that be long enough to adjust? What did he know— always a groom's man, never the groom. Geez, what exactly should a guy say in response? I am sorry? It'll get better? How about them Cowboys?

"So are you going to the Denim & Diamonds Ball this evening?" She filled in the silence on the line.

Damn! Jack knew he'd forgotten something. The ball was an annual fundraiser for West Texas Regional Hospital. "Truth be told, I'd forgotten all about it." He winced at the thought of wearing a tux.

Kate sighed. "It's for a really good cause. All those poor indigent children. They deserve medical treatment as much as those of us who can pay for it."

"True, maybe I'll mail in my check this year instead of presenting it at the ball."

"I'm glad to write the hospital a check, but they're insisting I show up. I'd rather be anonymous."

"Same here." He cradled the phone between his chin and shoulder, as he returned the file to its original place.

"I guess they want to encourage the other big pockets to donate." Silence hung on the line again.

Jack cleared his throat. "Yeah, well have a good time."

"Would you mind?" Her voice was almost a whisper.

"Mind what?"

Kate giggled, making his eyebrows climb. "This is embarrassing, but I couldn't scrounge up a date for tonight." She coughed. "So I was thinking, maybe we could go together. You know, help each other survive the evening. But I don't want to impose on you."

Jack bit back a groan. Dang it, he had to do the right thing. "Oh why not, I've got a tux, I might as well use it. I'd be happy to escort you."

"You're such a gentleman," Kate said. "I'll have to think of a way to make it up to you."

"You don't have to do that."

"What's the fun in doing things I have to?" she said with a laugh. "See you at six thirty."

Kate must have been watching for him, because she emerged as soon as Jack pulled up. He whistled softly under his breath. She looked model beautiful - tall and slender, with spun gold hair combed into an elegant up-do. The setting sun glittered off the diamonds at her ears and neck and splashed onto marble smooth bare shoulders. He straightened the lapels of the tux and hoped he passed muster.

Her look said, admire, but don't touch.

Unbidden, Lynn's face filled his mind: her impish grin, warm eyes and scatter of freckles— a face so touchable. Where else did she have freckles? Probably all over. He'd love to play connect-the-dots with his finger, tongue. Jack sighed and returned to reality.

Kate's icy-blue eyes met his, cool and measuring. He couldn't imagine joking around with her or mussing up her hair. Oh well. She was a good neighbor. And this was just a matter of convenience, not a date. He leapt out, ran to the other side of the pickup, and held the door open for her.

She stopped and her smile wavered. "Would you mind if we took my car? It'll be hard to get in and out of the pickup in this dress."

Jack nodded, eyeing the clingy pale blue sheath that showed off her sharp curves. How did she move in that thing? Then his eyes fixed on the deep V of her décolletage. Diamonds and soft woman. Now that's what's called Icy Hot.

Her hand smoothed down her side, before reaching into a tiny purse. She gestured with keys in her hand.

Jack gulped and turned to where she indicated. This time, he whistled appreciatively loud and clear. The polished-silver Lexus was a beaut of a car. As he slid into the passenger's seat and buckled himself in, Jack realized no amount of washing and spit polish could make his pickup compare to this sleek machine. He breathed in the warm leather smell of the interior. *Nice.*

Kate peeled out of her drive and screeched onto the highway, interrupting his Zen moment. Damn, where's the fire? He glanced at the clock to make sure they weren't late. As the speedometer leaned further and further to the right, the car's gentle purr climbed into a roar that reverberated in his blood. He pressed his right foot to the floorboard and stifled the urge to snap at her.

"Haven't seen too much of you lately," she said.

"Busy farming." He gulped and swallowed the scream that tried to claw out.

"All work and no play makes Jack a dull boy."

He glanced at her and caught her looking at him from beneath thick lashes. Her lips curved into a smile. He shrugged, trying to look relaxed.

"Got to finish harvesting before …Um, there's a sharp curve coming up."

She swerved hard, banking to the left. Jack grabbed the dash while his heart threatened to run off without him. Maybe he could walk to the damn party.

She laughed.

He couldn't believe how soft and genteel she sounded despite the car careening on the road. How could she be so cool, with the car almost out of control? Missed her calling as NASCAR driver.

"You never did take time for fun," she said. "In fact, you never noticed anything beyond your physics books."

He kept his eyes on the road and clutched the edges of

his seat. "Like what?"

She drove in silence, slowing slightly. "Like me."

Okay. Call him clueless. "You were one of the popular girls in high school," he said, breathing easier. "Didn't think you noticed me."

"Not notice a Callaghan?" She turned toward him with one sexily raised eyebrow.

Keep your eyes on the damn road, woman. He fiddled with his tie. "I remember my dad and your dad came up with that great scheme of sending us to the prom together."

Laughter shook her shoulders. "Yeah, I think they even picked a place for our wedding."

Heat flamed across his face. "I was mortified and refused to put you into that position."

"So you asked that ...What was her name? That strange Goth chick."

"Kendra." She'd been new to the school. Her dad was an oilfield worker who moved from place to place, so they weren't around for long. Too new to know all the baggage that came with the Callaghan name. Best that way. Lynn was new too. New and without any preconceived notions. Excitement buzzed up his spine.

"Didn't realize until then what a softie you were," Kate said. "It was nice of you to ask her. I guess we all felt sorry for her."

He shrugged and stared out at the darkness rushing by. Sorry? He hadn't felt sorry for her. Kendra had been like him. They didn't fit in. She didn't look like the other girls and he was a nerd on top of being a Callaghan.

As a bonus, he'd completely horrified his father. Jack smiled into the dark. Kendra and he had split early from the party and ended up star-gazing on Mount Nebo, the only-decent sized hill for miles around. He'd had his first kiss that night. He licked his lips remembering the taste of spearmint gum. What would it be like to kiss Lynn?

"Well, I have to admit I was kind of disappointed."

He took in Kate's sharp profile. Other memories, like the whispers and name-calling he'd endured for being a Callaghan, the fights he'd gotten into because of all that, bubbled up. "Actually, given the Callaghan reputation, I'm surprised you or your dad even considered the idea."

"Dad came from a long line of bankers, he was always in favor of a good merger," she smiled. "As for me, I just wanted a taste of the tall, dark and dangerous Callaghan."

Flash bulbs popped, blinding him as soon as they walked in. Damn photographers. Must be a slow news day or something. Kate's grip on his arm tightened. She nodded and beamed, completely overshadowing him. Not a problem, since he didn't like being the center of attention anyway.

Kate leaned close. "Hey, we might make it into the *San Angelo Herald* society page or the hospital newsletter."

Her whisper tickled his ear and Jack shifted to put some distance between them. "Yay us."

"Did you see the TV cameras?"

"Kinda hard to miss." He looked around the hall, taking in the twinkling white Christmas lights, the giant clear plastic snowflakes that shone like melting ice and the clouds of billowing gauze.

Someone had performed a miracle. He'd attended plenty of sausage suppers, auctions and other fundraisers in the hall and usually nothing could hide the ugly cream walls and the cold glare of fluorescent lights. He turned to Kate. "Who decorated this place?"

"I think it was that new artist in town, Jennifer Delgado," Kate said. She dragged him toward a table.

He made a mental note to compliment Jen next time he saw her. Little glittery snow globes propped up snowflake-shaped names tags on white china. Jack pulled out Kate's chair. He nodded to the six others at their table— a who's who of the old money in the area. Hands down the two of them were the youngest.

The lights blinked until the music and noise faded. Then the emcee stepped up to the microphone and started talking about the importance of the fundraiser. When his name came up, Jack flushed and ducked his head. Geez, could they move on?

Kate's name rang out into the room. She stood, looked around and nodded a few times, waved and smiled. Too bad she didn't have a tiara and a Miss Whatever sash. Jack grabbed his water glass and took a drink. Kate definitely handled attention better than he did, and especially well for someone who claimed she preferred anonymity.

After the applause had died down, Amos Tavistock raised an eyebrow at Jack from across the table. "A shy Callaghan? Hard to believe. All the Callaghan men before you didn't balk from taking credit —whether they deserved it or not— especially your great grandfather and grandfather. Sharpest wits in the west, we used to say."

"Hush," Elsie Tavistock leaned close to her husband. "If you can't say anything nice, keep your mouth shut."

The older man colored and patted his wife's hand in silent apology. Tiny and thin, with silver hair and bright twinkly eyes, Elsie looked like a pretty bird perched in her wheel-chair.

Jack shrugged. Tavistock had to be ninety if he was a day and had likely known the older Callaghans. What he said was true enough. Not exactly complimentary, but true. Jack eyed the empty wine goblet next to his sweating water glass, and willed the waiter to appear. It was going to be a long evening.

The band struck up a waltz. Not wanting to hear anymore about his family, Jack asked Kate for a dance. Congratulating himself on his escape, he put an arm around her and began to move, only to flounder when she snuggled up close and pressed her breasts against his chest. After the third time he stepped on her toes, Kate suggested they return to the table. Relieved, Jack shepherded her through the dancers, mumbling an apology for his two left feet.

He stifled a groan as they approached the table where an opinionated discussion about oil prices, stocks and shares competed with the strains of the waltz. Reminding himself why he'd come, Jack pulled out Kate's chair again and seated himself. Thank God someone had filled his wine glass. He sipped wine, devoured both his and Kate's chocolate cakes, and felt his mood go foul as conversation continued on business topics. Oil money constituted a big chunk of his inheritance from the Callaghan estate, but damned if he'd talk about it at a party.

Kate jumped into the conversation. "It's depressing. Oil prices are finally up and the wells are going dry." Everybody at the table nodded, much of their wealth also stemmed from oil legacies.

"This drought isn't helping any," another rancher added. "People are selling off their livestock to keep from seeing them starve."

The man's wife leaned in, wide-eyed. "Then there's the fires burning up all of Paradise Valley." A low murmur of agreement rounded the table.

"The only thing holding a breath of hope now are those city developers interested in the land around here,"

Kate said. "Some of their offers are mighty tempting."

"It's a laugh." Tavistock waved a hand as if shooing a fly. "They aim to section off the land into little ranchettes and sell them to city folk, who want to play cowboys." Nervous glances flickered left and right.

Kate sipped her wine and shrugged. "Times are changing and we have to change with them or be wiped out." People shifted uneasily in their seats, some nodded.

Jack couldn't stay quiet any longer. "Just to be a devil's advocate. What about water? We already have a water shortage here. The ranchettes will bring more people in, which will further strain the water supply."

Elsie beamed and Tavistock clapped. "Good point, Callaghan."

"But," Karl Humberg, a local attorney, cut in. "I think Kate may be right. I've heard these ranchettes are high-end development. So it's people with money who'll be buying them, people who will add to the tax base."

Mrs. Humberg nodded at her husband. "As for water, Abilene's developing a pipeline, and there's T. Boone Pickens ready to sell his water to whoever wants it. If we have the money here, the water will come."

Jack almost gaped. What faith in the mighty dollar. "It's not just about money," he said. "It's also about management of our resources."

The faces around the table stared at him. Aged, grim faces. "A time may come when it won't matter how large our tax base is, if we don't have any water to meet essential needs," Jack said.

Elsie's reedy voice followed his, "When water is as rare as the blooms of a Century Plant, the resources will go to the highest bidder and it may not be us."

Tavistock shook his head, playing with his gold wedding band. "We're losing a way of life."

A twinge of jealousy passed through Jack. While everything else might be lost, Tavistock would always have Elsie.

"Maybe I am being simplistic, but I don't think progress is a dirty word," Kate said, her voice a calming purr. "I think if we work with the developers, we can make it work for us. The key is management, don't you agree, Jack?"

He sat up straighter and met Kate's steady gaze. "Depends on who's running the show."

His cell phone vibrated. Excusing himself, Jack found a quiet corner and answered it. Jen's voice —rough and panicky— came across the line. "Jack, we have an emergency."

Jack stiffened. "What's up?"

"Um, there's a broken water pipe and we don't know what to do," she replied. "Can you please come? We're drowning here."

"I'm on my way." He snapped the phone shut and glanced at his watch. Nine thirty. Not too bad. He'd spent a decent amount of time at the event. Jack strode back to the table in a lighter mood. He whispered to Kate that an emergency had come up and they had to leave. She stood and started saying her goodbyes. Couldn't she hurry it up? Jack shook hands and nodded at everyone, feeling like a bobble-headed doll. He relaxed once he breathed the night air.

In the car, Jack filled Kate in on Jen's situation. She nodded sympathetically. "It's hard to be a single woman at times. Jen's lucky to have such a helpful landlord."

Who did Kate call for her plumbing problems? Actually, that was none of his business. Jack drummed his fingers on the center console during most of the drive, wanting to be at Jen's and fixing things. When they arrived at Kate's house, Jack jumped out. He apologized again for cutting her evening short.

"Tell you what, I'll let you take me out some other evening to make up for this." Kate leaned forward. Her sweet, flowery perfume tickled his nose, making him dizzy and nauseous. Too close for comfort.

"Ah, sure," Jack said, taking a step back. "I better go before my rent house goes underwater."

"Good luck," she called to his retreating back.

"Good night," Jack answered, without turning around. He didn't slow down until he reached the pickup and climbed into the driver's seat. What just happened? Had Kate wanted him to kiss her? Talk about surprises.

He started the pickup and got the hell out of Dodge.

CHAPTER 10

What a disaster. Lynn kneeled in cold ankle deep water and peered at the pipes under Jen's kitchen sink. She could do this. *Just stay calm.*

A spray of water from the broken pipe splattered her face. She turned away, coughing, and blindly grasped the pipe until her hands covered most of the hole. The water pulsed and fizzed against her skin, sneaking out wherever it could. Nope, this wouldn't work. Taking a deep breath, she let go. Water sprayed everywhere. She grimaced and swallowed the curses dancing on the tip of her tongue. What the hell had made her think she could do this?

In the beginning, it seemed so manageable. She'd volunteered to do the dishes and left Jen, who had a cold, tucked on the couch. Soon afterwards, cold water licked her toes. Even with the faucet turned off, water still streamed out.

Jen had hovered in the doorway. "Anything I can do to help?"

"You want to get pneumonia? I've got this covered." Lynn wished she felt half as confident as she'd sounded. "Go back to your couch."

"I think I should call Jack."

"No!" Lynn had rolled her eyes. Jack to the rescue yet again? No way. "I can handle this."

Yeah, right. She had handled it all right. Handled it with as much finesse as only a clumsy dragon could. Lynn had tried unsuccessfully to find the water meter and the turn-off valve. Next, assuming that the pipe was leaking from a loose joint, she tackled it with a pair of pliers.

A stomach-wrenching noise later, the rusty pipe had developed a jagged, yawning hole. Water sprayed her. Lynn shot away from the pipe, slid and landed with a significant splash on her bottom.

Jen dialed Jack.

"Traitor," Lynn grumbled, half-listening to the one-sided conversation as she came up with her next strategy— duct tape. Her butt hurt and her pride hurt even worse. Jack must think she was a chronic damsel-in-distress. So much for great impressions.

An image of him taking off his fire helmet and smiling at her came to mind. What a smile. The memory of their tangled gazes steamed through her. Lynn started at the feather-soft melting inside her. Guilt tapped at her conscience. Here to hunt for duct tape, remember? Focus on the problem. She found the duct tape in the same drawer as Jen's gift wrapping paper and scissors. The girl needed serious help.

Grabbing the purple tape, Lynn ran back to the sink.

She needed to get the problem fixed before Jack showed up. Water pelted her as she struggled to wrap duct tape around the offending crack. She worked quickly and wove lengths and lengths of tape about the pipe, her arms moving up, down, and sideways. Finally, out of tape, she sat back on her haunches and grinned. She'd tamed the beast! The water was down to a trickle and a few half-hearted spits. Temporary fix, but not bad.

She grabbed a mop and shoved it back and forth across the wet floor. *On a roll now.* The water would be gone before Mr. Callaghan showed. After a few minutes, Lynn stopped and leaned against the handle. Oh, her muscles ached. A massage would be heaven. Of course, she instantly recalled his fingers work their magic on her foot. She closed her eyes. In her mind, Jack smiled and placed his big hands on her back. His hands moved, spread warmth and tingles. They inched up and under her shirt, to the front and up, up until they reached and cupped her breasts—

He's a suspect. Her eyes flew open and she vigorously mopped a patch of floor until it winked back squeaky clean and shiny.

A loud knock, followed by the hum of conversation. Jack. She headed for the door, before coming to a standstill. What was she, a teenager? No, that was the dragon in her. Lynn blew out a breath and grasped the mop for support. Remember the difference. She counted backwards to slow down her heart to regular speed.

Jack appeared in the doorway, dressed in some sort of formal wear. Every muscle in her body quivered. She almost expected him to say "Bond. James Bond". Lynn licked her lips and stared at him. Okay, roll tongue back up and close mouth. She took a deep breath. "Wow, you, um…You really cleaned up."

Jack leaned against the doorframe and grinned as Lynn gaped at him and nervously licked her lips. Oh yeah. For once he wasn't the mess. "I put this on just for you."

Her answering grin sparked a fierce desire to kiss her. He shifted to shove his hands in his pockets and hide the sudden bulge in his pants. His eyebrows inched up as he whistled. "Your new look suits you."

Maybe he should have his head examined because he actually meant the compliment. She did look cute and sexy.

A barefoot Lynn, wearing cut off jeans and a faded gray t-shirt, glared at him while clutching a mop. Her hair, twisted and held up by a clip, ended in a fountain of spikes. She scowled. "You like the water-logged monster look?"

He grinned. Lynn, the wet and wild punk-rocker maid. His eyes drifted back to the dripping wet t-shirt. Hmm, maybe he wasn't so crazy after all. Nothing cute and harmless about her curves. With an effort of will he turned toward the problem he'd come to fix.

A massive ball of duct tape hung from the pipe under the sink, looking like a very weird, very malignant growth. What on earth? He squatted and peered at the purple mass.

"What *are* you wearing?"

"It's a tux," Jack said, standing. "Haven't you ever seen one before?"

"Not like this one," Lynn replied, taking a few steps toward him. "You're wearing jeans, for Pete's sake."

Jack stood and did a turn, the way he imagined a model would. "You are looking at a Western tux. Note the long coat with tails, a string bolo tie instead of a stupid bow tie, the jeans and boots. I'm all decked out."

Another step closer. She reached out and touched the brim of his hat. "And yes, a black cowboy hat." Lynn's dark eyes glittered. "It should be white, you know? Heroes always wear the white hat."

She didn't know the Callaghans. A bitter taste filled his mouth. Jack looked away from her, at the hissing pipe. Heard her stumble, felt cool air between them.

"So what are you going to do about this?"

Jack couldn't resist. He looked down at his clothes, then her. "Nothing. I think you have it under control."

Her beautiful eyes widened. "What?"

"Just joking," Jack chuckled. "So why didn't you turn off the water to the house?"

Lynn mumbled something.

"Didn't catch that."

"I couldn't find the meter," she said, biting out each word. Her lips pushed out in a sexy pout.

Something growled within him. A wild urge to grab her, nip those pink lips, and taste her gripped him. Jack took a deep breath as he rocked on the edge of control. *Down boy, down.* "You're such a city girl." He grinned to hide the turmoil inside him. "There's no meter because we use well water out here. There's a valve by the well."

Jack hurried out the door. He liked having fun, but these emotions were new, different.

After about half an hour, and after getting completely drenched, he'd fixed the leak and helped clean up the kitchen. By the end of all that, when Lynn offered him a dry towel and a cold beer, Jack figured he'd definitely earned the reward.

Jack threw the towel onto the seat and sank into the recliner. He took a drink, and let out a deep sigh. "It's been a long day."

"Sorry about spoiling a nice evening for you," Jen said.

"Thanks for the rescue," Lynn said in a tiny voice.

Jack grimaced and shrugged. He filled them in on the shindig, minus Kate and her surprises. "The fundraiser's for a good cause, but it was kind of stiff and I was ready to get out," he said. "So in a way, you rescued me too."

Jen sneezed and Lynn jumped to get her more ginger-infused tea.

"Talking of rescue," Jen croaked. "Rescue me from this over-zealous nurse, will you?"

"Stop complaining," Lynn said, going into the kitchen. "I'm just doing what needs to be done."

Jen shook her head. "This is your vacation, I can't let you spend it playing nurse." She leaned towards Jack and whispered, "She's driving me nuts. Do something."

"Why should I? You ragged me about my tux."

"I'll buy you a case of beer. Shiner Bock, your favorite." She cast a desperate look towards the kitchen. "That ginger tea is vile."

"I'll see what I can do," he replied. When Lynn returned with the tea, Jack offered to take her sightseeing the next day.

"Oh, I can't leave Jen, as sick as she is." Lynn shook her head at both of them.

"Yes, you can," Jen said. "It's settled. Pick her up at nine!"

Lynn blushed again. "Jen, behave," she said. "I can't impose on Jack."

This time Jack shook his head. "I really don't have much going on tomorrow. The machine parts still haven't come in," he said. "Besides, it'll be my pleasure." He'd enjoy showing her around, getting to know her, exploring all possibilities. He pushed to the edge of the recliner hoping she'd agree.

Jen added further endorsements. "He grew up here, so

you'll have an authentic, native tour guide. He'll take you off the beaten path."

Jack grinned wickedly. "Wear comfortable shoes, darlin'."

CHAPTER 11

Lynn almost spewed coffee as she stared at the *San Angelo Herald's Society Page*. A large black and white picture of Jack and a blonde stopped her from flipping to the comics section. The woman, identified as Katherine Harrington, clung to his arm and flashed a movie-star smile. Jealousy clouded her mind. The dragon bristled. Hands off. *Now*.

She sputtered and coughed as coffee went down the wrong pipe, making Jen glance away from the early morning scene she was trying to capture in watercolor. Her painting already looked like a photograph of the view outside the kitchen window. "Are you okay?"

Lynn nodded, ducking her head as common sense flooded her. She had no right, no right at all, to be jealous. She and men weren't meant to be. Hadn't her experience with Rob taught her anything? In fact, she shouldn't even care who Mr. Callaghan socialized with, unless the woman turned out to be his partner-in-crime. She narrowed her eyes, studying the woman's perfect up-do. Jack was nothing more than a nice guy, an acquaintance. A suspect. She flipped back to the front-page news stories.

"Are you sure you're okay?" Jen squinted at her. "You look kind of peaky."

Lynn raised the mug to her lips and took a careful sip. "Must be catching your cold." Truth be told, she'd had a restless night. Her stomach muscles clenched as she remembered her early morning dream. Jack, her, and a giant out-of-control water hose. It was a wet dream in more ways than one. Heat spread downward from her face.

Fortunately, Jen had turned back to the window and to her work. "There's Jack!" she called out.

Lynn popped out of her chair and spotted a cloud of dust approaching. God, how was she ever going to face the man? She whirled toward her room. Maybe she'd pretend to be sick. And lose the chance to interrogate him again? No way, no how. Lynn drew up her shoulders and turned back toward the approaching green pickup. Get a grip. The dream was nothing more than a case of nerves strained by the plumbing disaster of the century.

Or maybe Jack was totally to blame. The surprise of seeing him clean would have been too much for anybody. The way the tuxedo jacket had hung off those broad shoulders and molded to his wide back, tapering at the waist, and the way the jeans showed off the long lines of his legs, that very nice ass.

Her temperature had spiked to dangerous levels when

he'd returned from the living room sans tux, shirt and cowboy hat. All the contours and planes she'd imagined laid bare. Her fingers had tingled with the need to run them through his hair, across his sculpted stomach. While he'd worked, she'd checked him out. Seen his muscles contract and relax under smooth skin, drops of water shine and sparkle caught in the swirl of dark hair that disappeared into his tight, tight jeans.

Warm, melting sensations shivered through her.

She scowled as she swung her backpack onto her shoulder. The dragon's raging hormones kept throwing her off her game. Once she'd woken from the dream, she'd tried a cold shower, then meditating. Neither had worked.

"I just need to get the guy to answer some questions," she muttered. "Then he'll be a) behind bars for arson, b) burnt toast, or c) riding into the sunset with the blonde." A reedy breath skittered out of her. "Then I can stop—" Stop what? The involuntary flutters she experienced every time Jack came in view? Stop dreaming? Ha, good luck.

"What?" Jen said, frowning.

"What? Oh, ah…, Jack's here." She scrambled to open the door.

A giggle stopped her mid-step. "Have fun!"

Fun? Oh no, what was Jen up to? Initially, she'd been embarrassed at her friend's insistence that Jack play tour guide. Then her practical self had re-asserted itself. Whatever Jen's intentions, hers were all business.

Lynn stuck out her tongue at her friend. "Don't wait up!" She turned to face Jack as he held the truck door open for her and her insides turned to mush. He wore a sexy grin and tight Wrangler jeans. The Dream Cowboy. Yeehaw!

Jack watched Lynn saunter up to the truck. The sway of her hips, the way her gray t-shirt clung to her curves, those flashing dark eyes— oh yeah, she was *hot*.

She stopped inches from him, the apple scent of her perfume tempting him to step closer, bury his face into her nape. "So, where are we off to?"

How about my house? Or, more specifically, my whirlpool, couch or bed? "There are some Indian drawings at a ranch near the town of Paint Rock, about an hour away," Jack said. "In fact, the name Paint Rock comes from those drawings."

"Sounds interesting," Lynn said, climbing into the truck. "I minored in anthropology in college, so this is right up my alley."

Jack started the truck and glanced at Lynn. The excitement shining in her eyes made a smile balloon inside him. He'd been nervous that Lynn might not like the hike. He gave her points for dressing practically: jeans, a t-shirt and hiking boots. No make-up and hair pulled into a no-nonsense ponytail. She looked beautiful.

Desire tugged at him. He wanted to kiss her. Better not jump the gun and spoil their first date —F—first date? His mouth went dry and he swallowed a couple of times. Let's see, he'd offered to show her around, she'd accepted. Now the two of them were spending the day together. If it walks like a duck and quacks like a duck...

"What's Natural Farms Inc.? I just noticed the sign on your truck."

"Yeah, I need to wash it more often." He pulled out onto the road. "Natural Farms Inc. is my business," he said. "We only grow organic products." He stuck his right hand out. "I'm the CTO."

"What's a CTO?" She grabbed his hand and shook.

A buzz rushed his head. "Chief Tractor Operator."

Lynn laughed and looked at the countryside zooming by. "So, do you farm all this land?"

He stared out of his window. Once, all of it had belonged to the Callaghan family.

"No, there's my place, then the Callaghan-Avery ranch, owned by my sister and her husband, and a few other owners scattered all around us," he said. "I farm about seven hundred acres and that's more than enough." People shook their heads when they talked about his grandfather and dad selling the Callaghan legacy piecemeal whenever the need for money grabbed them. You know what? Good riddance. Too much work.

They passed the occasional abandoned home falling apart into the weeds, rusty tractors missing parts and windmills standing still. Jack fell silent. His gaze flicked over at her. "The rubble of people's dreams," he said, staring forward again. "Each of those abandoned houses is a sign of somebody giving up."

Jack frowned harder as he drove past a large Hope Developers sign.

Lynn had seen several of those signs dotted around the countryside during the drive. All of them featured a sketch of a fancy house —large glass windows, corrugated roof, and stone columns— next to a picture of a laughing, picnicking family. It announced: *Coming Soon! Paradise Point— your escape to a better life.*

She had the sudden urge to smooth out Jack's scowl. She wanted to kiss his worries away and tickle him until he cracked a smile. Instead, Lynn sat on her hands to keep from touching him. Damn it. This was crazy. *You don't know what he's thinking. He could be planning his next fire.* "Well, I guess the new subdivision will revitalize the area."

He cut her a sharp look. "No, they'll just turn it into yet another over-crowded, over-commercialized faceless suburb. Mow down the wildflowers to put up Starbucks and shopping strips."

The bitter tinge to his words left a bad taste in her mouth. She swallowed past it. "I thought there was a children's park in the plans."

A thin laugh. "Instead of climbing trees, the kids will climb monkey bars, but where will all the wildlife go?"

His anger seemed to suck the air in the cab. Lynn fidgeted in the uncomfortable silence.

"I'm sorry," he said finally. "I just hate seeing the land abused like that."

She cleared her throat. "It's understandable. Being a farmer, you're close to land and nature." After a beat, she added, "Farming must be hard. Is the profit worth the work?"

"You definitely don't get into it for the money nowadays," he said, "with the water shortages and droughty weather we've been having for the last nine years. Not to mention the developers buying up land at prices farmers can't even dream of paying."

A lump formed in Lynn's throat. "Why did you go into farming?"

Jack shrugged. "I like working outdoors with my hands," he said. "I can't imagine being stuck behind a desk all day."

Lynn glanced at him and saw his knuckles were almost white as he grasped the steering wheel. His lips pressed together in a thin line. She could sense his pain, see its impression on his face. The word "suspect" whispered in her mind, over and over again. *Eternal damnation.* Lynn turned her face to the window. "So were you born into it? Are you carrying on the family tradition?"

He barked out a laugh. "Can't imagine too many of my forefathers willing to get dirt under their nails. Nope, I'm forging my own path." Jack leaned forward and snagged a brown envelope from the dash, then handed it to her. "Oh, before I forget."

"What's this?"

"Open it."

She discovered her article. Jack had cut it out of the paper, mounted it on a piece of black cardboard, and laminated the whole thing. Pleasure at his thoughtful gift fizzed through her.

"Thanks, that's so nice of you." She smiled at him. "Are you always so nice?"

"Once in a while. Just to throw people off," he grinned, then turned serious. "It's a real good story, and I wanted to make sure you had a copy."

"You really liked it?" She ran a finger over her name.

Jack nodded. "I was there and I know how it ended, but even I felt compelled to read it," he said. "You're a natural storyteller."

Lynn ducked her head. She put the article back in the envelope and carefully resealed it. Jack's words warmed her from the inside out. He couldn't be the rogue. She didn't want him to be.

They drove up to a metal gate with a cattle-guard underneath it. Jack stopped the truck and got out to open the gate. Heat flamed Lynn's skin as her gaze settled on his ass. Flashes of her dream —his tanned, lean body against hers, his mouth on her breasts, her fingers wrapped in his hair, her mouth tasting his salty skin— played in her mind. She looked away when he turned and headed back to the truck. Damn teen dragon. Why didn't she get over the hormones already?

The truck door creaked open and he settled into his

seat.

Lynn cleared her throat. "The ranch owners won't mind us looking around?"

"They're family friends and I called them ahead of time. But they also open it up for the public from time to time."

Jack stopped the truck again, so that he could shut the gate behind them. But Lynn hopped out and closed it.

They drove a short distance and parked. "We'll have to hike up to the rocks," Jack said. "It should take us a couple of hours to look around."

Lynn followed Jack's lead along a trail heading up into the high bluff. He jumped rock to rock, nimble and goat-like.

"You really know your way around this place."

"Like the back of my hand," he called back. "The owners' son and I spent many Saturdays adventuring among these rocks."

Jack pointed out the different pictures among the rocks as they threaded their way along. The sun had faded the ones that were more in the open; but others, that lay hidden behind crags and other rocks, still held rich colors: ocher, red and sometimes a greenish tinge. Some stood out starkly in black and white. Lynn identified a few hunting scenes, involving deer, arrows and men. She spied a cross with the date 1643 on it.

"How old are these?"

"Most of the pictographs probably date from about 1400 A.D.," Jack said. "Some, like that cross, were made by Spanish explorers."

"How do you know that?"

Jack shrugged. "I'm into history, both local and wider range. So I'm always reading about things."

The sun beat down at them from the center of the sky

as they headed back. High noon. Sweat beaded her hairline and heat radiated from her. She glanced at Jack. Sweat definitely worked for him. Tendrils of his dark hair curled against his neck, while his damp t-shirt clung to his broad back. She drew in a sharp breath as her heart thudded, heavy and loud, and the dragon coiled in her stomach. She wanted to taste him, feel him. She wanted to know Jack Callaghan. Lynn closed her eyes for a moment. No, she didn't want him. The dragon was the horny one.

"Ready to eat?" Jack asked as he stepped onto level ground.

"Hell, yeah," Lynn answered, glad that her face, already red from exertion, wouldn't betray her embarrassment.

Jack grinned as he lowered the tailgate of his pickup and climbed on. He tossed Lynn a thick blanket and asked her to pick a picnic spot.

She spread the blanket under a shady oak near the water, and Jack plopped himself and the cooler down on it.

"Ahh, ice cold drinks," Lynn sighed, grabbing a Diet Coke. Jack took a Sprite. He wrapped his bandana around some ice and used it as an ice-pack to his brow and neck. She pressed the cold, wet can against her hot forehead and cheeks, before grabbing a foil wrapped sandwich.

Crusty French bread peeked out at her as she unwrapped the top. She pulled the rest of the foil away and bit into the sandwich without waiting for Jack. The zing of spicy mayo burst over her tongue. It was quickly followed by the savory flavor of roast chicken layered with creamy avocado and peppery arugula. Shredded carrots added just the right amount of sweetness.

"Mmm," she said. "This is gooooood."

Jack responded with a gallant bow. "Me and the local grocery store at your service."

He'd made a meal for her. No guy had ever done that. Did he have to be so nice?

After devouring the sandwich, Lynn looked around. A gentle breeze fingered her hair as she watched a white crane fishing in the shallows. A perfect moment of peace. It'd be a shame to spoil it, maybe she could pause her investigation for a bit. Enjoy the sunlight, nature and the company. "This is a beautiful place."

"Yeah, that's actually why I packed lunch," said Jack, slicing up an apple with his pocket knife. "I loved picnicking here as a kid." He offered her apples and chunks of Cheddar cheese.

"So what was it like growing up out here?" Lynn asked nibbling the fruit.

"Great," Jack said. "I ran around barefoot and shirtless all over the ranch. So for the first six years of my life, I was this spindly, brown kid with hair bleached blond by the sun."

"Blond?" Lynn asked. "But your hair is dark brown now."

"Things changed," Jack said. "Hair became darker and I had to start wearing shoes as I grew older and started working with the horses."

"You grew up on the ranch?"

"Essentially," he said. "Besides working on the ranch, I also enjoyed the countryside. There's a clear water pool in the area, with large trees on the edge. It's great for swinging into. I spent a lot of hours fishing, invading planets and catching frogs."

"Sounds like an ideal childhood," Lynn said.

His lips pressed together into a thin line. "It was what it was."

They munched in silence for a while.

"Would you go back to it if you could?" she asked.

Jack shook his head. "Nah. I'd rather see what lies ahead," he said. "Besides, we have a saying: 'It's never the same river.' Things keep changing."

Lynn turned towards the green waters of the Concho. A piece of driftwood floated by. A snapping turtle emerged from the waters and laboriously clambered over some rocks jutting out of the river. The turtle lay there, sunning itself without a care in the world as a couple of dragon flies hovered around it. She wished she could be the turtle.

"So, what was your childhood like growing up in a Japanese-American household?" Jack asked.

Lynn flushed. "I'm impressed you picked up on my Japanese background. Most people think I'm from the Philippines or Mexico."

Jack smiled and shrugged. "Actually, I asked Jen."

Her breath caught in her throat. What else had Jen told him? Maybe he already knew about her suspicions. No, didn't feel like it. They wouldn't be this comfortable with each other. He wouldn't keep glancing at her or smiling at her in that melting way. Damn, she'd miss Jack's flirting when she left. Lynn managed a laugh. "I like your modesty too. Most guys would just take credit for guessing right."

"Yeah, well, I'm not like most guys," he said. "And I don't take undeserved credit."

Their eyes met and held. Lynn found herself dog-paddling in a fathomless ocean of green. Time slid into a slow waltz. Warmth unfurled deep inside. She broke eye contact and stuffed her hands in her pockets. Why did life have to be so complicated?

"So, are you going to tell me about that childhood or

would you rather we discussed something else?"

"I didn't have much of a Japanese upbringing," she said. "My grandparents were sent to an internment camp, as part of the forced relocation of Japanese Americans."

Jack turned his head and looked at her. "Pearl Harbor."

The sweep of his gentle gaze, warm with sympathy, almost stole her breath. Where the touch of his fingers sent electricity sizzling through her, this was quieter, deeper. More dangerous. Like a real hug that promised safe harbor and unconditional acceptance, an embrace you never wanted to escape. Lynn nodded. "My mother was six years old," she continued. "But their lives became a nightmare even before the camp."

She'd replayed the story many times in her head, imagining the different players. Imagining herself in their shoes. Her voice shook as she finally told another person about her grandparents living in fear as they waited for their summons while stories of Japanese Americans being arrested, questioned and sent to camps were whispered all around them. The houses being searched for subversive materials, which generally meant anything Japanese, the ominous knocks on the doors.

Jack covered her hand with his, creating a warm cocoon. She should break contact, but she left it in his. How could something so wrong, feel so right?

Then Jack said, "My mother came from a German background and spoke the language exclusively until eight years of age." He paused and plucked a wild dandelion, twirled the stalk between his fingers. "My grandparents stopped speaking German during the war. By the time I arrived, no one in the family remembered much of it."

"War can make people react in so many different ways."

Her grandfather had been angry and wanted to return to Japan when they were released from the camp, but he knew they'd be treated as shameful pariahs there as well.

"My grandmother tried to teach people about the Japanese, cut through their fear by creating a fusion of Japanese and American experiences." She laughed. "Ever had tuna casseroles with a side of seaweed salad and wasabi? It's pretty good."

But her grandmother never lost control, never lashed out as a dragon. No matter how hurt, how scared. Oh *Obaa-chan.*

"You'll have to make it for me." His tone held meaning, a quiet hope.

Their gazes tangled again for the length of a heartbeat.

"Someday." *I hope.* She glanced away from him. "My mother reacted by becoming as American as possible—demanding ketchup instead of soy sauce, gyrating to Elvis rather than learning the tea ceremony." She sighed. "Not all of it can be blamed on Americanization, my mother never really got along with her mother."

"Sometimes parents and children don't fit together, can't relate, despite belonging to the same family." He looked away at the river.

Lynn couldn't believe she was telling Jack all this. She hadn't talked about her grandparents experience even to Jen, and definitely never to Rob. Strange. She'd met Jack just a few days ago and he came from a totally different world, but Lynn could talk to him. She trusted him. It didn't add up, didn't make logical sense, but she trusted him.

"My grandmother taught me all she knew, like how to create bonsai and some of the traditional dishes, and she told me Japanese folk stories." Revealed family secrets, taught me everything I know about life. "She died too soon."

Jack gave her hand a gentle squeeze and Lynn found the strength to continue.

"I took language classes in college and found out all I could about the Japanese culture. I toyed with the idea of going to live and work in Japan in search of my roots, but then I realized that I'd always be an American there because, well, I am American."

"I know what you mean," Jack nodded. "I took German classes in college too, hoping to rediscover a piece of my heritage," he said. "Though I have German and Irish in me, when I think of myself I'm a Texan, pure and simple."

Lynn smiled. Maybe she and Jack weren't that different after all. Again their gazes collided, held, melted into one another. His thumb drew circles on the inside of her wrist. Silent quakes of desire burst through her.

"Hey, how about climbing up to the peak?" His question came out in a hoarse croak. "The view's spectacular."

She needed to put distance between them. Before desires —crazy, insane desires— overtook her reason. "Last one up is a rotten egg," Lynn yelled, racing ahead. She embraced the touch of the wind on her skin, her hair, the pure physicality of the action.

Jack laughed as he streaked past her. Almost to the top, he twisted toward her, grinning like a fool, and held out his hand.

Lynn stared into his eyes, took a deep breath, and put her hand in his.

Once on top, they stood panting, surrounded by sky.

Paradise Valley stretched below, the Concho River glistened like a sequined scarf over its gentle green and brown slopes. Lynn shivered next to Jack.

Thinking she was cold, he wrapped his arms around her shoulders. Her soft, apple scent teased him, drew him closer. She leaned into him. He closed his eyes and bit back a gasp. They stood like that for a long time watching birds sweep across the perfect blue sky.

Jack wanted the moment to last forever. The wind played with tendrils of hair that had come loose from Lynn's ponytail. He glanced down and saw the beautiful curve of her cheekbones glowing in the molten sunlight. The need to taste her skin, nibble and kiss his way down to her neck and shoulders overwhelmed him. Could he stop at that? He forced his eyes away from temptation and caught the brilliant colors of a rainbow to the right. Cicadas serenaded them. Nature seemed to be outdoing herself to create the perfect setting. Kiss the girl.

Fine, I get it. His head sank toward Lynn's half-smiling mouth.

Her face turned towards him. The smile disappeared and her dark eyes swirled with emotions. The desire he saw in them made his own flare. Her ragged breathing, or maybe his, filled the silence. Jack kept his gaze locked onto hers as he moved closer. His heart rode hard inside his chest. He stopped inches from her lips, letting their breaths mingle, giving her a last chance to decide if she wanted this, wanted him. When she didn't move, he closed his eyes and let himself fall.

She shifted in his arms.

Jack's eyes flew open as his lips pressed against a cool, soft palm. Lynn stood, eyes closed, the back of her right hand pressed against her mouth. How could such a soft, delicate hand be such a formidable wall?

Disappointment stung over and over, like an angry wasp. He sighed and pulled his emotions under control.

She trembled against him. He moved his mouth to her ear. "Rainbow at three o'clock."

She looked at him. Her eyes glittered with emotion. "Jack, I'm sorry, but—

He pressed his fingers to her lips. Pillow soft lips. "Nothing to be sorry about," he said. "And you really are missing a great rainbow." He turned her to face outwards.

He stared at the rainbow without really seeing it. Lynn filled his mind. He could be clueless at times, but not this time. She'd wanted the kiss as much as he did. He'd seen his hunger reflected in her eyes. What had gone wrong? Why had she stopped him?

CHAPTER 12

During the drive back to Jen's house Lynn's mind replayed the almost-kiss over and over again.

Having his strong arms around her had made her feel safe, feminine. It'd been nice to not think of herself as a dragon, a protector of the weak and innocent, but just as a woman. Did he have to smell so good? The scent of clean sweat and evergreens, warmed through with a hint of musk, intoxicated her. A jumble of emotions —that she didn't feel brave enough to untangle— roiled through her. On top of that, silence squatted between them like an invisible troll. She hadn't meant for things to go that far.

Lynn peeked at Jack. He looked lost in thought, his face a blank page with shadows. Her gaze fixed on his full lips. With each breath she drank in another intoxicating whiff of his rich, warm male scent. Desire swirled in the pit of her stomach. What would his kiss have tasted like? Would it have been gentle and playful or raw with hunger and need?

The truck slowed and stopped. Lynn dragged her gaze to peer outside. The early evening sun painted a pretty picture around a two-story building, constructed of native stones and adorned with the standard façade of a past era.

Despite the peeling paint, boarded up windows and graffiti on the walls, the structure still displayed graceful federal pillars, an arched pediment over the main entrance and beautiful moldings. A flat-roofed gallery with a saw-tooth edged awning —now tattered and dusty— wrapped around the building.

"Wow, that must have been really beautiful," Lynn said, eyeing the swirly leaves decorating the concrete cornice. "But what's it doing in the middle of nowhere?"

"That's the Range Hotel, one of the fanciest in all of West Texas at one time," Jack said. "From the early 1900s until 1970 this area was considered a health center because of its dry climate and remoteness. The government built the State Tuberculosis Sanatorium here, and hotels and motels sprang up between what was known as Sanatorium, Texas and San Angelo to cater to the families and friends of the patients."

Lynn took in the copper gutters glowing in the sunset. "What happened?"

Jack shrugged. "New medical advances and drugs almost wiped out TB in the United States. The state hospital was converted to the San Angelo State School to serve mentally handicapped men and women," he said. "Over the years, the Range changed hands and ran down. Now it's a transients' hangout."

Her gaze moved over several bedraggled and grimy

homeless men loitering on the steps. Their stooped and worn bodies crumpled together. Some looked away, others stared back with vacant eyes. A tingle of fear crept into her mind. Was the man stalking her around town among them?

Lynn shook her head. "It's sad to see it falling apart like this." She searched the faces. "But, at least it's still providing shelter to some."

"Yeah." Jack started the pickup.

Lynn kept her eyes on the huddle of men as they drove away. A familiar figure in a tattered coat emerged from among the pillars and planted himself on the road. Lynn's spine went rigid as her gaze met his. The man raised a shaky hand and spread two fingers into a V. He pointed at his eyes, and then aimed them at her. *I'm watching you.* A breath hissed out of her.

"You okay?" Jack glanced at her.

"Just a leg cramp," she answered massaging her right calf. Lynn glanced back and smiled. She did have another suspect.

Cannon bounded to the door to greet Jack, welcoming him home with loud woofs and sloppy licks.

"Why can't girls be more like you?" Jack said, burying his face into the dog's hairy neck. "Uncomplicated and enthusiastic."

Cannon turned his head and gave him a sympathetic look. Jack grinned and scratched behind the dog's ears. Hot breath puffed into his face and he pulled away. "Phew! Dog breath. Okay, I'm glad she's nothing like you."

Jack threw himself on the couch, his mind churning. He replayed different parts of the day over and over again. He'd definitely enjoyed himself. He thought Lynn had too. They'd laughed a lot. That was a good sign, right? He raked fingers through his hair. And they'd talked about all kinds of things. Strange, despite coming from very different places, both their families had much in common. Lynn had looked so strong, yet vulnerable, speaking about her grandmother. He'd wanted to hold her tight. Okay, truth be told, he'd wanted a hell of a lot more.

Jack leaped up and paced the room. But he'd settled for holding hands. Much less forward. Anyhow, she hadn't pulled away. Yeah, if you'd asked him things had been going damn great. He stopped and frowned. "So why didn't the kiss happen?"

He shook his head and stalked to the library. He ran his fingers along the spines of some books. His father had shelved them alphabetically. He started pulling books out, and piling them according to subject matter. Time for a little change around here.

Maybe she wasn't interested. Her face, flushed with desire, filled his mind. A jolt of answering need speared through Jack. He stopped and leaned against the bookshelf. Oh yeah, no denying the attraction. He gulped and strode to another section of the library. Pulled more books out.

Okay, he wanted her, she wanted him and both happened to be consenting adults. So what was the problem? He ran a hand over his face and sneezed. Damn, he needed to dust this place. Maybe she didn't want a short and sweet fling, but a relationship. Lynn seemed like a nice girl, the kind who'd want a meaningful relationship, the kind that deserved romance.

He sank to the floor and sat Indian style among the precarious towers of books. Yeah, that must be it. She wanted a relationship. Jack propped up his face with his hand. Nothing wrong with nice women having fun, not everything had to be serious. He considered himself a nice guy and he'd never had a long-term relationship. Somehow, all the females he'd dated had been passing through his life on their way somewhere else. And what was wrong with that? Both parties had fun. Nobody got hurt and people continued with their life.

Images of his sister Annie and her husband Glenn, working together on the ranch, rocking on their porch swing, and laughing, popped into his mind. Jack shook off the loneliness that gripped him. Yeah, some people had happily-ever-afters, some had romantic interludes, and then others got stuck in unhappy marriages, like his mother and grandmother. He sighed.

He pulled out Annie's wedding album and flipped through it. She'd been so happy and beautiful that day, glowing and beaming at everybody, including her annoying little brother. He stopped at a picture of her and him dancing together. Then Jack moved onto a picture of her and Glenn's first official kiss. Thank God, Annie had found love and happiness. He pictured himself and Lynn in the same place. Did he dare hope for Happily-Ever-After? Would she have him despite his being a Callaghan? Could she love him? Could he love her the way she deserved?

A relationship. Did he want a relationship with Lynn?

His breath caught and an odd stillness welled up inside. The sound of his heartbeat amplified and echoed in his head, silencing all thought.

Yes.

Shaking, Jack stood and stumbled away from the books. He flopped into the chair at his desk and took a few deep breaths. A relationship. Talk about new frontiers. He switched on the computer and pulled up the internet.

He didn't know if he was relationship material or not, but he planned to give it a hell of a shot. He typed her name, grinning like an idiot as his heart did a drum roll. Googling her. What next? Passing her notes?

Jack skimmed the first thirty references. A fairly recent engagement announcement in the *Houston Chronicle* caught his eye and he clicked on it. After an unbearable wait, a black and white photograph formed. A smiling Lynn and a Robert Uriah Neff III stared back at him.

"Fuck." He shoved away from the desk.

"Stupid bitch!" The dragon master hurled the empty beer bottle at the wall. Shattering glass brought him a few moments of calm. How dare Lynn like someone else?

Didn't she realize what he could offer her? Maybe she wasn't good enough for him. Any woman with taste and standards would choose him— the artist, the man who controlled the dragon. He let out deep, jagged breaths, hating himself for feeling like the ten-year-old whose best friend just dumped him to hang out with the cooler kids. He could have any woman he wanted.

With shaking hands, he lit another cigarette and took deep, desperate pulls. The aroma, the taste, the heat of the fire filled his breath, enveloped his body. The smoke caressed him with soothing touches. He grasped at the comfort offered by the dragon. He sighed and leaned back in his chair. Damn it, he wanted Lynn.

Her face, her body, filled his mind. His heart slammed against his ribs. How could a woman with fire in her spirit choose anyone but him? Every time their eyes met, her nature called to his. He shook his head to clear his thoughts, wishing he could ignore her siren call. Oh for silence, blessed silence.

The thought of being without Lynn left him cold. He took another drag of the cigarette, inhaled the dragon spirit deep within himself. Last night he'd dreamt of the dragon again. All gleaming black, breathing an inferno.

But this time, there'd been another. A jewel-toned blue-green female. They'd circled the autumn moon, great wings flapping, singing the fire song. Then —he licked his lips— then, they'd mated.

Want shivered through him as he recalled the vision of the two great dragons writhing and wrestling among the clouds. Their raw passion stirred up a storm, until winds chased clouds from the sky, lightning crackled and thunder boomed. He groaned as his own lust burned bright at the memory and his jeans tightened uncomfortably. Fingers strayed to his erection.

He must have Lynn. The dragon meant it to be so. What else could the dream mean?

Lynn. He'd sensed fear in her. A hesitation. He smiled into the dark and crushed the cigarette at the edge of the growing pile of butts on the table. Of course, he was the dragon master. Perhaps she was awed. Perhaps she couldn't imagine he'd want her.

He laughed as the solution came to him. She was a woman, his woman, and he'd have to woo her.

All he needed was a little bit of time. Then she'd see the truth and choose him.

Pushing out of the chair, he stumbled across to the cooler to get himself another beer. He twisted the cap off and took a swig. Cold, bitter liquid tumbled down his throat, relieving some of the disappointment that his mate wasn't as perfect as he'd thought. She'd see her error. Otherwise, she'd pay. She and her friend would burn.

If he couldn't have her, no one could.

But the drink didn't quench the dragon inside. The

need for a fire gnawed at him. Yes, he could wait for Lynn, but something had to burn soon. Very soon.

The dragon's roar ricocheted in his head.

CHAPTER 13

Lynn woke drenched in sweat, her heart going like a jackhammer. A scream stuck, half-uttered, in her throat. Her gaze darted about the dark room, trying to see into the shadows. Her sleep had been fractured by fits of troubled dreams and pulse-pounding awakenings.

Fires. Fires everywhere. The entire countryside pockmarked by bonfires.

What had woken her this time? A noise? Did the phone ring? She forced herself to lie still, listening. Seconds slid into minutes and seemed like eternity. Nothing, except for the loud ticking clock.

Dreams or warning? Unease tingled under her skin like the buzz of an electric shock.

Lynn kicked off the sweat-dampened covers and

swung her legs to the floor. *Serenity. Courage. Wisdom.* She'd repeat the mantra for as long as it took to fight off the fear. She pushed her fingers through her hair and glanced at the bedside clock. Three freaking a.m. Again. She closed her eyes and groaned, knowing sleep wouldn't come.

Hugging herself, Lynn decided to walk around the house, double checking the windows and doors. Uneasiness reverberated inside her as she made her way through the dark, silent house. Dragon genes made it easy for her to see, but nothing undue caught her attention. Yet she was aware of a presence. A large, dark presence hovering on the edge of her mind.

She stood undecided on the threshold of the back door. Part of her wanted to run back and dive under warm, safe covers. Another part tensed, determined to face an unknown adversary. She had vowed to stop the rogue and she would. Huffing out a breath, Lynn grabbed her backpack, unlocked the door and stepped onto the dew-wet grass.

An unnatural silence greeted her. She cocked her head this way and that, listening. Why weren't the cicadas and katydids singing their night songs? It wasn't cold enough yet to kill them off. Lifting her face to the full moon, she sniffed. No tell-tale smell of smoke.

She glanced about her, searching.

Brilliant stars glittered in the dark velvet sky. Night in the countryside, without any artificial lights, was breathtaking. But tonight a sense of danger edged her wonder. Perhaps it was nothing but her paranoia. Still, no harm in an aerial patrol. She stripped off her PJs and stuffed them into her backpack, shouldered the straps, and stood naked under the moonlight.

Closing her eyes, she concentrated on her breathing.

As her muscles relaxed, Lynn cleared her mind of niggling worry and called the dragon. The change rushed through her veins, charging her with its energy, renewing her essence. Power filled her limbs and cells as she took on dragon form.

Lynn coiled her muscles into a tight bunch and leapt toward heaven. Her powerful wings flapped until they caught the wind and rode. She decided to circle all of Paradise Valley. Thinking of the strange homeless man she'd encountered twice, she headed for the derelict hotel.

When she reached it, darkened windows stared like unseeing eyes. Nothing moved. Again a whiff of anger and dragon musk tinged the air. She circled the building twice, peeking into windows. Bodies huddled together or curled up alone on dirty floors.

Shifting with the wind, Lynn changed direction, skated higher, and continued on her patrol. The beauty of dark land and shimmering river glimpsed through a constantly-shifting veil of gray clouds soothed her. She stretched her neck, spread her wings as far as she could, and gave in to the exhilaration.

Lynn gazed below at the dark, clustered rectangles she identified as buildings and landmarks around town. She passed several spires and crosses, naming each church under her breath. She hoped none of the townspeople were awake. What wild tales might flourish if someone caught her silhouetted against the silver moon?

She scanned both the skies and the land beneath. Wariness rode between her shoulders and drove her forward. A movement far below caught her attention. Lynn hovered in the air, her gaze fixed on the shadows. A pickup shot out of the darkness. Even though the headlights were turned off, its body gleamed ghostly pale in the silver moonlight.

A breath hissed out of her. Someone else seemed to be awake. Someone who didn't want to be too obvious about his or her whereabouts. Could it be the arsonist? She tracked the vehicle from above as it weaved between buildings, through shadow and light. Once the pickup left the town environment and hit the open road, it became a lot easier to follow. She paced herself to match the truck's speed.

When it passed Jen's house, Lynn hazarded a guess. Jack's home was next. Could the unknown driver be headed there? Could it be Jack or was it someone who wanted to hurt Jack? With a burst of adrenaline, she shot forward and raced ahead. Her heart zipped.

The ranch house and its surroundings stood still and dark. She dropped down into the trees edging the property, hoping Cannon wasn't running loose. Breathing ragged, she waited a few minutes. No barking, leaping, licking dog attack. She shifted.

Lynn cursed as she dug through her backpack. She'd forgotten to pack a new change of clothes after the last time. Shit. Shivering in the chilled night, she changed back into her pajamas. Then, hidden in the trees and bushes, she crept closer to the house, squatted in the shadows. Lynn fidgeted to keep the blood circulating in her limbs. Pins and needles would not only be annoying, but a damned hindrance if she needed a quick escape.

The soft rumble of the diesel engine thrummed in the air.

The pickup pulled into her view and parked. Lead cold betrayal dragged through her as she recognized the vehicle. She scuttled forward, carefully parted some of the branches with her fingers and peered through. The door opened and the overhead light inside the cab lit Jack's face.

A dull ache spread inside her. Where had he been this late? And why was he driving around without headlights at night?

Her eyes and nose burned, heralding tears. What the hell? She'd expected this development. Or at least should have. Jack was a suspect. Just a suspect. Nothing more. Now he was even more suspect.

What she hadn't expected was her own reaction. Somewhere along the way she'd started to think, hope, he'd be a good guy.

She shook her head to clear away the emotional jam and realized he'd already disappeared inside. Annoyance and curiosity quivered inside her. For half a second, she considered hammering on the door and demanding answers. A quick glance at her outfit changed her mind.

What if Jack had a plausible reason for being out and about? How the hell would she then explain her lurking in his bushes in the early morning hours in hot pink Tinker Bell pajamas?

Turning away from the house, she looked up. A faint lightness smudged the dark. Dawn approached fast. No time to wallow in what-ifs.

Lynn had just slipped back into Jen's house and locked the door, when the phone rang. Unease bubbled in her gut. Early morning calls didn't often bring good news. A mad dash later, she snagged the receiver before a second ring. "Hello."

"You owe me." The familiar dark whisper made her stomach roil.

"Who is this?"

"I took care of your problem."

"What are you talking about?"

A soft chuckle. "You'll know soon enough."

The call ended. Icicles formed along her spine, chilled

her to the core. Lynn dropped the phone back to its cradle and paced. Who was this caller? Was it Jack? Her heart stopped.

What had he done? What did he want? She pressed her hand to her lips. Did he know about the dragon?

The radio beeped and crackled in the kitchen. Heart pounding, Lynn ran toward the noise. A door slammed and footsteps thumped behind her. She and Jen careened to the radio just as it announced a five-alarm structure fire at the Range Hotel.

CHAPTER 14

Tears filled her eyes as Lynn watched the beautiful old hotel, engulfed by flames, burning bright like a torch against the dawn sky. The fire highlighted a face here, revealed a detail there, in unusual clarity while shrouding others in pitch black shadows. Bedraggled transients huddled in silence while the firefighters bombarded the flames with water.

The fire department was winning, but it was too late for the building. The early morning light revealed a burned out hull— all smoking wood and blackened bricks, a mausoleum, surrounded by pools of water.

Lynn took a deep breath. The sharp stink of charred wood cleared her head, reminded her she was on the job. Hernandez would definitely want this story. She snatched a pen and pad from her backpack and took notes.

Jen had set up her station and was busy handing out water and cookies to the homeless. Lynn picked out Anderson by his trademark Stetson hat and Roberts stood next to him. Both men watched the fire, their backs to her. Like it or not, she'd have to try for an official quote. See if she could find out the cause of the fire.

An October chill had finally set in. She zipped her jacket to the neck and made her way toward them.

"Too bad they let this building turn into a dump," Anderson said.

Roberts shook his head. "Lit up like fireworks."

"Dry wood, trash brought in by the homeless," Anderson said. "Nothing but fuel. Add cigarettes and make-shift fires to that... Boom."

A man clutching a leather satchel jogged up to them. "Sorry, I was in the middle of a foaling when the call came."

"Poor sod's beyond help, but glad you're here," Anderson said. "Come on, let me take you in."

Lynn hurried up to Roberts. "Who's that?"

"That's Jim Grayson. He's a local vet and the precinct Justice of the Peace."

"Justice of the Peace?"

Roberts jerked a handkerchief out from his jacket and wiped his sweaty face. "He'll officially pronounce the man dead."

Dread choked her. Lynn couldn't make a sound. She swallowed and tried again. "Dead? They found a body?"

Roberts nodded. Grim weariness lined his face.

"Who?"

"A homeless guy who'd been camping out here like the rest." Robertson glanced around at the group crowding Jen's station wagon. "Unlike the others, he didn't make it out."

Her heart fluttered in her throat. She wondered if it was the same homeless guy she'd been seeing around. She turned and searched the crowd. No sign of the man.

Roberts rubbed his hands together and blew on them. "I spoke to the guy a few days ago."

"You knew him. I'm sorry."

Roberts let out a short, joyless laugh. "Can't say I knew him, but we'd spoken. He spun me quite a tale."

"What'd he say?"

Roberts looked at her, a wistful smile on his lips. "He claimed he saw a dragon."

Her heart plummeted. What? When? How? A dark whisper echoed through her head, *I took care of your problem*. She licked her lips. "Huh. So, what started the fire here?"

"We think the guy must have got drunk and fallen asleep while smoking." The sheriff sighed. "We found empty liquor bottles and cigarette butts around the body."

Cigarette butts again. Guilt bellyached inside her. A man was dead, she should tell the police about the cigarette butts she'd found. "Are they the same brand that you found at Jen's?"

"Can't comment. It's an ongoing investigation."

"Thanks for what you did share." She unzipped her back pack and dropped her pad and pen inside. Her hand lingered, touching the plastic bag hidden within. The sheriff wouldn't be happy about her poking around.

She zipped the bag and turned away. Took a few steps. What if the butts she'd collected could help catch the guy doing all this? What if it could have prevented this death?

A breeze played with her hair, brought the scent of smoke to her. Lynn whipped around and marched back to the sheriff.

He watched her, a quizzical look on his face.

Her fingers hurried to outrun her doubts. Lynn pulled the evidence bag out and held it out to Roberts. "Do these match any of the cigarettes you found?"

He stared at the bag like she was holding a live scorpion. "Where did you get this?"

"I was driving by Jack Callaghan's house and I thought I saw somebody skulking among the shrubs." The words ran out like water from a leaky faucet. "So I went back later and investigated. I just took a few, there's more there by the bushes in the front."

CHAPTER 15

The axe blade glinted, sharp and silver, in the sunlight. Jack adjusted his grip, hoisted it over his shoulder and brought it down with a satisfying thunk, splitting the log in two. He threw the pieces onto the growing pile, and placed another log on the stump.

Heat steamed off his back and sweat drenched his shirt. He had enough firewood for two winters, but he didn't feel ready to stop. He needed hard, physical labor, mind-numbing work, anything to keep his mind off Lynn.

Engaged. The wedding announcement said she'd be married in less than a month. No wonder she'd balked at kissing him. He gritted his teeth. She could've told him. Instead, she'd played him for a fool. He put extra force into the next swing and was rewarded with a satisfying thwack!

He should have stuck to the occasional bar waitress who just wanted some fun. But no, he had to fall for Lynn. Gone out on a limb and risked everything for a relationship. What the hell for? To be lied to or manipulated into a damn pretzel? Suffer like his heart had been tossed down a dry well?

No thanks. He'd take fun and meaningless with a dash of honesty. He thwacked the log again.

The sound of car doors slamming echoed from the front of the house. Shit, he wasn't in any mood for friggin' visitors. He hacked at the next log.

"Morning, Jack."

He turned and wiped his forehead with the back of his arm. Sheriff Roberts and his deputy, the hulking Jenkins, stood behind him. Since he couldn't confront Lynn, might as well scratch his itch by taking on these guys. "What do you want?"

"A concerned citizen reported seeing some suspicious activity around the front of your house." Roberts smiled and shrugged. "Thought I might check it out, if it's okay with you."

Jack's grip tightened around the axe handle. Concerned? Make that nosy and ugly. People needed to keep themselves out of his damn business. "You got a warrant?"

Roberts' lips flatlined. "You got something to hide?"

They stood soldered together by twin glares. Jenkins' cleared his throat.

The sheriff's body sagged. "Look, I'm just trying to do my job."

A soft breeze kissed Jack's heated skin, soothed some of the anger away. Dang, he was being an ass. "What kind of suspicious activity?"

"Someone lurking around."

He leaned the axe up against the house. "Let's go check it out."

"With all the strange goings on around here, we can't be too careful," Roberts said leading the way.

"Yeah." Jack walked, his back stiff, between them. Jenkins loomed behind almost breathing down his neck.

When they reached the front of the house, Jenkins slipped like a shadow and joined Roberts's search in the bushes and trees. *What the hell did they expect to find?*

"Sheriff!" Jenkins pulled out a camera from his coat pocket and snapped picture after picture.

Jack hurried after Roberts and saw some cigarette butts scattered under the azalea bush.

"Smoking's real bad for your health," Roberts said over his shoulder.

A muscle ticked at Jack's jaw. "I don't smoke."

"Well, somebody does and he's been peeping in your windows."

Jack gritted his teeth as anger twisted through him. Somebody had been on his property. Spying on him. His hands bunched into fists. He wanted to stomp the damn butts into the ground and then do the same to the peeping Tom.

Jenkins took out an evidence bag and tweezers from another pocket, and went after the smokes. Jack exhaled as he unclenched his hands. "Can I see one of those?"

Jenkins stood, closed the evidence bag and held it up for him.

He reached for it, but Roberts stopped him. "We don't want your fingerprints on it."

Jack sighed and peered at the see-through plastic bag. He made out a bit of a printed logo. "Can I smell them?"

Jenkins and Roberts exchanged a glance. After a nod

from the sheriff, the deputy cracked the top open.

Jack leaned forward and took a deep sniff. A sharp bite of tobacco laced with a hint of licorice. Anger battered at him. He stumbled backward. "I've smelled that before."

Roberts' eyes widened. "Details?"

"Sam White, the foreman at the Callaghan-Avery ranch, smokes something like that."

Jenkins gnawed his lower lip. "Sam White and probably three-fourths of the county. Even I smoke the same brand."

The man had a good point. Didn't mean he'd have to like it. "Oh, well then. Sorry can't be more help."

The sheriff and deputy ambled toward the car. Jack followed to make sure they got the hell off his property.

Roberts stopped and popped the trunk. He pulled out a pair of broken-in boots and held them up. "Look familiar?"

"Look like my old work boots that went missing from the barn a few weeks back," Jack said. "Where'd you find them?"

"Downtown," he said, tossing them back into the trunk. His eyes stayed on Jack. "You want them back when we're done with them?"

Why would he want back boots with worn off soles? And why did the sheriff want them? He shook his head.

Roberts shut the trunk and crunched across the caliche to the driver's side. "Planning any trips anytime soon?"

"No."

"Good. Let us know if you do."

Lynn slammed down the phone into its cradle harder then she'd intended.

Reporters working around her borrowed-cubicle

popped up like gophers and threw curious glances her way. While the newsroom came with many resources, it didn't afford her the privacy of Jen's guest room. Her face burning, Lynn threw a new notebook into her backpack and headed for her assignment— a re-election announcement by Commissioner Ward on the County Courthouse steps in downtown San Angelo.

She'd just left a fifth message for Henry Chase of Hope Developers and not heard a peep out of him. The guy had to be avoiding her.

A carnival atmosphere greeted her on the courthouse lawn. Red, white and blue balloons and streamers adorned the antique-looking lampposts and wrought-iron stair rails at the main entrance. Rousing marching music played from a boom box. The candidate stood surrounded by men in suits and jeans, and coiffed and manicured women. Lynn watched the popular man smile and handshake his way among the crowd.

She had her notepad flipped open and pen poised when the music died down and Ward made his announcement. Applause greeted his words. She needed a live quote from the man, something spontaneous rather than practiced. If that wasn't asking too much from a politician.

Seeing an opening, she pushed forward and shoved her hand forward. Ward gave her a hearty handshake.

"Commissioner Ward," she began.

"Call me Mike. Everyone calls me Mike," he said, smiling.

The man could do a toothpaste ad. "Lynn Alexander from the *Herald*. Why are you running again?"

"It's the satisfaction of serving my community," Ward said. "Besides, the monthly stipend of seventy-five dollars is my cigarette money. My wife won't give me any."

Lynn chuckled at his little joke. "Any ongoing projects you want to see completed?"

"Oh, there are many," Ward said. "A short-term and long-term solution to our water problems, the proposed Paradise Valley development, adequate facilities and equipment for our local law enforcement and fire departments, better pay for everybody including employees and so on."

She looked up from taking notes. "So you think the land development will be a good thing for Paradise Valley?"

"Money and jobs coming into the community is always a good thing."

Jack's take on the development floated to her mind. "So you've no concerns about over-development or the ecological balance?"

"Well...." He tugged at his tie. "Like any proposal, it bears scrutiny." Ward's gaze wandered over her shoulder. He waved and nodded at someone. "I need to mingle."

"Anything you'd like to add that I didn't ask?"

"No, except that people need to go out and vote," he said. "They can vote for anybody they like, but they need to vote."

A whole lot of nothing. Lynn thanked him and stowed her pad and pen into her bag. He tried to give her a campaign button.

"Sorry, Mike, I have to be impartial," she said. "Good luck."

As she headed back to the office, her stomach growled, reminding her she needed to grab breakfast. She decided to detour to Diego's Burrito Shack. Walking in, she spotted Sam, the ranch manager she'd met at Jack's place. An ugly scowl lined his face as he talked in soft tones to another man. The only other customer sat hidden behind a newspaper. She wished she had a handy newspaper. Lynn ducked her head as she hurried to the counter and ordered a chorizo and egg burrito. The transaction took only a few minutes.

Brown bag clutched in one hand, she tried to sidle by but Sam's words snagged her attention.

"Yeah, the Callaghans are having trouble," Sam said. "Serves them right. Ill-gotten gains are always hard to swallow."

"If you can't stand them, why do you work for them?" the other asked between bites. "Anyway, the sister's an Avery now."

Sam slammed his palm down on the table. "Once a Callaghan, always a Callaghan. It's the blood." He sat back and pulled in a couple of deep breaths. "I work for them because they're enjoying my inheritance and I might as well squeeze 'em for what I can."

Dreading the encounter, Lynn nevertheless pivoted and presented herself at the table. "Hi, I couldn't help overhearing you and I have to ask— will you repeat what you just said?"

Sam glowered at her. "I have no problem repeating the truth, but what's it to you?"

She pulled out her notebook and pen. "I'm writing an article for the paper on the proposed land development, and part of the research is tracing the families with land stakes in Paradise Valley." She smiled. "What do you mean the Callaghans' are enjoying your inheritance?"

Sam eyed her suspiciously as she dropped onto the bench next to his more even-tempered companion. "I don't have to talk to you."

"Well, if you don't want the world to know your side of the story…"

He hunkered forward. "Part of the land they own used

to be owned by the White family. My great-granddaddy homesteaded the place."

"His grand-dad lost the farm in a drunken gamble."

Sam tossed his companion a heated look, then turned back to Lynn. "Yeah, well, a more honorable man than a Callaghan wouldn't have taken advantage of the situation. He ought to have thought about the family."

Maybe he had a point, but shouldn't White have thought about the family before risking the land? Lynn kept her opinions to herself as she jotted down notes. "Do you have proof that your family owned the land?"

His gaze skewered her. "I'm telling you like it is. Why do you need proof?"

She shrugged and threw full blame on Hernandez. "The editor requires it."

Sam looked down at his gnarled and dirt-encrusted hands. "Yeah, my dad tried to sue and the paper covered it. I'm sure the *Herald* still has those old articles."

Probably stored in the archives, or as the news staff referred to it— the morgue. "How much land are we talking about? What's it worth?"

He grimaced as if he'd just bitten something bitter. "It was a decent-sized farm, about one hundred sixty acres right by the river."

"With the developers sniffing around, it'd be worth some money today," his friend chimed in.

"All of which would go into Callaghan pockets instead of mine," Sam growled.

"Have you tried talking to Jack Callaghan or his sister? Maybe they'd sell you the land." Lynn packed the tools of her trade into the backpack.

"Buy back what should be mine? I don't think so!" Sam attacked his burrito with a vengeance.

The man next to her, obviously an old friend or just

164

foolishly fearless, snickered. "There's also the issue of being able to afford it."

Sam lurched to his feet, swearing and cussing. Lynn said a quick goodbye.

She exited the booth and turned toward the door just in time to see Jack racing for the door. He carried a folded newspaper. Shit.

"Jack!" She rushed after him.

By the time she exited, he was already in his truck.

She flew to the window and knocked on it.

He turned an unsmiling face to her. After a moment, the window rolled down.

"I can explain," she blurted.

His icy stare didn't change. "No need. You're curious like all the others about the infamous Callaghans."

"I'm just doing my job."

His lips curled into a sneer. "Well, your nosiness isn't appreciated. And watch out who you trust, Sam White is neither stable nor reliable." He paused and let out a deep sigh. "We employ him out of a stupid sense of obligation."

The window went back up and the truck rumbled to life.

Lynn jumped back and watched him squeal out of the parking lot. Something inside her grew heavy and sank to the bottom of her stomach and she felt an overwhelming need to cry. Fool. She was only trying to find other suspects, and a disgruntled employee seemed like a good candidate. A long-drawn breath surged out of her. It didn't matter what he thought of her. She was in Paradise Valley to help Jen and catch the rogue. Not to mess around with Jack.

Abby, the *Herald* receptionist, greeted her with a mile-wide smile and an impressive bouquet of red roses. "Someone's got an admirer."

"Huh?" Lynn hurried forward. The roses' sweet, heady fragrance made her feel woozy. "Who sent them? Is there a card?"

"There is." Abby plucked it out from the back and handed it to her.

Lynn held the small innocuous cream envelope like a dragon egg in mid-hatch. Could Jack have sent them? The man got an A+ for romantic follow up. She wished again he hadn't overheard her conversation with Sam. Her heart thudded at the base of her throat.

"So, open it!" Abby leaned over the counter, her eyes shining.

Lynn pinched one end of the envelope and tore a section open. Spasm after spasm rocked her nervous system. True warning or haywire dragon? She opened her mouth and gulped in air, then grabbed the vase. "I'll just take them to my desk."

Abby's smile dimmed. "Well. Enjoy your secret!"

Clutching the vase to her chest, Lynn tried to hold back the nausea stirred up by the roses and dashed into the newsroom.

A wolf-whistle stopped her. Hernandez leaned in his doorway, grinning. "Somebody must like you!"

"I guess."

"So who is it then?"

Lynn's gaze darted like a trapped fly. "I don't know."

"Hmm, a secret admirer." He rubbed his hands together. "I like mysteries."

She'd been afraid of that. "Got to go, lot's to do." Lynn trotted past him.

"Are you going to the Paradise Valley Picnic and fundraiser Wednesday?"

"Yes, I'll write up a story for you," Lynn answered without stopping.

"Good," Hernandez called after her. "Maybe your admirer will reveal himself there."

"That'll be news." She dumped the vase on her desk and slammed into her chair. With shaking fingers, she tore open the envelope and pulled out the card.

An ink sketch of a dragon adorned the heavy cardstock. No signature.

CHAPTER 16

Frisky banjo tunes and the mouthwatering smell of barbeque greeted them at the park entrance. Even though she could've flashed her press pass and entered for free, Lynn dropped twenty dollars into the hand-lettered *Donations* box at the entrance. The money would help the Jarvis family. Jen —carrying the brightly-wrapped bicycle for Timmy from the two of them— hightailed it to the work area to help with the set up, while Lynn got sucked into a whirlwind of people.

The Jarvis family took turns hugging her, and she hugged them back— glad to see them happy again. Being politicians in an election year, the county commissioners made sure to shake her hand. She waved at Timmy as he raced by.

She wove through the crowd, stopping and chatting with several of the firefighters, except the one she wanted to see. Where the hell was Jack?

Lynn spotted a familiar face. The statuesque blonde from the newspaper photograph. The one who'd been draping herself all over Jack. She seemed to be in an intense conversation with someone, leaning close to a man, who for the most part stood hidden behind a life-size cardboard cut-out of Ward giving everyone a thumbs up. Did he have to put the damn sign there? Lynn zigzagged toward them, trying to get a better look at the woman's companion. Was she with Jack? Had to be. She'd recognize his relaxed stance anywhere.

Anxiety gnawed at her. Lynn didn't want to interrupt, but she wanted to ask him about his late night trip and the Range Hotel fire and clear the air between them. As soon as the conversation ended, she'd pounce on Mr. Callaghan.

She positioned herself behind the sign and hovered over the table of desserts. Bits and pieces of the conversation floated to her.

"The Range was a dump. It needed to be razed," he said. "I don't know why everyone is so worked up about it?"

Shock rippled through Lynn. *A man had died.*

"It's a historical building, something that can be a tourist attraction and an asset," the woman's tone cut like a rapier. "In other words, it's worth money. A lot of money. I assume you can grasp that."

Fire was, no pun intended, the hot topic around the area lately. But Jack had told her he loved history. She inched forward.

"Why are you lurking there?" The cool, cultured voice poked at her.

Lynn flushed as she stepped out and joined the couple. Swallowing, she turned to the man. Henry. Not Jack. The knot in her shoulders eased.

The developer's representative had exchanged his suit for crisp blue jeans, a white shirt, black cowboy boots and a black Stetson. Jack-style attire, except for sunshades perched on the hat. The statement she'd heard earlier didn't seem as surprising now. But, wow, the two sounded alike.

"Well, what do you have to say for yourself?" The woman stood with her hands on her hips.

Lynn took a deep breath and counted to ten. "I'm just waiting for you both to finish talking." Then sticking out her hand, she added, "I'm Lynn Alexander, with the *San Angelo Herald.*"

The woman's gaze remained glacial even as her lips curved upward. "I am Kate Harrington," she said, shaking hands. "So you're the one I should thank for the Jarvises continuing to be my neighbors."

The man pushed his right hand forward. "Hi, I'm Henry Chase, with Hope Builders."

Lynn shook his hand and improvised. "I know who you are. I was waiting for my chance to speak to you."

Kate excused herself and sauntered away after a speculative look at them. Lynn, for her part, pretended not to notice and turned her full attention on Henry.

"Sorry, I've been meaning to return your calls." He smiled as he gave her the slow once over. "So what can I help you with?"

"You have some exciting plans for Paradise Valley I'd love to interview you about." She batted her eyes. "When can we get together?"

Henry's eyes widened. "Oh, so you've heard about the development. How did you manage that?" His gray gaze zeroed in on her.

She tried to imagine herself as Hernandez and shrugged. "I have my sources and you just confirmed them."

"We aren't ready to have a news story about it yet."

"You're confusing news with advertising."

Henry shook his head. "I guess I do owe you for rescuing me from that conversation." He glanced at the crowd. "Some of the people here don't like what my employers want to do, so they take it out on me."

Lynn glanced away. While she felt bad for the guy, she also happened to agree with Ms. Harrington. The old building had been beautiful and an asset, and not just for the economic value. And it had nothing to do with the guy's employers. Should she change the topic? She met his gaze. "She did have a point."

He grinned at her. "I know," he said. "I don't know why I sometimes just argue for the sake of argument."

Lynn laughed. "They expect the worst, so you fulfill their expectations?"

"It's fun watching people get all worked up... sometimes." Henry stepped closer. "Where are you from?"

Lynn grimaced as she realized that she still stuck out like a sore thumb in Paradise Valley. "Houston."

"Yeah? Me too." The strains of a fiddle sailed through the air. A band called The Howlin' Hound Dogs played on the stage. "Want to dance?"

He dragged Lynn to the dance floor despite her protests of not knowing how to two-step. "Come on, we have to represent Houston," he said. "It'll be fun."

However, Lynn kept tripping up because she was laughing so hard at the outrageous comments Henry kept making. For a moment, a whiff of dragon musk tweaked her nose, then it disappeared, replaced by her partner's spicy aftershave and the mouth-watering smell of barbecue in the air. They discussed the life-draining long Houston commutes and compared notes on the meat-market aspect of the club-scene, including the cheesiest pick-up lines they'd ever heard. Toward the end of the song, Henry whispered his version of the lyrics into her ears: "*Mah dawg died and I got the shingles, the missus she left me and she took the pork rinds and Pringles.*"

Her laughter, he said, was like the night song of cicadas. Insistent and continuous, and something that'd keep him awake all night.

The music ended and before Lynn had the chance to catch her breath, Jack came and stood next to them. She looked into his eyes. They were wintery green and unreadable. He glanced at her partner. "Mind if I cut in?"

Henry's grip tightened on Lynn's waist. His gaze locked with Jack's.

In return, Jack squared his shoulders and took a step forward, almost between her and Henry. His hands curled into fists.

Hot, dry desert heat rose in waves around them as if October had suddenly switched to deep summer. Lynn struggled to breathe and think in the stifling air heavy with the strong, musky scent of male dragon. Her muscles tensed, pulsing to change. Scales calcified one by one on her abdomen. What on earth?

A little girl squealed as she rushed by, pigtails flying. Timmy bumped into Lynn, then ran around her, waving a stick with a wooly caterpillar perched on it. The world shuddered and moved again. Lynn sucked in a lungful of cool, refreshing air.

Henry smiled, or rather bared his teeth, and released her. "Be my guest, as long as you return her."

Jack responded with a steely stare.

Her heart twirled as she found herself caught up in Jack's arms and settled against his muscular chest. The minute they touched, her insides turned liquid. "I really don't know how to two-step," she said.

Had Jack called the heat and the pheromones? Was he the dragon? She took a deep whiff. He smelled of mesquite smoke, musky and warm, from working the grills. His scent enfolded her, worked its way under her skin.

Jack showed her the basic steps. "Just relax and follow my movements." The music started up again. The band was playing an old favorite, *"Silver Wings."* Henry stood at the edge of the crowd, watching them, his face expressionless.

"You look beautiful darlin'." Jack's whisper tickled her ear, shot a shiver down her spine. His tone echoed admiration, and maybe a tinge of regret. Why? Her insides churned with mixed emotions.

Soon she was only aware of Jack. Lynn discovered her head came up to Jack's collar bone and fit neatly under his chin when he leaned forward a bit. She snuggled in and relaxed. What would it be like to do the deed with a male dragon? She shivered and he tightened his hold.

They moved effortlessly around the makeshift dance floor. Two people fused into one. Lynn couldn't think of anything save his hand at her waist, the touch of his body against hers, his warm breath playing on her hair.

She noticed Brenda and Tom dancing by. Brenda had her head on his shoulder, and Tom leaned down over her. Brenda's hair was held in a ponytail by a yellow ribbon, its fluttering end whipping around Tom's nose from time to time. They seemed to be in their own world.

Lynn sighed. This felt so right. She settled in and enjoyed the sway of their movement, and Jack's possessive grasp on her. She closed her eyes and imagined they were a couple. She became just a woman, a much desired woman caught in the embrace of her handsome admirer.

Before she knew it, the music ended and they pulled apart. Why was he so quiet? So cool and distant? Was he still angry at her? His winter gaze burned into hers and they stood inches apart even as a new tune started up. Sweat beaded through her pores and pooled underneath her breasts.

She wanted to reach up and touch his face. She wanted to tell him everything —about dragons, fires and suspicions— and hope he'd understand. Her nerves skittered every which way. Damn, had she hurt him? She took a deep breath and gathered her courage. A well-manicured white hand settled on Jack's shoulder.

"I believe you promised me this dance," Kate laughed.

Lynn turned away and ran smack into a broad chest. Henry.

"Ready for the next dance, m'lady?"

She laughed. There were other men. Jack and his bad temper suddenly seemed too much work. Of course, she needed a man about as much as her dragon needed to get laid. "Only if you commit to an interview first."

He chuckled and gathered her in his arms. A whiff of warm orange and bergamot swept through her, relaxed her. A voice whispered in her head. *No reason you can't enjoy the company of a nice guy.*

"You are relentless," he said.

"Yes, I am. The relentless reporter." That sounded so good that she almost believed it. She quirked an eyebrow at him.

He pulled in a sharp breath, his gaze fixed on her. "Okay, let's meet for drinks on Monday."

Laughter spurted out of Lynn. "The way an interview works is I ask you questions," she said. "I think I want my wits sharp for that."

He dipped her, held her off balance for a minute. "Are you saying you're done in by one drink?"

Relax. When she was upright and looking into his eyes, she cleared her throat. "I'm saying I don't mix business with pleasure."

Henry whirled her out and pulled her close again. "Okay, I'll have a beer and you can have San Angelo water. Believe me, that's not a pleasure."

A giggle burst from her, and then Henry swung them around the dance floor. Her gaze found Jack and Kate dancing. A lightning bolt of jealousy shot through her, followed by a tumble of emotions. Better matched in height, Kate looked into Jack's eyes as they waltzed by.

Henry blew into her ear. She raised her head from his shoulder and saw a teasing smile on his face. *Live a little.* "Made up your mind about Monday yet?"

Say yes. Say yes. What was wrong with a little bit of fun? Henry was a nice guy. So he didn't make fireworks go off inside her, but he made her feel good, made her laugh. "Sure, when and where?"

After cheering Timmy on as he blew out his candles and cut the cake, Lynn grabbed her piece and found a seat. Elsie Tavistock clapped a hand to her heart and beamed. "Oh you looked so happy on the dance floor."

"It tired me out," she laughed and wiggled into a comfortable position.

"You know, dancing is one of the things I miss the most," Elsie looked down at her lap. "This danged arthritis has taken so much from me."

"Oh." Panic gripped Lynn as she stared at the metal rims of Elsie's wheel chair. What could she say that wouldn't sound trite? "I-I'm sorry. I hope you had many dances before."

Tavistock settled on Elsie's other side, and handed his wife a glass of punch. "Aye, that we did." He kissed her on the forehead. "Enjoyed every one of them. And Elsie was the most beautiful woman there, still is."

Elsie laughed and leaned into her husband. "He's partial to me," she said. Her bright blue eyes turned serious. "Make good use of every chance life gives you to dance."

The words slipped inside her head, resonated, called up an answering twinge of emptiness. She nodded. They were joined by Jen and a tall, pretty woman with a cloud of auburn curls held up by a gigantic silver clip.

Jen introduced her as Annie Avery, Jack's sister. On hearing Lynn's name, Annie squealed in delight. "I read that story you did on the fire at the Jarvis house."

Lynn smiled as warmth spread through her. "I hope you liked it."

"Oh yes, I cried," Annie said. "But it was funny to see my brother portrayed as the hero."

"Well, he was rather heroic," Lynn replied.

Annie laughed. "I'm sure he was, but it's still funny to me." She proceeded to regale the table with a "you-wouldn't-believe-what-Jack-did-as-a-young-'un" story.

Apparently, Jack was twelve when Annie got married. "Half-way through the reception, the family couldn't find Jack. "Imagine me clutching my puffy wedding-cake dress up a mile from the dirt as I tottered around." She shook her head. "But he was a hot-headed tyke with a tendency to get into trouble, so we wanted him found."

An uneasy tingling spread through Lynn and grew to a burning point as Annie stopped and took a drink of water. "Finally, we discovered him at the back of the hall playing with matches. Drunk as a skunk that had fallen into a barrel of moonshine!"

Laughter roared out of Annie, filled Lynn's head, crashing over her mind, drowning out sanity. "I just find it funny that he went from nearly burning down my wedding hall to this heroic firefighter," she said, wiping tears from her eyes. "Miracles do happen."

The others at the table also laughed, some snickered, but Lynn's guts knotted. Parts of what she'd researched about serial arsonists, warnings she'd known about dragons and shape-shifters, crowded in to roost in her mind.

Hernandez was right. A lot of arsonists, or people who are attracted to fire, did join fire departments, especially the volunteer ones. Many of them had childhood stories that involved them starting fires or playing with matches. The motive in many instances involved being a hero.

Lynn excused herself and pushed away from the table. She tossed her half-eaten cake into the garbage. A chill seeped into her, spread inside her veins contaminating cell after cell. She'd lived through the quick-trigger temper and all the trouble that came with it, before *Obaa-chan* had taken her in hand and trained control into her.

She stumbled through the crowd. Her eyes searched for Jack, passing from face to face. Finally, she found him. He was dancing with the tall, blonde Kate Harrington. Again.

The dragon churned inside. Her thoughts gathered in her head in a large, screeching, pulsing cloud of darkness. Jack liked historical things. Maybe all that talk about history was a cover? He wouldn't burn the hotel. But they caught him playing with matches. He wouldn't let a man die. Or would he? Did she know Jack Callaghan at all?

CHAPTER 17

Lynn sat still at her desk, surrounded by open files and books on arson. Phrases and words tumbled and collided inside her head. She shoved her fingers in her hair, grabbed a handful and tugged. The sharp bite of pain silenced the crazy thoughts and doubts for a moment. As her fingers loosened their hold, the whirlwind started again. She had to find some answers.

She snatched up the phone to call Anderson, but stopped halfway through punching in his number. The man wasn't exactly media-savvy or friendly. Maybe she'd have better luck getting information if she cornered the investigator in his office.

A brisk walk in the nice, crisp morning could also help clear her mind. Lynn grabbed her notebook and a couple of pens and set off for Tom Green County Sheriff's Department, where Anderson's office was located.

The repeated trill of a bicycle bell caught her attention, drew her eyes. The homeless man in the black, tattered coat wove his bicycle back and forth on the other side of Harris Avenue, almost parallel to her. He gave her a gap-toothed smile and a lazy wave.

The dragon growled deep inside, wanting to lunge across the four lanes of flowing traffic. Lynn fought the urge, eyeing the man. Bulging plastic bags tied to the back of his bike swayed as he slowly pedaled forward. For an instant their eyes met and held. Then he passed her, sped up and turned the corner. Breath petered out of her as she resumed walking. Dragons and ghosts. She really needed to end this.

Taking a last gulp of the smoke-scented fall air, Lynn climbed the three steps of the drab, flat-roofed, one-story building that housed the Sheriff's Department. As she pushed through the door, three pairs of eyes turned toward her.

Two deputies and a clerk hovered behind a Formica countertop. The scratchy tones of the police monitor bounced off the metal desks and file cabinets, and added to the chaos in Lynn's mind. She parked herself at the front counter and asked for Anderson.

The clerk made a discreet phone call. "He'll be out to get you in a minute."

The soft whir of overhead cameras tempted her to wave and make funny faces. If they were going to record her every move, might as well give them something to talk about. Then again, maybe not the best plan.

Finally, Anderson emerged and led her deeper into the belly of the building, to his office. Her nose twitched at the sweet scent of tobacco lacing the air and she fought back a sneeze as she settled into a plastic and metal chair with no padding. Anderson obviously didn't want visitors to hang around and chitchat. He pinned her with a cool stare. "So what can I help you with?"

Lynn flipped open her notebook and clicked her pen. "I have a few questions about the fires in Paradise Valley," she said. "I'm collecting information for an overview story I'm working on."

Eyes fixed on her pen, Anderson leaned back in his chair and crossed his arms. "Shoot."

"Are these fires related?"

Anderson's cold blue eyes returned to her face. "Why would you think that?"

Nerves danced a jig in her stomach. She mustn't lose control of the interview. Lynn squared her shoulders. "Well, you've been at all the recent fires," she said.

He nodded. "I like to be present at every fire scene, just to check things out."

"Do *you* think these recent fires are related?"

Silence. Lynn willed herself not to break it. Anderson and she calmly gazed at each other across his desk littered with files and stacks of paper. Finally, Anderson sighed. "We're investigating that possibility," he said.

"Have you found anything suspicious at any of the fires?" For it to be on the record and her able to report it, he'd have to mention the footprints and the cigarette butts.

Anderson steepled his fingers under his chin. "This is an open investigation, so I can't talk specifics," he said. "Let's just say the frequency of the fires is disturbing."

Lynn took a deep breath. She racked her brains to glean something helpful from all the research she'd done.

"Experts say there are generally two types of arsonists— the amateur firebugs and the organized serial arsonists. What do you think we have here?"

Anderson sat up straight. His eyebrows rose in surprise. For a moment, he chewed at his lower lip, making his mustache jog. "Off the record?" he asked.

"Sure," she said. "But we might have to revisit the issue later for the record."

"We think we might have an amateur whose habits are escalating," he said.

"What do you mean?"

He mentioned a series of grass fires and abandoned building fires had preceded Lynn's arrival. Then there was Jen's fire, an occupied home. "He seems to need bigger and bigger thrills as time passes."

He pulled out a cigar and lighter from a desk drawer. The flame drew Lynn's gaze like a magnet.

"It could also be that the person is trying to keep down the danger but his fascination grows and his willpower fails," Anderson said, then paused to chuff out a couple of puffs of sweet scented smoke. "Fire is dangerous. And now we have a dead body."

Dread scrabbled down her spine and crouched in her stomach at his words. "Do you think there could be more? Are people in danger?"

Anderson held up a finger. "Let's not cause a panic," he said. "But catching this person is a priority and the department is working on it."

Lynn's writing hand shook. She slid lower in her chair to keep her notebook out of Anderson's view. The rogue needed to be stopped and time seemed to be running out. Would she be able to handle it? She didn't have a choice. Lynn said a silent prayer. An unbidden thought blipped into her mind— and at the end of it all, she'd have a heck of a story. Front page, top half. A different kind of excitement flushed through her. My hunt, my story, and I will handle it.

"I need something on the record," she said. "Do you have a suspect?"

"Yes."

When Anderson didn't add anything else, Lynn tried another angle. "A lot of times the amateur fire bugs turn out to be part of volunteer fire departments."

Anderson leaned forward and fixed her with a glare. "Part of that impression is created by the media," he said. "More stories are written about firefighters who turn out to be fire-starters because of the irony of the situation."

Without missing a beat, Lynn countered, "So, you are saying there isn't an issue of arsonists joining fire departments?"

Anderson shifted around in his chair. "No, that's something we do have to watch out for," he said. "All new trainees and volunteers are carefully screened."

She asked him to elaborate on the red flags.

"You know, fascination with fires or a disregard of rules and safety," he said. "If somebody is over-eager or keeps showing up first on the scene."

Fear squeezed her lungs until it hurt to breathe. Jack. Images of him standing in front of the burning hotel rolled through her mind. She forced herself to ask the next question. "Do you suspect anyone in the Paradise Valley Volunteer Fire Department?"

"No comment."

She asked her standard, "Anything else you want to add?" and ended the interview. Lynn quickly explained that she was still in the information-gathering stage and would call Anderson again when she was closer to writing the story.

"That's fine," Anderson said, handing her a business card. "If anything else comes up, I'll let you know."

Cannon barked hard and furious, startling Jack out of his Tom Clancy novel. Seconds later the doorbell rang. Excitement sprinted through him. Jack jumped up. Lynn? No reason for her to come calling. Just get over the girl.

He trudged across the room, grabbed Cannon's collar with one hand, and opened the door with the other. Henry Chase stood on the porch, leaning casually against a post in the universal pose of studied idleness. An image of him dancing with Lynn pushed into Jack's mind and made his grip tighten.

Henry broke into a big smile, stuck his hand out and stepped forward.

Cannon lunged for him and Henry skipped back.

"Down boy!" Jack wondered why the usually friendly dog was acting up. "I'll be with you in a second. Let me put him in the bedroom."

He returned to find Henry strolling around staring at the deer heads in the family room. Jack gritted his teeth. Why hadn't the man waited on the porch? He let out a breath and willed himself to relax. After all, he *had* left the door open. "So what brings you here?"

"Just wanted to talk some business with you."

Jack knew Henry was the San Antone developer's representative and that he was in town wheeling and dealing for land. But he couldn't imagine what business the man could have with him since he wasn't interested in selling.

"Why don't you come into the office?" He turned and led the way.

Jack had run into Henry hanging out with some of the off-duty volunteer firefighters at local bars. His talents included buying drinks and telling funny stories. Seemed like a nice guy. Yet, Jack's hands itched with the urge to punch him. Jack flexed his fingers. How much of his dislike of the guy had to do with Lynn? Jealousy? That was a new one.

Henry let out a low whistle as he entered the library. "Nice."

Jack glanced around. "Thanks. It's the family homestead."

Henry caressed the top of one of the armchairs. "Family heirlooms. Treasures." He peered into the display case.

Jack eased into the seat behind the desk. Surely the man hadn't dropped in on him to talk furniture and knick-knacks. "So, what did you want to discuss?"

"Wow, you're all business, aren't you?" Henry flopped into a chair.

Jack leaned forward, not saying anything, and stared at his guest.

"Okay, okay," Henry held up his hands. "I am here to make you an offer."

"I'm listening."

Henry reached into his satchel and pulled out a neatly bound Hope Builders' concept plan for the Paradise Valley area and laid it on the desk. "We are looking for land and you have a lot of it. I think we could work together for mutual benefit."

"Sorry, you wasted a trip. I'm not interested in selling."

"How come? We're open to price negotiations."

"It's nothing to do with money, I'm just not selling."

Henry threw him a puzzled frown and scratched his chin. "I don't get it," he said. "From what I hear, you aren't exactly a popular person in these parts. Why don't you just take the money and make yourself a better life elsewhere?"

Jack's temper flared. How dare this —stranger— listen

to gossip and draw assumptions about his life? Would Paradise Valley never accept him for who he was? He looked down at his nails and stayed silent for a long while until he felt the anger tamp down. Then he looked Henry in the eye. "Because this is my land, my family's land, and I will not be run off it by anybody."

Now Henry leaned forward. "Some people would contest that claim." He shrugged. "From what I hear."

Jack clutched the arms of the chair, to keep himself from leaping across the desk. He needed to control his temper.

"Also, heard the Callaghans before you didn't hesitate to sell and make a quick buck." The other man laughed.

The sound grated on Jack's nerves like the whine of a dentist's drill. He pulled his pen knife from his jean pocket and flicked it open, counting to ten as he cleaned his fingernails with the blade. He'd been working on his temper, and wasn't about to be goaded into losing it. "Well, I guess I am different from the other Callaghan men."

Henry looked around the room again. "Come on, man, everyone has a price. We just have to find the right one for you." He fingered the carved grooves in the arm rest. "Tell you what, I like some of this old furniture you have. How about I come up with a handsome figure to relieve you of the land, the ranch house and the furniture?"

Jack squinted at Henry. "Not interested."

"Think about it," Henry tried again. "You'll be free as a bird, with cash to burn."

Jack rose out of the chair until he towered over Henry. "Since you've been prying into my life, I am surprised you haven't heard how stubborn I am," he grated out. "Me and the rest of the Callaghans are legendary. You are wasting your time, Mr. Chase."

Henry flashed him a switchblade of a smile. "Family," he said. "Don't worry, I've studied the Callaghan family history rather well. I'm going to find your price sooner or later. You're a Callaghan, after all."

It took a shitload of control not to punch the guy. Jack prided himself on being a gentleman, but he was about to throw Henry out. He shook with barely suppressed rage. I am *not* my father or my grandfather or my great-grandfather, he repeated silently. He took a few deep breaths and felt the calm return.

"Mr. Chase, you've run out your welcome. Leave."

Henry rose from his chair and tipped his hat to Jack. "Until we meet again."

Jack had just slammed the door shut, when his cell phone rang. Damn, he was popular today. He snatched the phone out of his pocket like it burned him. "Callaghan."

"Hi there, sweet thang," Annie said. "You alright?"

"Yeah, just peachy," Jack bit out. "Why?"

"I just had a feeling you were upset."

Damn. Annie had an uncanny sense of knowing when things were off with him.

She interrupted the silence. "You were in demand at the picnic last night, dancing with all those single gals."

The feel of Lynn in his arms shot through him. He gritted his teeth and stalked back to the library. "Well, you're always after me to be social, that's what I was doing."

"I think Lynn Alexander might have a crush on you," Annie said. Once his sister set off, it was hard to derail or distract her. "She made you out to be quite the hero."

Jack barked out a harsh laugh. "She was just doing her

job," he said. "Writing up a story good enough to sell papers."

"She is a good writer, but I still think there's some personal interest."

"Whatever. I'm not interested." *Liar, liar pants on fire.* He huffed out an impatient breath.

"Well," his sister paused for a too-brief moment. "I have to tell you about this other really interesting conversation I had at the picnic."

"Who with?"

"Kate Harrington."

He slumped into a chair. "Should I guess what was said or are you going to tell me?"

"Well, she had a lot of questions about you," Annie giggled. "Like if you were seeing anyone. She's definitely interested."

Jack laughed at his sister's silliness and shook his head. "Maybe she was just making conversation."

"Yeah right, she said you'd make a good couple. Both from old ranching background, both mature, both single."

"What did you say?"

"I agreed." She paused. "I hate seeing you waste away all by your lonesome."

"Don't worry about me," he said. "I have better things to do."

"Like what?" she retorted. "You're both single. She's attractive, classy, intelligent and interested. You could do a lot worse, especially since this area isn't exactly hopping with eligible women."

Jack hesitated. Kate wouldn't quite fit fun and meaningless either. And, his heart ranted, she wasn't Lynn. The memory of their dance broke to the surface of his thoughts. Jack had felt a shiver of pleasure as soon as he'd held Lynn in his arms. He recalled the sweet apple aroma of her scent, the softness of her body, the warmth of her breath.

His jeans tightened. Again. He needed to stop acting like a hormone-crazed teenager. Get a grip. But how could he stand being in Lynn's vicinity without going stark raving mad? Maybe Kate would be a good distraction. "You have a point."

"So you'll ask her out?"

"I'll think about it," he said, ending the call.

CHAPTER 18

Pounding on her door jarred Lynn from a deep sleep. She burrowed deeper under the warm covers. The noise continued. "Jen?" she called out in the dark.

"Phone call! Somebody from the paper," Jen said, poking her head in.

Lynn pushed out of the blankets and glanced at the radio-clock next to her. "At four in the morning? On Sunday?"

"Something about an emergency they need you to cover," Jen said, holding out the phone toward her.

A sigh leaked out of Lynn. "I'll be right there," she said, rolling out of bed. One good thing about working in advertising and plugging away at the never-ending novel— assignments never came this early. She stumbled to the door, rubbing her eyes, and took the phone.

"Hello?" She mimed out writing. Jen nodded and disappeared.

"I've a surprise for you. A special gift." The deep, dark voice wrapped around her like a dense shroud, sending a shiver flickering through her. She stumbled against the door frame and leaned on it for support.

"Who's this? What do you want?" The questions came in sharp bursts as she clutched the phone.

He laughed. A soft, relaxed chuckle. "It's okay, Lynn," he said. "I know what you are and I want to be your friend." He paused for a breath. "And more."

A shadow crossed her mind and she barely suppressed a shudder. Who the hell was this? What did he know? Had he sent the roses? Was it Jack? She couldn't tell. Something seemed to be muffling and distorting the voice.

Jen returned with pen and paper. She snatched them from her.

"What the hell are you talking about?" Act tough and he'll sob out a confession. Maybe.

"Language, language." Amusement laced his voice. "You're a beautiful woman, you should act like one."

Lynn swallowed the expletive stomping on her tongue. Fine, two could play that game. "I don't have friends without names."

"In time, you'll have it. Along with my heart."

Crazy with a capital C. Lynn's throat turned cotton-dry. She swallowed a few times. "Are you the fire-starter?"

"Fire," he whispered. "You should come see this fire I built for you. It's burning so bright."

Fuck. Lynn dropped the pen, scrambled around on the floor and found it. "Where— where is it?" Her heart thundered inside her as she jotted down directions. "I'll be right there."

The fire was at the Tavistock ranch. Memory of the outspoken rancher and his charming wife haunted her. Please let them be okay. She gripped the backpack in her lap so hard that her nails bit into the leather.

"Fucking crazy dragon! He did this to win me? How dare he use me as a reason?" she seethed as the car jumped forward.

"Crazy dragons don't need reasons," Jen said, stepping on the gas.

Lynn let out a breath. The problem was the man seriously believed she'd be impressed by arson. So in a roundabout way, she'd caused the latest fire. Concern for the Tavistocks filled her. *Please, please let them be okay.*

They arrived at the scene at the same time as the fire department. The firefighters tumbled out of their vehicles and rushed towards the burning ranch house. Lynn spotted Jack's truck already parked just outside the gates. He must have got here earlier. Was he here as a volunteer firefighter? Or had he been the one to call, the first one on the scene? Doubt made her heart freeze and shatter into a million shards. Jack. So it was Jack.

Seeing them, Jack emerged from his pickup; he wasn't in uniform. His gaze latched onto hers as he stood framed by the house engulfed in flames.

"Stop right there!" A gunshot echoed into the night, freezing everybody. Tavistock, dressed formally in a Western tux, a black Stetson perched on his head, stood on the porch. He lowered his gun from its raised position and pointed it at the approaching people.

"What the hell?" the fire chief roared.

"This is private property. And you all can't come in," Tavistock replied.

Lynn, following Jen and the firefighters at a discreet distance, stared. Geez, could the situation get any more screwy? Her cell phone —a loaner from the *Herald*— rang, earning her glares from all around. She grabbed it from the backpack and stabbed the button. "I can't—"

Hernandez bellowed in her ear. "Where are you?"

Lynn bit her lip. Maybe she could use this to her advantage. Holding the phone to her ear, she stepped further away from the others. "At the Tavistock ranch."

"Great, we definitely want this story."

"Got it." She clicked off and slipped into the shadows of the ancient oak grove surrounding the property. Lynn packed away the phone, then shouldered the backpack. She took a deep breath and broke into a run. Zigzagging from one dark, warped trunk to another, she circled toward the back of the house.

Lynn breathed in the musty smell of dew-soaked earth and rotting leaves, edged with the sharp scent of the new fire. A tremor raced along her spine as she crept through the patchwork of moonlight and darkness. The wood smoke clouded her thoughts, stirring the dragon into a frenzy. Keeping her eyes on the distant glow flickering among the trees, she crept closer.

A whisper of movement from behind rooted her to the spot. Was someone following her? Jack? The hair on her arms and neck stood to attention— in warning. She dropped to the ground, into the dark embrace of a cedar bush and willed herself invisible. Lynn crouched still, barely breathing, and waited.

Minutes ticked by. Her muscles cramped. She craned her neck and looked this way and that. Nothing moved. No one there. Then an armadillo scurried through the leaves inches from her hands. Lynn swallowed her scream and released the breath she hadn't realized she'd been holding.

The cool air carried the arson investigator's voice. "Amos, your house is burning down. We are here to help."

Tavistock's answer followed, weighed down with a sad finality. "It's my property and my responsibility. I tried to put it out and couldn't. I guess I'll go out with it."

Lynn cringed. Tavistock stood to lose everything he owned and worked for because of her. No, because a crazy dragon had fixated on her. Either way, she seemed to be at the root of the problem. Her stomach knotted in guilt. She had to do something. She straightened and moved forward.

After a moment's silence, Anderson spoke again. "Amos, did you set fire to your house?"

"No! My ranch and the house is all I have, I wouldn't destroy it," Tavistock's voice cracked.

"It doesn't have to be this way," the fire chief chimed in. "We can put out the fire and try to save your house."

Another gunshot ricocheted in the quiet of the early morning. "I don't want to shoot anybody," Tavistock said. "But I don't want you all trespassing either."

Lynn stopped at the iron fence and gate separating the backyard from the grove and stared at the blazing house. Hungry flames poured out of windows and cracks, licking the air, beckoning to her. The dragon lunged inside, wanting out. Wiping her hands on her jeans, Lynn grasped the cold metal bars and climbed up and over the gate. She dropped to the dirt and ran toward the house, stopping inches from it as the radiating heat beat against her.

Invisible or not, her human form didn't come in

asbestos. Sighing she squinted at the backdoor through the roaring flames. So near, yet so far. She closed her eyes and willed the dragon.

The fluid shift and stretch of bones, muscles and mass zinged through her, took her breath away. A warm, caressing heat lapped at her core and spread. Scales rippled across her skin. Twin billows of steam whooshed out of her nostrils. *Ready or not, here I come.*

Lynn lumbered forward, crashing through the door. She stopped at the threshold of the smoke-filled living area and adjoining kitchen, and swiveled her head from side to side but couldn't spot the rancher.

"Into your hands I commend my body and my soul, amen." The words floated out of a darkened doorway.

Lynn sniffed at the air. The smell of smoke, age and dust tickled her nostril. Taking a deep breath, she shifted back into human form and hurried toward the opening. Good, her invisibility still held. She found the rancher and Elsie seated on the bed, his bald head touched her silver one. Lynn squared her shoulders and approached the couple.

"Are you sure about this Elsie?" Tavistock whispered.

Tears streamed down wrinkled cheeks. An unspoken thought wafted into the room. *How long can you live on the edges of life? You're nothing but an empty shell of the woman you were.*

What the hell? Dragon mindspeak. Lynn tiptoed closer and glanced at the figures. Were either of them dragon or part dragon?

End it. End it now.

"Yes, this is what I want." Elsie said. "But you should get out."

No, no. He needs to stay. He's your soul mate.

"You know I'd never leave you," Tavistock answered.

A sob broke from Elsie as she slumped against her husband.

Holy Sh— Lynn bit her tongue and glanced around the room. The whispers came from someone else. Was he inside and invisible like her? The rogue dragon? She turned and looked behind. Fat fingers of fire appeared at the door. Heat and smoke poured in. Must save one insane couple *now*. When she turned back, Elsie lolled in Amos' arms, passed out.

"Amos," she called in a half-whisper.

The gray head jerked and jumped, as he searched the room. "Who?"

"Amos, you need to get out, you need to save Elsie."

"Who are you?"

"Your guardian angel." Never in a million years had she envisioned using her invisibility to play an angel. *Obaa-chan* must be rolling in her grave and laughing her ass off.

The man slumped across the still form in the bed. Lynn rushed to him and shook him. "Amos?" No response. Coughing, she searched and found their pulse. Amos and Elsie Tavistock were out cold. Great. She glanced at the door. The fire was spreading into the room. No time for subtleties. She rolled the couple up in the bed cover, leaving an opening for their heads for them to breath, tied a knot to keep it from coming undone. Then dragged the bodies to the floor. Would the other dragon try to stop her? She'd deal with him when she had to.

Once again she willed herself to change. This time the transformation came slower. Weariness weighed her limbs down. Damn, she'd have to sleep for a month to recover. Grabbing a mouthful of the covers between her teeth, she stumbled backwards and dragged the

Tavistocks out of the room feet first. She figured the closer their heads stayed to the ground, the better.

She came up against a wall and pushed back. With a groan the wall crumbled and crashed at her feet. The movement of air caused the fire to flare brighter, creating a wall of flames between her and safety.

Her energy wavered, then surged again. Horror filled her as her invisibility fell away and revealed iridescent blue-green scales reflecting the fire's glow. Fortunately, her form blinked out just as quick. Shit. She'd overdone the changes. How much longer would she be able to hide? Would she have enough energy to change back to human form before she faced the others? No matter, she had more important concerns right now.

Lynn's gaze fell to the inert forms lying lumped together and hidden by the covers. A memory of her grandmother lying so still on the warehouse floor careened through her head. She whooshed out another breath and adjusted her hold. Whatever happened, she had to save Amos and Elsie. Then fanning out her wings to create a barrier between the Tavistocks and the flames, Lynn pulled them through the fire.

Her energy flickered again, making her stumble. A dizzying rush of cold wrapped around her as she fell to the ground in a tumble of bodies and limbs. Moaning, she curled up in the dirt, inches from a pair of black boots. Then darkness swallowed her.

Lynn came to surrounded by paramedics. "Where?"

"Lay still ma'am," said one, checking her pulse. A soft squeeze of her hand made her turn and find Jen standing next to her.

Soft, heart-breaking sobs from her right made her turn her head again. She hissed as a sharp pain lanced through her. Her eyes found Amos leaning against an ambulance.

Anderson let out a breath and placed an arm around the man's shaking shoulders. "Crazy old coot," he muttered as he took Tavistock off the firefighters' hands. Jack came and stood on the other side of Tavistock and put a firm hold on the man as well. Lynn heard him trying to calm the old man down.

Gingerly, she sat up, leaned against Jen for a long while until the world stopped swimming.

"Maybe you should rest for a bit longer," Jen whispered.

"I'm fine," she said. "Just help me up."

Jen braced Lynn as she stood, supported her weight as she took her first steps. "You're lucky I followed your ass and found you, dressed you, and called for help."

Lynn glanced down at herself. Old sweat pants, a soft sweater and slip-on canvas shoes from the backpack. Her gaze shifted to Jen's familiar black boots. "Thanks."

They stumbled to the crowd, pushed through. A grim-looking emergency medical tech jogged up to Anderson and the chief. "Elsie didn't make it."

A wave of sadness rippled through Lynn and her throat tightened. She almost sobbed out loud. She'd failed, failed again.

"Dang sad," the chief muttered. "She die in the fire?"

The EMT shrugged. "The fire I'm sure contributed."

Finally, Anderson cleared his throat. "Well, we'll let the JP and ME figure out the cause of death," he said.

He pulled out a cell phone and called the Justice of Peace on duty to come and perform coroner duties. "The medical examiner needs to be notified and we'll need to get the body to him," he said into the phone. Then he called the Sheriff's department and asked them to send a detective from the Criminal Investigations Division and someone from the Crisis Intervention Unit to deal with Tavistock.

Lynn huddled next to Jen. Even though the fire had been put out and the immediate danger had passed, grief weighed her down. She glanced at Jack, standing next to Tavistock like a bodyguard.

His gaze collided with hers. Was he responsible for Elsie's death? Confusion and anger drifted into her soul as he held her attention. When he blinked and looked away, she swallowed. Had the arsonist followed her too? How much had he seen? Was Jack the crazy rogue? The rogue had killed Elsie, and almost killed Tavistock. Her guts fisted. She needed to talk with Jack.

As the Paradise Valley VFD vehicles pulled out, two other sheriff's department cars, an ambulance, a station wagon and a green Chevy suburban arrived on the scene.

"What's going on?"

Jen nodded at the new vehicles and identified everybody for her: the Criminal Investigations detective, the Crisis Intervention Unit volunteer, emergency medical technicians, the JP and the body transporter, respectively.

"They are going to transport the body in a suburban?" Lynn asked. "Don't they have to use an ambulance or a hearse?"

Jen shook her head. "Anything that can fit a body will do," she said. "And the transporter the county contracts with happens to drive a suburban."

Lynn watched in silence as the techs loaded a black body bag into the suburban.

Tavistock let out an anguished cry. "No, Elsie! Elsie! Don't take my Elsie away!" he cried. The old man leapt forward, his thin body wracked by heaving sobs.

Gritting his teeth, Jack grabbed the old rancher in an

awkward one-armed hug and forced him away from the body and the smoking house. The crisis intervention officer, a soft, round-faced woman, stepped forward and helped lead Tavistock back to the ambulance. One of the EMTs stepped forward and handed Jack a blanket. He wrapped it around the sobbing man. "Oh, Amos, Amos," he said.

The EMTs took over. They'd give Tavistock something to calm down. Jack and the CIU volunteer stepped away from the ambulance.

"Well, he's going to the West Texas Regional Hospital right now, but after the next few days...I need to call around to the Salvation Army and other places," she sighed. "He'll need a place to stay temporarily. Too bad he doesn't have any family."

Jack looked back at the lost old man surrounded by busy med techs. "Well, he's got friends," he said. "I have got room at my house. He's more than welcome to stay, if that's okay with y'all. And I'll look into nursing homes."

The CIU volunteer looked visibly relieved. "That's mighty good of you."

Jack nodded and mentally added, for a Callaghan. Shame pinched him. The woman hadn't said that. Stop imagining more trouble than there already exists. He touched the brim of his hat in goodbye and turned away.

A yawn escaped him as he flexed and stretched his aching muscles. Damn, he was tired. He looked around and caught Lynn watching him. A tightness gripped his chest. *Lynn.* Emotions surged through him. His heart had almost stopped when he'd heard Jen screaming for help, seen Lynn and Amos lying so still on the ground, near Elsie wrapped up in bed covers. What the hell had she been thinking? Putting herself in danger like that was irresponsible. Amazing. Incredibly stupid. So very brave.

A need to touch her, reassure himself she was okay, overwhelmed him. Damn, he should walk away. Instead he stalked toward her.

Danger. The dragon inside Lynn coiled and tensed. The fury shading Jack's face made her want to fight or flee, but instead she stood her ground and waited. Good, she wouldn't have to chase him down.

He stopped in front of her, glowering. "What the hell were you thinking going into that burning building?"

"You guys were thinking and arguing, I decided to do something," Lynn said. Wait a wasabi second. She should be the one asking questions.

"We might have had to rescue three people instead of two," Jack said. His voice shook with rage, and...she almost thought worry.

"Well, you didn't," Lynn shot back. "In fact, you guys didn't need to rescue anybody thanks to me." God, she sounded like a self-important brat. The man threw her off her game.

"You could have been hurt. You could have died in there and no one would have known." His voice cracked.

Did he really care? This was too weird. She looked away, then back. Her eyes met Jack's anguished ones. "How could this happen?"

A breath leached out of Jack. "Elsie's health started failing and apparently she's been in and out of depression. Amos said she set the fire, took an entire bottle of sleeping pills and told him to get the hell out."

"Why?" She knew why because she'd heard the ugly whispers. She wanted Jack's reaction, his reason.

"She'd had enough, Amos tried to convince her otherwise, but..." He shrugged. "Anyway, Amos said he'd respect her wishes but no way was he going to let her die alone." Jack's face was ashen with shock and sadness.

Lynn looked down at the dirt and shook her head. "I didn't do too much. I saw him trying to drag her out and tried to help."

"Yeah, Jen told us."

"She still died." The words burned her throat, left her nauseous.

"You tried," Jack said. "I feel so sorry for him."

They stood in silence for a while. Lynn struggled to make sense of the chaos around her. Should she believe Jack's words, the sadness and concern she sensed in him, or the gnawing suspicion growing in her gut?

"Were you first on the scene?" she asked.

He nodded, staring at the charred ranch house.

Lynn's glance lingered on his sweaty, tired face. Would the rogue look so broken? Could the crazy beast care about anyone? Either Jack was a great actor or he had a split personality or something. Panic rattled through her. Maybe the dragon controlled him.

"How did you get here so quick?" she pressed.

He glanced at her. "I was on my way home when I saw the orange glow of the fire, so I headed for it."

Where was he coming from this early in the morning? She heard herself asking him the question.

He flushed. "I was out by the mermaid. I needed some downtime to think about things."

The mermaid statue on the banks of the Concho in downtown San Angelo. He'd shown it to her during the tour. A romantic spot with the river and trees. It all seemed a life time ago. What kind of things? She wanted to ask, but didn't. "Anybody see you there?"

His eyes narrowed at her. "Excuse me?"

Lynn forced herself to hold his gaze. Her heart pounded in her chest. "Were there other people around the mermaid? Did you talk to somebody?"

Jack shifted and planted his hands on his hips. His shoulders stiffened. "You mean witnesses. Why? Do I need a lawyer?"

"You tell me." Her heart thundered in her ears as she tossed him a defiant glare. If he could prove he'd been at the mermaid, there's no way he could've been at the ranch whispering nonsense to Elsie. Her mouth dried as she waited. She almost broke down and apologized as fast as she'd accused him, but she couldn't dismiss her suspicions so easily.

He stalked away from her, his stiff-legged gait kicking up dust. Then he turned back and stopped inches from her. "You are a fine one to point fingers. And speaking of fingers, when the hell were you going to tell me about being engaged?"

Lynn stumbled back as if he'd hit her. What? How'd he find out about Rob? A wave of nausea swept through her. Not that it mattered, of course, because the engagement had been broken. Rob was no longer in the picture, and Jack appeared to be her suspect. If so, he was on his way to jail. She lifted her chin. "That's none of your business."

"I suggest you make it the next guy's business."

"What next guy?"

His expression hardened. "Henry. I saw you two dancing together."

"As did the rest of Paradise Valley." She pushed her face closer, so they stood nose to nose. "And I danced with you too. What of that?"

They glared at each other.

Then he grasped her face between his cold hands and pressed his lips over hers.

A smothered yelp burst from her as she stumbled, but

he held on. A flash-fire second of panic, then his rich, male taste filled her mind. Dark and smoky. Sexy as hell. His tongue explored her mouth, tangled with hers. She shuddered, her thoughts melted in the heat of the kiss. She pressed back, savored his essence, explored in turn. A throaty growl, deep with hunger and yearning, rumbled through her and poured into him. He trembled against her.

When he shoved her face away from his and let go, Lynn could only stand and pant as she stared at him. More, she wanted more.

His eyes darkened with anger and confusion. "You should have told me. Somehow, at some point, you should have told me."

Damn it, what was Jack's game? Lynn dropped her gaze. "You're right. I'm sorry, I should've told you about Rob." She closed her eyes and then opened them. "You didn't have to declare your feelings by setting this fire."

"What?"

She shoved past him and took her turn pacing. "What do you expect me to think? The attraction between us, then the phone call telling me you wanted to be more than friends, that you've a surprise for me." Lynn stopped and stared at the smoking ruin of the ranch house. "How could you think setting this fire would impress me?"

"I didn't call you and I didn't set this fire." A cold, hard glaze settled on his face. "According to Amos, Elsie did."

"Yeah, but you helped things along. I heard you." The words rushed out before she could think better, fueled by the volatile mix of grief, guilt and anger at another death. Lynn's gaze fixed on a twisted and scorched patch of prickly pears lit by morning sunlight.

He grabbed her upper arm and yanked her to him.

Face to face, he said, "What are you talking about?" He huffed out a breath as he let go of her and dragged his fingers through his hair. "And if you overheard or saw something suspicious, then you should tell the Sheriff."

Gnawing on his lower lip, he stared at her. "Do you really think I would—" He cleared his throat. "I would help things along?"

She stood inches from him; close enough to wrap her arms around him and kiss away his hurt. Press herself against his warm chest and listen to the beating of his heart. She held his gaze, not knowing what to think, what to do.

Jack shot her a disgusted look and walked away.

CHAPTER 19

It was after nine when Lynn dragged herself to the *San Angelo Herald* office. Lack of sleep jumbled her thoughts, plagued her with the images of body bags and corpses as she reviewed and organized her notes and impressions. But that wasn't what left her insides hollow. Lurking behind every thought, every word she typed, was the unrelieved bleakness of Jack's long, silent stare. She pressed her palms against her burning eyes and released a sigh. Focus on the story, for now nothing else matters.

Words fought their way onto the page as she relived the Tavistock fire. Elsie's death and the distraught man made the story painful. By ten o'clock, she was drained and headed for the newspaper's library to do some research on Tavistock. Maybe she'd find something to jump-start the words.

Standing among the rows of metal file cabinets almost as tall as her, Lynn hunted for the Ts. When she found them, she pulled open the drawer. A soft musty ancient scent greeted her. Brown envelopes, normal letter size, lay stacked tightly in the drawer. Each envelope was labeled with a name and held the relevant details of that person's life. Some of the more important people had two or three envelopes to their name. Her fingers brushed across the tops, searching.

People's lives reduced to a bunch of clippings, stuffed into envelopes and stored in the morgue. A fog of sadness clung to her as Lynn dug through and pulled out Amos Tavistock's envelope and walked back to her desk. She needed a hit of caffeine to clear her head, so she stopped and grabbed a Diet Coke from the vending machine.

Missy, the cop reporter, worked at the adjacent desk. She glanced over curiously at the brown envelope in Lynn's hand. "What's that?" she asked. "Do you have an obit to write?"

Lynn grimaced. "Sort of," she said. "I'm doing some research for my Tavistock story."

The other girl looked away. "Oh."

Why go all shifty-eyed here? "I figure I need some background on Tavistock and his wife for the story," she said.

"The whole situation is so sad." Missy shook her head and stared at her hands. "Elsie always seemed so happy despite her health."

Guilt ate at Lynn for staying silent about what really had happened at the fire. How could she explain the voice she'd heard to Missy? She couldn't. She managed a shrug. "People often keep their pain hidden."

Missy cleared her throat. "I think you should just keep it short."

Lynn sat up straight in her chair. She bought herself some time by opening the Coke and taking a sip. "Well, I'm going to put in the facts of the fire but I also have to include some information about the Tavistocks," she said, careful to keep her tone neutral.

"I just feel Mr. Tavistock should be left with his dignity," Missy said. "I mean, nothing can be changed about his wife being sick and setting the fire. Now they'll bury her and move on. I don't think the public needs to know all the sordid details."

Lynn shook her head in disbelief. It appeared the story about Elsie's state of mind was already out in circulation, even without being in the paper.

She looked at Missy. The petite blonde was born and bred in San Angelo. She knew the community and was part of it. Lynn understood her discomfort and point of view, but she also saw the need to report fully. Celebrate the two lives most affected. Perhaps being an outsider was an advantage. It helped her to be more objective when it came to reporting on the community. Maybe there was such a thing as being too close to the news.

"I understand where you're coming from and I feel just as bad," Lynn said. "But I can't just do a short blurb on the fire. The Tavistocks were a part of the community and Elsie should be remembered."

Missy nodded, squinting at her computer screen. "Yeah, I guess," she said. "I would just hate to see Mr. Tavistock hurt anymore." She scrunched up her face and started typing her story. A ferocious click-clack of keys filled the air.

Lynn turned back to her envelope and sifted through the clippings. She found Tavistock's birth date, his high-school graduation and college graduation pictures and information, some family and ranch history and, finally, a wedding picture.

The younger Elsie Ann Tavistock had been a beauty. Lynn took in the pretty oval face, big eyes and gently smiling mouth. Her blonde hair was brushed into an elegant French twist. She was dressed simply but attractively in an embroidered skirt suit.

Tavistock stood next to her, grinning ear-to-ear. He stared at his bride with unabashed happiness, his arms holding her possessively. They made a handsome couple. Lynn studied the picture. The two seemed to have eyes just for each other.

She found it hard to believe that the cynical old man she'd first encountered in the parts' store could ever have been so young, handsome and happy. His eyes twinkled in the picture. She remembered other encounters. Amos' eyes had always twinkled around Elsie.

Lynn read the wedding announcement, while half-listening to the chatter of the police scanner in the background. It described the outfit the bride wore and details of the reception held afterwards. From all accounts, the event had been lavish. Held in the Range Hotel ballroom, wine and food had flowed. The guest list included several big names from back then.

"Hello?" A cool female voice broke through the scanner static and usual conversations about traffic hold-ups and quiet beats.

"Mike here," a man said. "Listen, I can't go through with this."

Lynn flipped over to a blank page and grabbed a pen. She transcribed the conversation. You never knew what could turn into a news story.

"Calm down. What's the problem?"

212

"Wheeling and dealing is fine with me. I know how to do business," the man said. "But endangering lives isn't." Lynn leaned closer to the scanner and sucked in a breath. Missy pushed forward, too.

"Don't worry about it."

"Don't worry? People are dying," the man said. "I don't want to take risks like that."

"You really aren't. Why don't you take care of your end and let other people worry about theirs?" the woman said. "And if it makes you feel better, our associate has been reprimanded for the risk. He's back in control."

"He better be."

A blaring horn interrupted the conversation.

"What's that?" the woman asked.

"Oh, somebody I know just drove by," the man said.

"Damn it. Call me on a land line." The woman hung up.

Lynn and Missy exchanged a glance, complete with raised eyebrows and conspiratorial smiles.

"That was interesting," Lynn said.

"More interesting than the usual calls picked up by the scanner," Missy said, putting away her notebook.

"It sounded like it could be about the fire…at the Range Hotel," she added quickly when Missy turned to stare at her.

Of course, the rest of the world blamed poor Elsie for the Tavistock fire. But she'd heard the oily whispers, urging, pushing, needling Elsie toward her choices. Just as she'd heard a voice on the night Obaa-chan died. No one had believed her then, and probably no one would now. But damn it, the voice had been real, so real that she'd felt like the speaker had been standing inside her head. "I wish I knew what it was about and who the people were."

She jotted down the time and date and snapped her

notebook shut. Mike. The name rang a bell in her memory. Could he be Mike the county commissioner? Could he be involved with the arsons? Maybe. It was a common name. But she'd still check on it.

Hernandez stopped by their desks and tapped his watch. "Tick-tock ladies, more typing and less talking. Deadlines approacheth."

Lynn shared an eye-roll with Missy, and turned back to the almost-empty envelope. She'd have to worry about the phone call later, first she had a story to finish. She found another picture, this one was a candid of the new couple dancing. Again, their eyes stayed steadfastly on each other. Elsie's words about dancing floated back to her and the photograph trembled in her hand.

She laid the wedding photograph and the new one side by side, on top of all the news clippings about the Tavistocks. Looking at the pictures, Lynn realized she'd found some sweet moments from the life of Amos and Elsie. She hoped the Tavistocks had had many.

A certainty gripped her, a need to know for sure. She tucked the two pictures of the couple into her notebook and grabbed her backpack. She needed to talk to Tavistock.

Lynn knocked on Hernandez's door. "May I borrow one of the Herald cars?"

"Is this in pursuit of a lead?" At her nod, he continued. "Sure, if the keys are there the cars are available, but check the log to make sure no one's already booked them."

After Lynn found a free car, she snagged the corresponding keys and lit out the door. It turned out to be an old clunker with the Herald's logo printed on the sides. She'd stick out like a summer dress in Antarctica, but hell if it drove she was happy.

Questions about whether she was doing the right thing plagued Lynn during her drive. Fifteen minutes later, she arrived at Jack's ranch house still unsure. Part of her scolded herself for intruding on a grief-stricken man. The other part argued that the man had clearly been head-over-heels in love with his wife and there was a story there.

"I'm just going to give him the opportunity to tell me the story," she said to herself. "If he doesn't want to talk to me, I'll respect that and leave him alone." Taking a deep breath, she stepped out of the car.

She found Mr. Tavistock sitting on the porch swing and staring into space. Lynn climbed up to him and wished him good afternoon. He looked at her absently and nodded.

"I found something I wanted to show to you," Lynn said, and held out the photographs. "She really was the most beautiful woman at the dances."

Tavistock's hands shook as he took the photographs and looked at them. "Yes, she was."

Lynn twisted her fingers together so tight they hurt. "I'm writing a story about the fire for the paper and I wondered if you'd talk to me about Elsie, since she's part of the story."

A door opened behind her. Lynn turned to see Grandma Edith, the matriarch of the Jarvis family, step onto the porch. She wore a faded flower-print apron and carried a broom. "Hi Lynn," she said. "Jack's out working his fields."

"What are you doing here?" Lynn asked.

Grandma Edith shrugged. "I do part-time housekeeping for Jack," she said. "Something I can help you with?"

"Oh, I needed to talk to Amos," Lynn said.

Grandma Edith pressed her lips together into a thin line. "Amos probably needs his rest and shouldn't be bothered right now."

Lynn's face turned hot with embarrassment.

Tavistock looked from one woman to the other. Then he shook his head. "It's okay Edith, I need to do this."

Grandma Edith looked at him. "If you're sure," she said. Seeing his nod, she cleared her throat. "I'll get some lemonade for the two of you."

When she'd left, Lynn sat down next to Tavistock. "Are you sure?" she asked. "If you're not up for it or don't want to do it, you don't have to."

Tavistock turned tired blue eyes on her. "I want to."

Grandma brought out the lemonade and then disappeared into the house. Lynn got her pen and paper ready. "So, tell me about her."

Tavistock spoke about how much he'd loved Elsie and she'd loved him back. How she'd stood by him when the stock market crashed and he'd lost a lot of money in investments, then through the fifties' drought. She'd taken part-time jobs to help the family. How they'd both weathered the death of a child by being there for each other. "You know she never wavered in her love for me, right till the end she tried to make me leave her in that burning house," his voice choked into silence.

"Tell me about the night of the fire," she said.

He seemed lost in thought for a bit. Then he shook his head as if to clear out the thoughts jumbled in there.

Earlier that evening, Henry Chase had visited Tavistock trying to convince him to sell his property. They visited on the front porch, since Tavistock wasn't going to let anyone into the house. "The house is mine and Elsie's," he said. "I don't want any strangers tromping about."

They'd said goodbye at about 8 p.m. and Tavistock retired an hour later. At midnight, he woke up when Elsie shook him awake and smelled the smoke. She told him what she'd done, begged him to let her die. He'd tried unsuccessfully to put out the flames. In the end, when he couldn't budge Elsie, he'd decided to join her. Then Jack Callaghan arrived on the scene. "He'd been driving by when he saw the flames and stopped," Tavistock said. "I tried to get him to leave but he wouldn't. Bullheaded Callaghan. He's the one who called the fire department."

Lynn stopped taking notes. Both Henry and Jack had been on the scene. One of them had to be the dragon, the whisperer. Hope flickered in her. Maybe Jack really was innocent and his presence merely a coincidence. Unfortunately, she didn't trust coincidences. Henry seemed like a harmless flirt… could he have a darker side?

Why did the both of them have to turn up on the scene? Would Jack have called the fire department if he had wanted the fire? Didn't the arsonist call her?

"Did you mention Henry and Jack to Anderson?" she asked. Tavistock nodded. Good, the arson investigator could figure it out.

"How did you and Elsie meet?"

The old rancher's face broke into a happy grin. "My dad actually introduced us. I laid eyes on her and knew she was the one. Happiest day of my life."

"She was a very lucky woman."

Tavistock took a long drink of his lemonade. "We were both very lucky that we found each other and found love."

Lynn leaned over and covered one of the old man's hands with hers. She gently squeezed. "Yes, you were both lucky to have found that," she said. An aching need blasted through her, she remembered how she'd felt dancing with Jack. Would she ever feel that content again?

Tavistock looked up and smiled. "Yeah, nothing else matters."

Lynn thanked him for sharing his story, collected her photographs and left. As she drove away, she saw Tavistock gently swinging on the porch and smiling to himself.

Back at the office, Lynn focused on the facts. She reported the fire accurately and mentioned that Elsie set the fire and died at the scene. Conscientiously, Lynn put in that the county sheriff's department was still investigating and that the Justice of the Peace was waiting on an official autopsy report from Lubbock.

She wrote a second story focused on the love between the couple. She reported how they met and how they stood by each other. For all concerned, Mrs. Tavistock had been a well-loved and loving spouse. What she did in the end didn't matter, not to the love story.

Lynn wrote about Mr. Tavistock, who loved his wife deeply, perhaps so much that he gave in to Elsie's last wish. She wrote about his anguish at her death. She wrote about the serene smile that lit up the old rancher's face as he relived the memories of his wife. By the time she ended, Lynn had tears in her eyes and a lump in her throat.

After reading the story once more, she sent it to the editor. She'd done her best. Hopefully, her best was good enough. Lynn hoped she'd portrayed the couple with respectful dignity. She really didn't want to add to Tavistock's pain. The story was good, but the people involved were more important. A yawn escaped as weariness rolled over. Folding her arms on the desk, she rested her head. When she closed her eyes, Lynn saw Amos and Elsie dancing. Another couple whirled close by — Jack and herself.

Lynn jumped out of bed at 7 a.m. and scooted out the door. Only to find Jen already sitting on the porch with a neglected cup of coffee and the paper.

She looked up with red-rimmed eyes and thrust the paper at her. "You're up early."

Lynn almost stopped breathing as she grabbed the paper and eyed Jen uneasily. "Is my story in there?"

Jen nodded.

"Did you read it?"

Another nod.

"Well?" Lynn asked, exasperated.

Jen burst into tears. "It's so sad," she wailed. "It's so... so... beautiful."

Lynn shuffled her bare feet uncomfortably, shivering in the morning air. "So do you think a lot of people might be upset by my story?" she asked. Then in a whisper she added, "Do you think it was tasteless of me?"

Jen took a tissue from her pocket and wiped her face. She shook her head vigorously. "No, no," she said. "I think it's very moving. I think you've paid a great homage to their love."

Lynn's whole body loosened in relief. "Oh good," she said. "That's what I was trying for."

After Jen left for the studio, Lynn finally looked at the paper. Hernandez had run the picture of the dancing couple on the front page. After reading the story, Lynn quickly changed and left for work.

She hurried into the office and slipped into the unoccupied desk near Missy. The buxom blonde looked up, smiling, and held out a blueberry muffin. "For you."

Her stomach growled, reminding her that she'd missed breakfast. She grabbed the muffin. "Thanks. These are in your diet plan?"

"Yup, these are low-fat— I baked them myself," Missy said. "Low in fat, but not on taste."

Lynn looked dubiously at the muffin. In her opinion, most low-fat and no-fat foods tasted like cardboard. Her stomach rumbled again and she bit into the muffin. Mmm, she had to agree with Missy.

"This is really good," she said, swallowing her first mouthful.

Missy grinned back at her. "Hey, listen, I'm sorry for poking my nose into your story yesterday," she said. "You did good."

Lynn nodded. "Thanks," she said. "And don't be sorry. I'm glad you talked to me yesterday. Made me think about the story more."

They both turned back to their respective computers. Lynn pulled out her arson file with a pang of guilt. She was no closer to identifying the fire bug. Henry or Jack? Well, nothing better than tackling it with a vengeance now. Maybe she'd catch up with missed work and make some progress.

The Society Page picture of Kate Harrington and Jack lay right on top. Why had she saved this crap? She pulled it out intending to toss it in the trash, but found herself zeroing in on the woman's face. Kate just rubbed her wrong. Could she be jealous? Lynn dismissed the notion —she didn't have a jealous bone in her body— and tapped her fingers on the desk. Okay, she was jealous.

Lynn typed in Kate's name in the search engine. Let's get the deets on the competition. Soon she had some court records— divorce and bankruptcy filings. She let out a low whistle.

Missy stopped typing. "What?"

"She's divorced."

"Who's divorced?"

"Um, Kate Harrington." Lynn pushed hair out of her face. "I-um-met her at the Fire Department picnic." *Divorced meant single and available. Not good.*

"Oh my, you had the pleasure of meeting the Queen." Missy shot her a grin.

"She is kind of intimidating."

"You could say that." Missy glanced this way and that. "I call it looking down her nose at everybody like she's too good for this town."

Lynn studied the screen again. The records were filed in Dallas County. "Looks like she'd been in Dallas for a bit, but chose to come back to Paradise Valley."

At this, Missy popped out of her chair and leaned over the cubicle wall. "She didn't exactly have much choice." Her voice lowered to a whisper. "The divorce was messy and she got saddled with the ex-husband's gambling debts."

"Oh." That explained the bankruptcy filing. "Good thing her family's ranch is held in a trust."

Missy nodded. "Yeah, otherwise she'd have lost it too."

Before Lynn could ask anything else, Hernandez stepped out of his office and bellowed Missy's name.

As the other reporter hurried to the editor's office, Lynn turned back to her computer. She'd wasted enough time on Kate, time to turn her attention to Henry. With a sigh, she typed in his name and hit enter. Nothing happened. She grabbed her mouse and clicked like crazy. Nothing. No, no, no. She let her head fall forward and land on her desk with a thump. A collective groan echoed around the room. The system had crashed.

Her stomach screamed in hunger. Not sure what to do next, Lynn grabbed her bag and a newspaper and walked to Fuentes.

The restaurant was packed. Instead of waiting for a table, Lynn hopped onto a stool at the bar and placed her order. She unfolded the paper and looked around the room. A familiar pair caught her attention. Tom Jarvis sat at a table just a few feet away with another man. Henry Chase stood next to them, three-quarters turned away from Lynn.

She opened the paper at random and buried her head deep into the pages. Lynn wasn't in the mood for Henry's bantering and flirting. At the same time, she couldn't help wondering about the group. She peeked from behind the paper and tried to catch the conversation.

"Yeah, I read about the fire in the paper," Henry was saying. "I'm very sorry about your loss."

"Not as sorry as I am," Jarvis muttered.

"Well, the offer still stands." Henry spread his hands, smiling wide.

Jarvis stood up and got into Henry's face. "Well, I'm still not selling." He used his finger to drive home the point.

Henry snarled and pushed close to Jarvis. She couldn't catch what he said, but the other man dropped back into his chair. Next, Henry pulled out a card and tucked it into the man's shirt pocket. "If you change your mind," he said. "It's easy money Tom. Think about it." He tipped his hat and left.

Seconds later, Jarvis pulled out the card, crumpled it and threw it on the table. Then he and the other man got up and left as well. Interesting.

Lynn's food arrived. She picked up her fork and dug

into it while wondering about the exchange. Her mind kept returning to the nasty smile she'd caught on Henry's face as he strode out. Of course, Tom got rude first…but she'd expected Henry to deal with it with his usual humor.

Instead, he'd been…what? Scary. His movements, his smile, even his words now that she thought about it, had exhibited a cool viciousness. Lynn shivered. It was as if she'd just seen the Mr. Hyde part of Henry. Maybe she'd get more insight at their interview Monday.

CHAPTER 20

Lynn gaped through her windshield at the hand-lettered red and white sign attached to the roof of the restaurant. Maybe she'd misread it because of the dying light of dusk, the peeling paint and bullet holes. She squinted and read it again, aloud, slowly. "Jim Bob's Beer, Bait & BBQ."

Somehow, when Henry had mentioned a cozy, quaint restaurant on the shores of Lake Nasworthy, removed from the pedestrian city life, this was not what she'd pictured. She huffed out a breath and rested her chin on the steering wheel. The mustang, she'd wanted to rent something with style, stuck out like a perfectly manicured cherry-red thumb. Neither the sun-bleached wooden shack, listing to the left and billowing smoke, nor some of the patrons emerging from rust-bucket, diesel chugging trucks, inspired her confidence. Well, she couldn't sit idling in front of the door while she thought things through. Changing gears, she drove to the far edge of the lot to give her vehicle plenty of personal space, half-hidden by a stand of mesquites.

Maybe it would have been wiser to cancel the interview. Henry's face from Fuentes filled her mind along with a shiver of unease. What if he was the rogue? What if he was the caller? She pressed her lips together. Damn. The fires were driving her crazy, making her suspect everyone and everything. Or was she so desperate to clear Jack, that she'd started to suspect everyone else?

Focus on the present. Should she go in to the bar or not? Lynn pinched the bridge of her nose. To be fair, the mouthwatering aroma of cooking meat and the packed parking lot indicated the place might have some merit. The front door flew open and a mountain of a man dragged another out by the scruff of his neck and threw him into the dust. "Git outta here, you sorry ass drunk!"

Or maybe not.

At least, there seemed to be security of sorts. And while she could take care of herself, no sense in pulling a horror-flick move and walking into trouble. Something told her a single female would invite too much attention, unwanted attention. She glanced at her watch. Six forty-five. Arriving early had seemed like a good idea: she could grab a table and work on the questions she wanted to ask about the development. Probably not such a good move. She sighed, fingering the grooves on the steering wheel. Best to wait for her seven o' clock appointment and watch for Henry from the safety of her car.

A gleaming black and chrome pickup squealed into the parking lot. She watched the gravel fly as it pulled into a spot closer to her than the other vehicles. Apparently, the driver didn't want his vehicle dinged or scratched either. Henry hopped out and slammed the door. Dressed in faded jeans and a black button-down shirt, he peered into the side mirror and fixed his hair.

Lynn grinned and exited the car. Gripping her backpack under one arm, she hurried toward him. "Hi Mr. Chase!"

He whipped around. After a few seconds, a Colgate white smile appeared. "Did we backslide or something? I thought we were on a first name basis."

"Right, Henry." She giggled because that's what he seemed to be expecting. "I wasn't sure if I was at the right place, but this is the address you gave me."

Henry laughed. "Yeah, it doesn't look like much, but it's the best kept secret in the West."

His hand rested at the small of her back as they entered the dimly lit interior. Lynn considered putting a bit of space between them, but given the environment, maybe Henry was just being careful and a gentleman. He nodded to the man behind the makeshift counter/display case featuring all kinds of fishing lures. Recognizing his scowling face from the parking lot, she sidled past, allowing Henry to steer her toward the back, past couples dancing to juke box tunes, to the tables.

On the way, they stopped by a kitchen window and placed their orders. They stood a few minutes reading the menu tacked to the wall. A pink-faced woman, wearing a sauce-splattered apron, appeared at the window with a pad and pen. "What'll it be hon?"

"I'll have a brisket sandwich, fries, and a cold Shiner Bock, and just a glass of San Angelo tap water for the lady," Henry said.

"Hey!" Lynn glared at him, a smile twitching her lips. Part of her was relieved to find that the mischievous

Henry had returned.

He grinned. "Decided to mix some pleasure with business after all?"

She narrowed her eyes at him, then turned to the waitress. "An order of barbecued chicken and coleslaw with a Diet Coke, please." Lynn turned back to Henry. "I'm so looking forward to grilling you." The server handed Henry their drinks and a wood chip with a number.

They settled on a table in the less crowded part of the room. She tore some paper towel from the roll on the table and dusted off crumbs and peanuts shells from her chair before sitting.

Henry rested his elbows on the table and leaned forward. "So, what's a pretty girl like you doing in a place like this?"

A part of her enjoyed his easy flirting, but she had more important concerns. Lynn pulled out her note pad and pen. "Getting some answers from you about Hope development."

He laughed. "I meant, what brought you to West Texas?"

She arched an eyebrow. "And I meant, let's get down to business."

He smirked as he eyed her. "Yes ma'am." He sipped his beer.

She flipped her notepad open to a fresh page. "So who'll be able to afford all the $400,000 houses that your company is planning on building?"

"This is what we call a high-end development." Henry sat straighter. "We're marketing them as ranchettes to people in big cities like Houston, Dallas, Los Angeles and New York."

"Why would people leave such exciting cities to come

to the middle of nowhere?"

"Lower taxes." Henry took a swallow of beer. "Actually, a lot of people are getting tired of fast-paced cities and searching for a simpler life. Paradise Valley, with the Concho River running through it, the old trees and the mesas in the background, can be an ideal setting for the right development."

Lynn bent her head and wrote his answer. "Number 52!" rang out into the room. Henry scraped back his chair, grabbed her half-empty glass and headed for the kitchen window. She watched couples whirl by— some had the bright flush of new romance, others the practiced grace of years of dancing together. Her heart ached. Would she ever find a man to grow old with, to dance the years away with until the two moved as one? The smell of smoky Mesquite overwhelmed her senses and memory of dancing with Jack followed in its wake. Impossible. Stop yearning for the impossible. She blew out a breath. Her hormones had clearly gone haywire.

"Trouble in Paradise?" Henry's voice made her jump and straighten. He slid her plate in front of her. She'd been so busy feeling maudlin, she'd completely missed his return. Lynn smiled her thanks and scribbled "Tavistock" in her notebook. Underlined the name a few times.

Henry arched an eyebrow at her as he set her Diet Coke down.

She gulped down some soda, glanced at her notebook and back at him. Time to dig deeper. "What? Do you know him?"

He placed the tray on an empty chair at the table and sat. "Made him an offer soon after I got here. Maybe I'll visit him again." He bit into his sandwich.

She tapped her pen against her chin. "I heard you visited him the day his home burned down."

He chewed and swallowed. "Where'd you hear that?"

"Tavistock told me when I interviewed him after the fire," she said, taking another fortifying drink. "So what were you doing there?"

Henry washed his food down with some beer. "Trying to do my job," he said. "I upped the offer, but he still turned me down."

"Why?" Lynn sipped some coke, waiting for his answer.

"He's a stubborn old fool."

An image of Amos and Elsie floated into her mind. Lynn blinked back the moisture stinging her eyes. "Why did you approach Tom Jarvis again? He's already turned you down too, right?"

Henry leaned back his chair and studied her. "You following me?"

Inane laughter bubbled out of her. "Nope. Just happened to be in the right place at the right time."

His gaze shuttered as he played with a gold ring on his right ring finger. "Yeah, I approached him again thinking the fire at his house might have changed his mind, but I was wrong."

Something whispered through her mind and a strange languor grasped Lynn, weighing her down. Lynn leaned back her head, making her hair dance around her shoulders and gazed at Henry under heavy-lidded eyes. "And you're still plan to go back again. Why?" Her tongue seemed to trip on itself.

With a bemused smile, Henry propped his head with a fisted hand. The shiny gold band glinted and gleamed at her, inviting her to touch. "Life's taught me to go after what I want."

Not sure how to respond, she glanced away. A glint of gold caught her attention.

"Nice ring."

Henry stilled, a red flush spreading across his cheeks. Looking down at his hands, he shrugged. "Just a memento of my mother's."

"Somehow I'd have never figured you for a sentimental sort." She giggled and leaned forward.

"There's a lot you don't know about me." He flicked an errant curl that'd tumbled across her face. A finger brushed her cheek, the touch echoed deep inside, a stroke against her thoughts. "So are we here to talk about me or Hope Development?"

Lynn pushed herself straight. "How would the development impact the local economy?"

Henry washed his food down with some beer. "First of all this is a $120 million project but that's just the beginning." He shot her a practiced smile. "We'll be hiring all local firms and labor to build it, we'll purchase a large amount of the materials locally and then we'll be selling these ranchettes to people with great spending potential." His smile widened. "The county's tax revenues are going to rocket."

She jotted down his answer, but her writing resembled bird tracks in the dirt. The letters swam in front of her eyes. What was wrong with her?

Henry pointed at her plate. "All work and no food will make Lynn starve." He stood and grabbed her empty glass. "I'll get you a refill."

That's it— she needed to eat. Lynn finished jotting her notes and set the notebook aside. She picked up her chicken leg, took a bite, and almost moaned. Juicy meat with a smoky mesquite aroma. She tried the coleslaw. Cool and sweet with a bite of horseradish. Mmmmm.

Henry returned to the table as she licked her fingers. "Finger lickin' good?"

She giggled. "My faith in your ability to choose a restaurant is restored. This is good."

Henry grinned. "Glad to hear that. So, how about dinner tomorrow?"

Lynn choked on her bite. Coughing and sputtering, she stared at him. Finally, after a drink, she cleared her throat. "Are you asking me out on a date?"

Say yes. Say yes.

"No, I just like to eat." His gray eyes danced with mischief. "Especially, with beautiful women."

She rolled her eyes. "Like I said, I don't mix business with pleasure."

"When's the story coming out?" He leaned forward, his gaze boring into hers.

"Wednesday."

"Let's have dinner Wednesday night."

Her heart twisted as Rob, then Jack came to mind. "I-I can't."

"Thursday then."

Geez. "You weren't kidding about being persistent."

"I don't mind being patient at all, as long as I get what I want in the end." He stared into her eyes and leaned closer.

Warmth shivered through her. *Give this a chance.* Jack's words —*I suggest you make it the next guy's business*— echoed in her head. She dropped her gaze to the peanut littered floor. "I really shouldn't, I'm not ready for a relationship." She sighed and wiggled the fingers of her left hand at him. "In fact, I ended an engagement not too long ago."

"Then there's Jack."

Lynn's head shot up so fast that the room spun a few times. Her gaze locked with Henry. Was she that transparent? "Then there's Jack."

Henry's face hardened. For a moment something cold and cruel peeked out. Lynn suppressed a shudder. Then it was gone, replaced with his usual amused expression. "Well." He leaned back in his chair and swigged his beer. "I was asking you to dinner, not for your hand in marriage."

She searched his gaze for any hint of anger, but only found amusement. Maybe she'd imagined the menace? Her recent experiences had her spooked. "I know." She shrugged. "I, I just wanted us to be on the same page."

He nodded and drank some more beer. "No reason we can't be friendly." He smiled. "Hey, we Houstonites need to stick together." He raised his beer bottle. "To friendship."

After a few attempts, Lynn clinked the bottle with her Diet Coke. She took a gulp, enjoying the sweet, fizzy taste. Henry really was a nice guy.

The soulful strains of "*Silver Wings*" emanated from the jukebox. Henry's warm hand covered hers. "How about a dance?"

Dance? She could barely stay awake. "Don thin so."

He stood, pulling her. "Come on, we know you can dance. Be nice."

Nice. It'd be nice to dance with a nice guy like Henry. Lynn stumbled to her feet and followed his lead. He wrapped one arm around her waist and the other around her shoulders, pulling her close against the line of his body. She sank into his steady, strong solidity. They began moving. Her head throbbed as the room swayed, the lights flared and dimmed, and the other dancing couples blurred together. She cushioned her head against his shoulder and closed her eyes, losing herself into the slow, sensuous rhythm.

His lips grazed an ear, a wet flick of the tongue. Her

eyes flew open as she jerked away from him or tried to. A reptilian chill permeated her thoughts and set her shivering. Lynn's legs had turned to rubber and vertigo gripped her. Within seconds, she'd slumped in his arms.

"Are you okay?"

The room bucked and her stomach heaved. "I don't feel so good," she muttered into his shoulder.

His grip tightened on her. "Come on, maybe some fresh air will help." He gathered up her things, cuddled her close and half-carried her through the crowd and out the door. He was so strong. Lynn ran an appreciative hand over the arm she clung to. "Shanks."

"My pleasure."

The night air caressed her face with soothing coolness. The playground song *Henry and Lynn sitting in a tree* popped into her head. Lynn glanced at Henry.

Shadows darkened his face and hid all expression. He leaned her against his truck and opened the door. His arms tightened around Lynn as he tried to lift her into the cab.

Lynn batted at his shoulder. "My car…"

"I don't think you should be driving," he said while he struggled with her flopping arms

The damn lyrics of the song circled inside her head. Lynn slumped in the seat, gazing at Henry. He smiled and closed in. *K-I-S-S-I-N-G!* Where'd that thought come from? A memory of the searing kiss she'd shared with Jack earlier razed the moment. Lynn turned her face away, eyes closed. "No."

A cool gentle caress crossed her face, ran along her neck and seeped inside, until she felt it deep within herself. "You know you want it," a soft whisper in her ear. The smell of dragon musk built until it laced every breath. The dragon inside arched and stretched, panting.

Lynn shuddered.

"Oh my God, you smell," she whispered. "You smell like a dragon."

He stilled.

She focused on him as horror flooded her insides. Her tongue lay thick inside her mouth, refusing to form words. *How come I didn't smell you earlier?*

A dark flush tinged his sharp cheekbones. *I'm usually better controlled, but around you sometimes not so much.*

Oh God. Mindspeak. All those telltale hints rushed to her. She should have listened to her intuition. She should have stayed the hell away from him. She lay still, passive, in his arms.

Do you like smelling my need for you?

Ghost fingers stroked her inside out. He was inside her…no, no, that wasn't possible. The dragon pushed close to the skin as forced desire quaked through its coils. Woman and dragon burned up with a hungry heat. A soft growl rumbled from her throat.

His eyes glittered in the dim cab. His head lowered again and soon Henry's mouth grazed her neck, the soft roughness of his lips broken by gentle nips. In her mind's eye, she saw Jack holding her, kissing her, driving her wild. Desire flooded through her veins. A groan escaped her as her body buckled upwards, to press against him. The spicy tang of exotic aftershave overrode the musk, pushed through her dreaminess. Not Jack. She put up her hands, flat against a muscled chest, and pushed— only to find herself clinched tighter. "No."

He was holding her too tight. She couldn't breathe, couldn't think. Damn her head hurt as if clenched by an unseen hand. A wail of pain tore from her. He pushed his face into the nape, taking a deep breath. "You're mine."

Mine. Mine. Mine. The dragon's enraged roar drowned

Henry's voice as it thrashed inside, caught in that invisible grip. She needed to do something, she didn't know what. All she wanted to do was curl up and sleep. But the dragon persisted with an angry roar. Her head flopped forward, resting on Henry's shoulder.

What the hell did you drug me with?

A soft chuckle bounced around in the nooks and crannies of her brain. *Oh a little something to make things easier.* A smile tugged at his lips. *I don't usually use drugs, I'm the dragon master. I can control dragons, I can control you.*

His words chilled her, forced her to muster the many frayed threads of her being and pull together. Breath sawed out of her as she focused on curling her fingers into a fist and strike at her him. The wimpy blow glanced off the side of his head, but a blow nevertheless.

Lynn gasped as Henry shoved her against the seat and grasped her face with one hand, cold fingers pressed skin to bone. The pressure, the pain cleared some of the fog in her head.

Henry smiled lazily at her. "Stop fighting me little girl. You want me, desire me," he said, staring into her eyes. "Tell me you want me."

Fear whispered down her spine. Recognition flooded her. Henry's voice, dark and seductive, thick and sticky. Familiar. *Little girl.* Oh God. It was him. Henry had called her the night of the Tavistock fire. He'd whispered to Elsie. Henry had called to her the night *Obaa-chan* died.

No, life wouldn't make it that easy for her to find redemption. Was her mind playing tricks on her like everyone believed? Or had her shadowy nemesis been real? But why the hell couldn't she move? Drugs and...could Henry really control her? Or was he delusional and crazy? Either way, she was in trouble.

Her gaze darted around. For the first time she realized

how vulnerable she was. The parking lot was dark and empty. They were quite a ways from the bar and the trees hid them from view.

"I -I thought you wanted to be my friend," she said.

He laughed. "I want to be more, much more."

"No." The word shot out as soon as it formed in her head. Lynn couldn't stop the shakes shuddering through her body.

Fury darkened his gaze. "What do you mean, no?" he said. "You can't say no."

The viselike grip tightened. Pain and cold wracked her body, making her shake as if jolted by continuous volts of electricity. Fight back for God's sake. But she couldn't move, couldn't call the dragon, even thinking was becoming hard. Cold, so damn cold. She didn't know how, but he seemed to be freezing her inch by inch.

"Say you want me." Spittle landed on her throbbing face. "You want me."

"I-I want you." Waves of desire washed through her. She blinked and stared at Henry. Why the hell had she been resisting him? He smelled like a dragon, a virile, male dragon ready to mate. Her breath came in short pants as she spread her legs apart.

He pressed his mouth down on hers. Hard. Lynn tasted blood where his teeth bit down on her lips. Desire receded from her, until all she felt was the physical kiss. Wet and hungry. All teeth and tongue. She closed her eyes and desperately tried to remember the self-defense moves she ought to know by heart since Obaa-chan had spent years drilling her, training her, but her mind still wasn't completely free. Gagging as his tongue burrowed deeper into her and the smell of stale cigarettes overwhelmed her senses, she pushed futilely against Henry's hard, unmoving chest.

When he finally broke the kiss, Lynn gulped a lungful of air and pushed herself back against the passenger door.

"Tell me you love me."

Anger with an underbelly of dread lay heavy inside her. The dragon reared back unhappy with the manhandling. A rare agreement between woman and beast. Lynn drew strength from her dragon's ire and raised her head, met his gaze. "You can't force love."

His hand shot forward, imprisoning her neck. He gazed into her eyes as he slowly squeezed air out of her. Something dark and lethal fisted in her head. "I can."

CHAPTER 21

The support against her back vanished and she found herself falling, only to be stopped by another body. Hands grabbed her, pulled her out of the truck, shoved her out of the way.

Darkness swarmed her vision as she landed against something hard and flat. Her palm grazed the rough pavement and pain shot up her arm. She lay limp, waiting for, almost welcoming, oblivion.

A rush of cool sweet air washed over Lynn. Her eyes fluttered open and slowly focused on the glittering night sky framed by the windshield. Curses and grunts seeped into her awareness.

Moments later an inferno blazed through her as the dragon screamed in rage and tore its way out of her. Free at last. Claws erupted as scales rippled across her skin, her jaw ached as teeth elongated and sharpened. Muscles, joints, bones trembled with strain as they stretched and bulked. Heat built up until the pressure inside her head threatened to smash her skull into a million pieces. Wrenched and disoriented by the rushing shift of molecules and matter, she stumbled forward, shot out a breath of fire. The two figures rolling around on the asphalt stilled.

Lynn could only make out dark silhouettes, locked in a frozen embrace. Henry. Hot fury boiled through her as she remembered how he'd toyed with her just moments before. Reduced her to utter helplessness. A plume of fire flashed from her mouth.

With a cry, the figures broke apart, stumbled and ran in the same direction, trying to get away from her. With a hiss, she swung back the entire muscled and plated length of her tail and lashed at them. Her tail connected with thick, heavy slap to a body, lifted it up in the air. Like a straw doll, the man bounced onto the asphalt and cracked his head on a concrete barrier. As he lay there, blood ran from his head and stained the concrete, the other broke into a run. Lynn blinked, shuffled forward, then lowered her head to the still figure. She breathed in a familiar warm, musky scent laced with a clean, soapy smell. One breath and the fog in her mind cleared. Jack. Oh shit. She'd hurt Jack. Lynn's head swiveled between Henry's disappearing back and Jack's still form.

A bitter taste filled her mouth as her dragon shuddered and receded. She'd given in to her beast and hurt an innocent man. Drenched in sweat, she dropped to her knees and hung her head low. Lynn reached inward for the beast. Found it curled into a ball, trembling. Her anger gave way to concern. For the first time, her dragon was afraid. She'd never encountered something like Henry. He smelled like a dragon, but he called himself a dragon master. He got inside her head and wrecked havoc. What was he? All she could call him right now was crazy, beyond crazy, frightening. She didn't want to chase him into the night.

Shivering in the chilly night, Lynn stared at Jack's still form. A warning echoed in her head. Must get out of here. A half-naked woman and a bloody man would raise questions. Lots of questions. Nausea and nerves tangoed inside her. Lynn turned to her side and vomited her guts out onto the asphalt. She looked away from the smelly mess and wiped her mouth on a tattered sleeve. A tremble raced through her. While not exactly a fan of puking, it did make her less sluggish, cleared her head.

She gazed at Jim Bob's. No one had come running out to investigate yet. Probably the jukebox and the general level of inebriation drowned the commotion in the parking lot. However, somebody had to come out at some point. She staggered to her feet and grabbed Jack's collar. Wincing and cursing, she dragged him to the mustang, and loaded him up in the passenger seat. Her backpack lay abandoned on the pavement. She ran back to it and found her spare clothes.

Music and laughter peppered the night as a couple emerged from the bar. Lynn crouched in the shadows, behind the trunk. The man drunkenly serenaded his companion. The woman giggled. They swayed and stumbled to their truck, never even glancing at her corner of the parking lot. Breathing easier, Lynn opened the trunk and quickly changed. The baby powder scent of the clean t-shirt soothed her nerves. She balled up the soiled remains of her former outfit and stuffed them into a plastic bag, planning to dispose of them later. Shutting the trunk, she ran to the driver's side, slid into her seat and started the car.

"Where to?" She muttered, pulling out of the parking space. She glanced at Jack, relieved by the regular rise and fall of his chest. "Something tells me, I'll have a lot of explaining to do once you come around."

Would he freak out? Most likely. Her glance lingered on the blue shadows on his still face. The real question remained would he fight or flee? Either way, she needed to control the situation and make him understand that something worse than her roamed Paradise Valley. Her first impulse was to drive him home, lock him into a room and force him to listen. She gnawed on her lower lip and cast a quick glance at Jack. The blood and his being unconscious worried her. She ought take him to the Emergency Room and let doctors check him out. West Texas Regional, the nearest hospital, was a fifteen minute drive.

Lynn grabbed her cell and called Jen.

"Are you back home or still in town?"

"I'm at the museum for the exhibit opening. Waiting on you."

Relief flooded Lynn. Jen was in San Angelo. "Meet me in front of the hospital ER and hurry."

The sight of Jen's station wagon, parked curbside near the ER entrance, untangled the tension balled up in Lynn's chest. Her friend must've hauled ass. She parked right behind, hopped out and ran to the passenger's side.

Jen sprinted over and glanced in at Jack through the window. "What happened?"

"Long story short: Henry and Jack got into a fight, he got hurt and I think he probably should be checked out by a doctor." Lynn ran a hand through her hair. "You need to take him in."

Hand on hips, Jen cocked her head to one side and looked her over. "Wait, I think you left a few important details out. Why can't you take Jack to the ER? And when did you decide on an outfit change?"

The man in question groaned softly and shifted in his seat. Lynn cursed and whipped around then back again. "I can't because he saw me turn dragon, and I'm afraid if he comes to and sees me, he'll freak." She kicked a pebble lying next to her foot and sent it flying. "I'd rather avoid a public scene."

"Ah," Jen said as she opened the door and reached for Jack. "You owe me girl. Damn he's heavy. You grab the legs."

"I have a better idea," Lynn said. "Why don't you run in and ask for a wheel chair or a stretcher or something."

Lynn stood by the open car door, praying that Jack wouldn't come around too soon. Within minutes, orderlies rushed out wheeling a gurney at high speed. Jen led them to the Mustang and Lynn stepped back and out of the way. As they wheeled Jack off, Jen grabbed her. "Come on, you can sit in the waiting room."

Lynn was half-way through her third Styrofoam cup of coffee, when Jen came out of the swinging doors that hid most of the ER busy work. She leapt up, spilling some of the tepid coffee on herself, and ran to her friend. "How is he?"

"Well, he's awake and they're running some tests on him just to make sure everything is all right." Jen slumped into a chair.

Lynn sat down next to her. "Um, did he mention anything about dragons?"

Jen shook her head. "Seems like he's got temporary

amnesia. Both he and the doc bought my story about finding him injured next to the road." She bit her lip. "Of course, the doc also kidded him about brawling. Some of the injuries indicated something like that."

"What about the bleeding?"

"That's a superficial cut he got when his head hit something sharp," Jen said. "Like a rock."

Or a rough-edged parking bump. "Shit." Lynn finished her coffee and shot her empty cup into the wastebasket. "Talk about being in the wrong place at the wrong time. What was he even doing there?"

Jen rolled her head side to side. "That I know," she said. "He came by looking for you within minutes of your leaving. Said he really needed to talk to you." She stopped and rubbed her chin, remembering. "When I mentioned that you'd gone to meet Henry at Jim Bob's Bar, his face darkened and he almost growled at me before stomping off."

Lynn stared at Jen. "You made that last bit up."

"No way *Jose*." Jen straightened herself and leaned forward. "I've never seen Jack so worked up."

"Wait, how did you know I'd be at Jim Bob's?"

"There's only one place on Lake Nasworthy," Jen said. "Now, what really happened tonight?"

A shudder threaded through Lynn. How would she explain mind control to Jen when she didn't quite grasp it herself? "Henry slipped something into my drinks. I don't know what, but I felt like crap."

Jen shot out of her chair. "The *asshole* drugged you? *Madre de Dios.*"

Lynn twisted her hands in her lap. "And I forgot one of the basic safety rules: don't let strangers near your drink."

Jen crouched in front of her and placed a hand on her

knees. "Are you okay? Did that asshole hurt you?"

"No. Yes." Fear cracked her voice. Lynn grasped her head in her hands. "It-it wasn't just the drugs, there was something else. I mean the drug disoriented me until I couldn't tell my left from my right, but it was like something alive and evil had entered my head and got a chokehold on my thoughts, my will." She hugged herself, remembering the awful cold, the slippery feel of alien thoughts and desires, the frozen helplessness. Had he really invaded her? Or was she suffering the effects of the drug and the power of suggestion? Bile pushed up her throat again and she gagged.

Jen jumped into the seat next to her and hugged her tight. "Do you need to see the doctor too?"

Lynn shook her head. "No, I'm all right. The dragon managed to fight him off in the end."

"Is he the rogue dragon? Is he the one setting the fires?"

A long breath whooshed out of her. "I think so," she said. "Henry talked like the guy who called about the Tavistock fire, so I'm pretty sure he's the one setting the fires."

"But?"

"But, the last one was technically set by Elsie. It sounds far-fetched to say he controlled her, but I believe he did." Like she'd believed there'd been another dragon with her grandmother and herself. Could she get anyone else to believe her this time? "Henry called himself the dragon master. I don't know what that means," Lynn slumped in the chair. "Whatever he is —plain crazy or mind-control freak— it's damn scary."

Jen squeezed her hand. "So what do we do now?"

Lynn shrugged. "Depends. Are the doctors leaning toward keeping Jack here under observation?"

"No, they definitely made noises about sending him home as long as there was a friend to watch over him," Jen said. "I volunteered."

Lynn smiled. "Thanks. I know he'd appreciate it and I think it's important for at least one of us to be there when he remembers and freaks."

"Well, I'll try and calm him down for you, but you need to do the explaining," Jen skewered her with a firm gaze. "I saw that hot kiss you both shared at the Tavistock fire."

Heat suffused her neck and face, as Lynn shifted her gaze to a pretty pastel of a fishing scene. "Let's not go there. I can't risk being disappointed and hurt again." She sighed. "I just need to accept I'm meant to be alone."

Jen reared up in her seat. "Don't even think like that. You deserve happiness."

Memory of Jack trying to get away from her rose up like a specter. "Well, I think my priority should be figuring out Henry." She stood. "I'm going to the paper to do some research. Then I'll come to Jack's and take over the watch."

Jen's face paled. "I don't know if you should be running around on your own tonight." She rubbed her arms. "Henry's still out there."

The image of Henry running into the woods chased through her mind. "I think I scared him bad enough that he won't come after me tonight." Lynn unclenched her jaw. "But yes, he's still out there and I'm scared." She folded her hands under her breasts and planted her feet firmly on the ground. "I don't like being scared."

CHAPTER 22

A caravan of vehicles, spewing exhaust into the chilly night, greeted Lynn in the back parking lot of the San Angelo Herald. Distributors waiting to pick up bundles of newspapers for delivery. She glanced at the clock. 11:45 p.m. The paper probably wouldn't be ready for another hour or so. Glancing at the crowd of men and women, Lynn relaxed and breathed easier. Henry wouldn't dare make a second attempt here among all these people. Would he?

Crazy people could do anything. She parked the mustang near the door, found the key she needed and exited. Her heels tattooed the pounding of her heart as she crossed the cement loading dock.

Light and shadows danced over the dull steel door

making it difficult to see the keyhole. Nerves made her fingers clumsy as she stabbed at the lock with her key. *Open, open, open.*

The feeling of being watched spider-crawled down her spine and tears threatened. On the third attempt, the key slid in. Lynn twisted and pulled the heavy metal door open, then slipped into a well-lit entryway. The door snicked shut behind her and she heaved out a breath. *Safe.*

To her left a narrow flight of stairs led down to the basement press area. On the right lay a darkened corridor, the red glow from the overhead exit sign painted a faint pathway to the door at the far end. The Editorial department lay behind that door.

Squaring her shoulders, Lynn forced herself forward one step at a time. The shimmering red reflection of the light spilled on the linoleum in front of her like a pool of blood. Another darkened corridor branched to the left. This one led to the circulation area, now shrouded in thick shadows. Goosebumps raced along her skin.

Henry could be waiting in the dark, waiting to get her in his clutches again. Sweat beaded her upper lip as she stood rooted in anxiety, unable to move. She shivered. Did the air suddenly turn cooler?

Stop it. No one could enter a locked building without a key. She grimaced. Yeah, just like dragons didn't really exist. Shit. Pulling on sheer will power, Lynn rushed through the darkness in a mad sprint for the door. Panting, she jammed the key into the lock and twisted. How secure was it to have the same key for two doors? *Stop thinking.* She pushed through and groped blindly at the wall for the light switches. A gasp escaped her as her fingers encountered the tell-tale bumps, a quick flick upwards flooded the newsroom with cold white fluorescent light.

Lynn stood and surveyed the room. Empty. She stumbled to her usual desk, fell into the chair with a sigh and grabbed the emergency Butterfingers she'd stashed in the left hand drawer. Her entire evening had been a series of emergencies. Ripping open the package, she bit into the chocolate. Sweetness flooded her mouth, soothed her senses. After a few chews, she breathed evenly again.

Still munching on the bar, she pulled out Henry Chase's card from her Paradise Valley Development folder and set it on the desk. Then she rolled over to the computer and logged on, clicking her way through cyber space. Time to run Henry's name through the online research services the paper subscribed to and see what came up. Should have done this before the interview, she mentally slapped herself.

She first tried the Bexar County system and couldn't get anything beyond a current address in San Antonio and his birthday.

Then armed with the birth date and name, Lynn tried the Harris County system. Bingo! The man had a record.

She scrolled through the report. A couple of minor assaults, what appeared to be bar brawls, and then an arrest for arson. Lynn stopped breathing for a minute. The report didn't have much beyond the legal details, such as date of arrest, date of arraignment, sentencing etc. She wanted details. A click on the print button and the printer shuddered and wheezed to life.

Next Lynn tried LexisNexis, a subscribed program which allowed the paper to search news articles printed on specific topics. She typed in Henry Chase, arson, and Houston. She received five hits— articles printed in the Houston Chronicle about seven years ago.

She read through them all. An electronics shop in Houston had gone up in flames at about midnight. By coincidence an off duty police officer had been driving around the area and saw the blaze and Henry Chase, the suspect, lurking in the area. The cop called the fire in and the police. Then he tackled Henry. Within minutes fire trucks and police cars were on the scene. The cop reported that Henry had seen him and tried to run.

But the off-duty cop, who had been driving around aimlessly after a fight with his girlfriend, had apparently used all his pent up aggression on chasing Henry down and subduing him. Thank God for girlfriends.

She continued reading. In the sentencing phase, Henry Chase had implicated the owner of the shop, one Ben Barton. Barton also happened to be Chase's brother-in-law. Because of his testimony, Chase received a reduced sentence of one year. Barton received three years.

Lynn searched some more to see if she could find anything else. When she didn't, she printed out the most complete story in the selection. Then she leaned back in her chair and closed her eyes. She recalled the Paradise Valley picnic where she'd mistaken Henry for Jack from behind. And she'd been way off course about Henry being just a nice guy.

Hernandez's voice echoed in her head: Do your homework. Yeah, now she needed to figure out who else might be involved. Next step would be to ferret out information from the county clerk's office using the Freedom of Information Act. Lynn typed up an official FOIA letter requesting phone records and meeting minutes for the last six months. Then sent it to Hernandez for his approval. That done, she stuffed the print outs into her bag and hefted herself out of the chair.

Lynn turned off the lights and pushed out the door, then dashed down the corridor and exited the building. The cool night air kissed her perspiring face. The dock now had a few heavily-muscled press guys loading stacks of papers as each vehicle moved up in line. She pulled in deep breaths of the chill air, wished them good night and climbed into her car.

Jen had left the porch light on for her. Thank God. Even though the meager light shone like a lost boat in the night. A darkness filled with God knows what. Stop being a ninny. Her encounter with Henry had her jumping at shadows. Some dragon she was.

Lynn squared her shoulders and stepped out of the car. She slammed the door behind her, as if the noise would send the fear skittering away. Nope, instead whispers and rustles filled the night. It was the wind, just the wind. Gripping her bag tighter, she ran for the door illuminated by the light. Shadows seemed to grow and move alongside her, keeping pace.

Panting and puffing, she raised her hand to bang. Jack needed to be woken up regularly anyway. But the door swung open.

"I heard the car door," Jen said.

Her hand dropped. "In the middle of the boonies, I'm sure you can hear every little noise." Lynn pushed past her friend.

The musk scent of a male dragon assaulted her nose—dark and dangerous, filled with the warm promise of sex. Dizzy, she braced herself against a cool adobe wall. The recent volatile change appeared to have left her hypersensitive. Her eyes scanned the darkened hallway, lit on the aged wood beam framing, a fire blazing in the hearth off to the left. She hadn't seen this part of the house before. Nice for a dragon's lair. She sucked in a breath. Yup, she stood in a freaking dragon's lair. Jack had to be at least part dragon.

Cannon, followed by Jen, trotted over and goosed her with his cold nose. Then he jumped up and licked her face.

"Well, I feel safer knowing Cannon is here to lick all intruders to death," Lynn said pushing the dog down.

Jen laughed and led the way into the kitchen.

Moss green walls and dark cherry cabinets greeted Lynn. She stumbled to the breakfast bar and perched on a stool. No fussy knick-knacks, or cute cookie jar in sight. Instead, sleek, shiny copper canisters, each neatly labeled, lined up like soldiers near the stove. A masculine kitchen, warm and inviting in a no-nonsense way. She could imagine Jack at the stove cooking up a spicy pot of chili. Wearing only a pair of faded jeans and apron with the legend Kiss The Cook. *Erm, where'd that come from?*

Lynn dove into her backpack and searched for the article. She pulled the pages out and sorted them into a neat pile on the counter, ready for discussion. Then she folded her arms on the cool granite and rested her head on them. The mouth-watering aroma of coffee relaxed her. Her gaze drifted to the copper pots and pans hanging from an ornate pot holder overhead. The metal winked at her merrily in the kitchen light. Yup, the man liked shiny things as much as her. Great, she had a dragon and a mind-control freak to deal with.

"Did you find anything useful?" Jen poured coffee into a mug and placed it in front of her.

Lynn took a swig of coffee and shoved the papers to Jen. "Take a look for yourself." Cupping her hands around the warm mug, she watched her friend speed read through the material.

Finally, Jen looked up. Her eyes sparkled. "This is great," she said. "You've enough to give to Anderson so he'll take a close look at Henry."

How tempting. She'd love to dump Henry into Anderson's lap and let him be someone else's problem. Yeah, a couple of million dollars would be nice too. After another sip of coffee, Lynn hung her head. "I can't share this with Anderson."

"Why?"

For a moment, the memory of Henry whispering in her mind, making her do things, feel things, burned like an unhealed wound. The niggling idea that she'd heard his voice before, long before, resurfaced. She had to be sure that Henry had nothing to do with *Obaa-chan's* death. If he did, she was going to take care of him herself. She shivered and wrapped her arms around herself. "He's too dangerous," she said. "Despite being a dragon, I had a hard time resisting him. I can't let innocents get hurt."

"Shoot." Jen gnawed on her thumb. "Wait, if he can do the mind control thing, why aren't all the people just selling him the land as soon as he asks?"

Lynn swallowed her coffee, and stared. "Good question, unfortunately I don't know the answer."

"Didn't *Obaa-chan* communicate with you telepathically? Maybe it's a dragon thing."

The notion prowled around her head. "Yes, dragons can talk to each other telepathically. We call it mindspeak, but this was different." She shook her head. "*Obaa-chan* never tried to control me."

Jen downed her coffee in one gulp. "Yeah well, *Obaa-chan* also baked cookies and had a conscience."

Lynn grimaced in acknowledgement. Uneasiness stalked her. She was missing something, but what? "I don't think he's a dragon. I mean why didn't he turn dragon on me?"

"Your mom can't turn dragon." Jen shrugged. "Maybe he can't either."

"Maybe." Lynn tugged on her lower lip. "Too many damn maybes and questions. I can't go to Anderson or Roberts without knowing more." She sighed. "What's bugging me is how I totally missed the ball with Henry. In fact, Jack came across as more of a dragon than he did."

Jen gawked at her. "You thought Jack was the rogue dragon?"

"I considered the possibility." Her answer earned her a glare.

"Are you nuts? He's been nothing but nice to you since you got here. Was I a suspect too?"

"Don't be silly," Lynn said, folding her arms across her front. "And I had my reasons." She listed a few: always first on scene, childhood history, arsonists.

Jen shook her head. "You can't reduce people to statistics and patterns. You have to see them for who they are. You have to see with your heart."

Anger flared inside Lynn. "You asked me to find and stop an arsonist. Investigations don't involve the heart."

Sorrow colored Jen's face. "You're afraid."

Lynn slammed her empty cup onto the counter. "Of course I'm afraid. I'm dealing with a dragon and a mind-control freak."

"You're afraid of falling in love, being vulnerable," Jen said. "You're afraid of your human side."

"This isn't helping. Can we save the psychoanalysis for after we've nailed whoever or whatever is burning up Paradise Valley?"

"Fine." Jen drew in a deep breath. "Now that you've been investigating, do you still think Jack is the rogue dragon?"

"No." Not the rogue, but still a dragon. Was he working with Henry? Somehow she didn't think so.

Gathering both empty cups, Jen asked, "So what's

next? What do we do?"

"Thanks for the coffee." Lynn climbed off the stool and grabbed the mugs from Jen, who protested indignantly, then headed for the sink. "As for what we are going to do next is, you're going to get some sleep and I'm going take over the Jack watch for the next few hours."

"That's your plan?"

Lynn rinsed out the mugs and placed them on the drainer. Wiping her hands on the dish towel near the sink, she turned. Jen stood there with hands fisted at her hips. "You got something better?"

"No." Jen sagged against the counter. "But what about Henry? What if he disappears?"

"He's already disappeared for tonight," Lynn said. "I don't think he'll be returning to his apartment. Even if he does, I'm not ready to confront him."

Lynn watched Jack sleep. His regular breathing, neither too deep nor too slow, reassured her enough to let her study him. His face looked young and peaceful on the milk chocolate pillow. Her gut insisted he didn't know about his dragon heritage. But how could that be?

Her eyes traveled along the line of his throat, the tanned muscles of his arm and over the exposed part of his chest. Jen must have helped him undress. A stab of jealousy flared through her. She pulled her gaze back to his face.

His dark hair spilled over the large bandage on his forehead. Her fingers itched to reach out and touch him. She remembered her tail smacking into Jack, lifting him up and flinging him, the sickening thud of his landing, then the dark spill of blood. Lynn bit back the whimper threatening to emerge. Unable to sit still any longer, she shut her book and rose from the chair. Wincing at the ache in her back, she tiptoed closer to him.

Her gaze traced the lines of his face, taking in the thick, dark brows, the square, strong jaw. She swallowed. God, he was delicious. And she was dangerous. She'd hurt him.

Lynn turned away and returned to her book and chair. Both looked about as inviting as a trip to the dentist. She bit her lower lip and glanced at the bed again, at the man who lay tangled in chocolate sheets and sky blue quilt. A liquid warmth spread inside her, rushed her senses.

Trembling, she lowered herself into the chair. A twinge of protest ran through her muscles in anticipation of her cramped position. She shot out of the chair. "Stop being an idiot," she muttered. The bed was big enough and Jack lay on the far left side of it. She could easily sleep on the other side without disturbing him. "We are both responsible adults here." She ran a hand over the soft cotton sheets. "Tired, worn out adults."

Giving into her tiredness, she sank onto the soft mattress.

Lynn woke to darkness and the feel of a warm, hard masculine body spooned against her back. Heavy, muscled arms wrapped around her. A large hand cupped her right breast. She stiffened. She needed to get out of bed and away from him. But Jack's heady scent, spicy and male, intoxicated her, lulling her into lying quietly in his secure arms.

He stirred, pressing his stiff erection against her behind, squeezing and massaging her breast gently. Thank God for her t-shirt. The thin cotton was a flimsy barrier, but at least it was there between her skin and his. Her mind screamed danger, but she found herself pushing her traitorous ass against him, responding to the slow rhythm of his hands.

A soft groan escaped him. His breathing increased as she continued to grind herself against him. His hands slipped under her t-shirt. Lynn shivered at the friction of his calloused palms against her peaked nipples. Warm breath and a brush of lips against her neck had her arching back. The graze of teeth on skin set her on fire.

Half-swallowing a moan, Lynn twisted and turned in his arms to lie face to face with him. "Jack?" she whispered on a breath.

He fisted his fingers in her hair and tugged her head back. Then Jack's mouth covered hers. His body pressed against her. Hot need boomeranged between them, back and forth.

The kiss was warm and urgent. Lynn's body melted and molded to his. She kissed him back hungrily. She wasn't aware of anything but the surge of hot, searing pleasure rushing through her. Once again dragon and woman met in rare agreement— this man felt right.

Fiery desire razed her. She wanted more. Her hands roamed across his warm skin, exploring every dip and curve, slid lower. He shuddered beneath her palms. Lynn stopped when the top of his boxers met her fingers, hesitated. Sanity spoke up, told her to stop. This would be a mistake.

His lips traced their way down her neck, opened wide and latched on. Teeth and tongue nipped and sucked at her skin. Lynn cried out, spasmed, wrapped her fingers around his erection. He groaned and shoved himself more fully into her hand. His mouth reclaimed hers.

Her fingers fumbled, found the opening, slipped inside. Her hand grasped his hard, hot sex, slid over smooth satin skin.

Suddenly the kiss became gentler. His tongue, which had been tangling with hers, circled lazily. His fingers let go of her hair. She let go of him, pulled back her hand. When his lips slipped from hers, she wanted to cry.

"This isn't a dream is it?" His voice, thick and heavy with lust, lay between them in the dark.

Lynn couldn't answer.

He reached over and across her and switched on the lamp on the bedside table. Lynn crunched her eyes shut against the flood of brightness, then slowly opened them. Jack stared at her with soft, sleepy eyes and mussed up hair.

Kiss me. She reached out to touch his face.

Kiss me. A soft feminine whisper, full of need, rolled around Jack's mind. He skittered away from Lynn fast, landing with a thump on the floor. "Get out of my head."

They stared at each other.

He looked down at his bare chest. Who'd undressed him? Slowly he raised his gaze to meet inscrutable dark eyes.

Lynn sat on the bed tugging her t-shirt into place. A simple white t-shirt that clung to all the right places and set off her tanned skin perfectly. A t-shirt that she didn't wear much under as he'd discovered. His cock stirred at the thought and warmth spread across his face. Thank God he still had his underwear.

Wait a freaking minute. This was the woman who'd turned into Godzilla. He took a deep breath. Okay, maybe not Godzilla. Something smaller and prettier, but still scary with sharp teeth and fiery breath.

"Jack, what is it?" Lynn's brows puckered as she tilted her head to one side. "You're making strange faces."

"What are you doing here?" Waiting to eat him. That

would be an effective way to keep her secret. His gaze darted around the room. The chair. She lay between it and him. The lamp? Somehow he didn't think a lamp would faze the beast. Why the hell didn't he stash a fire extinguisher in his bedroom? God, he sounded loony toons.

She sat still, her gaze wary. "You have a concussion and the doctor wanted someone to wake you every two hours. Jen and I are taking turns." She scooted toward the edge of the bed.

Jack scrambled back and up. Concussion…maybe that explained his crazy thoughts. "Uh, gotta go." Clutching the sheets to himself, he dashed to the bathroom and slammed the door shut.

CHAPTER 23

Once the lock clicked into place, Jack sagged against the bathroom door and rested his forehead against the unyielding cool wood. His head seemed stuffed with packing peanuts, each thought cushioned and indistinct. What exactly had happened?

Ironically, he'd thought about their conversation at Tavistock's ranch and reached the conclusion that he needed to talk to Lynn, figure out what she meant by "I heard you."

Jack stumbled to the sink, wrenched open the faucet and splashed some water on his face. The icy cold water on his skin, made him gasp, cleared his thoughts a bit. Pull your shit together. He grabbed a towel and buried his face in its softness. He'd decided she was important to him and he couldn't let her go without a fight. Of course, as soon Jen had told him that Lynn was out with Henry, he'd gone all primal and rushed off to stake his claim.

Instead, he'd found her struggling with Henry and a rage —more fierce and hot than anything he'd ever felt— had shook him to his soul. Jack took a deep breath and ignored the whisper of heat his recollection called up from deep within. *Focus.* He'd pulled Lynn out from the asshole's truck. Then turned to deal with Henry.

Jack rubbed his sore jaw. Henry had turned out to be quite a little fighter. And then there was this monster. He'd looked around for Lynn. But there was just this thing, breathing fire, watching him through cold reptilian eyes. He shook his head, before stopping as the pain gonged through his head. Had he already had the concussion and imagined the beast? He touched his sore ribs and winced. The injury was real. But how had he been hurt?

He stared at the bathroom door. The person on the other side probably had some answers. All his muscles bunched up and tightened. Every time he thought of her, the image of the beast came crashing through his mind. Impossible. People couldn't change into beasts. Could they? Jack raked a hand through his hair, groaned when his fingers brushed a sore spot.

After a couple of calming breaths, he snagged his robe hanging behind the bathroom door and pulled it on. Ridiculous as it was, that single layer of cotton made him feel less vulnerable. He tightened the belt. There had to be a rational explanation, and he meant to get it.

Jack sauntered out of the bathroom and made a beeline for his closet, giving Lynn a wide berth. Had he really heard her whisper in his head? Kiss me. He focused on the floor, on putting one foot ahead of another. If he could avoid looking at her, he'd be able to think straight. He threw the doors open and searched through his shirts.

"Do you want me to leave?" Her voice, low and throaty, whispered over his skin. He barely suppressed a telltale shiver.

"No." He fingered a cotton blue and white striped shirt. "We need to talk."

"About?"

Clutching a gray sweatshirt, a white t-shirt and jeans, he turned to face her. She lounged in the bed, supported by a bank of pillows, and watched him. In his bed. Memory of skin sliding over skin threatened to overwhelm him. He swallowed. "About what happened."

"You mean the kiss?" She folded her arms across her chest and raised her chin.

"Ah, no." His mouth tingled. He touched his lips, then dropped his hand as if burned. Maybe the sweatshirt would be too warm. Did he need to open a window?

Lynn swung her legs off the bed and walked to the door. Damn, the woman had a nice ass. She turned and leaned against the door jamb. Her eyes, dark and cold as winter nights, stared from an impassive face. "Oh, you mean my turning dragon."

The clothes dropped from his hands as a strangled laugh pushed from this throat. "Dragon?" *No one can turn into a dragon.*

"I did." The quiet conviction in her voice stunned him.

He blinked. Had she heard his thoughts? Jack bought himself some time by gathering up the clothes. "That's not possible."

"People used to think it wasn't possible to sail around the world either."

He rubbed his jaw, the rough scratch of stubble on

skin helped anchor him to reality. "That's different," he said. "People just didn't know enough of the world."

"There's still a lot people don't know about the world."

Jack studied her, taking in the dark circles under her eyes, the bleak expression on her face, and the stubborn-set of her chin. "Is this some kind of a weird joke?"

"I'm not joking," Lynn said. "Trust me."

Okay, she was crazy. Or he was. One of them was crazy and delusional. "Give me a reason to."

"You're in your house, alive and in one piece."

Reason warred with his fear as images of the beast filled his mind. Standing in the doorway, she'd effectively cut off his escape. Her words sat heavy and true between them. If —that was a big if— she could really turn dragon, she could also have killed him at any point between his losing conscience at Jim's and waking at the hospital. Presumably, it was Lynn who'd got him to the doctors. He owed her.

His mind whispered: *Predator*. Goose bumps danced across his skin, but he forced himself to stand still. "Fine. I'm listening."

She bit her lip and glanced over her shoulder. "Would you feel better if I called Jen to be part of this conversation?"

He did *not* need someone to hold his hand. "No thanks. This is between you and me."

"Okay, watch me." She took a deep breath and closed her eyes.

The air shimmered and boiled around Lynn, thickening, almost becoming tangible. Energy snapped and crackled, filling the room with soft, whispered noises. The temperature grew warm, warmer, hot. He swiped sweat off his brow.

Iridescent blue green scales rippled across her skin and encased her like some new-fangled armor. Her fingers shot out curved claws, dark and deadly, like the razor-sharp beaks of birds of prey. Holy Shit! Jack bit down hard on his tongue to kill the scream building inside, to make sure he was awake. Pain flashed along his nerves then disappeared. She stood there still, alien and frightening.

Her body pushed to stretch, as if struggling to escape its prison of skin and bones. The writhing and contortions looked painful. His throat snapped closed and he struggled to breathe. His brain yelled run, but his legs refused to move. He stared at her, demanding answers without words.

The t-shirt tightened across her body, seams popped. Lynn's eyes flew open and she stared at him through glowing, cat-like eyes. She breathed in short, heavy spurts. "Like whaat you seeeessss?"

The tortured, hissing words rasped across him like sandpaper, awakening him to an unreal reality. With a half-strangled shout, he stumbled back into the closet. No escape. His hands searched for something, anything, to use as a weapon.

"I guessss notssss." She closed her eyes again.

Should he barrel past her? He'd played football once and he knew how to sprint and body slam someone. The chances of him pulling it off were pretty good. His gaze flew to those scythe-like claws. Or maybe not.

Suddenly the claws retracted and disappeared into human fingers. As he watched, Lynn grew smaller and returned to her familiar height and shape. The scales receded like waves rushing from a beach, leaving behind only golden, unmarred skin.

"Fuck." Breath, he hadn't realized he'd been holding,

whooshed out of him. This time when her eyes opened they were the familiar black, but no more comforting. Jack glanced away from their cold, dark depths.

She took a tentative step forward, and he backed further into the unyielding hardness of the closet. Almost climbed onto the shelf.

"I'm not going to harm you." Her voice sounded quiet and normal.

How could she change so fast? How could she change at all? What was she? None of this made sense.

She took another step forward.

"Stop, stop right there!"

"I won't harm you." Her voice cool, empty, cracked at the end. It was that bit of dissonance, of vulnerability, that finally seeped into his conscience.

"I know, but you're damn scary."

Lynn looked away and stared at the wall. She wrapped her arms around herself.

He'd hurt her feelings. Could a monster even have feelings? A real monster, not the Disney version. He shook his head. "Okay, a part of me knows you won't eat me, but the rest of me is just reacting without thinking."

"Yeah, your body seems to do that around me."

An image of her in his arms formed, then erupted into a monster, all spewing flames and snapping teeth. He almost made a break for it, but crossed his arms and forced himself to stand his ground. "Look this is some crazy shit and I'm trying to deal with it the best I can." His face warmed as a heaviness settled inside him. "We need to talk about everything."

Oh God, I've been lusting after a beast.

She flinched as if struck, then straightened her back and faced him. "Yeah, I guess we do," she said. "The kiss was nice, but I don't have time for such distractions. I'm here on serious business."

Shameful relief spread through him at her words. He just couldn't imagine being with her, now that he knew what she was. *Beast.* A shiver trembled through him. No, don't go there. "What business?"

"Figuring out who's been lighting fires all over Paradise Valley."

Adrenaline spike through his veins. He leaned toward her. "Do you know who it is?"

She shrugged. "I have an idea."

Curiosity overrode caution, he strode within inches of her. "Tell me." He'd make the bastard pay.

"Why?"

"I want to help you get him." He bunched his fingers into fists. "He's wrecked havoc with people's lives and I want him punished."

"What makes you think the arsonist isn't a she?"

The thought hadn't occurred to him, but it was possible. Apparently anything was possible. "Whatever." He licked his lips. "I want to help bring this person down."

She unfolded herself from against the door jamb and stuffed her hands in her jean's pockets. "Then stay out of my way."

Jack gaped as she pivoted and sauntered down the corridor. He followed at a safe distance. "This is my town, my people, I'm not going to be ordered around by a —*beast*— a stranger."

She stopped in front of the opening leading to the kitchen and looked back. "Oh, sorry to break it to you, but you are part beast too." She smiled. "Have fun researching the family tree."

With that she turned the corner and disappeared from his view. A tremble quaked through him at her words.

Jack swayed and teetered, then his legs buckled.

CHAPTER 24

After a quick change of clothes, Lynn fled to her car. She didn't even stop to say goodbye to Jen. Just grabbed her backpack and keys and ran.

"The gall of the man." She revved the mustang and screeched out of Jack's yard. Gripping the steering wheel hard, she wished her fingers were on his neck. *He'd* started the kissing and manhandling. *She* hadn't asked for any of that. The two kisses they'd shared— her lips tingled as warmth hummed somewhere between her breasts at the memories.

A montage of his reactions tumbled through her thoughts— fear, revulsion, relief. No room for doubt. Damn dragon senses. Jack seemed to make every nerve ending in her body come alive, every sense leap to new heights. A tremor danced through her. She'd heard his thoughts as clearly as if he'd spoken them inside her head. She'd smelled his emotions —the sour tang of fear; the cool, wet scent of relief— as if she'd had her nose pressed to his warm, naked skin.

She almost ran the car off the road. Her hands shook as she pulled to the side and parked underneath a golden-leafed pecan tree. Every little breeze created a shower of leaves. Every little thought set off a flutter of feelings. *Obaa-chan* had once said if two dragons were emotionally close —really close— the connection could be amazing, like being one. Her breath stuck in her throat— a painful, pregnant pause. *Close. When had she become close to Jack?* She didn't want to be close. She knew better.

He'd called her a beast. *Beast.* The word sank like a cold, hard rock and settled into the murky depths of her stomach. What else would he call her? After her thirteenth birthday, when she'd first started changing, she'd been curious. Curious enough to stand in front of a mirror while undergoing her transformation. She'd seen the dragon. And yes, it was a beast. No denying the truth.

Anger seeped out of her, replaced by soul-chilling emptiness.

A sprinkling of tears landed on her hands, arms, clothes. She snuffled like a horse as she wiped away the telltale wetness. Releasing a shaky breath, she restarted the car. Work. She needed to focus on work.

Lynn arrived at the *Herald* extra-early, 7:45 a.m., and found Hernandez's approval of the FOIA letter waiting for her in her email inbox. She opened the document for a final review and was half-way through it, when her cell phone rang. Startled, she dug through her backpack, grabbed the phone and flipped it open. "News," she barked.

"Hello, Lynn?" Her mother's voice came faintly across, soft and unsure. Totally unlike her.

"Mom?" Lynn said surprised. "What's going on?"

"Everything is ok now," Ayako replied. "But I'm calling from the hospital."

"What happened?"

"Your dad had a heart attack. But he's been stabilized."

"Oh my God. Oh my God." She reached for her backpack. Her fingers traced the flying dragon carved into the red leather flap. Dad had spent an entire weekend hand-tooling the backpack for her sixteenth birthday. Worry flailed inside her.

"He's ok Hana-chan. His doctor said he'll be as good as new in a few days."

Lynn took a deep breath. She searched for a piece of paper and pencil on her desk. "Are you ok?"

"Yes," Ayako replied. "Especially now that your dad's out of danger. But I'm tired."

"I'm coming home," Lynn said. "I'll come today."

"You don't have to rush," she said. "I mean, you have your work and Dad is getting the care he needs."

"Mom, I want to."

Her mother cleared her throat. "Well, it will be nice to see you," she said. "We both miss you."

Lynn found an empty piece of paper and a pen that wrote, and balanced the phone in the crook of her neck. "Ok, give me details, like hospital name, room number and name of doctor." She scribbled down the answers. "I miss you both too," she said and hung up.

She looked up and met Missy's worried eyes.

"Everything ok?" Missy asked.

Lynn shook her head and felt tears stinging her eyes.

She hurriedly blurted out the news. "I have to go home."

Missy nodded. "Is there anything you want me to take care of?"

Lynn looked across at Hernandez's darkened office. "Oh, where is he?" she said. "I can't leave without talking to him."

"Don't worry," Missy said. "You just do what you need to do and I'll fill him in."

"Thanks," Lynn said. She made a quick call to Jen and updated her. Since most of her things were in Houston, she planned to head straight there from the office. Jen made her promise to be careful.

Next she did a public data search on Henry's brother-in-law, Ben Barton, and got his current address in Houston. She printed both the address and the FOIA letter. She shoved the address in her jeans pocket and sealed the letter in an official *San Angelo Herald* envelope. Before hurrying out, Lynn gave Missy all her contact information in Houston. Then she hot-footed it to the county clerk.

The county clerk's cheerful smile shriveled up as she read the letter. "Wow, that'll be a lot of paper." Martha put the letter down and pursed her lips. "It'll take time to pull together."

Lynn nodded. "I know it's a lot of work and I really appreciate your help," she said. "Anyway, you don't have to rush because I'm not sure how long I'll be in Houston." She proceeded to fill in Martha about her father.

A look of sympathy flooded the older woman's face. "Oh no," she said. "You just go be with your dad and don't worry about this. I'll have it ready when you get back."

"Thanks, Martha. You're a sweetheart." She headed

for her car and Houston.

If it weren't broad daylight, she'd have turned dragon and flown. San Angelo, a one-airline town, didn't even have a direct flight to Houston. Forced to drive the rental, Lynn made it back in five hours instead of the usual six or seven. She pulled into the visitors' lot at the hospital, parked the car and ran to the front entrance. The merry jingling of a bell and the Salvation Army Santa attached to it stopped her. With a start Lynn realized it was already November and Christmas was right around the corner. Time flies when you're fighting off bad guys and getting your heart broken. Jack's face loomed in her memory, about to kiss her one moment, wide-eyed and scared the next. Tears trembled through her, leaked out the corner of her eyes. No time for this. She had to see her dad.

Lynn opened the back pack and scrabbled around in it until her fingers found a pack of tissues and some change. After discreetly swiping at her eyes, she tossed her change into the red kettle and continued on her way.

"God bless you!" the Santa called out.

Please let Dad be okay. She hurried to the elevator and punched the button for the third floor.

Lynn checked in at the nurses' desk. The woman on duty smiled sympathetically and gave her directions. "Perfect timing," she said. "Your Mom's with your Dad."

As she rushed through the corridors, Lynn barely noticed the Christmas decorations the hospital had put up and they did nothing to cheer her up. Her eyes scanned the numbers and names on the doors. Finally, she arrived at room 315, the name "John Alexander," her dad's name, was written in green marker on the board next to it. Pulling in a breath, she opened the door and stepped into the darkened room.

Her father lay with his eyes closed in the hospital bed, hooked up to various monitors and IVs. The hushed beeps of the machinery mixed in with his rasping breaths. Her mom perched on the bed, her back to the door, holding his hand. They both glanced at her as she tiptoed to the bed.

"How's my intrepid journalist?" His voice came across in a dry, scratchy whisper like old, fragile paper. It warned: handle with care, or all that preciousness would disintegrate to dust.

Lynn rushed over and hugged him, careful not to squeeze him too tight. "Not feeling too intrepid at the moment," she mumbled against the regulation gown. "I hate seeing you in a hospital bed."

Her father put his arms around her. "I hate being in one."

"It's good to see you." Her mother's cool, calm, polite voice interrupted the moment.

A frisson of resentment sparked through Lynn. No matter what happened, whether dealing with *Obaa-chan's* death or a crying, broken mess of a daughter, Ayako Alexander remained professional and in control. Well, at least she knew Dr. Mom was fine.

Lynn managed a nod at her mother.

"I better go check on my other patients." Her mom gave her dad a quick kiss and rose from the bed. She turned to Lynn. "I'll see you later for dinner?"

"Yeah, meet you at the house."

As the staccato clip of her mother's steps faded, Lynn took her place on the bed.

Her father took her hand in his. "So how are *you*?"

A stab of pain tore through her heart as she remembered her encounter with Henry, a fight she'd almost lost but for Jack. The pain twisted inside. Jack.

Then the phone call about her dad. Life could be better. Another thought dogged the first— it could also be worse. At least, she hadn't lost it again and ended up in a hospital bed herself. Lynn met his gaze and answered honestly. "Much better than when I left here," she said. "It's been great hanging out with Jen and the job's wonderful."

"We've been reading you. Your mother's taken out an on-line subscription to the paper," her dad said, and then broke into a wide grin. "Ok, tell me all the juicy, off-the-record stuff."

Lynn regaled him with stories about all the various assignments and their sideshows. She told him about traffic-stopping livestock and the interesting characters she'd covered, like Tavistock. While her words skipped over Jack, her mind taunted her with images. She told him about the fires, including her leads and her hunch about the culprit.

Her father let out a low whistle at the end of her monologue. "That's one heck of a story," he said. "Just be careful, ok?"

She nodded, taking in the dark circles under his eyes, the shock of gray hair, the tired smile. He looked old. Vulnerable.

"I'm thinking of moving back to Houston soon."

Her father raised his eyebrows quizzically. "Why?"

Lynn took a deep breath as she straightened his covers. "I'm your only child and I feel I should be nearer to you... in case you need me," she said. "I want to be here for you."

Her father recaptured her right hand in his left. His grip felt warm and strong. "You know what's the best part of us all being adults here?"

Lynn shook her head.

"We can all lead our own lives and still be family." After a pause, he cleared his throat. "The best gift you can give me and your mom is to live your life to the fullest."

She looked at him, her eyes burning hot with unshed tears.

"That way we don't worry about you," he said. "And you can stop worrying about me. This heart attack was a wake-up call. I fully intend to take better care of myself and to really listen to your mother about diet and exercise."

Lynn grinned.

He grinned back. "So we got a deal?"

"Deal," Lynn said and sealed it with a hug.

Lynn's stomach growled, reminding her that she'd missed lunch, so she grabbed her Houston map from the car and walked to a deli near the hospital. After ordering, she found herself a window table overlooking the sidewalk.

She spread the map on the table and pulled the piece of paper bearing Ben Barton's address from her pocket. Her food was delivered just as she had hunkered down to study the tangle of throughways, freeways and byways that made up the Houston road system. She thanked the waiter, bit into her sandwich and continued planning. By the time lunch ended, she'd figured out the most straightforward route to Barton's apartments on South Gessner.

Somehow, knocking on the door of a perfect stranger and asking questions seemed less daunting than returning to Paradise Valley and facing Jack again. Or, in the more immediate future, having dinner with her mom. Only the two of them, without her dad to play referee. Yeah, going to a known criminal's apartment and asking intrusive questions sounded downright appealing.

CHAPTER 25

Lynn found Barton's apartment complex quite easily. There was nothing green about Green Haven Apartments. The buildings looked aged and shabby, with yellow paint peeling off in places and graffiti decorating the walls. The strings of colored lights and faded plastic decorations dotting many of the balconies made the atmosphere even sadder. The hot Houston sun beat down on the cracked pavement alongside the buildings, denying that Christmas was less than a month away.

She pulled into a parking spot in front of the building, hopped out, and locked her car. A few feet away a group of six young men worked on a low rider. Loud Tejano music blared from the car's interior. All of them stopped what they were doing and gave her the once-over. Some smirked and one gave her a lazy wave. Lynn ignored them and continued on her mission. She found Barton's apartment on the top floor and jabbed the door buzzer.

A lean, muscular man in a sleeveless undershirt and frayed jean shorts opened the door. He stood barefoot. A heart tattoo, with "Angie" written across it, decorated his left arm. He wiped his hands on a faded dish towel. "Yeah?"

Three curious children peered out from behind him, shoving and giggling. He shooed them away and turned back to her.

"Ben Barton?"

After a beat he said, "Yeah. What do you want?"

She smiled and held out her hand. "Hi, I'm Lynn Alexander, a reporter with the *San Angelo Herald,* and I'd like to talk to you about the fire—"

The man sneered, showing teeth. "For God's sake," he said, "can't you all leave well enough alone? It was seven years ago and I've done my time."

Lynn panicked as the door started closing. She hadn't come all this way to leave without talking to Barton. She was a journalist after a story. An intrepid journalist. Before she knew what was happening, Lynn found herself jamming her foot in the crack of the door and pushing back.

"It's not about you," she said. "I want to talk to you about Henry Chase."

Barton stopped pushing and eyed her suspiciously. "What about him?"

Not about to waste the temporary reprieve, Lynn rushed on. "He's now in San Angelo, where I work, and there've been a number of mysterious fires there recently. I know he was in jail for arson once, but I want to make sure that wasn't a one-time mistake before I do a story linking him to the fires." She took a breath. "I wouldn't want to hurt an innocent man."

Barton laughed and opened the door. "Ok, Miss Reporter, I'll talk to you," he said. "It'll be my pleasure."

She entered the sparsely furnished apartment. The three children —about twelve-years-old down to five or six— pored over books at the kitchen table. On the wall behind them, a large red and yellow tin sign advertised "*Eva's Palm Reading.*" Decorated with a large hand, the crescent moon and stars, the sign added a retro-coolness that was out-of-place with the ordinary apartment. "Nice sign," Lynn said.

"Family heirloom." Barton turned to the kids. "You lot, take a break from homework. Go on down and play, but stay near the apartment."

They put away their books and then filed out the door lickety-split. Barton pulled out a chair and sat down at the kitchen table. Lynn followed suit.

"Their mother works full time," he said. "I'm a handyman, and I look after the kids."

Lynn nodded. "Bringing up kids is an important job."

Barton shrugged. "So what questions did you have?"

Taking a deep breath, Lynn pulled out her notebook, pen and tape recorder. "I'd like to record our conversation," she said. "And the interview is on the record, for printing. Are you ok with all that?"

He stared at the black recording device for a long moment and then nodded. "Yeah, sure," he said. "I don't have nothing to hide."

Lynn smiled at him. "Ok, so tell me about the fire at your electronics shop."

Barton's shoulders hunched and he pulled away from the table. He narrowed his eyes and pressed his lips together. He looked pissed. "I thought this wasn't about me."

"It isn't," Lynn said. "I just want to hear your side of the story."

Barton exhaled and slumped in his seat. "You know about the fire?"

"What I read in the papers."

He nodded. "Well, that was pretty much like it was."

"So you asked Henry, your brother-in-law, to burn down your shop?"

Barton gazed down at his hands, clenched together into fists on the table. "Yeah."

"Why?"

He looked up, surprised. "For the insurance money."

She heard the unspoken *"Duh"* loud and clear, but plowed on. "Yes, but what did you want the money for?"

Barton sighed and slid further down his chair. "Angie was pregnant with our third child. It was a hard pregnancy and she was on bed rest. So she couldn't work and the store wasn't doing well."

He paused and looked away at an empty wall. "Having had two kids, I knew how expensive a baby could be and I was worried about money," he said. "So, I thought up the insurance scam."

Lynn looked up from her notebook. "Weren't you afraid of getting caught?"

Barton shook his head. "I knew Henry's reputation."

"And what was Henry's reputation?"

Barton shrugged. "He's been playing with fires ever since he was a kid. As he grew up, Henry hung out with a rough crowd and he'd do fire jobs for money."

Lynn's pulse quickened. "So he'd been involved in arson before?"

"Oh, yeah."

Lynn cleared her throat. "How come the news articles

don't mention that? I mean, they treated your fire like his first."

Barton let out a raucous laugh. "Nah, Henry wasn't a virgin when it came to fires," he said. "He was just so good, he never got caught before."

"So what happened?"

Barton got out of his chair and then sat back down again. He gnawed his left thumbnail for a bit. "My bad luck," he finally said. "That off-duty cop happened to be at the right place at the right time. Then Henry seized his chance and played it like his first time. And I did my time."

Lynn put her pen down and looked Barton in the eye. "I appreciate you talking to me but, being a journalist, I have to ask you if you have any proof of Henry's other involvements."

Barton held her gaze for a moment. "I think I do." He scraped back his chair and left the room.

A few minutes later, he emerged from the bedroom carrying a battered bible. "My wife's," he said, setting it down on the table. He flipped through it and brought out a yellowed newspaper cutting, which he pushed toward Lynn.

It was an article from a Louisiana paper, about twenty years old. A fatal house fire had killed Peter and Eva Chase. The only survivor was twelve-year-old Henry Callaghan Chase. The article mentioned the fire was under investigation.

Lynn wrote down the details in her notebook. She was surprised by the middle name, but didn't remark on it.

Barton cleared his throat. "Eva was Angie's mom. They investigated and questioned Henry a few times but couldn't ever find anything," he said. "Me and Angie were already married then and he came to live with us after that."

Wow. "Weren't you uncomfortable having him live with you?"

Barton shrugged. "He was family and a kid," he said. "We had our suspicions and we made sure never to leave him by himself. Then he started hanging with his friends and was hardly home."

"Do you have anything else?"

Barton shook his head. "That's it."

"Do you know where I could find some of his friends?"

"Nah. Troublemakers, all of them," Barton said.

Lynn studied her notes for a while and then cleared her throat. "Where did Henry get his middle name? Is Callaghan a family name?"

Barton shrugged. "Angie's mom used to be Eva Garcia, and for a while she went by Eva Garcia-Callaghan, before she married Peter Chase," he said. He flipped to the front of the Bible until he came across a penciled in family tree. He turned the book towards her.

Lynn's pulse quickened as she pored over the names. She frowned. Eva's parents were Tomas and Rosa Garcia. "How did she end up with the surname Callaghan?"

Barton scratched his chin. "Well, the story I've heard is that some rich West Texas rancher by the name of Callaghan got Eva pregnant and then paid her to leave town. She moved to Louisiana with a nice little nest egg, added Callaghan to her name, and set up her fortune-telling business in New Orleans." Barton waved a hand at the palm-reading sign.

"Fortune-telling?"

"Yeah, Eva claimed she was psychic." Barton snickered. "She claimed all sorts of things."

"Like what?" Lynn rested her arms on the table and

leaned forward.

"Like knowing I was trouble." He laughed. "Claimed she could sense a winning scratch-off or a lottery ticket."

"Was she right?"

"Sometimes, but never about any big jackpots worth real money." He shrugged. "I think she just got lucky."

"Then what happened?"

"She raised Henry and ran the business, met Peter." He scratched his jaw. "Whatever money she had, her and her husband blew on drinking and gambling."

Lynn studied her notes. "I'm confused. Where does Angie come into the story?"

"Eva had her as a teenager with some man by the last name of Schultz. At least, that's the name she gave Angie. Grandma Rosa raised her, which is why she's so normal." He glanced at the clock and stood. "I've got to start supper."

"Can you tell me anything else about this Callaghan connection?" she asked, rising from her chair.

Barton shook his head. "Nope, told you all I know."

Lynn nodded and chewed her bottom lip. "Where did Miss Garcia live before Louisiana?"

Barton shrugged. "Someplace called Ben Ficklin."

Disappointment pooled in her gut. She'd been sure he'd say Paradise Valley or San Angelo. "Where is that?"

"It used to be a community a few miles south of San Angelo, got wiped out by a flood."

Bingo. Lynn put away her things, and held out her hand. "Thank you, Mr. Barton, I really appreciate you speaking to me."

This time Barton shook her proffered hand. "Good luck with your article."

She hurried back to the car. Lynn's thoughts churned as she tried to process all the information and connect all the dots. Were Jack and Henry related? Did Jack's womanizing grandfather get a young woman pregnant and then pay her to leave town? Or was it another rancher called Callaghan? Somehow, she didn't believe in coincidences.

CHAPTER 26

Lynn arrived at her parents' house juiced on the adrenaline of a good hunt. The puzzle stood on the brink of solution, if she could just place all the pieces in proper order. But for some reason, the solution eluded her. She slammed the car door shut and trotted up the driveway.

Halfway, she stopped and retraced her steps to stand in front of the house. *Obaa-chan*'s apartment, a mother-in-law addition, peered out from the back. Maybe one of her grandmother's books would give her some clues about Henry's kind of creature. Lynn dashed to the back and clattered up the stairs.

The thought that *Obaa-chan* wouldn't be there, waiting with a cup of green tea, sucker punched her at the door. She stood on the landing, breathing hard. She hadn't entered the place since the night her grandmother had died.

Heat swirled around her and memories —long repressed— clamored for attention. Her legs wobbled as dizziness almost swept her off her feet. Lynn grasped the railing. The touch of cold metal pulled her back to the present. *Your fear is only as strong as you allow it to be, Obaa-chan's* words haunted her. She shook her head to clear the film of fear clinging to her mind.

Lynn stared at the tarnished brass door knob. It's just an empty apartment. Heaving out a breath, she reached out and grasped the knob. Twisted and pushed, to no avail. Locked. Damn it.

Her shoulders sagging, she turned around and returned to the main house. Shame and relief seeped through her, making her miserable. She unlocked the front door and walked inside, dropping her backpack next to the coat rack.

"I'm in the kitchen!" Her mother's voice bounced down the hallway, accompanied by the mouthwatering savory scent of fried onions and chicken broth.

Lynn trudged into the pristine white-and-blue kitchen, and flopped into a chair.

"Tired?" Ayako looked over the pot of boiling soup.

She managed a nod. "Long day. Anything I can do to help?"

Her mother eyed her hands. "Wash your hands first."

"Yes, ma'am, Dr. Mom," Lynn replied, pushing out of the chair. She made sure to scrub her hands for twenty seconds. Her mother abhorred germs.

By the time she finished, Ayako stood slicing chives for garnish. "Get some bowls, please?"

Lynn swallowed a sigh. Her mother's forced cheerfulness and careful politeness added a different kind of strain to their relationship. Why couldn't the woman just relax? Her conscience pinged her. At least she's trying to make dinner civil and pleasant.

Facing the blue dinnerware, Lynn practiced smiling. Then she rolled her head from side to side, did a restrained shimmy, and grabbed two deep bowls. Next she found a couple of soup spoons and took them to her mother. "Smells good!"

Ayako shot her a smile. "Let's hope it tastes good." The smile wavered. "With my mind on your dad, I can't seem to remember simple things, like where I left the keys or whether I put salt in the soup."

Lynn managed a Jen-like careless wave. "Salt's overused anyway," she said. "It'll be healthier."

"Oh, so you *do* listen to me sometimes." Her mother's face shone red from the steam.

"Sometimes." Lynn headed to another cabinet and snagged two glasses. "Milk, right?"

Receiving a nod, Lynn went to fridge and poured milk into the glasses, then carried them to the table. The soup bowls were already in place and Ayako sat waiting.

Lynn dropped into her chair and bent her face into the warm aroma floating up from the bowl in front of her. Fat Soba noodles, bits of chicken, slices of mushrooms and green onions floated in clear broth. It reminded her of simpler times from her childhood.

Her mother stirred some hot sauce into hers. "So, are you going to call Rob now that you're back?"

Lynn's spoon froze mid-air. Luckily, it was empty. Calm. Stay calm. "Rob and I are no longer seeing each other."

"He told me you were angry at him for some mistake. He seemed really sorry."

"Did he explain to you what the mistake was?" Lynn's

voice dripped icicles— cold and sharp.

Her mother shook her head, then dropped her gaze back to the soup.

"Would you like the sordid details?" Damn, she sounded bitchy.

Her mother pursed her lips and gave another head shake.

Lynn counted backwards from ten. "Mom, Rob's a big boy and he doesn't need, or deserve, an advocate. This is between me and him. Stay out of it, okay?"

A nod. If her mother bowed her head anymore, she'd get hair in the soup. Why the hell was she being so conciliatory?

Lynn sighed. "I know you liked him and you're disappointed. I'm sorry."

Ayako met her gaze. "I'm sorry too. I did like him, but mostly because he seemed to make you happy."

"He did make me happy for a while," Lynn said. "Trust me, I decided what was best for me." The best thing for her would be to find a cave and stay the hell away from men. The faces of all the guys she'd been involved with —failed with— paraded through her mind. Her thoughts lingered on Jack and the two kisses they'd shared.

Her mother slurped a noodle into her mouth, chewed and swallowed. "I do trust you. Now, tell me about Jen and Paradise Valley. Have you met anyone there?"

Bile pinched the back of her throat. Just the thought of discussing the Jack debacle made her feel sick. She gulped down some milk to wash the bitterness from her throat. Her heart ached. How could she miss someone who thought she was about to eat him for a snack? She was so never going to discuss Jack. Especially with her mom. "Oh before I forget, do you have the keys to *Obaa-*

chan's apartment? I tried going in there and it's locked."

Ayako rubbed an invisible spot on the table. "Yes, I locked it. I guess I'm not as trusting as your grandmother." She coughed. "I didn't touch anything. Well, aside from cleaning out the fridge."

"You didn't sort through her things? Why?"

Fiddling with her spoon, her mother gave a half-hearted shrug. "I just thought you could deal with everything once you were ready."

Thanks for leaving me the hard job. Lynn stared over her mother's left shoulder at a silk scroll on the far wall. An orange and black koi swam in the pale blue waters of a quiet pond next to a weeping willow. If only she could escape to that serene spot.

"I mean, you were close to her." The additional words drew Lynn's eyes back in time to catch her mother's glance dart to her and away again. "I— I didn't want to intrude."

Intrude? Did her mother really feel like she'd be intruding on *Obaa-chan's* privacy? That not being dragon somehow made her not good enough? "I don't think she would have minded."

Ayako picked up her glass with a trembling hand and gulped some milk. "Mmm," she mumbled, then dabbed at her lips with a paper napkin. "Maybe. But I think she'd have preferred you to do it."

Lynn rubbed the bridge of her nose. Baggage. Why did everyone have baggage? "It's going to be hard for me," she said. "I would really like some help."

Her mother's spoon dropped with a splash into the soup. "Are you asking me to help you?"

Tears welled as Lynn bit her tongue —literally— to stop the smart-alecky reply that pounced to the ready. She nodded. "Yes, I want you there with me."

Ayako wiped up the soup splatters on the table with the napkin. "Of course. Of course I'll help." She looked up. "When did you want to do it?"

Weariness —from the emotional turmoil of the past few days, the long drive, and this final conversation— descended on Lynn like a vulture coming in for the kill. She yawned into her hands. "Tomorrow will be soon enough."

Jack's skin itched under all the dust and sweat covering him in the musty attic, yet he didn't stop pawing through box after forgotten box. The piles of old clothes, scraps of paper and photographs just kept growing. All these years, he'd only made trips up to grab or stow Christmas lights. Everything else he'd ignored. Junk, just ancestral junk. Now, he searched for answers.

The naked overhead light bulb gave off a feeble glow. Shadows edged the small pool of light like doubt. Would there be anything to find? The entire idea seemed too fantastic. He wanted to dismiss what Lynn had said, forget everything. He wiped the sweat from his brow. Unfortunately, he couldn't dismiss what his eyes had seen. Twice.

An image of Lynn half transformed into dragon pushed into his mind. He'd never forget it. Awake or asleep— didn't matter. Whenever his eyes drifted shut, that picture woke him. In other instances, another image —of soft skin and willing lips— haunted him. His fingers curled around an old, grimy rubber ball. He threw it against the far wall with a grunt of frustration. After a plaintive squeak, the ball thumped to the floor.

He pulled out a tattered black notebook. Probably another ledger of accounts from the old dry goods store. His ancestors apparently counted and recorded every penny spent and earned. That was before his spend-happy grandfather and father got into the picture. Without bothering to open it, he tossed the notebook to the relevant pile and continued digging. This time he found one of his father's old pipes. A faint smell of sweet cherry still clung to the empty bowl.

Jack froze. He turned and stared at the ball. Half deflated, it sat forlorn on the floor. That'd been one of his old childhood toys. He'd loved it as a child. And now the pipe. This box must be from his father's time. Slowly, he twisted around and grabbed the notebook. The age-worn cover made it look much older than most of his father's books. He flipped it open. Faded blue-inked words sprawled across the yellowing pages.

Settling into a cross legged position, Jack began to read. Just a few sentences later, recognition slammed him. He remembered lying in bed as a young child as his father had read him these stories— of dragons who sacrificed themselves so their loved ones could escape, and others who fought with courage and fire, of caves and treasures, adventures in the sky and foreign lands. As he grew older, he'd started asking for other stories. He'd always assumed the story was printed in a book, but it was handwritten. The book slipped from his sweaty palms and bounced on the floor. The precarious seam split some more, and a few pages spilled and scattered. "Shit!"

Jack scrambled to gather the pieces. Among them, he found an envelope. He held it a moment. He'd take the notebook downstairs to the library, take a shower and look through everything in better light. Instead of returning the small envelope to the damaged book, he slipped it inside his shirt pocket.

So, he was a coward. At least he was man enough to

admit it. After a long, hot shower, Jack prowled around the desk, eyeing the notebook. As if, any moment, it'd transform into a dragon and bite him on the nose. He needed to read the words, needed to find answers. Instead, he remembered his promise to visit Tavistock at the assisted living facility in San Angelo. Grabbing his hat, he lit out the door.

As soon as he knocked and entered, the old man switched off the television and flashed him a toothy grin. "I see, you finally remembered me."

"Oh, I've thought of you often, it's just that life had me by the throat." Jack sank into the comfortable lounge chair next to the bed.

"Or has a certain young reporter kept you busy?"

Jack stared at his fingers twisting his hat round and round. "Nothing like that."

Silence forced him to look up into Tavistock's worried gaze. "Y'all had a fight?"

Enough with the questions. Maybe the visit hadn't been such a great idea. "No. So, how are the nurses treating you?"

Tavistock made a face. "Fuss over me like I'm a baby."

"Anyone young enough to fuss over me?"

The old rancher shot him a sly smile and his chin jutted out. "You can't fool me. I saw you and Lynn kiss at the fire. Reminded me of Elsie and me in our younger days."

Jack leaned his head back and closed his eyes. Shit. Apparently there would be no avoiding the topic. "We aren't right for each other."

"Really?"

"Yeah, really."

"Ya' know…"

Jack's eyes popped open as he sat up straight. "I don't want to talk about it."

Tavistock stared at him, then nodded. "What *do* you want to talk about?"

Placing his hat on his knees, Jack leaned forward. "The old days."

Raising a gnarled finger, Tavistock tapped his temple. "Everything's in there. What do you want to know?"

"You knew my great-grandfather and grandfather, right?"

"Yeah, I knew 'em."

"I want your take on them."

"You've heard stories."

Jack nodded. "I want to know what you thought of them. The good and the bad."

"The good and the bad." Tavistock leaned back into his pillows and steepled his fingers. "You've heard most of the bad, so I won't repeat things needlessly."

Jack's knees jitterbugged with his hat. He forced himself to still.

"To tell the truth, I was kinda jealous of them for a long while."

The hat flew to the floor as Jack jerked in surprise. He picked it up and dusted it off. "Jealous? Of what? Their money?"

"Nah, my dear old dad had plenty of that." He chortled. "The Callaghan men had something else. Just something special about them."

Jack's throat grew as bone-dry as West Texas dust. "What do you mean?"

"Confidence. Pure one hundred percent proof confidence." Tavistock shook his head. "To a young tadpole like me back then, ungainly and unsure of myself, that was a thing of envy."

"Confidence?"

"Oh yeah, they'd walk into a room and you'd feel their energy like the sun beating down on us mere humans. For a long time I wanted to be just like a Callaghan."

A bitter laugh burst out of Jack. "Then you found out what villains they were."

The old man regarded him with laughter in his eyes. "No, then I found Elsie."

The change in topics left Jack floundering to follow. "Elsie?"

In reply, Tavistock shrugged with his palms held up. "I figured if I'd won Elsie, I couldn't be that lacking. The right woman does wonders for a man's confidence."

Heat invaded Jack's skin. "Oh."

"Ya' know…" Tavistock held up his hands at Jack's glare. "Don't worry. I'm just talkin' about the old days."

Jack's shoulder's climbed down as he settled into the chair to listen.

"This town's always been full of gossips," Tavistock said. "Just like they talked about the Callaghans, they talked about anyone else given half the chance." He cleared his throat. "Did you ever hear about how Elsie and I met?"

He laughed at Jack's sheepish look. "I guess you have. Well, it's true."

The hat landed on the floor again. According to rumors, Elsie had been a lady of the night when she'd met Tavistock. "True? I always chalked it up to meanness." He cleared his throat. "We might be talking about two different things."

"I may never have been a Callaghan, but then again given the stories almost everybody in Paradise Valley might be some part Callaghan." Laughter shook his shoulders. "Anyways, I caused my share of trouble."

Infected by Tavistock's glee in the story, Jack couldn't help grinning back. "What kind of trouble? Wait, I thought your father introduced the two of you. At least that's what you said in the paper."

"So he did! He took me to Miss Hattie's bordello for my eighteenth birthday for some manly experience, if you get my drift," Tavistock said. "Elsie was my teacher that night."

"Whoa, too much information there pal."

"Stop blushing, I'm not giving you any details," Tavistock shook his head. "Anyhow, I became a regular and eventually proposed."

A low whistle escaped Jack. "That must have been interesting."

"You can't imagine the hoopla!" Tavistock wiped at his eyes. "On one hand was my father, the respectable banker, and on the other hand was this very stubborn woman. Imagine how pissed they were to find themselves on the same side."

"On the same side?"

"Yeah, neither wanted me to go ahead with my crazy idea of marriage."

"So, you actually had to work to win her love."

"Oh no, I'd won her love all right. But at first she said no."

"Why?"Jack asked, intrigued despite himself.

Tavistock shook his head. "I came from a prestigious family. She didn't. She was worried about all that, her job and her not being good enough."

Jack nodded. "Well, there were a lot of differences between you two," he said. "Different backgrounds, ages, and marital status. And her, um, job."

Tavistock waved his hands dismissively. "Those differences don't matter," he said. "I mean, I didn't ask to be born into my family but I was. And she didn't ask for hard times and a room in the brothel. Those things just happened. And we certainly had no control over which years we were born in."

He paused and swallowed. "What really matters is the feelings," he said. "If two people feel differently about each other, than there's not much to work with. Luckily, Elsie and I loved each other."

Jack's thoughts swam as if Tavistock had banged him on the head with a frying pan. Lynn hadn't asked to be born a dragon, just as he'd never asked to be born a Callaghan. God, he'd been a shithead.

He needed to think. He scuttled out of the chair. "I gotta go."

"Jack."

Fighting his need to rush home, Jack turned at the door.

"Ya' know, you've got some of that Callaghan confidence," he said. "Now go find that girl and get the rest."

He left Tavistock cackling in his room. The sly old fox.

Jack's heart gladdened as he pulled up to the house. Bright, cheery light blazed from the windows, welcoming him home. Light streamed out into the night, carving out the nearest trees and shrubs. Moths fluttered and fawned in that yellow spill. Wait....He'd never leave so many lights on. His fingers froze on the pickup's door handle. In fact, he hadn't.

Jack flung the door open and flew out of the truck. Crouching low, he ran under the cover of shadows close to the house. Of course, all those damn lights would make it impossible to hide for long. He stepped into the brightness and swung the back door open. As he slipped inside, he cursed himself for not locking up. Until today, he'd never felt the need to. Where was Cannon? Usually, the dog greeted him at the door wagging his whole body in excitement. Goddammit. The intruder had better not have hurt Cannon. Anger and worry torched the blood in his veins. He strode through the house, calling and whistling for the dog.

Something between a whimper and a whine answered him from the kitchen.

Jack broke into a run.

He skidded to a stop right inside the kitchen. Cannon cowered underneath the kitchen table, low to the ground, face nudged between his front paws. His tail swished in a halfhearted wave.

What the hell had scared the dog this bad?

Jack grabbed a doggy treat from one of the counter cabinets and approached the table with soft steps, then crouched down to be closer to Cannon. Holding the treat out, he called the dog in friendly, happy tones. "Here, boy. Look what I got you? It's a treat. A treat! Come on, boy."

With another whine, Cannon scooted forward on his belly.

Keeping the treat just beyond his reach, Jack was finally able to draw the dog out. He stood with the dried twist of beef held high.

Barking, Cannon bounded to his feet and lunged for it.

Jack fed him the treat and rubbed Cannon's shaggy coat with both hands. Fear dissipated into the air. The dog didn't seem to be hurt. After a careful once-over, Jack rewarded Cannon with an extra treat to make up for whatever fright he'd endured.

Even though his gut said the intruder was long gone,

he locked the back door before checking out the house. He started with the library.

"Holy Shit."

Books, papers, knickknacks lay scattered all over the floor. Someone had attacked the chairs with something sharp. White stuffing and springs pushed out like entrails. Paintings and animal heads had been pulled off the walls and thrown willy-nilly.

"Shit. And double shit."

He waded through the debris to the desk. No notebook.

Like a wild boar, he charged here and there, searching under different piles, stirring up the mess and reforming it, until at last he stood in the center of it all, panting to catch his breath.

No notebook.

As an afterthought he went over to the display cabinet. The scale, the antique gun and all the coins were missing. Gone, all gone.

His heart jumped and jived in his chest as he dashed out of the room, around the corner and down the hallway to his bedroom. Another mess greeted him there.

He ran to the bathroom. Wrenching open the lid of the laundry basket, he pulled out a handful of clothes. A grin spread his lips as he caught sight of the soiled shirt he'd been wearing earlier. One hand shot to the left breast pocket and encountered the stiffness of the envelope.

With a half strangled cry, he sat on the edge of the tub. His fingers trembled as he pulled the yellowed envelope out of the pocket. Blank on the outside with something inside. Sweat spiked his upper lip as he flipped it open, and found two pieces of paper. He unfolded the first to reveal a map of the old Callaghan property. An X marked a location that seemed to be on one of the hills on land that he still owned. That's lucky. He squinted at the map. Or maybe not. His father and grandfather had sold away bits and pieces of land, but somehow always kept the hill and its surrounding areas in Callaghan hands.

Curiosity gnawed him and he unfolded the second paper. It turned out to be a letter to him. From his dad. Tears blurred the writing. Jack hurriedly swiped at his eyes. He remembered his dad rambling on his deathbed about family and dragons. He'd been half listening, squeezing his father's hand, trying to say goodbye. He'd dismissed his dad's words as nonsense, a fragment of something from one of his books. Worse, he'd resented those books.

Taking a deep breath, Jack gazed down at the letter. The missive was simple.

Dear Son,

I hope you find this letter and the notebook, for this story and all it reveals belongs to you. Also, to your sister. Though, she is more like her mother and less a Callaghan. In the ledgers I've kept meticulous accounts of all the lands sold at nominal cost to family. Anybody with a drop of Callaghan blood. Your grandfather and I tried to make amends for generations of wrongs. Now you must continue what we started. Almost everything is lost, but what remains can be found in the cave. It is now yours to protect.

God bless and good luck,
Your father.

CHAPTER 27

He'd have much rather spent his time watching Lynn, but stalking Jack had paid off. Henry flopped on his bed and cracked open the notebook.

This time he'd savor every word.

The story was told from a dragon's point of view. A dragon who had barely escaped the crusades and St. George's wrath, and made his way to Ireland, adopted the name Callaghan then moved on to the New World. A dragon who, in human form, experienced seasickness on a ship journey, survived the Indian wars and subsistence farming. Luckily, he had been able to bring at least part of his treasure horde. A dragon who'd taken a Native American woman as his mate and started the Callaghan dynasty.

He finished reading the story at three a.m. Laying the book on his belly, Henry folded his hands underneath his head and stared up at the stained popcorn ceiling. Weariness burned his eyes, but his thoughts ran on full battery.

An imaginative attempt to glorify the family? Or truth? Most people would chalk the tale up as fantasy, but he knew better. He knew the truth of dragons.

All these years, he'd dreamt of the black dragon. Imagined it breathing, pulsing, fuming inside his body. All his life, he'd heard its roars and whispers of fire, flame and destruction. Sometimes he'd thought he was crazy. Most other times, he imagined this beautiful, powerful creature had somehow been trapped inside his body. Cursed to serve him, and only him, forever. All this time, he'd considered himself the dragon master.

A giggle escaped into the night. Now it all made sense. The dragon wasn't a separate being, but a part of him. Not the dragon master, but the dragon. If only he'd known this earlier, how much more powerful would he have been today? Rage sparked inside for all the wasted time. If only his father had done his duty and claimed him, shared the family secret….

He strode back and forth across the threadbare carpet. His foot sent an empty beer bottle rolling across the room. The old woman had tried to tell him. But he'd dismissed her words as more foolish ideas, just like her ideas about honor and responsibility. He thought she'd been trying to tempt him to give up his power and follow rules. Rules were for ordinary people. He'd played along, and then destroyed her.

He grabbed a fistful of hair, tight enough to pinch the skin on his skull, and closed his eyes enduring the pain as punishment for his own foolishness. If he'd only listened to the old woman….

No matter. The girl could change. His mind played back Lynn's transformation from human to dragon. Beautiful. Powerful. Unreal.

A smile flickered to his face. But, of course, it was real.

At Jim Bob's he'd acted a fool and fled screaming like a little girl. He tightened his fist and grimaced at the pain. He'd thought he'd been prepared. But he hadn't expected interference from the Callaghan brat, he hadn't expected Lynn to rise above the drugs and his control to turn dragon. His control had never failed before, but something about this godforsaken Paradise Valley affected him. When she'd started shooting flames, running away had seemed the safest option.

Henry sighed, dragged his fingers from his hair down his face. Next time, next time he'd make damn sure to be ready. There'd be no freaking surprises. Lynn would be his. And she would show him how to turn dragon, and come into his Callaghan heritage.

Hah, the old man left him a valuable inheritance after all. He rubbed his chin. But he wanted more, deserved more. He wanted it all.

Henry strode to the bed and threw himself on it, next to the notebook. He flipped through the pages until he found the bit about the dragon's treasure.

Six thousand pieces of gold and ten thousand drachmas of silver, a handful of diamonds from India, golden amber and ocean colored turquoise from Egypt, rubies and emeralds and other precious stones from the land of Persia.

Treasure. The word created a frisson of excitement in his veins. The sound of it echoed and swirled in his mind like motes of gold dust. Thoughts of it filled his mouth with a golden sweetness, until saliva leaked from between his lips.

He swallowed as he wiped his chin. Of course, he'd searched the house and found nothing. But deep in his bones he knew there had to be treasure. Jack had probably hidden it somewhere.

Henry settled his head back onto the pillow. But what would make Jack lead him to it?

Fortified with a hearty breakfast, Jack gathered together some essential items— axe, hacksaw, trash bags, rope, first aid kit, flash light, protective glasses, pocket knife, bug repellent, cell phone, a flask of water, a box of crackers, the map. He surveyed the pile. "Come what may, I'm ready."

He packed most everything into a backpack. The axe he decided to carry— handy to hack through brush, enemies, and, possibly, dragons. In case there was more than just Lynn. He dressed in a long sleeved shirt and thick jeans, then donned his fire suit. Next, he jammed his feet into hiking boots, shouldered the backpack, and slid his hands into heavy gloves. As a finishing touch, he slipped on the protective glasses and slammed his hat — the fire helmet seemed a bit of overkill— on his head.

With a sigh, he stomped toward the door and made the mistake of glancing into the hallway mirror. Sheesh, he looked like a cross between Indiana Jones and an alien. Any dragon he came across would be too busy laughing its tail off to give chase. According to Jen, Lynn happened to be out of town. Small blessings.

Shaking his head, he stepped outside and climbed into his truck. Within moments, the engine rumbled to life. Jack headed for Fire Mountain.

After a fifteen minute bumpy ride, he stood at the foot of the craggy hill and stared toward the top. Somewhere up there was a hidden cave. What was in the cave? A man-eating monster? Treasure?

Whatever. Grasping the axe handle tighter, he began to climb.

Loose gravel skittered beneath his boots, rolling this way and that. He used the axe like a pole for extra leverage as he worked around boulders and pushed through thickets of overgrown scrub and cacti. From time to time, he hacked at particularly tough patches, careful not to create large noticeable gaps. Obviously his ancestors had wanted this place hidden for a reason. He'd give them the benefit of the doubt and discover the reason before telling the whole world.

While the thick fire suit protected him from the wicked cacti needles and rough branches, it was like an oven around his body. Sweat rolled down his face, and back, making the clothes stick to his skin. The suit was slow cooking him to death. Jack stumbled more and more often.

He missed his footing and lurched backwards, starting a small avalanche of debris. His arms flailed in front of him, his fingers wrapped around a gnarled cedar branch. For a moment, he remained at a hundred and thirty-five degree angle, swaying on the heels of his boot. "Freaking hell!"

If he'd rolled down the hillside and broken his neck, no one would have a clue. Maybe he should call his sister so she would at least know where to look for his body. The thought of Annie worrying killed that idea. No other option, but to survive.

Gritting his teeth, he pulled himself upright and onward. His gaze locked on the ground ahead, every step measured.

Once he reached more level ground, he stood panting

a few moments, enjoying the feel of firm dirt under his feet. Then continued his journey.

At the halfway point, he stopped and leaned against a large rock. Taking off his hat, he swiped at the sweat on his brow and gazed again at the top. It still seemed far away, out of reach. Whatever was up there better be worth the trouble.

His throat ached, protesting the lack of moisture. Jack lumbered out of the pack and snagged the flask. He fumbled with the top, finally unscrewed it, and tipped back his head. Cool, wonderful water ran down his throat, his skin. He splashed some of it on his face and head. Then, grinning like a wet fool, he just sat there on the rock like it was the comfiest recliner. Somewhere a mourning dove cooed.

Life was good. He didn't need the treasure. He didn't need any more riches because financially, he had enough. What he needed was another type of treasure. Lynn. And she was not at the top of the hill. He almost started back down, but he remembered his father's words that whatever was up there was his to protect. Well, he wouldn't fail his dad this time.

Taking a deep breath, he pulled himself straight and started climbing again.

Almost to the top, Jack noticed an outcrop of rock that resembled the head of a dragon frozen in mid-roar. He chuckled. Everything reminded him of dragons. Yet something about the rock caught his attention and ignited his intuition. He pulled out the map from his backpack and looked it over. Bingo! Using the axe, he hacked his way through the thorny underbrush, and found a dark opening hidden beneath the ledge.

Someone had tried to fill the hole in with rocks and crumbling mortar. He attacked the plug with his axe, tapping at the stone with the back of the head. By the time he'd dismantled the barrier, the banana suit and hat lay discarded in a heap.

He stared down into a man-sized hole in the dry earth and caliche. No answers floated up. He could make out some details in the dim interior. The passage stretched downward like a long throat waiting to swallow.

Blinking, Jack looked up into the clear blue sky. The sun was already rolling toward the horizon. He pushed his glove top out of the way and glanced at his watch. Four in the afternoon. His stomach growled in hunger reminded of the lateness of the day.

His gaze returned to the inky blackness of the hole. Forget dragons, what about the native West Texas frights like scorpions, rattlesnakes, and spiders? He stumbled back. He could return the next day and finish the exploration. Then he glanced down at his truck parked way below. Or not. Jack trudged to his backpack and found the flashlight and the rope. Good thing he'd brought along a good bit. He tied the rope around the nearest large boulder, double knotted it, and tied the other end around his waist. Then, clutching the lit flashlight in one hand, he lowered himself into the opening.

He rappelled down, using the dirt walls of the shaft to steady himself, past crooked roots sticking out of the earth and striations of rocks. Dust rained down on his head, slipped under his clothes. The grittiness made his skin itch like mad. Jack grasped the rope tighter and tried to ignore all distractions.

Finally his boots touched ground. He looked up, the hole framed a circle of West Texas sky. A desperate longing, for light and fresh air, tore through his lungs and almost sent him scrabbling back up. Swallowing the panic, Jack let go and untied the rope from his waist.

So, he stood in a dirt tube. An old mine shaft or well? Whatever, he was stuck at the end of the road. Now what?

The ground seemed to slope. Nosing around with his boots, Jack discovered another opening at the base. He pressed his back into a wall and lowered himself, letting his feet slide along the tilt. He'd have to lie down on his back to get through. Momentum carried him off and bounced him into another tunnel. He wiggled and slid forward. Gravel and rock dug through his clothes into his skin. He ignored their sharp bite as well as the growing sense of doom. What the hell had he gotten himself into? Would he make it out alive?

Just as he'd decided to throw himself an all-out pity party, the new tunnel widened. Jack curled into a sitting position, then struggled upright. He dusted himself off as best as he could and looked around at his surroundings. He stood in a cave, which opened to other caves in different directions. Stalagmites and stalactites formed luxurious solid drapes and twisting spires, frozen butterflies and gothic icicles.

He turned off the flashlight. The cave and its fantastic architecture glowed with a soft luminescence. The quiet trickling of water reached his ears. Tightening his hold on the metal barrel of the flashlight, Jack followed the sound. He stopped at every turn to scrape out an X on the wall to his right. The thought of defacing the natural caverns didn't settle well with him, but the idea of being lost underground seemed a tad more disturbing.

After many twists and turns, he emerged into a larger cave, rounded with a great pool of water at its center. Water ran off a high ledge and down a wall into the pool, which narrowed at the opposite end and meandered out a smaller tunnel. A cobweb of light danced on the smooth, green surface.

Jack tipped back his head and studied the dome. A million little perforations let in light. Cracks among the rocks outside? Tension tightened his neck. How fragile were the walls? Could he be buried alive in the next moment?

He glanced back at the tranquil pool. The light swooped and peaked in a definite pattern. Not natural, someone had put in a lot of thought and work to create just the right effect. Breathing easier, Jack walked around the perimeter of the pool, careful to stay near the wall where it was dry and less slippery. The moisture in the air made it a damp seventy degrees or so. He sniffed. The musty smell was gone too.

The path curved and as he rounded the bend, he saw another cave opening. At the far end, he could just decipher something large and ghostly white. Jack flicked on the flashlight.

Bones. Bones bleached white by time formed a hulking skeleton, half-buried in a drift of scales. Shimmering scales, twins to the one in the library. Silence hovered in the air as possibilities multiplied within his mind. Jack stepped closer, reached out a hand and ran his palm over one smooth surface. He angled himself and pushed between two of the ribs. It felt like standing inside a giant bird cage. His heart ached, seeing the truth at last.

All around him, the bones glistened. Large bones, small bones, narrow ones and flat ones forming the outline of a dinosaur-like creature. Except there were the wing bones to consider. Dragon. Lynn's questions about the scale in the library now made sense.

Touching this ridge and that curve, he stood silent inside the remains of a real dragon.

The last full-blood in the family.
Great, great grandpa Callaghan.

CHAPTER 28

Jen parked El Burro in front of Grandma Edith's house and tapped the horn twice.

In response, the front door flew open and Timmy tore down the path to the car. Arms, legs, muffler and backpack flailed in all directions. Brenda stood in the doorway smiling at her son's hurry and mouthed, "Thank You."

Answering with a grin, Jen leaned across back to unlock the door behind her. Tommy climbed in. She twisted around to make sure he'd buckled in, all safe, before starting the car.

Many cheery shouts of goodbye punctuated the air and heralded their leaving.

"Ready for our date?" Jen inquired of her temporary

charge. The Jarvis family planned to clean up the burnt shell of their house and didn't want to drag their son through the destroyed wreck. So she'd offered to keep Timmy for the day.

"Oh yeah!" Timmy's voice vibrated and rose like the whine-bark-yelp noises made by one of those super hyper terriers. "Are we going to Kids' Kingdom Park? Can we go? Please? Please."

Looked like she was in for a super exciting time. "Aye, aye Captain."

As soon as they were out of sight of the house, Timmy pulled off his knit cap with a pompom on top and tossed it to the front. "This is so babyish."

"I don't know, I think it makes you look cute. Cute enough to kiss." She puckered up and made smoochy noises.

"Miss Jen!"

A glance in the rearview mirror revealed the boy's face had turned the purplish red of a ripe prickly pear fruit.

Laughter bubbled out of her. She pointed the car toward San Angelo and sped up. Jimmy reeled off lists of things he hoped to do and places he really wanted to go. Yup, there'd be plenty of options.

As they neared the narrow Lone Wolf Bridge, she slowed down. Another casualty of the many fires plaguing the area. The charred markings still on the frame and rails of the bridge filled her with sadness. What kind of rage led people to such meaningless destruction?

Close to the end of the bridge, Jen stepped on the accelerator. The rapid-fire ringing of a bicycle bell jangled in her ears. A blur of salt and pepper passed her.

Then time slowed to a series of freeze frames.

An arm swung out to the left as did the bike.

Ice cold fear wrapped around her, like something

dangerous had slipped inside the car and taken control. A continuous scream filled her head. Clutching the steering wheel, Jen jammed her foot down on the brake.

Instead of stopping, the engine rumbled and the car bucked forward. Shit.

A dull thud shook the car. Her airbag exploded. Her feet scrabbled. This time she found the brake.

For a moment, Jen sat still, breathing in the sharp, biting odor of gun powder brought tears to her eyes. The wailing scream seemed to be coming from the backseat. Oh God, Timmy. She twisted around.

Eyes scrunched shut, mouth open wide, the boy wailed.

Jen backed up the car slowly, parked and ran around to the rear door. She fumbled with his seatbelt, managed to hit release and pulled Timmy into her arms. She hugged him tight and spoke soft words of calm until he became quiet.

"Do you hurt anywhere?"

Timmy sniffled, but shook his head.

"Are you sure?"

He nodded.

"I'm so sorry, Timmy." She let him go and stood to stare at the still bundle of clothes and human on the road in front of her car. The mangled bike lay a little bit further. *What have you done?* Madre de Dios, her conscience actually had a voice. "I've got to check on the man."

Timmy scrambled after her, managing to latch onto one of her legs. "Who is he?"

Lynn shrugged as she dragged herself and the boy forward. "I'm not sure." He looked like one of the vagrants she'd seen hanging around downtown.

As they drew closer, the stink of stale sweat, urine and

alcohol assaulted her. Definitely one of the homeless winos. *Still a life, a human being.* A whisper inside her head. She tried to pry the child off her leg. "Why don't you wait in the car?"

Wide-eyed, Timmy shook his head. "Where'd he come from?"

Step closer. The siren call of an invisible force grabbed her, urged her forward.

Jen sighed and straightened, then continued her slow progress. "I don't know. Maybe he'd been fishing under the bridge and rode his bike up from there."

They stood over the wretched form in silence.

"Now what do we do?" Timmy whispered.

Jen squatted next to the man. "Let me check his pulse. Then we'll take him to the hospital."

Timmy sidled next to her, peering down.

Her fingers closed around a grimy, warm wrist.

Eyes popped open. A startling cool, gray gaze bored into her own, reminding her of stormy winter skies.

The wrist tore from her grasp and flew toward the boy. The other hand flew out from beneath the coat. A whirlwind of flesh and cloth.

Timmy yelped as fingers clinched like handcuffs.

Jen stared at the struggling boy and then at the gun now pointed at her.

"Good to see you, Jen."

Henry's voice. A whisper left her lips, "*Madre de Dios.*"

CHAPTER 29

Burdened with cleaning supplies, Lynn followed her mom up the stairs to Obaa-chan's apartment. Her planning had paid off and she wouldn't be the first to step inside. Dread had eased a bit, but grief and loss still lodged inside.

"What exactly are you looking for?" Her mother called over her shoulder as with a quick twist of the key she unlocked the door and pushed it open.

"Reference books on mythological creatures," Lynn said clattering across the last step and onto the landing.

"Dragons?" Her mother flicked on the lights.

"Dragons and others." Lynn fixed her gaze on the maroon and yellow patterned carpet as she stepped inside and shut the door.

"What kind of others?" Ayako strode over the bookcase and stopped.

"I'll know it when I read the description." Lynn's gaze traveled over a mass of photographs arranged on the wall across. Most were of her at different ages, a scattered few of other family members. Finally, she settled on a photograph of *Obaa-chan* and herself at Lost Maples State Park. Two sweaty, red-faced grinning fools framed by a breathtaking canvas of fall colors. Totally oblivious that a month later *Obaa-chan* would be gone.

A sob caught in her throat. She padded to the picture and caressed the cool glass with shaky fingers.

Ayako came and stood next to Lynn, pulling her into a gentle one-armed hug. "Are you okay?"

Lynn nodded, taking a deep breath. Her mother's soft honeysuckle scent soothed her nerves. "I just miss her."

"I miss her too." Her mother smiled at Lynn's quick, sidelong glance. "I loved her in my own way and she loved me as much as she could."

The question, always inside her, elbowed out. "Why didn't you two get along?"

Ayako went still, as still as the photographs facing them. "I disappointed her."

"How?"

"By not being a dragon." Lifting a finger, she skimmed the dust of a frame. This one held a picture of three generations— *Obaa-chan,* Ayako and Lynn as a baby. "But it's okay, I think I made up for it by giving birth to you."

Heat peppered Lynn's skin. The heat of shame and guilt sunk her head low on her shoulders, but she pushed more words out. "How did I end up a dragon? I mean if you aren't and dad isn't…"

A pretty laugh sang through the air, unwinding the twisted, knotted tension. "I agreed to go out with your dad when he first asked because he was as un-Japanese as could be and I thought that'd upset both my parents." She shook her head. "You're a good child. I, on the other hand, was a pain."

After a soft glance in her direction, Ayako continued. "I almost dumped your dad, when *Obaa-chan* not only liked John, but actually advocated for him to your grandfather. Of course, *Obaa-chan* could sniff out dragon blood, no matter how hidden."

"Hidden dragon blood?" Curiosity ramrodded Lynn's spine.

"Recessive genes. Your dad comes from one of the Germanic dragon families."

"What? How come I never knew this?"

"In case you haven't noticed, your father is a very laidback kind of a guy. To him, being part dragon is just like being part German. He doesn't think about such things. Just accepts it and goes on with life." Ayako shrugged. "I'm sure if you asked him, he'd be happy to tell you all about it."

Lynn rolled her eyes. "It'd be like one of his fishing stories. The dragons will keep getting bigger and fiercer every other sentence."

Mother and daughter, leaned closer, laughter shaking through them.

Another thought occurred to Lynn. "Wait, what made you change your mind and not dump him?"

Her mother blushed, turning cherry blossom pink. "Somewhere along the way I'd fallen in love with him."

The words fisted around Lynn's heart. Somewhere along the way, somehow, she'd done the same. Holy wasabi, she'd fallen for Jack and fallen hard. She pressed a hand to her lips, remembering their kisses.

"I realized dumping him would be as your

grandmother would have said: *Cutting off your nose to spite your face.*"

A giggle sprinted out of Lynn. "She had a saying for every occasion."

Smiling, her mother nodded. "The woman did like getting the last word."

Then she turned herself and Lynn back toward the bookcase. "Come on, there's work to do."

Lynn dragged over some empty cardboard boxes. "I want anything on mythology. Any type of mythology."

They sorted the books in piles. Mythology, anything unusual and interesting, Japan-related, and the giveaway pile. At the end of a good hour, Lynn sat back on her haunches, smiling. "I'd forgotten how much she loved those romance novels."

Her mother laughed. "The patients in my ward will be tickled pink to get their hands on these. Even the guys read them."

Each of them grabbed a book from the mythology pile.

"I'm looking for a creature that can do mind control," Lynn said, settling into a cross legged pose.

After an hour of leafing through books, Lynn stood and stretched, popping her spine. She'd found no clue regarding Henry.

Her mother held up a hand. "A little aid, please."

Grasping her hand in hers, Lynn helped her mom off the floor. Ayako bent forward, a hand on her back. "Growing old is a pain." She looked down at the heap of books they'd just worked through. "Are you sure none of what we found fits your creature?"

They'd come across vampires and Brazilian water creatures, extraterrestrial beings, and Japanese goblins.

"He's not my creature." Lynn tucked a loose curl

behind an ear. "And no, nothing fit."

Ayako made a disgusted noise, followed by a shrug. "Why don't you tell me more about this thing as we sort your grandmother's clothes?" She shuffled off toward the bedroom.

Lynn stood still, unable to move. The air thickened and boiled like soup. She struggled to breath. The room had been *Obaa-chan's* sanctuary. Every afternoon and night she'd disappeared into it to catch up on her beauty sleep.

It'd been easy to pretend *Obaa-chan* had been napping in the other room as they sorted the books. Now, she couldn't lift her feet and step across the threshold. She couldn't face the lie.

Her dinner churned in her stomach in a great tsunami of nerves and liquid. It rushed upwards. Lynn dashed to the kitchen sink and retched out her guts.

Ayako thundered to her side. She held fast as Lynn washed out her mouth and helped dry her hands and face with paper towels. Finally, she half carried Lynn to the couch and sunk down beside her. "What's wrong Hana-chan? You seemed okay."

Sobs stormed out of Lynn. She held tight to her mother as she cried. Finally, she could breathe again. She still didn't loosen her grasp. "I'm sorry mama-chan."

"About what?"

Her mother's cool fingers stroked her hair. Lynn listened to the steady rhythm of heartbeats marching along underneath her head. She wished she could freeze the moment forever. "I should have saved her."

Ayako stilled, drew out of her arms. Cold air filled in the space.

A hand lifted her chin, until mother and daughter stared into each other's eyes. "You tried."

The truth burned her tongue. Scorching her gums, the soft insides of her cheek until she wanted to fling the words out, be rid of them finally. But the other part cowered in fear. She remained silent until the taste of ashes filled her mouth. "Sometimes I think I killed her."

Her mother pulled her into a tight embrace. "I know, the Dragon Council fools almost had you convinced."

"Maybe they had a reason to believe—"

The hug loosened as her mother pulled back and looked her in the eye. The familiar steely glint was back in place. "I don't care what those fools believed, I know you didn't."

"But you weren't there."

"True, but I know you."

Her steady gaze shone with truth, enveloped Lynn in bone-deep warmth. She nestled in against her mother. "I should have done more that night."

"What more could you have done?"

"I don't know," she sniffled. "That's the thing. I should remember every detail, but I only have these bits and pieces that flash through my mind, make me sick."

"Trauma does that." A soft kiss blessed her forehead, a gentle hand stroked her back. "What do you think *Obaa-chan* would want?"

"I don't know," Lynn mumbled.

Ayako laid her head on top of hers. "Do you think she'd want you to live your life full of regret? Do you think she'd want you to try and save her at the expense of your life?"

"I just feel like such a worthless piece of dragon shit." Lynn cringed. Her mother considered curse words to be right up there with germs. "Sorry. But I mean, look at my life. I haven't done anything worthwhile beyond surviving."

A sigh puffed across her hair. "What about what you're doing to help Jen and the people of Paradise Valley?"

Lynn plucked at her t-shirt. "I'm not sure how much help I'm going to be in that situation." She couldn't even figure out what Henry was, how on earth would she fight him?

Her mother shifted into a more comfortable position. "Why do I feel you didn't give me the whole story about Paradise Valley?"

Heat flushed through Lynn. How exactly did you tell your mother about close encounters with two different men? Plus, she hadn't wanted to add to her mom's worry. Fine, the story was more than a bit sketchy.

"Even though I'm not a dragon, I might be of some help," Ayako said. "But I need all the details."

Those words, the need to affirm her non-dragon mother, the need to cement this new, fragile mother-daughter bond, had her nodding. "Okay, I'll tell you everything."

Her mother pushed out of the couch. "How about you tell me everything as we clean up the rest of the apartment?"

By the time the entire story —from scenting dragon musk at Jen's fire to her interview with Barton— spilled out, clothes had been packed away into garbage bags, dishes had been wrapped in newspaper and then put in boxes and every surface of the apartment shone. Of course, Lynn had still skirted around several Jack situations. She figured no mother really wanted graphic details of her daughter's unsuccessful love life. Plus, it was over. No use talking about a guy who didn't want to be in her life.

Ayako flopped down on the couch. "I think I could

give you a scientific explanation for Henry."

Lynn, who'd collapsed on the floor at her mother's feet, jerked upright. "What?"

"It's just a hypothesis, of course."

"Mo-m."

"Remember we were talking about recessive genes?" Her mother patted the seat next to her.

Lynn joined her on the couch. "And?"

"Well, if it worked for us, why not for the Callaghans?"

"So whoever's part Callaghan is also part dragon?"

Ayako nodded. "Possibly, if they got the right gene."

"Well, that kind of explains why I've been getting almost drunk on dragon essence in Paradise Valley." She thought of Jack's womanizing ancestors. "But why didn't I smell it all the time then?"

Her mother's brow pinched in thought. "From what you've told me, the musk seems to be triggered by intense emotions, like at the fire or in a confrontation."

Her tongue lay thick and swollen in her mouth, but finally the words whispered through her lips. "Jack seems terrified by the idea and doesn't seem to have a clue about his dragon blood."

"Our family —on *Obaa-chan's* side—actively tried to marry into dragon blood to keep the trait as strong as possible, but what if the Callaghans didn't?"

Tension rocked her back and forth. "Why?"

"Well, maybe because of lack of opportunity and knowledge, they mated without worrying too much, which eventually faded their dragon abilities."

"And somewhere down the road, they forgot."

Ayako spread her hands. "Of course, that could also mean that on accident they might have brought in other recessive dragons and/or other traits, creating hybrids with a whole new combination of abilities."

Goosebumps rushed her skin as the idea gelled with her memories of Henry. "But Barton didn't seem to think too highly of Eva's psychic abilities."

"Layers." Her mother placed one hand on top of the other, building layers in the air. "What if, again unknowingly, they ended up layering the same trait?"

Lynn pressed a fist to her forehead. "English, please?"

"Well, dragons can mindspeak, right?"

Lynn nodded.

"So, what if they mated with somebody with some psychic abilities, this strengthened the Callaghans' mental powers, then someone else with similar traits came in later down the line?"

"Like Eva."

"Like Eva or someone else and so on. As a result, the trait got stronger and somewhere along other recessive dragon genes may have been pulled into the mix."

"And so we have Henry." Triumph burst through like fireworks painting the night sky, then faded. "Wait, if Henry could almost control me, why isn't he having better luck getting people in Paradise Valley to sell to him?"

Her mother leaned her head back on the couch and stared at the ceiling. "Henry's hold on you broke when Jack interrupted, right?"

"Yes." Lynn wondered where her mother was leading. Her pulse ratcheted up. Had Dr. Mom guessed about her and Jack's weird mental connection?

"Again, hypothetically speaking," Ayako said. "Maybe sharing the same genes, or at least some of the genes, makes one family member immune to another."

"So Jack can resist Henry."

Placing her hand on her knees, Ayako struggled off the

couch. "Given what you've told me, maybe anybody with Callaghan blood would be resistant, or at least have some level of resistance."

Now if she could just call up an army of legitimate and illegitimate Callaghans. Henry would so not be a threat. Lynn gave a weary shake of her head.

The shrill tones of her cell phone cut the air. Lynn leapt up and ran for her backpack. Fumbling, she pulled out the phone and brought it to her ear. "Hello?"

"Hi Lynn, it's me." Jen's voice quavered like a bird shivering in the cold.

"What's wrong?"

"Henry's got Timmy and me." The words almost got swallowed by a sob.

Shit. Shit. Shit.

Whispers in the background.

Lynn's dragon clawed at flesh and skin, wanting out.

"He— he wants you to return to Paradise Valley." Jen hiccupped. "Now."

"Okay. How am I going to contact him once I get there?"

More whispers filled a long, terrible moment.

"Hi Lynn." A smoother, more dangerous voice filed down the line, turning her blood cold. "Don't make the mistake of calling the police. Come alone. I'm looking forward to seeing you."

Anger hissed in her breath. "Don't you dare hurt them."

A smug laugh. "Are you really in any position to make threats?"

She drew in a deep breath. Let it out. "What do you want?"

"I'll contact you." A quick click, and the phone went dead.

Lynn ran back to the main house to grab her car keys. Her mother fluttered behind, caught up in her old panic. She wanted to stop and comfort her mom, she wanted to say goodbye to her dad, but adrenaline whipped her on. She needed to be in Paradise Valley.

"Why can't you just call the police and tell them to take care of it?"

"He said not to call the police." Lynn pushed through front door.

"You don't have to listen to him." Her mother sounded near tears. "Is this that mind control thing?"

Lynn stopped and searched the small shelf in the hall. Where had she put her keys? "No, but I don't want to rile Henry up even more."

"He sounds dangerous," her mother wailed, following her into the kitchen.

The keys lay on the kitchen table. Lynn snagged them and turned to face her mother. "Don't worry, I'll take a Callaghan with me."

"But he told you to come alone."

"You just told me not to listen to him."

Mother and daughter stared at each other.

Lynn smiled, not a happy smile but an understanding one. "And you told me that my surviving the fire was a good thing because I was helping Jen and others," she said. "I have to do this."

Ayako sighed, then leaned forward and kissed her forehead. "Be careful."

CHAPTER 30

Flyers with Timmy and Jen's smiling faces greeted Lynn from light posts and shop fronts as Lynn drove into Paradise Valley. The word "MISSING" printed in bold block letters. Lynn stopped at the *San Angelo Herald.*

She paused by the mail slots and absorbed the hum of activity— the cheerful chatter of several conversations going at once, the constant but discordant clicks of the keyboards and rings of telephones, the rush of people in pursuit of stories. The noise and energy washed over her in a warm welcome.

The knots inside her loosened a bit. Lynn emptied her overstuffed mail slot into her backpack and made a beeline for Missy's blonde head.

As she approached, the cop reporter looked up, then

jumped out of her chair to hug her. "You're back! How's your dad?"

"Fine, thanks. What do you know about Jen and Timmy?"

Sadness shaded Missy's face. "I'm so sorry, first your dad and now your best friend." She sighed. "They went missing sometime yesterday. No one got worried, until they failed to return to have dinner with the Jarvis family at six. They tried calling Jen, but no answer. Some kids later found her cell phone in a ditch by the Lone Wolf Bridge and turned it in to the Sheriff."

Lynn tugged at her lower lip. "Any suspects?"

Missy turned and messed around with some papers on her desk. "Just Jen."

"What?"

Missy lifted her chin and shrugged. "Well, the cops haven't found any evidence of foul play. She could have lost the phone, or chucked it. The car's gone too. And Timmy was last seen with her."

"Crap." Feeling lightheaded, Lynn sat down in Missy's chair. "What's being done?"

"The Sheriff's put out a BOLO."

Lynn craned her neck. "A what?"

"Be On the Look Out notice," Missy explained. "The volunteer fire department, San Angelo police and fire, DPS and community volunteers are all searching."

"What about Jack?"

Missy scrounged up her face in thought. "Can't say I've noticed him, but I've also been mega busy." She shrugged. "He's bound to be in the thick of things. He always is."

That's exactly what she was worried about. Henry was a Callaghan. Did he want revenge on the family? If so, was Jack in danger? Or had the two been playing her and the rest of Paradise Valley? Doubts picked at her mind.

Lynn thanked Missy and said goodbye.

Despite the dread curling her intestines, she headed for Jen's place. The cottage looked orphaned without her colorful friend. Lynn parked the car and found her cell phone. Turning it silent, she pressed 9-1-1 and kept her finger poised over the send button. Then she slid out of the car and approached the porch with measured steps. She didn't want to be surprised.

The smell of dragon musk and old cigarettes stained the air, making the hair along her arms bristle. She stopped and glanced around. Nothing out of the ordinary caught her attention. Finally, she stepped onto porch and marched to the door.

The sense of danger thickened, but she pushed through it and stared at Jen's doormat.

Henry had left her a message.

The word "welcome" spelled out in cigarette butts.

Lynn stumbled backwards and almost ran off the porch. At the last moment, her anger kicked in and held her steady. She would beat Henry. She'd get Jen and Timmy back. Somehow, some way. She snapped a picture of the message with her cell phone and emailed it to her newspaper account. Nothing wrong with extra precautions.

Still holding her phone at the ready, she glanced around again at the late afternoon shadows. Nothing. Sighing, she shrugged her backpack off and found tissues and plastic bags. Then she squatted and collected evidence. *Déjà vu* hit her, reminding her of a similar moment at Jack's house. Had Henry been skulking there too? Or had he been on a smoke break in between scheming with Jack?

Hurriedly, she stuffed everything in her pack, zipped it

closed and shouldered it. Then, lurching to her feet, she stared at the door. Did more surprises wait for her inside?

After a deep breath, she unlocked the door and pushed it open. The familiar sitting room with Jen's comfy couch and chair, colorful cushions and scatter of magazines seemed tinged with menace. Leaving the door open, she tiptoed through the house.

She searched through every room, under every piece of furniture. Nothing had been disturbed until she'd arrived on the scene. No surprises, no clues, no more messages. Disappointed, she locked the front door, slipped her phone into the backpack and headed to the kitchen. A cup of tea would help her think as she considered her options.

Turning on the faucet, she leaned against the sink and watched the rush of water spiral down the drain. Tension sucked her energy just as fast and left her depleted. She washed her hands and put the kettle on the stove.

Might as well do something useful while she waited for the water to boil. She slumped into the kitchen chair and pulled out the unread mail from her backpack. The first few turned out to be advertisements, and those landed in the trash. The press releases went into a To Be Read pile. Her fingers stopped sorting when she came across a thick manila envelope from the county clerk's office. The cell phone records. She'd have to compliment Martha's fast turnaround next time they met.

Her pulse zipped as she tore open the envelope and pulled out the sheaf of papers. She flipped through them, scanning the entries for Mike Ward's call. She found several calls made to a San Antonio number. While Hope Development didn't pop up, it could be someone's private line. Finally, she found the date she'd jotted down and the number the commissioner had called at 7:05 p.m.

Lynn grabbed a pen from her backpack and circled the entry.

She lugged out the heavy cross directory of the area Jen kept by the phone and searched the listings in Paradise Valley. Her finger stopped as she found the match. The directory listed Katherine Harrington as the owner of the number. The queen of Paradise Valley.

Adrenaline arrowed through her, similar to the quivering excitement her dragon felt on the hunt, but different. A more intellectual thrill triggered by the name. Recognition that she'd found a crucial link, another piece of the puzzle. But how was Kate linked to Henry and the developers? Lynn slipped the papers back into the envelope and replaced it in the safety of her backpack. Her treasure chest.

Lynn's fingers brushed against something cool and soft. Curious, she grabbed the thing and tugged it out. *Obaa-chan's* journal from the apartment.

She stared at the sky blue silk cover and hesitated, not wanting to read her grandmother's private thoughts. What if she discovered something awful— like she'd disappointed *Obaa-chan* by her slowness to embrace her inner dragon, her clumsiness in the *dojo* or air, or in a myriad of other little ways. Or worse, she might have to face all her grandmother's love and dreams for her and know, in the end, she'd failed.

The kettle whistled, granting her reprieve from her thoughts. She fixed herself some soothing green tea and headed back to the table. She opened the journal and flipped through until she found the entries from the month of *Obaa-chan's* death. She would start with the most recent and work her way backwards. Maybe she'd find some clue to her grandmother's state of mind, some explanation about what she'd been doing at that warehouse located in Houston's port area. Not the usual hangout for little old ladies. Even dragon ones.

Inhaling the fragrant steam, Lynn began reading. Instead of a depressed mind or a delusional one, she found one charged with excitement. Her grandmother had found a young dragon. A misguided dragon needing direction.

A twinge of jealousy and regret pierced through her. Had her grandmother replaced her? Around that time, she'd been so focused on work and climbing the corporate ladder, she'd cut down on her visits. Could she blame *Obaa-chan* for finding a substitute? She wrapped her hands around the warm cup. No, even if she'd lived right next door still, *Obaa-chan* would have taken the stray under her wings. That would be just like her.

Lynn sipped her tea and pictured her grandmother's most protective mother hen instincts taking over. She continued reading, keeping an eye for a name to pop up. Why didn't she call him by his name?

The diary revealed her grandmother's ideas about dragon obligations and duties, the dangers of power without understanding, the importance of sharing wisdom and support through mentorship. Of course, she'd heard these ideas before, been lectured on them time and time again. She smiled and bet this other young dragon got lectured too. Soon the journal proved her right.

Obaa-chan seemed happy that Henry—

Her heart slammed up from her chest and into her throat, and a wave of nausea followed right behind. Lynn blinked and read the name again. Henry. Shit, shit, shit. She forced herself to read on. Henry, at the start wary and disbelieving, seemed to be thawing, listening and responding. She had hopes for this one, including introducing him one day to Lynn. Apparently besides being a mentor, she'd been considering a matchmaking role too.

A shudder of dread passed through her as she remembered being stuck with Henry in his truck. She pushed on. The text switched to a darker, tenser tone. Shorter sentences. Agitated words pressed deep into paper.

Her grandmother had been worried. She'd sensed fire and sensed the young dragon at the center of it. He'd promised her he wouldn't prostitute his talents and dragon powers anymore. He'd been so eager to start learning from her, though the first meditation session had seemed to disappoint. Yet, she felt it in her blood that he'd regressed. The last time they had spoken his words had smelled of lies. After sleeping on it, she knew she had to confront him.

That was the last entry.

Oh God, could her grandmother's Henry be the very same Henry Callaghan Chase? Lynn slammed the book shut and leapt from the chair, tipping over the half empty cup in the process. Cold tea soaked through her t-shirt turning her skin as cool as her insides. Henry was a young dragon, a misguided one, and from Houston.

She cleaned up the mess, then rushed to her room and changed shirts. Grabbing her car keys, she headed out the door. Time to find Jack.

CHAPTER 31

Lynn launched out of the car, up the porch and jabbed at the door bell. Continuously. Open, open, open damnit. The air around her smelled musty, carried the scent of dead and decaying vegetation.

The door squeaked open and revealed Jack in a rumpled shirt, jeans and bare feet. Dark circles lay under his eyes. His lips flatlined as his gaze settled on her. They stood staring at each other in silence. The smell of dragon musk filled the air as liquid heat rushed her veins.

Leave. The word bounced inside her head as if he'd shoved the thought in there.

Despite the cozy warmth of the late afternoon sun, panic chilled Lynn. Holy wasabi, the man was downright unhappy to see her and she was getting all hot and bothered over him. How low could she go? She fought down the tears welling inside, the urge to turn and run, and pulled in a deep breath. This wasn't about her and Jack. This was about saving lives and stopping Henry. "We need to ta—"

Henry pushed into view, a gun pointed at a gagged and bound Timmy.

"Perfect timing. I was just about to call you." Henry tipped his head to one side. "Come on in."

As soon as the door was shut and locked, Henry herded the group back into the living room. Jen sat gagged and tied to a chair. Her eyes widened and she emitted some muffled noises. Ignoring her, Henry picked up Timmy and tossed him onto the couch and then pushed Jack toward it, trailing ropes. "Take your seat again."

Kate sat ensconced in one of the armchairs with a blank, bored look on her perfectly made-up face. Was she truly bored or being careful to hide her thoughts? One hand held a slim, silver gun pointed at Jen, the other half waved, the fingers shiny with rings. "Great, Lynn is here. Can we get the party started?"

"What's the point of all this?" Jack whirled on Henry, only to have the gun dance over Timmy. He pulled in couple of deep breaths and unclenched his fists.

"Impatient, impatient." Henry laughed and inclined his head. "If you both will have a seat."

Lynn and Jack sank into the couch, careful not to touch each other.

Henry swaggered to the center of the room and struck a pose. "This is about my inheritance, my rights as a Callaghan heir."

Jack blinked at him. "Callaghan?"

"You didn't notice the family resemblance?" Henry

smoothed a hand through his hair. "Can you guess who's who in this picture?"

Tired of all of Henry's games, Lynn snorted. "He's your uncle, and the illegitimate son of your grandfather and Eva Garcia, a local psychic."

Henry glared at her, turning a deep shade of red. "Excuse me, I'm telling the story here."

Lynn crossed her arms and settled back into the couch. "Get to the point."

Henry pulled the empty chair forward, turned it and then straddled it. The gun rested on the chair back, casually pointing at the couch. Jack leaned forward.

Maybe I can rush him and get the gun away.

Don't.

Already on the balls of his feet, Jack tottered at the edge of the couch while staring at her.

Lynn slapped him on the back. "Breathe. Breathe. I think he's having a seizure." She leaned over Jack and thought hard. *Dragons can mindspeak.*

A snicker. *Pretty convenient isn't it.*

Lynn's head jerked up and knocked against Jack's. Both their heads swiveled in the same direction.

So when you said you heard someone whispering to Elsie…

Lynn figured there'd be no secrets among the three of them. *He convinced her.*

Elsie was easy. Henry smiled at them, shared a wink.

Muscles bunched as Jack tensed. "You fucking bastard."

Henry flinched, then turned cold "Any other interruptions and I'll shoot somebody. Maybe I'll start with Timmy's toes."

The child whimpered. Lynn's dragon rattled its scales and gnashed its teeth. She could feel the sharpness edging her skin. She focused on her breathing, visualized a soft, glowing light. Let it expand and fill her mind. Then she leaned over and patted Timmy.

"As I was saying, my mother was used and discarded by your grandfather. The great John Drake Callaghan himself." He paused to flick imaginary dirt from his shirt. "He paid her off as if she was nothing more than a whore and could be bought."

She took the money and ran to New Orleans.

The thought earned Lynn a poker-hot glance from Henry.

Didn't say a word. She smirked.

"She died penniless." The sentence ended in a growl. "Do you know what a hard childhood I had? How many nights I went to bed hungry, forced to wear hand-me-downs from charities?"

Jack cocked his head, listening.

"What?" Henry looked around.

"I thought I heard violin music. My mistake."

The gun went off, blowing a hole in the ceiling. Muffled shrieks sounded from Jen and Timmy. Plaster and dust rained down on them. Lynn thought harder about the light. Every time her thoughts threatened to slide into her mind, she shone them out.

Henry stood up and strode to the couch. Looming over Jack, he grinned. "You're going to reimburse me for all those years."

They locked stares. Jack shrugged. "All you had to do was ask. I'll call the lawyers and give you your share.

Henry hawked up a spit ball and let it land right by Jack's foot.

The man didn't even flinch or change expression.

"You are not going to give me anything, I take what I want." Henry leaned closer. "Let's start with the treasure."

"What treasure?"

Lynn's head swiveled between the two men. *Treasure?*

A mad light glinted in Henry's eyes. "The dragon's treasure."

All eyes turned to Henry as silence raged in the room.

"Did you just say dragon?" Kate arched a shapely eyebrow.

"I said Callaghan treasure." Henry licked his lips, and focused on his partner. "The operative word being treasure." *Treasure. You want treasure. Heaped piles of gold and silver, glittering gems.*

Kate's lips slid into dreamy smile and her gaze softened.

Even though Henry's thought wasn't aimed at her, Lynn shivered as residual temptation brushed against her mind. For an instant she drowned in the allure of rings on her fingers, gold necklaces dripping from her neck, and coins in the counting house.

Jack's growl broke through the mental fog. "There is no treasure."

"Don't lie to me." Henry struck Jack with his pistol hand, leaving a long red bruise along one cheekbone.

Jack gritted his teeth.

Lynn gasped and reached for Jack.

"Don't touch him." A dangerous tremor laced Henry's voice, threatening to spill over into something more volatile. *You're mine. Mine.*

Lynn shrank back.

Henry refocused on Jack. "Tell me where the treasure is."

"There's no treasure."

Henry shot the couch, Kate shrieked and all the others jumped.

Bits and pieces of stuffing wafted in the air, belched

out of the gaping hole between Lynn and Timmy. The boy sat there shivering and sniffling. Lynn glared at Henry as she scooted over and put an arm around Timmy's small shoulders.

Jack leapt from his seat.

Lynn cut her eyes to Jack. A vein throbbed on the side of his neck. She wanted to press her fingertips to it, smooth away the tension.

Henry backed up, the gun aimed at Timmy and Lynn. "Next one will be in the boy."

Jack ran a hand through his already disheveled hair. *Nothing in the cave is worth anyone's life.* "Fine, I'll take you to the treasure."

"Good thinking." Henry motioned to the others. "All right everyone, time to travel."

Jack let out a harsh laugh. "It's not exactly easy to get to. You can't go up a mountain with an entourage, especially when some of them are bound and gagged."

Lynn stared at him. What was he doing?

Henry rocked back on his heels. "What did you have in mind?"

"Let everyone else go and we can head up to the treasure." With a casual wave he included Kate and Henry.

Kate jumped up from her seat.

Henry chuckled. "Sorry, not happening. Not that I don't want to whoop your ass. Again."

Jack growled in frustration.

Henry grasped Lynn's arm and pulled her off the couch. "I've got a better idea." Nodding to Kate, he said, "You stay here with our collateral, while Lynn accompanies us."

"I don't get it." Jack shook his head. "Why do you have to drag Lynn along?"

Henry cast a lingering glance at her. "She knows my reasons."

Jack stomped toward the laundry room, and they followed.

Lynn looked over her shoulder at Jen and Timmy. Their shiny eyed gazes stayed pinned on her. They had nothing to do with treasure and dragons, but everything to do with her. The blame always came to roost on her shoulders. Sighing, she turned away. She had to get them out of this mess.

At the back door, Jack reached for the axe leaning against the wall.

Henry stiffened. "What are you doing?"

Jack froze. "Need this along to clear some overgrown brush out of the way."

Henry gestured with the gun. "Fine. Just remember I can shoot you dead."

After a sharp glare, Jack grabbed the axe and pushed out the back door.

They climbed into his truck, with Lynn sandwiched in the middle, warmed by the press of flesh. Her dragon trembled like a dousing stick sensing water, surrounded by an overload of male testosterone. Jen and Timmy's frightened faces crowded into her mind, squelched all inkling of desire.

A wild energy burned the air in the small cab as the truck bumped and jostled down a caliche road, stirring up dust. Twilight colored the sky in shades of mystery. Her gaze latched on to the Evening Star shining out of reach like hope.

The bottom of the backpack vibrated in her lap. She swallowed her yelp when she realized someone was calling her. "I'm hungry." She slipped her hands inside the backpack searching. Her fingers found the phone. She turned the phone over and under other things, before pressing the talk button. Otherwise, the bright light of the phone would be an instant giveaway. With the other hand she pulled out a package of crumbled crackers and tossed them onto the dash, before resuming her fumbling around.

"How can you be hungry?" Henry shook his head.

"When I'm scared or nervous, I eat." She pulled out a pack of chewing gum. "And having a gun pointed at me is scary. Anybody want some?"

Jack shot her a glare, while Henry just chuckled.

She tossed it back in. "What's going to happen to Timmy and Jen at Jack's place?"

"Nothing if both you and Jack cooperate with me."

"How can you be sure? What if Kate shoots them?"

Henry shook his head. "She's one of the few people in this area who actually listens to me and follows orders."

She pulled out a package of beef jerky, ripped it open and settled back. Gnawing on the spicy meat, she crossed her fingers that whoever had called had hung on long enough to hear their conversation and do something.

The truck ground to a stop at the base of a hulking hill.

Lynn stared into the deepening shadows. "Are we going to climb that in the dark?"

Henry pulled a flashlight from his pocket. "I'm tired of waiting."

Sighing, Jack grabbed the axe and a heavy duty flashlight. Then he shouldered past them, leading the way.

They climbed single file, feet slipping and sliding on the rough trail. Clothes got caught on prickly bushes, skin got scraped and scratched. Muttered curses and the crunch of gravel under their shoes created a discordant symphony.

Every time Lynn stumbled, she'd clutch onto Jack. Henry's hand would immediately be on her body, steadying her. The hot, hateful glares exchanged by the two men left Lynn singed.

Finally Jack stopped and shone his light on an overhanging rock. A shiver ran through her as Lynn's gaze followed the outline of a dragon's head, mouth opened to throw a flame. Where were they?

The light traveled lower and shone on a thick tangle of brush. "Here we are."

Henry shifted next to her. "Where?"

"There's an opening hidden behind the brush. All you have to do is clear it." Jack's voice slid along her skin like the cold metal flat of a knife.

Henry laughed. "Okay Axeman, go get 'em."

Jack tossed her his flashlight. Both she and Henry followed the glint of metal and light flying toward her.

For some reason, her head jerked back toward Jack. Lynn watched the edge of the axe head glint silver in the moonlight as it arced into the night. At the last moment, Jack twisted around, the blade rushing at Henry. *Must keep Lynn safe.*

With speed fueled by desperation and dragon genes, Henry threw himself into a back flip and fired a shot. The loud crack drowned out the soft noises of the evening. The sting of gunpowder and hot scent of fresh blood splashed the air, flooding her senses. The flashlight landed at her feet and rolled around creating a dizzy pattern of illumination.

Through it all, she saw Jack grab at his right arm, blood seeping between his fingers.

Woman and dragon entwined in agitation. Lynn grabbed the flashlight, found herself next to Jack, her hands on him. Before she could think it through, she threw the flashlight at Henry, but he ducked. "You shot him!"

"I should have shot him in the damn nuts." Henry glared as he picked up the flashlight. "Either of you try anything like that again, and I'll aim there next."

Fuck it. She should have attacked Henry instead of flying to Jack. Talk about stupid moves. She cut her eyes at the man lying next to her. Mr. Callaghan was so not good for her. Lynn rummaged through her backpack, and pulled out a purple and silver pashmina scarf, saved as a memento of Obaa-chan. She grasped the soft material with regret. Jack needed it. Sighing, she tied it tightly around his wound.

"Enough with the nursing." Henry rested on a boulder. "Get to clearing."

When she reached for the axe, Henry tut-tutted. "No need to dirty your hands, sweet heart."

"Thanks for the offer." Grim faced, Jack lifted the axe with his good hand and hacked at the vegetation with a deliberate murderous rage. Sweat darkened his shirt as he stood panting finally, at the mouth of a dark opening in the rock wall. "There you go."

A rope tied around a boulder near the lip continued down the hole. Probably left there by a prior visitor. She glanced at Jack, but he stood staring away from her, sadness kissing his face. What was down there?

Henry pushed off the rock and aimed the gun at Jack. "Toss the axe down the hill."

Clenching his jaw, Jack complied.

All the air almost left her lungs as the axe disappeared from view, swallowed by darkness. With Jack injured, her chances against Henry didn't seem too good. A shiver rappelled up her spine as she remembered his alien takeover of her mind.

"Off we go down the rabbit hole." Henry extended his gun arm like a gracious host and smiled at Jack. "After you."

Nerves twitching, Lynn hovered by the opening. The darkness beyond lay shrouded in sinister warning. "I don't want to go in there."

"Frankly my dear, I don't give a damn." Henry sniggered at his own wit, then shoved her forward.

Like worms they crept and crawled through the dirt, deeper and deeper into the earth. Jack's movements slowed, turned clumsy. Lynn was glad she plugged the space between the two men. With Henry on the edge, she didn't want him to hurt Jack any more. The blood soaked shawl had turned a dark plum.

Finally, they emerged into a cave and stood up. Lynn stifled a scream as the flashlights lit up the pale stalactites and stalagmites, rising from the floor, bearing down from the ceiling. For a moment, she stood as if in a mouth full of jagged, sharp teeth.

"Cool." Henry turned in slow circles, his face bright with wonder.

Lynn stole a quick glance at Jack.

He stood swaying on his feet, then crumpled into a heap.

She ran to him, but an iron-strong hand wrapped around her hair and jerked her away. Henry held her next to him. "Another one of his tricks?"

"I-I don't know."

His hold eased on her. "Go kick him."

"No."

Kick him. Icy eels slithered through her thoughts, nudging and prodding, coiling around.

"N-no."

"Go kick him or I'll shoot him." *Go.* The silent word

347

shoved her forward.

Lynn dragged her feet to Jack, then barely tapped his body with one foot.

"Harder. Like you hate him."

The click of the gun chambering and an overwhelming shove inside her pushed her into action. She swung her foot back and kicked him on the topside of his back. Jack took it like a rag doll. His awful stillness tore something inside her, filled her ears with a silent scream.

"Come on let's go. We still have to find the treasure."

She stood a moment, staring down at Jack, struggling to think. Her mind seemed to be floundering in muddy waters. "We can't just leave him here."

Henry swung around and eyed Jack's form. "I could shoot him and put him out of his misery, but I don't want to waste the bullet."

Come. The word, insistent, demanding, echoed in the chambers of her mind.

Finally, an idea broke the surface, formed itself into words. Jack would be safer without her. Lynn shot away from Jack and returned to Henry's side. "What do you want from me?"

"Everything." Henry scanned the various caves facing them. "But first the treasure."

Hot, caustic words bubbled to her lips only to be staunched by the icy presence in her mind. She settled for a flinty glare.

He grabbed her arm and pulled her toward the sound of water.

As Lynn moved further and further away from Jack, fear infested her bones like termites feasting on wood. She moved along the cool earth walls, keeping to the shadows, alone with Henry once again.

They found the emerald pool, shimmering and glassy

like polished stone. Large enough for a dragon, or two, to swim in. Relax. Play.

"Make love." Henry nuzzled her ear. "Once you help me release my inner dragon, we will make love in these waters, under the pretty lights."

She tried to move away, but he snatched her against him. "I'll share the dragon's treasure with you, I'll make you my mate." He nodded at her. "You really should consider it, the relationship would be mutually beneficial. Special."

The sudden swings from borderline hysteria to seething anger to calm reason spread a chill in the pit of her stomach. Swallowing, she tried to focus, to imagine a single flame burning in the darkness.

Resistance is futile.

The trickling of water soothed her jittery nerves, stirred an old memory. She stared at the water rippling down the rock wall, merging with the deeper waters of the pool.

What will you get from resistance? Nothing.

Obaa-chan's voice whispered in her mind. *Be like the water, soft and flowing. Move with the currents, along the channels of life. Don't resist. And nothing will be able to resist you.*

Henry's voice resurfaced like oil rising on the top of water. *Don't resist.*

She dragged in a long, cold breath. Lynn turned the corner and bumped her nose against Henry's back who'd stopped moving. Peering around him, she gasped.

A full intact dragon skeleton shone under the twin beams of the flashlights. Shimmering white scales lay piled around the bones like untouched snowdrifts. Sadness bruised her heart and she wept inside for the dragon, for *Obaa-chan*, and for Jack.

Laughing with childlike glee, Henry rushed forward.

He darted around the skeleton, touching the bones, gathering up handfuls of scales and pouring them out. Listening to the dry rustle and clatter of the scales, his grin grew wider.

Perhaps she should have seized her chance and fled back to Jack, but Lynn found herself oddly mesmerized by this side of Henry. While she winced as he tramped around this sacred resting place, she also couldn't help being touched by the sheer force of his joy. She could almost like him again.

He looked up just then. His eyes sparkled as if sunlight danced on the ice in them. "Can you believe this? Isn't this amazing?"

She nodded, stunned silent by the enormous remains.

Henry ran back to her, traced a line along her cheek. "It's a dragon just like you."

"I'm not that big."

He'd already turned back to stare at the shiny bones. "I know, but you're just as magnificent."

You are beautiful.

Beautiful? Not a beast?

You are beautiful. Stop resisting.

She stumbled toward him, as if ensnared by an invisible lasso.

I will make you happy.

Her feet hurried.

Together we will rule the world.

She tripped over her own feet. *Power.*

Yes, imagine the power.

He caught her, swept her into his arms and danced a slow waltz.

Dizzy, she rested her head on his shoulders and closed her eyes. *Power without understanding.*

You will help me understand, come into my full potential. He swayed with his head laid on top of hers. "You have to help me release my dragon."

The fire inside her head flared, stirred by the memories of *Obaa-chan*. She had to know. "Why? Didn't you turn down my grandmother's offer?"

He stilled.

Breath got stuck right beneath her breastbone and fluttered there like a trapped moth. She focused on her breathing and waited.

Henry stepped away from her. "She told you?"

The dragon roared inside her head. Cracks spread at the speed of a lighted fuse through every wall she'd ever built between the beast and herself. "She tried to help you."

He sneered. "She tried to control me. Meddling old woman."

Flames slipped through the chinks with greedy, grasping fingers, pushing and prodding her. Stirring her anger. "You killed her."

He smiled at her then, a smile so cold that it coated the fire inside her with ice. "No love, you did."

The ground beneath her feet shook and she stumbled to her knees. Her eyes watered, and her throat closed in on itself, as the sharp smell of smoke whipped around the cave. Great big chunks of herself broke and tumbled into oblivion, then she remembered. Behind her clenched eyes, fire tasted the air with a hundred hot, hungry tongues. In the midst of this hell, lay her grandmother's tiny, unmoving human form like a discarded and broken doll.

In an instant, Henry's arms went around her and his head drew close. Soft, invisible fingers played among her thoughts, caressing and soothing. Touch, after seductive touch. Exploring. *I told you we were alike.*

351

Lynn's eyes flew open. "No." The word emerged from her as a moan.

He pressed kisses to her neck. *My fire would have devoured her eventually, but you couldn't wait.* He shivered against her. *I will never forget watching you breathe flames. So beautiful.*

The image of an angry jet spurting from her lips, igniting the slick, shiny floor. Flames splitting into an army, rushing like hell's hounds at her grandmother looped inside her head. Eyes open or shut, the ugly truth couldn't be avoided any longer.

Tears poured from her like a long-awaited rain storm.

The smell of smoke and something nauseous and oily. Slick and shiny floor. What was on the floor?

Gasoline. Henry's whisper sucker punched her, left her reeling.

More memories thundered through her. She'd burst into the burning warehouse. Too damn late. Spied her grandmother through all the smoke and flames and rushed forward. Until a word formed in her head. *Stop.* Surrounded by all that heat, she'd frozen.

Fear frosted her breath as she remembered something alien and ugly scurrying like a spider inside her mind. Lightning flashed illuminating the darkest nooks and recesses. As the flames had drawn closer to *Obaa-chan*, she remembered her feet had stumbled and pulled her in the direction of the voice. *Come closer little girl.*

The heat of panic had boiled away the fear, and burnt away the alien existence for a moment. That's when her breath had whooshed out in flames. Ignited the damn gasoline she hadn't realized covered the floor.

Why hadn't Obaa-chan turned dragon?

I trapped her mind before she knew what was happening. No point making things harder than necessary.

You.

The hand clutching the heavy flashlight flew up and knocked Henry's head back, drew blood. He ducked the second blow. She clipped his jaw with a jump front kick. He staggered back.

At the same time, the change flooded her, washing away the last of the wall, drowning out all reason, all humanity. Churning, boiling heat filled her veins. Claws slid out like well-oiled razorblades. Her human face elongated, filled with teeth ready to tear. Bones, muscle, and flesh distended and twisted, spread and stretched as if elastic, then started settling into dragon form.

A chill fog permeated her skin into her veins, until the energy flow slowed and thickened like honey left forgotten on the bottom of the jar. Her transformation sputtered, then stopped. She stood frozen, a mishmash of monster and human.

Henry had scurried back and now lay staring up at her. *What the fuck are you doing?*

What I should have done the night you killed my grandmother. With great effort, Lynn moved the muscles of her mouth, massaged her gums with her tongue, the resulting saliva melted some of the cold gumming her up. In her half-state, calling fire would hurt like hell as the heat burnt away any remaining human cells. No choice. She took a deep breath and blasted out a flame.

Henry rolled out of the way with lightning fast reflex, but the pungent odor of singed hair hung in the air.

Stop this! Show me how to be a dragon.

Her throat burned, her breath steamed in the air. *Never.*

We can be so much together.

Another fist of fire grew inside her. *Never.*

Unseen fingers sunk into the soft tissues of her mind.

You are mine.

Ice cold air shot through her nerves. Coated her throat. *Never.*

The vise-like grip tightened. *Then you will die.*

Her teeth chattered. *Fine.*

Gunfire whined in the air. Bullets hit hard against her frozen body, glanced off the scales.

"Fucking Useless Piece of Shit!" Henry shoved the gun into his waistband. "Don't worry, I don't need the gun for you. Just like I didn't need it for your grandmother."

The pressure built inside, choked her breath as freezing dark loomed around her. Her head, her jaw, every bone in her body hurt. Brain freeze. *Obaa-chan's* voice whispered in her head. *Stop fighting. Be one with the dragon.* Her eyes fluttered close as she willed her muscles to relax one by one. She imagined a single flame, then allowed it to multiply and burn until her mind held a bonfire.

Henry sidled up to her, cupped her face in both hands. *There is still time. Stop resisting me.*

She raised her arms —bands of scale erupted along broken skin revealing bone and blood red muscle— and snagged his shoulders, the sharp claws tearing through the thick cloth of his jacket, through the shirt and into skin.

"Hell!" Henry jerked.

She pulled him close. Eased her hold just enough to stop his panic, but still keep him in place. Forced the words to form. *You are mine.*

He stopped struggling and smiled.

All mine.

He relaxed his hold. The biting chill ebbed.

Heat flared inside, countered the cold, allowing her a

small respite that ebbed and flowed. One of *Obaa-chan's* long-ago stories whispered through the spill of memories. When cornered by the enemy, an ancient dragon shape-shifter had chosen to unite with his dragon, to build the flames until they became one and burst into a fire ball as hot and devastating as the sun up close. Suicide and revenge rolled into a final, fiery blaze.

She let the fire rage through her veins.

Henry stroked her scale-covered snout. *What next?*

Her tongue flickered out, tasted his desire. *I will show you how to be a true dragon.*

Focusing inward, she worked the fire. Blew on it with the wind of her will, stirred it with her sorrow and fueled it with her anger. Hot sparks and gray ash flew inside her as the heat grew bolder.

Lynn stood trembling on the edge of death, free of all fear, almost welcoming the end. *Obaa-chan* was lost. *Jack.* Sobs bubbled inside. Maybe Jack hadn't died, maybe he'd survive in the end. She hoped Timmy and Jen would be okay, that whoever had called her had called the police. Her parents would miss her. So many goodbyes left unsaid. But taking out Henry would be worth the cost.

Heat flowed up and down her veins, stoking the flames at her molten core. She called on the dragon and it roared in answer, a dry desert wind rose and churned inside, whipped her fire into an inferno. All thought, all sadness, eviscerated by the blaze.

"Ow, it's getting hot." Henry struggled against her. Thrashed her about the snout with the gun. *Stop it. Stop whatever you're doing.*

Blood flowed from her nostrils and lips. Tasted salty on her tongue. She closed her eyes and held on.

He pushed her up against a cave wall and wrapped his hands around her half-human throat, squeezing. His mental coldness stabbed her over and over like a bayonet. *Stop.*

Ice formed, steamed off, reformed in the folds of her brain. Darkness lapped at the edge of her conscious. She refused to let go, dug in her nails deeper.

The stench of sweat, blood and fear rolled to her nose. His or her own?

Sweat poured off her in waves. A quake started deep inside, then spiraled outwards building in strength. Soon, the earth beneath her feet shook, the cave shook. Rocks crumbled and rained from above.

Despite the sharp pain needling through her, the bite of hot and cold, Lynn focused on her breathing, her fire.

The grip around her throat slipped, disappeared. Oxygen and relief rushed through her. Air had never tasted so good. Lynn's eyes popped open.

Henry groaned and coughed as he lay sprawled at her feet. Jack stood over him wielding a huge ivory bone — was that a rib?— like a bat. He was alive. Why hadn't he got out?

Lynn glanced across Jack's face, taking in the sweat slick skin, the determined press of his mouth, the tic pulsing by his left eye. *Run.*

Jack's eyes blazed with anger and heat as he stared at Henry. Then he looked up and met her gaze. Then she noted worry and resolve.

Henry shoved to his feet and rushed Jack. She pulled in great big drags of air, as the two men rolled together on the floor.

Henry landed a hard punch on Jack's bullet wound.

"Damn!" Jack clutched his arm, his face turned ash gray. Blood poured between his fingers. Henry seized the chance and scurried away from them.

Lynn's tongue flickered out, tasting the blood in the

air. The heady scent filled her breaths, seeped into her own blood. Heat simmered in her veins.

The remaining physical changes rippled to completion. A sigh escaped her as she slid into full dragon form. She lumbered forward.

Henry's gun roared.

Jack jerked as a new wound erupted on his thigh. He moaned and rolled toward her.

Henry continued to back away, his gun pointed at Jack. "Come after me, and I'll shoot to kill."

Lynn watched him through a half-lidded eye. *I don't need to come after you.* She pulled in a deep breath and opened her mouth. Heat —all the heat she'd built and stoked— flared inside her like a beast gone mad, clawing and slashing to get free. Intoxicated on the need to burn, she let go.

Fire leaped out of her, wrapped around Henry, scorched the cave walls. Fire devoured with abandon. *Die, you bastard.*

Screaming, Henry danced away from them engulfed in red-yellow flames with cold blue hearts. He turned and twisted, fell to the ground and rolled. A flaming dervish consumed by fire.

His skin blistered red, split and popped, turned black. Leathery bat-like wings half-extended from between his shoulder blades. His face contorted into a monstrous jumble of black dragon and human, froze in a grimace as he fell into the pool.

Nausea rocked through Lynn as she breathed in the odor of burning flesh and hair, listened to the fading echoes of the screams. The sudden spending of all the heat and fury left her weak. She toppled to the ground her gaze pinned on the smoldering half-submerged blackened corpse that was Henry.

She lay there as her form flickered and shifted back to human, feeling strangely empty. Where was the triumph, the vindication? No matter how horrible a death Henry died, no matter how much he deserved it, none of it would bring *Obaa-chan* back.

A hand caressed her naked shoulder. She managed to turn her head and meet Jack's gaze. He'd dragged himself to her. His eyes shone as he stared down at her.

"I killed him." Her words rasped her throat raw. "I killed him in cold blood."

"You did what you had to do."

"Yeah." The dragon had taken over. In the end, she was a beast. She let her head fall forward, closed her eyes. "Henry was right. I'm just like him."

"You're nothing like him."

Lynn's head snapped up at the vehemence of his words, her gaze jumped to his.

Jack ran a light finger along her face, tucked an unruly curl behind her ear. "He would have killed innocent people, including an eight-year-old. He would have killed you."

"This thing inside me—"

"Saved us." He held out a blood and dirt covered hand to her. "Come on, let's get out of here."

CHAPTER 32

Trembling with pain and fatigue, Lynn and Jack leaned on each other and pushed to a stand. He groaned as his legs folded under and he fell to the dusty floor. "Leave me," he said. "There's no way I can make it back the way we came."

Bile churned in her stomach as Lynn took in his pale, sweating face, his jagged panting breath, the metallic scent of blood. He'd been shot twice and lost a hell of a lot of that precious fluid. She squinted into the mouth of the dark corridor. He was right, he wouldn't make it on his own, but no way was she leaving him behind. Alone, in the dimly lit cave, where other dragons came to die. "Strip."

"What?"

"Your shirt. I could use it as a tourniquet to staunch your bleeding."

He hesitated, then complied. "Maybe you should just use it to cover yourself."

Lynn looked down at herself suddenly aware of her nakedness. She busied herself tearing the shirt into strips. "That wouldn't be practical for the next part of the plan."

"You have a plan?"

"Yes." She wrapped the torn shirt around his wound and tied it as tight as she could.

Jack grunted through gritted teeth. "Want to clue me in?"

She sat back on her heels, wrapped her arms around herself. "Do you trust me?"

His steady gaze met hers, remained. "Yes."

"Then I could turn dragon and carry you as far as I can, then you'd just have to tough it out through the rest."

"Carry me how?"

Lynn glanced away at the skeleton. "I could grab you with my mouth and drag you along."

A strangled sound made her look back at Jack's horrified face. Apparently trust didn't stretch to include her mouth. "Or you could climb up on me and hold on."

"I think I prefer the second option."

She took a deep breath and called for the transformation. This time it came slower, tingling and sparking like an electric charge through her molecules. Back in dragon form, she lowered herself to the ground.

Hissing with pain, Jack levered himself up and onto her. His arms slipped around her neck as he settled in between her wings.

She rose up and lumbered forward making her way through the dark. Whenever they came to a tight tunnel,

Lynn would transform back to human form to drag and push Jack in turns. Inch by inch they worked their way toward the opening.

When they finally emerged back on the top of the mountain, Jack flopped on the ground, breathing shallowly and looking almost bloodless. A network of fine, bleeding scratches covered his bare skin. Lynn pulled in a deep lungful of fresh air and stood. She peered through the brush and looked down. "Oh wow."

"What now?"

Lynn stared at the flashing lights around Jack's house. "The cavalry's arrived, so Jen and Timmy should be okay."

She turned to face him. "Except how do we explain Henry?"

"I don't think we can explain Henry." Jack pushed himself up. "And I'd really like to keep the cave a secret."

"I'll call the Dragon Council to come retrieve the body."

Jack blinked. "Who?"

"I'll tell you about them later." She grimaced. "But that's part of their job and believe me they are discreet."

He gave a slow nod. "Fine."

Lynn hunkered down. "Okay, we still need to think up a story to explain Henry's absence."

Thinking might be a problem. "Um, right."

Lynn looked up to find Jack's heated gaze on her breasts, and finally back up to her eyes. His breath came fast and shallow through slightly parted lips. Warmth washed through her at the desire she sensed burning inside him. Images of his hands and mouths on different parts of her body flashed through her mind. Her own thoughts or his? For a moment he made her feel all woman. Then common sense kicked in and she shrugged off her backpack. She pulled her spare clothes out and shoved herself into jeans, tee-shirt and sneakers. "Sorry."

"Nothing to be sorry about," he winked. "I didn't mind."

"Whatever," she hurried up to him and pulled his uninjured arm around her shoulders. "Come on, we need to start down."

He hobbled along beside her. "But we don't have a story yet."

"We'll figure something out."

He squeezed her, gentle and reassuring. *And we can always mindspeak.*

Cannon's barks drew closer, and swords of light cut through the darkness as the search party worked toward them. Head down, Lynn concentrated on using the broken branch to eliminate footprints leading up to the mountain. Then leaving Jack slumped in the dirt, she ducked behind a boulder. For a moment, her limbs just sat there heavy and aching as she leaned against the solid comfort of the stone. Her body lay still, depleted from all the changes, her mind weary after having tangled with Henry and finally faced the truth. Tears leaked out of her eyes and ran down her cheeks. All she wanted was to sleep, to fade into oblivion.

Lynn. Jack's call made her jerk upright. *They're coming. I need you.* Both woman and dragon shivered in delight, responded with eagerness, melded together. Lynn dragged herself up, and ran to join him. If Anderson commented on her footprints, she'd tell him she'd been taking a damn piss.

Jack's eyes lit up as she stumbled to a stop next to him, slid down to the dirt and settled in. His dirt and blood covered hand grasped hers. *Ready?*

As ready as we can be.

Cannon bounded through the shrubbery and found them, then proceeded to lick and trample Jack. Roberts and his group appeared right behind. He radioed the good news and asked the medics to hurry. "You guys okay?"

"Banged up, but alive." Jack managed a lopsided smile, while Lynn just nodded.

Soon more people arrived on the scene. Medics shoved between them, moved her a small distance. Jack's hand slipped free of hers. She stumbled, unwilling to move, tried to voice a protest. But EMTs and medical equipment swarmed between them, filled in the space, hid him from view. He needed them more than he needed her.

Another set of medics hovered around her, asked her questions, cleaned up her cuts and scrapes. Someone thrust an opened bottle of water into her hand. The sight of it made her parched throat ache. She hadn't even realized how thirsty she'd been in the midst of everything. She chugged it down.

Anderson emerged from the crowd and watched her. The EMTs slid into their groove, settled into their routines and worked quietly and efficiently. Roberts stood tall surveying the chaos, with Hernandez directly behind him. Their grim faces had her heart careening. What were they thinking? What questions would they ask? Jack lay motionless on a gurney to her right, his face tilted toward her. The sight of him calmed her frayed nerves.

She set the empty bottle down, wiped her chin with the back of her hand. "Are Jen and Timmy okay?"

"Yeah, they are safe," Roberts said, ambling up to her. "Need to ask you all a few quick questions, you think you can handle that?"

"I-I think so." Jack's voice sounded weak and fading.

Anderson squatted down in front of her and skewered her with his steel blue gaze. "So what exactly happened?"

Lynn glanced at Jack. *Don't tax yourself. Let me do most of the talking.*

Fine. I'll jump in if I can help.

Carrying on two simultaneous conversations —one in her head and one outside— proved interesting. The most challenging part turned out to be keeping her expressions from giving away her thoughts. Lynn bit her lip, stared at the ground and had to stop and think a lot. The confused look came naturally under the circumstances.

"Where's my backpack?"

Somebody passed it over. Lynn opened it and pulled out the red folder. All the people crowded around her, pushing and shoving. She flipped open to the map of the planned development that she and Jen had marked up. She pointed out the overlaps with the fire scenes. "Looks like the San Antonio developers brought in Henry to convince people to sell any way he could."

Then she showed them the phone records between Kate Harrington and Commissioner Ward. "I'm not sure what Kate's motive was. I mean she seems to be well off."

"I can answer that," Roberts said. "She is up to her neck in debts. Both she and her ex seem to have a gambling problem."

Lynn shook her head. Then she pulled out the articles on Henry and told them about her interview with Barton and about the Callaghan connection.

"Why did you decide to go Jack's place?" the Sheriff asked.

"I thought Jack was in danger. I had to warn him."

While the law enforcement officials questioned her

and Lynn answered, Hernandez took notes. She said Henry's motive included revenge for the way Grandfather Callaghan had treated his mother and jealousy and this idea of a hidden treasure.

The sheriff gave a slow nod. "Kate Harrington said about the same thing when we arrested her. So then, y'all went off on a treasure hunt?"

Lynn wrapped her arms around herself. "Jack tried to tell him there wasn't any treasure, but Henry didn't believe him."

"So I decided to play him and take him away from the rest of the people." Jack spoke up. "My plan was to try and take him when it was just the two of us."

"Why'd he take you along for the ride?" Anderson scratched his face and turned back to her.

Heat painted Lynn's face. "He seemed kind of obsessed with me."

Jack reached out for her. People moved out of the way and Lynn found herself scooting close. His hand wrapped around hers again. "Of course, that complicated matters, but I had to go through with the plan. Not too many options at that point."

"Go on, what then?" Both the Sheriff and Hernandez leaned forward.

"I took us to Fire Mountain because couldn't think of anyplace else, kept him thinking we were heading for the treasure." His hand tightened around hers. "First chance I got I attacked him with the axe, but he pulled the gun out and shot me."

"Jack dropped the axe." Lynn spoke through a sob. "Henry went crazy, he grabbed the axe and started waving it around."

"He said he'd hack me to pieces for tricking him," Jack said.

"I-I couldn't let him hurt Jack anymore, so I tackled him from behind," Lynn put in. The gun shots tearing into Jack's flesh, her kicking his still body, Henry's screams as he burned rushed through her mind, overwhelmed her senses. Strangled sobs pushed out of her with a violence that surprised her.

Let me take over. "Then we heard the sirens. Henry took off, and I wasn't in any shape to give chase," he said. "Lynn refused to leave me and I didn't want her alone with him out and about."

"Where do you think he went?" Anderson's soft voiced question crashed into the crowd.

Lynn's mouth dried up as if she'd swallowed a dust storm. Sweat pooled under her arms. Memory of blackened skin and the smell of burning meat had bile rising in her throat. "I-I don't know."

"Kate's property borders mine at this end, maybe he escaped there," Jack said. A soft groan escaped his lips and he closed his eyes.

Lynn stared wildly around. "He needs to get to the hospital."

The West Texas Regional Hospital chopper clattered in the air above them, raising up a storm. People rushed around getting ready for the landing. Lynn closed her eyes to the chaos and let sleep claim her.

Lynn woke up in a hospital room. The drawn curtains created a muted glow, allowing her eyes to adjust and focus. All kinds of tubes and wires hung around her. And machines monitoring her pulse, her breath and god-knows-what-else beeped reassuringly. *I'm still alive.*

The smell of food tantalized her nose, stirred the hunger inside, and she discovered a covered tray on the table attached to the hospital bed. The *San Angelo Herald* lay on top of the cover.

Her gaze swooped to the headline: "Arson Snuffed Out." Lynn smiled as she read the byline. Hernandez had listed her name first. She ran a fingertip under her name Lynn Hana Alexander. Maybe she was an ego maniac, but she felt a rush of pure delight at seeing her name in print. She didn't think she'd ever tire of that experience.

She read the article twice and sighed in satisfaction. Connecting the dots, doing the research, pulling information from interviewees— all of it had been hard work. She held the paper like a trophy. Hard work yes, but also solid printed proof that she'd been on the good guys' team. She'd made a difference.

Her eyes found the clock. 2 p.m. No wonder she was starving. Lynn inhaled her lunch of cold vegetable soup, crackers, a warm fruit cup and canned orange juice. A knock sounded and a nurse came in. "Oh you're awake and fed!"

"Jack?" Her question emerged as a whisper.

"He's got a couple of bullet wounds and he did lose quite a lot of blood, but the doctors said he'll be okay."

She almost asked to see him, but swallowed her words. Why? She was a dragon and he…wasn't enough of one. They had no future together. Time to return to Houston and her life.

"People have been peeking in on you all day," the nurse said, changing the IV bag and checking the monitors. She took the empty dishes away with her.

Lynn lay back and picked up the paper again, when there was a knock at her door. Maybe Jen had come to visit. She sat up, ready for a hug. "Come in."

Another nurse wheeled Jack in. He carried a bouquet of sunflowers. "Hey."

"Hey, yourself," Lynn said. Yet again he sported a

spectacular black-eye. Her gaze lingered on his face. Dark hair curled at his collar. Stubbles spread a light shadow along the planes and angles of his face, giving him a rakish pirate look. All he needed was a gold earring and an almost unbuttoned white shirt. A ship and the wide open sea. The dragon inside her shivered. Stop being a fool.

He cleared his throat and held out the flowers. "Thanks for saving my life."

"You're welcome." Her fingers brushed against his as she took the bouquet. Desire steamed through her. She turned to the nurse. "Could you put these in some water please?"

The nurse took the flowers and grabbed the empty plastic pitcher on the dresser and disappeared into the tiny bathroom.

"How are you doing?" Lynn asked. The words sounded stilted and without emotion. She hated them. Hated herself for feeling desire and awkwardness. Weaker than usual, she should have left earlier. Called Jen for help and slipped out. Avoided this meeting.

Jack shot her a half-smile and touched the back of his head. "Been better, but could've been worse."

"You'll recover."

The nurse bustled about with bright yellow flowers looking beautiful, despite the Pepto-Bismol pink pitcher. She placed them on the dresser and snuck out.

Panic sank its claws deep inside. Alone with Jack. Shit. Lynn licked her lips. "You read the story in the paper?"

Jack nodded. "Every word," he said. "Heck of a story."

"Too bad he escaped."

"Yeah, the guy just had all kinds of help lined up."

Their eyes met. Held.

"It's a story," she said. "Some of its true, some isn't. But you know that."

"I have realized life isn't black and white, there's a lot of grays and different shades of gray at that."

What the hell did that mean?

Jack smiled. "It means, there are no absolutes and life is full of surprises."

Lynn took a deep breath. Damn, she'd forgotten about their connection. "Specifics please?"

Jack shifted around in his chair. "I thought I knew who I was, but there's a whole lot more to discover."

"I'm sorry I didn't break it to you more gently."

"Sugar coating wouldn't have helped." He shrugged. "It took a while for the words to sink in."

She nodded. Silence. Awkward, bulky silence. "I'll be returning to Houston soon." She smiled and pushed more words out. "I'm thinking of trying to get a job at one of the local newspapers."

"Oh." Jack looked down at his hands, which had curled into fists. He flexed his fingers, wiggled them about.

"What's wrong?"

He raised his head. His eyes darkened, reminded her of wild jungles. She could smell the iron tinge of nerves and determination. "I have no idea what it means to be a dragon, I had hoped you might be willing to help."

She clutched the bed covers. "How can I help?"

"You know more about dragons than anyone else I know."

Lynn recalled his horror-stricken face as he backed away from her. He thought of her as a beast. Could she accept being his mentor and nothing more? She shook her head. "I, I am sorry." She swallowed past the lump in her throat. "You might never be able to turn dragon."

"I know that." He rubbed his lips. "I'd still like to know where I came from, what it means. My father…" He laughed. "I can't believe I'm about to quote him."

"What did he say?"

"Without roots, a tree can't grow branches." Jack ploughed one hand through his hair. "I spent a lifetime ignoring him, but I think I'm finally beginning to appreciate the man."

As he spoke of his dad, his voice grew softer, more wistful. She could see the ghost of the young boy he'd been lurking just beneath the surface. Sense the importance of his sharing. She wanted to help. Her want bit deep inside her, leaving an aching imprint. "I guess I could sort of mentor you."

"That'd be great." His face lit up with hope.

"Yeah, I could go through all of *Obaa-chan's* teachings and books, and share what I think will help." She leaned forward, caught up in her idea. "We could be like modern day penpals, except on email."

Penpals? Not if I can help it. "I was aiming for something more up close and personal."

His words sucked all moisture from her throat. She blinked at him.

I want to explore the possibilities between us. I want to kiss you. Again.

She opened and shut her mouth. Beast. He'd seen her as a beast. The creature and she— Lynn drew in a deep breath to rise above the turmoil inside her. "I'm still a dragon. A beast. Can you accept that?"

He levered himself out of the chair, balanced on his good leg and leaned closer. Jack stared deep into her eyes. "Then I'm quarter-beast and, at times, a complete idiot." His tongue traced slowly over his lip. "Can you live with that?"

Their eyes met and held. Somewhere a clock ticked the seconds away. She managed a nod.

His lips found hers, his tongue sought hers out. Heat fire-balled in her stomach, a deep, desperate hunger spiraled through her. She tasted him again after what seemed forever. And she wasn't sure if there'd be a next time. So she dived into the kiss, submerged herself in it. Her hands slipped around his head and neck, fingers curled into hair. They kissed deeply for what seemed an eternity. And just when Lynn felt she'd melt and evaporate, he broke away.

"Wh-what changed your mind?"

"Time and good sense kicking in," he said. "When I saw Henry's hand around your throat, I just knew deep in my gut that you were in trouble." A haunted bleakness settled into his gaze. "I thought I might be losing you forever and I couldn't stand the idea."

She brushed his lips with light fingers. "I felt my entire world crash each time Henry shot you."

Jack grinned. "And watching you run around naked was pretty convincing too."

"Shut up while you're ahead." Grabbing a handful of his hospital gown, Lynn pulled him close. Their lips melded in a kiss as hot as dragon fire and twice as sweet.

Also by Mina Khan

THE DJINN'S DILEMMA

Rukh O'Shay, half-djinn and assassin, is used to taking out the bad guys. But his latest assignment, Sarah White, is nothing like he expected. A glimpse of her bright aura reveals her gentle spirit, while her luscious beauty clouds his mind and makes him long for only one thing— to taste her.

Sarah shares the feeling of raw desire at Rukh's touch. He can turn her on with a glance, and satisfies desires she didn't even know she had. But Rukh had been hired to kill her— and the only way to save her is to find out who wants her dead before someone else finishes the job…

"I'll take this hot assassin named Rukh trying to kill me any day ;) Oh yeah, he was that hot." — Bitten by Paranormal Romance review, 2011

A TALE OF TWO DJINNS

Akshay (Shay for short), warrior prince of the earth djinns, earns the title of Crown Prince at a high cost when he loses his best friend in a battle against ancient enemies, the water djinns. Heartsick, he escapes to Earth to mourn.

Nothing gets the biological clock ticking (and elders lecturing) like almost dying in battle, so Maya, princess of the water djinns, travels to Earth for some no-strings-attached sex to fulfill her duty and produce an heir. But the beautiful and tough warrior gets more than she bargained for when she meets Shay.

Their not-so-simple one-night stand is interrupted by assassins and the world, as they know it, is changed forever. As Maya and Shay pull together to survive, both are determined to have their happily-ever-after and bring peace to their worlds— warring families, shadow assassins, and nosy busybodies be damned.

*** Fifty percent of every purchase is donated to UNICEF in memory of Mina's father***

DEAD: A Ghost Story

A multicultural ghost story in which Nasreen —the Indian-American protagonist— grapples with her life and death in West Texas. This is *not* a romance.

About the Author

Mina Khan is a Texas-based writer and food enthusiast. She grew up in Bangladesh on stories of djinns (pronounced "gins"), ghosts and monsters. These childhood fancies now color her fiction. She daydreams of hunky paranormal heroes, magic, mayhem and mischief and writes them down as tales of romance and adventure.

Her first published work, The Djinn's Dilemma, won the novella category of the 2012 Romance Through The Ages (published) contest.

A Tale of Two Djinns won the 2013 Readers' Crown for best paranormal romance. It also won second place in the novella category in the 2013 National Excellence in Romance Fiction Awards (NERFA).

I love to hear from my readers, and you can reach me at...

Website & Blog: http://minakhan.blogspot.com/

On Facebook: www.facebook.com/Mina.Khan.Author

On Goodreads:
www.goodreads.com/author/show/5234352.Mina_Khan

On Twitter: @SpiceBites

A note from Mina

Thank you for reading WILDFIRE: A Paranormal Mystery with Cowboys & Dragons. I hope you enjoyed it.

WILDFIRE is my love letter to my adopted home in West Texas, and I had a lot of fun mentioning local haunts, history, and sharing all the details that make the place special. This book wouldn't have been possible without the help of many, wonderful people:

My darling husband, who is my inspiration for Jack, and does all he can to help support me and my writing in so many different ways. My kids, who are awesome cheerleaders. D. Michalewicz, Steve Mild, Ken Land, Brian Dunn and Russell Smith for information about volunteer fire departments, law enforcement and so much else. The talented and funny newspaper editors I was lucky to work with and learn from: Bill Miller, Scott Stanford (Tower), William Taylor, and Tim Archuleta. Hernandez is for all of you!

My most wonderful critique partner, L.J. Charles; and amazing beta readers who helped make this book better: Laurie G., Hasna S., Teresa R., and Michelle C. The San Angelo Writers for feedback. For editorial help, Maya Rock and Jennifer Boggs. For artwork, Ana of Kingwood Creations and my sister Fahmi Khan.

Also all the members of my awesome street team, who kept me sane, let me vent, and gave me all kinds of help. A special hug to Michele H. who came up with Jack's last name.All my writing friends who kept me going.

A heartfelt and huge "Thank you" to all of you!

www.ingramcontent.com/pod-product-compliance
Lightning Source LLC
Chambersburg PA
CBHW020323180626
46812CB00001B/27